Madeleine's Masterpiece

Carol Treacy

ISBN-10: 0-9964474-2-3
ISBN-13: 978-0-9964474-2-3

The characters and events in this book are fictitious. Any similarity to
real persons, living or dead, is coincidental and not intended by the
author.

Published by Carol Treacy

Cover design by Sue Slutzky

To Suzy and JoAnne
I thank you both from the bottom
and top
of my heart.

1

By the time Madeleine Mozart got home, her head was throbbing. She rarely got headaches. This one was a doozy. She had to talk to someone. Tell them what happened. She wanted to call Priscilla. It was almost 11:00 p.m. and, even though it was a Friday night, she hesitated. She sat on the edge of her bed for a few minutes before making her decision. After all, this was an emergency.

With the cellphone in her shaking hand, she closed her bedroom door, plopped down on the bed and dialed. It took three rings for Priscilla to pick up.

"This better be good."

"I woke you, didn't I? Sorry." Maddie lay back on her pillow and kicked off her boots.

"Yeah, you did. You caught me drooling on poor Mr. Peepers. He doesn't look too happy. What's up?" As soon as she said his name, the small Abyssinian cat opened his eyes and started cleaning himself.

"Hold on. My head is killing me. I have to get an aspirin." Maddie sat up too fast, making her headache worse. She groaned and pressed her hand against her forehead as she went to the bathroom.

Priscilla said, "You can't talk and walk at the same time? How old are you again?"

Maddie swallowed two aspirin with water and wiped her mouth. "I don't want Ray to hear."

Priscilla sat up straighter. "This is going to be good. Come on. Spill the beans, M&M."

Maddie closed her bedroom door. "I'm just going to say it.

Charlie Evans asked me out."

"*The* Charlie Evans?" Priscilla was now fully awake.

"Yup."

"Get out! Wait, you don't sound very excited. What's wrong?"

Maddie let out a deep breath. "It started when Tanvi convinced me to go dancing in the city."

11 HOURS EARLIER

"Thank you again for lunch. This is so nice, Maddie." Tanvi helped herself to another serving of salad. When work at the recording studio was slow, she would have lunch at Maddie's house. It was only a few minutes from Rocking Horse Studios, where Tanvi was an audio engineer. Maddie had loved having company ever since she was laid off from the Sausalito Herald, the famous city by the bay's only newspaper.

Maddie talked her friend into dining with her and sweetened the offer by making Tanvi's favorite meal: faux chicken salad on a bed of arugula. As a Hindu, Tanvi had been a vegetarian since birth. She was still on the fence about going vegan, so she loved it when Maddie cooked for her. It helped give her a gentle and tasty push into the plant-based cuisine.

Tanvi said, "How's the job hunting going? Are there any sales positions at the Marin Independent Journal?"

Maddie snorted. "First of all, I haven't been looking for another job, especially in sales. I am so burned out on cold calling and kissing clients' asses. Second, I would never work for the IJ. I went for a job interview there about, I don't know, five years ago. The advertising department was so depressing. It looked like a prison without bars. Really dingy. The carpet was stained and the desks were industrial looking and..."

Tanvi laughed. "I get it. It must be nice to pick and choose what you want to do. In the meantime, how are you living on unemployment? Isn't it paltry?"

"I saved up some money when I was working for the Herald and I'm still getting alimony. I figure I have about four months before I have to hustle and find a job. I have been doing a lot of painting." Maddie looked in the direction of her lawn, where an easel stood holding a partially finished painting. She took a bite of the salad. "I have to say, this fake chicken salad is delicious."

Tanvi followed her friend's gaze. "Hard to see from here. I do like the colors." She checked her watch. It was almost one. She'd have to leave soon. "So…dating anyone?"

Maddie stood up and stretched. When she did, Mick came over and stood under her hand, willing her to pet him. The four-year-old tan boxer with a splash of white on his chest was all muscle, right down to his nub of a tail. Maddie stroked his head. "Nope. My last date with Frank was over a week ago."

"I find that hard to believe. You must get hit on all the time."

"What world are you living in? Oh, wait, I did get propositioned by a guy when I was walking Mick this morning. He was in an old beater truck and had three teeth. He either yelled, 'you wanna git supper sometime' or 'ye winder is sippin fine.' Hard to understand him."

Tanvi said, "Stop joking. You need to get out more, my friend. Ava, Sylvie, and I are going dancing in San Francisco tonight. Come with us."

"That could be fun. Sure. What time?"

"How about I pick you up at eight?"

"Sounds good."

Tanvi grabbed her purse. "I have to get back to work. Thanks again for lunch. See you tonight." She gave her friend the once-over. "Please wear something sexy."

Maddie looked down at her outfit. "Since when is a faded yellow George Strait T-shirt, green sweats, and pink Crocs not sexy?"

"I will not dignify that question with an answer. Later."

Maddie cleaned off the table. As she did the dishes, Ray walked into the kitchen and put his textbooks on the table. The seventeen-year-old was slender, with a shock of golden brown hair, ears slightly too big, and eyelashes that women would die for. He had his father's small, straight nose and his mother's full lips. Maddie turned slightly, as she continued to wash the plates.

"Ray-man. How was school?"

"Scattered fun followed by dark clouds in calculus. I think I'm failing the class. Why do they make us take it, anyway? Am I ever going to use it?"

Maddie chuckled. "Not if you don't understand it. Don't sweat it. I was horrible in geometry. I'm thankful we weren't required to take calculus in high school. Do you have homework?"

Ray sighed. "Always. Before I do it, though, I had this great idea for a snack. What do you think about mixing raw almond butter with coconut cream, a little maca, cinnamon, chia seeds, and peanut butter chips?"

"I think I just gained five pounds thinking about it." Maddie finished the dishes and wiped her hands. She went over to her son and gave him a hug. "I know that one day I'm going to be walking down the snack aisle in Whole Foods and see your creations, but I won't buy them because you'll be giving me a lifetime supply, right?"

"Of course; now give me some fightin' room." Ray rolled up his sleeves and went over to the chrome refrigerator. He grabbed the almond butter and placed it on the counter, then opened the pantry. Maddie knew when Ray got started, the kitchen turned into a war zone. She exited quickly before she was hit with flying chia seeds.

It took her a while to try to figure out what to wear for her night out with the girls. It had been so long since she had dressed sexy. She believed it was on her first date with Frank. That was over a month ago. Maddie went through a few outfits before one of them struck her as appropriate. She settled on a lime green, sleeveless button-down shirt and black jeans. The shirt showed enough cleavage to entice but not enough to disgust. She was hoping they'd find a table to sit at because her three-inch heels were only going to last a couple of hours. After that, the black boots would turn into stylish torture devices.

While she prepared for the evening, Maddie had the television on, peripherally listening to *Entertainment Tonight*. As she applied her make-up, she could hear host Peta Noughton. "Hollywood has landed in San Francisco. Director John Vicente is filming his yet-to-be-named romantic thriller and crowds have gathered to catch a glimpse of its leading man and lady, Charlie Evans and Rachel Swanson."

Maddie was halfway applying mascara when she stopped and

went into the living room. On the screen, the stunning Rachel Swanson smiled brilliantly at the crowd. Her co-star, Charlie Evans, was signing autographs. The host continued.

"Bay area backdrops include San Francisco, Berkeley, and Mendocino. The shooting is expected to last at least two months. Back in Los Angeles, festivities are underway…"

Maddie turned off the TV. "What I wouldn't give for a roll in the sack with Mr. Evans. He is delicious."

From behind a closed door, Maddie heard, "That's gross, Mom!"

"Sorry, Ray. Sometimes these things just fall out of my mouth." She knocked on his bedroom door and cracked it open. A plume of smoke took advantage of the opening and rushed out of the door, smacking Maddie full force. She coughed. "I could get a contact high." Ray's eyes were quite red and at half-mast. He was sitting at his desk, doing homework. Next to the textbook was a plate full of his latest snack creation. Maddie shook her head. "I can't believe you can study like that."

Ray popped one of the snacks into his mouth. "These are so amazing. You want to try one? I'm thinking of calling it Almond Mantra." He handed one to his mom. She took a bite.

"Delicious! You really have a gift, Ray, and I love the name. Can I have another?"

Maddie was on her third Almond Mantra when she saw Tanvi pull up to the house. As she ran out the door, she yelled, "I'm leaving, Ray! I'll probably be home late. Be good."

"Later, Mom. Have fun."

"I don't know what you're wearing, but you smell yummy." Tanvi pulled away from the curb. The Lexus SUV silently came to a stop at the end of the street, then turned left onto the main avenue. Maddie pulled an Almond Mantra out of her purse and handed it to her friend.

"You're smelling marijuana smoke mixed with Ray's latest snack sensation. Try it. The snack, not the pot."

As Tanvi ate the treat, her large brown eyes got bigger. "I'm telling you, your boy is going to be famous someday if he markets these snacks. They're amazing."

"I know. He certainly doesn't get his cooking skills from me or Tommy. You look lovely, by the way."

Tanvi smiled. "Thanks. Not too provocative for a married woman?" She lightly touched the long-sleeved, hot pink satin shirt. It complimented her dark skin and black, shoulder-length hair.

"Nope. Does Sanjay approve?"

"He was too busy fixing the kids dinner to notice. I shouted out my good-byes and slipped out the front door. So, are you ready to have fun?"

"Yes, I am. It's long overdue."

By the time they parked and walked to the Purple Umbrella, one of the more popular nightclubs in the city, it was close to 9:00 p.m. The younger crowd had yet to show up, so there were plenty of places to sit. Soon after Maddie and Tanvi nabbed a table for four, the rest of their party arrived. At fifty-five, Sylvie Heard was the oldest in the group. She was followed by Ava Collier, the youngest at thirty-eight. Whatever Sylvie lacked in confidence, Ava more than made up for. She practically strutted over to Maddie and Tanvi and gave them both exaggerated hugs. She swept her long blonde hair out of her eyes and pulled down her short, fire engine red dress, its fabric hugging Ava's voluptuous figure. Wearing stilettos, the woman towered over her friends.

"Ladies, I'm in the mood for a chocolate martini. Shall I get four?"

"Sounds great," said Sylvie.

"Me, too," Maddie added.

Tanvi was the last to answer. "One martini will last me the whole night and I wanted more than one drink, so please get me a screwdriver." She went for her wallet, but Ava put up her hand.

"First one's on me, gals." As she walked to the bar, she openly scanned the crowd for available men. Her eyes lingered on a goateed gentleman sporting a suit. She smiled demurely and put a little more hip into her walk. It was so obvious, Tanvi let out a groan.

"Geez. Can't she be a tad more discreet?"

Maddie laughed. "Ava and 'discreet' have never been used in the same sentence before. Congratulations on being the first and most likely, the last."

Sylvie added, "She's certainly not shy. I wouldn't mind an ounce of her bravado."

Ava returned and shortly after, the waitress brought their drinks. Maddie held up her martini. "Let's toast to me being a single woman again."

They clinked glasses and after a sip, Ava said, "Didn't you go out with, was it Frank, for only like a month?"

"Yeah, but I really thought he could be the one."

Sylvie almost spit out her drink. "Come on, Maddie. He so didn't deserve you, plus he was butt ugly."

"His looks were definitely on the 'what are friends going to say behind my back' side, but that's what I liked about him. I really believed that a skinny guy with a light-bulb shaped head, nasally voice and gap between his teeth would be more sincere, more appreciative of me."

Ava said, "Jesus, where did you meet this guy, Tales from the Crypt?"

"He used to be a client," Maddie replied.

"A mortician?"

Maddie laughed. "Lawyer."

Sylvie chimed in. "So why'd you kick him to the curb?"

"I didn't do the kicking. He did. When you tell a man that you want to take it slow and he says, 'Let me think about it and oh, by the way, I think about sex 24/7,' that sound you hear is the doof kicking himself to the curb."

"While he masturbates!" Sylvie added.

Ava raised her glass. "I'll drink to that. Hell, I'll drink to almost anything!"

The women toasted again, raising their glasses high.

At a booth not too far away, Gretchen Brockner was squaring off with Donna Madden. Gretchen wasn't comfortable. She didn't want to be there, in a bar talking to an agent. The writer and director could afford to decline requests to 'take a meeting' from nearly every actor out there, even the megastars. She had been asked by the head of Paramount to please meet with Donna. The decision was up to her. In order to appease the president of the studio funding her next project, she agreed, but she wasn't happy. She felt way too old to be hanging out in a bar where twenty-something women exposed their midriffs and flaunted their fake breasts. And the men. They were so well-coiffed, she thought she was back in Los Angeles at one of those Sunset Boulevard nightclubs, where people go to rub shoulders with celebrities and, hopefully, score with one of them.

Hiding it flawlessly, Donna was just as uncomfortable as Gretchen, but for different reasons. Her client was one of the most sought-after actors in the world. He was offered parts without an audition. Why in the world he wanted to be in this film was beyond her, but she had no choice. When the client says jump, Donna leaps as high as her four-inch pumps will allow.

Gretchen took a peanut from the bowl and ate it. "I'm flattered that he loves the script. I still don't want him in my movie. I told him that last week."

Donna replied in her upper-class British accent, "Please, Gretchen. This means so much to him and his star power will only add to the film's box office draw."

Gretchen looked like she'd been slapped in the face. "May I remind you, Ms. Madden, that my 'star power' isn't too shabby? I won an Oscar for directing *Klansmen* and another for best original screenplay, *Night Sky.*"

"I'm sorry. I didn't mean to insult you. I just know that he loves your work and this part means a lot to him."

"Forget it."

"What have you got against him?"

"He's a lothario."

"Who uses the word lothario anymore? Wait, don't tell me. I bet you're a screenwriter." Charlie Evans, scotch in hand, walked out from behind the booth. He looked every bit the famous movie star he was, even sporting the requisite sunglasses and bright white smile with perfect teeth. Donna stood up and hugged him.

"Good to see you."

"You, too." He removed his glasses and looked directly at Gretchen, trying to charm her with his looks. He extended his hand and she reluctantly shook it. Once Charlie sat down, he turned to his agent. "How am I doing?"

Donna said, "Not good."

"Do I have to look for another agent?"

"Very funny."

Charlie once again cast his attention to Gretchen. "I've been in a lot of movies. Some bad, some great. It's rare that I come across a script that is perfection. It's moving and romantic and unforgettable. I just finished reading *Julia's Love Affair* for the third time. I am Danny Jensen."

Gretchen shook her head. She couldn't believe the man's audacity. He had a lot of nerve telling her that the part was made for him. "Charlie, you are not going to convince anybody that Danny can fall in love with an older woman. You've made a reputation dating young, beautiful airheads."

Charlie countered. "They're not that young and, besides, why wouldn't I want to date them? Show me a man who would refuse."

"Danny Jensen," Gretchen said.

"Bullshit. He would but he happens to meet Julia. That could happen to me, too."

Donna sat back, enjoying the discussion and thankful that she was no longer a part of it. She recognized Gretchen's talent as a director and writer. She also knew the woman's reputation for being stubborn and inflexible. She took a sip of her cosmopolitan, letting the alcohol soften the negative energy in the air. Being Charlie's agent had its advantages, though she recognized that he could also be determined and hard-headed.

Gretchen dug in her heels. "I'm telling you, it won't work. Danny sees Julia for who she is and she's not that."

Charlie followed Gretchen's gaze and it landed on a gorgeous, young girl. She barely looked twenty-one. As she walked by the booth, Charlie's eyes drank in every five-foot-ten inches of her, giving her his most dazzling smile. He watched her walk to the bar, where a man was waiting. She gave the man a kiss, then turned to Charlie and smiled. Donna observed Gretchen's growing irritation. Hoping she wouldn't be overheard, she mumbled, "You're not helping your cause."

Before he could respond, Gretchen said, "Hello! Invisible older woman is talking to you."

Unfazed, Charlie leaned toward Gretchen and said, "Come on. Did you see that girl? I wouldn't be a man if I didn't look."

"Look? Your eyes practically bored holes into her tight, little body. This is what I'm talking about. I want the audience to believe that Danny is in love with Julia heart, mind, soul, and body, which isn't going to look like some twenty-one-year-old with breasts that defy gravity."

Gretchen started to get up. "I'm done here, Mr. Evans. Please don't contact me again."

Still unfazed, Charlie said, "Did you see me in *Roughing it in Detroit*? I played a blind, homeless man."

Donna cut in. "He won an Oscar for that role."

"I know. Blind beggar who beats the odds. Blah, blah, blah. The point is that this is my movie, my baby, and I'm not giving the role of Danny Jensen, a sensitive and compassionate human being, to a man who once said that all he wants out of life is old scotch and young snatch."

Donna countered. "Really, Gretchen. That was a long time ago."

"Last June?" said Gretchen.

"I will give you the performance of a lifetime. Trust me." Charlie was about to recite one of the lines in the script, when two very striking women reluctantly came up to the booth. Both were wearing tight T-shirts and skinny jeans. The shorter of the two said, "We're sorry to interrupt your conversation, but could we please have your autograph?"

The other woman said, "I'd do anything for one."

"Define anything," said Charlie. On cue, his megawatt smile dazzled everyone within striking distance. Everyone except Gretchen. As the woman leaned forward and whispered in his ear, Gretchen was attempting for the second time to leave, but Donna convinced her to stay a little longer. The exchange wasn't lost on Charlie.

"I'll give you this one for free." Charlie took two cocktail napkins off their table, signed them and handed them over to the women.

Turning his attention back to Gretchen, he once again began to recite one of the lines from her screenplay. Laughter from a nearby table interrupted his soliloquy. All three turned in the direction of the outburst.

Gretchen said, "How old do you think that woman is with the long, dark hair and bangs?"

Charlie said, "The one with the green top?"

Gretchen nodded.

"I don't know. Around forty-five, forty-six."

"Do you find her attractive?"

"She's okay, I guess." Charlie took a sip of his drink, clueless where the conversation was leading.

For the first time that evening, Gretchen smiled. She sat back in the plush, dark green booth and said, "You want to play Danny? Convince me. Go out with that woman, exclusively. Woo her. Make it very public. Make it very realistic. I want to see displays of affection. I want to see fucking hearts popping out of your head over her."

Charlie and Donna looked at each other and laughed. Then Charlie said, "You're serious?"

"Yup."

Donna said, "Let's go, Charlie. You don't want the part *that* badly. I'm in negotiations with Scorsese for his latest thriller. He already said he was interested in you for the leading role."

Charlie was staring at Gretchen, who kept the smile on her face. "I don't want to do another thriller." He looked back at Maddie, then turned his attention once again to Gretchen.

"I'll do it. How long?"

"As long as you're filming in the Bay Area."

Charlie nodded. "Any other rules? Meet her mom and dad? Wait, they're probably dead."

Gretchen sighed. "When I wrote the part of Danny, I was thinking DiCaprio."

"He's good. I'm a lot better."

"Where do you actors get such chutzpah? Or is it just unabashed egotism?"

Donna said, "The second one."

Back at Maddie's table, all the women were on their second drink except Maddie. She was still nursing the chocolate martini, determined to follow it with a tall glass of water. She noticed that as she aged, her body's tolerance for alcohol decreased. Two martinis and they'd be scraping her off the parquet dance floor. Ava was flying a little too high, her voice a little too loud. She was entertaining her friends with tales of her latest fling. Overly expressive, hand gestures aplenty, Ava was relating how she finally relented and had sex with the man on their third date. Maddie chimed in. "It's nice to know that you can wait until the third date to go down on the guy."

Maddie expected a response. Instead, her friends, a few slack-jawed, stared slightly above her head. Confused, Maddie turned. To her horror, there was Charlie Evans smiling down at her. He put his hand on her shoulder.

"Is this a bad time?"

"Please tell me that you're a man who looks incredibly similar to Charlie Evans."

He shook his head. "It's me. Would you like to dance?"

Charlie held out his hand and Maddie took it. As he led her onto the dance floor, she turned to face her friends, giving them a look of utter shock.

The DJ's selection was appropriate. They danced to Lady Gaga's *Bad Romance.* Maddie was having difficulty concentrating. She was sharing a dance with one of her favorite actors. How many times did she fantasize about being with Charlie Evans? Almost every time she watched one of his movies. The man was breathtaking. His smile, his seductive eyes. Even his ears were perfectly shaped. She decided to spend more of her energy watching Charlie dance than try and look cool. He was a fair dancer. No Patrick Swayze, but no Pee Wee Herman, either. He swayed to the beat of the music, very well aware that he was being watched, not just by Maddie, but by nearly half the patrons in the nightclub.

The song ended and was followed by Sam Smith's *Stay.* She assumed she was allotted one dance and started walking off the dance floor. Charlie took her hand, pulled her close to him and began slow dancing. His left hand rested on the small of her back. His right hand caressed her neck. For Charlie Evans, Madeleine was a prop, a tool to be used for an express purpose. For Madeleine, this was a dance she would never forget.

"What's your name?" Charlie asked as they glided across the floor.

"Madeleine, but my friends call me Maddie."

"Maddie what?"

"Mozart."

"Really?"

Maddie laughed. "Yes."

"Great name, Madeleine Mozart."

"Thank you, Charlie Evans." She was about to ask him a question when he deftly twirled her. It felt so natural. The normally klutzy Maddie turned perfectly, like a ballerina.

"So tell me, Ms. Mozart, what do you do for a living, besides looking lovely?" The last thing she wanted to tell the mega star was that she was living off unemployment. He would have twirled her off the dance floor and back to her seat.

"Let's not talk work. Are you in San Francisco on vacation?" As soon as she said it, she remembered that he was filming a movie.

"I'm shooting a film. Right now, we're over at the Japanese Tea Garden in Golden Gate Park."

"I love the tea garden, especially when the cherry trees are in bloom." She inwardly groaned, chiding herself for sounding like a tour guide.

The song over, Maddie thanked Charlie for the dance. He gave her a small bow. As they walked to the table, he said, "Can I take you someplace quiet for a nightcap?"

"Thank you, but I came here with my friends."

"Can't they share you with me, just for tonight?"

Maddie mentally smacked herself on her forehead. What the hell was she thinking? Charlie Evans just asked her for a date, kind of, and she refused him.

"Of course."

As they approached the table, the conversation came to an abrupt halt. The topic of discussion was obvious. Charlie turned to the women and said, "Ladies, it was a pleasure meeting all of you. Ms. Mozart – I love that name! – I'll be back shortly."

Once he was out of earshot, the questions started flying. Sylvie had been so nervous and excited for Maddie at the same time, that she downed her drink and was on her third martini. The closest she had ever been to a celebrity was when she accidentally bumped her shopping cart into Don Hardy, the news anchor from KNBR, the local television station.

"I can't believe you danced with THE Charlie Evans. He is so damned handsome!" Sylvie had to practically yell to be heard over the ever-increasing noise level. It was after ten and the young folk were drifting in like gangs of marauding hormones. They were dressed to score, ready for action, and many of them would succeed.

Maddie wiped her forehead with her cocktail napkin. "He asked me to go out for a drink. Tonight."

Ava looked offended. "You told him you were staying here with us, right?"

Before Maddie could answer, Tanvi said, "Are you crazy? Who would you rather be with, a group of slightly smashed women or the hottest actor in the world?"

"Really, Ava. What are you thinking?" Sylvie shook her head. "Have a blast, my dear, and do everything I would do and more."

Ava knew exactly what she was thinking. She tried not to look too upset, but she couldn't figure out why Charlie Evans picked Maddie and not her. She was younger and prettier and sexier. She glanced over at the booth where Charlie was in an animated conversation with two women. She would have loved to know what they were talking about.

As Maddie and Tanvi went off to the restroom, Gretchen was grilling Charlie on his new conquest.

"Congratulations. You got her to go out with you."

"Yeah, like that was going to be tough. Her name is Madeleine Mozart. It's going to look great in the tabloids."

Gretchen rolled her eyes. Charlie continued.

"I want to thank you, Gretchen."

"Why?"

"I couldn't have chosen a better way to prepare for the part of Danny, especially getting into bed with an older woman."

Gretchen said, "You need preparation for that?"

"And a handle of Jack Daniels. I know what an older woman's body looks like. I once saw my mother naked." He shivered.

Gretchen's opinion of Charlie dropped even lower than before. "What about you? You're no young stud anymore. You have wrinkles, don't you?"

"Sure, but they look better on men."

Donna said, "Even I find that offensive, Charlie, and I'm only thirty-five." She took a sip of her cocktail and continued. "Tell me, when this is over and you win, and I have no reason to believe you won't, how do you stop people from assuming that the only reason you dated this woman was to prepare for a role?"

Charlie turned to Gretchen with a look of inquiry. She thought for a moment, then said, "I'll tell the press that I chose you because of your relationship with an older woman, not the other way around."

Charlie smiled and said to Donna, "She's good." He turned to Gretchen. "You're very good."

Donna's cellphone rang. Normally, she wouldn't answer it during a business meeting, but she assumed that it was nearly over. Whitney Hyland's name flashed on the screen. She was one of Donna's latest clients, an aspiring actress. She knew what the phone call was about.

"Excuse me, but I need to take this. I'll be right back." Donna answered the call. "Whitney. Hi. Hold on. I can't hear you."

Donna walked in the direction of the bathroom. As she did, she passed Tanvi. Following the exit sign, Donna opened the door and entered a quiet zone.

"Love, are you still there?" asked Donna. "Great...yes, I am with Charlie, but I didn't have a chance to ask him about you...of course you're his type: young, talented, and gorgeous...you're welcome. The reason I couldn't ask him is because, and please keep this to yourself, he'll be dating an older woman in an attempt to prove to Gretchen Brockner that he could convincingly fall in love with this woman. Her name is Mozart...No dear, that's her last name...it's for the lead in Gretchen's new film...yes, he wants it that badly. As soon as Gretchen calls off the bet, he's dumping the woman and then he's all yours...I don't know. It could be a couple of months. Personally, I don't think he'll go the distance. She's probably in her mid to late forties...I know! I must be going and don't forget, you have an

15

audition at CBS next Tuesday with Kent Yulman. Sure…you, too. Bye."

Donna applied lip gloss and brushed her hair, then went back into the nightclub. When she heard the door close, Maddie walked out from behind the dumpster. She had been taking a breather, trying to wrap her head around the events of the evening. It now made perfect sense why Charlie Evans would pick her out of a sea of younger women. She felt nauseous and embarrassed. Her first instinct was to call Tanvi on her cell and meet her at the car. She didn't even want to look at Charlie again. She also didn't want to have to explain to her friends why a hot movie star really asked a woman like herself out.

Slowly, Maddie made her way back to the table. Charlie was there, regaling the women with a story. She took a deep, courageous breath and walked over to him. Charlie flashed her a big smile.

"There she is. Are you ready to paint the town red, blue, white, and perhaps even purple?"

"Sorry, but I have a splitting headache, so I'm going to pass. Thanks, anyway."

Undeterred, Charlie said, "I can get you some aspirin." He started to walk to the bar, but Maddie stopped him.

"Really, it's okay. I'm going to go home and sleep it off."

"Why don't you give me your number so I can take you out on a real date?"

"I don't know."

Maddie's friends were listening and couldn't believe what they were hearing. One of their own was chosen to go out with one of the most famous actors in the world and she was balking. They were all flummoxed. Sylvie couldn't stand it.

"For God's sake, woman, give the man your number. If you don't, I will!"

Charlie laughed. "I think you should listen to her, Madeleine. Otherwise, I'll follow you home and I would prefer not to take up stalking."

Smiling weakly, Maddie gave in. She dipped into her purse and pulled out one of her old business cards and a pen. On the back of the card, she wrote down her number.

Charlie took the card from her like he was being handed the Holy Grail. "I'll call you. I promise." And with the first hurdle under his belt, he walked back to the booth where Donna was waiting. Gretchen had already left, practically bolting out of the loud and raucous venue. His agent wished Charlie good luck. Though the words were dripping with insincerity, he welcomed them anyway.

Maddie watched as Charlie showed Donna her business card. She felt like going over and ripping it out of his hands.

"What the hell has gotten into you, woman?" Sylvie was lit and with it came unbridled honesty. "All it takes is a headache to turn down Charlie Evans? I'd have to be headless to refuse the guy, I mean Adonis."

Tanvi was next. She knew how enamored Maddie was of Charlie. On the way to the restroom, she couldn't stop talking about him, plus the attention she received from the women in the bathroom was enormous. These cute, young girls were fawning over her, asking her what it was like to dance with a movie star. It was intoxicating for Tanvi and she was peripherally involved. Somewhere between the restroom and the table, Maddie had a change of heart and Tanvi had no idea why. She put her hand on Maddie's shoulder. "Do you really have a headache or did you fall in the bathroom and now have amnesia? You nearly turned down the most sought- after man in…everywhere!"

Ava didn't say a word. She sat back and silently stewed. She would have loved it if Maddie refused Charlie's advances. It would have been Ava's cue to offer to show him her version of a night on the town. Instead, Sylvie had to ruin it, shaming Maddie into compliance. Damn her.

"Sorry, gals," Maddie said as she put her hand to her forehead. "My head really is killing me. Besides, what's the point of going out with Charlie when all he really wants to do is get laid. Once that happens, I'm history."

Sylvie yelled a little too loud, "That's the point, damn it! Sleep with him. I want to know what it's like to fuck a megastar!" A few people close by turned their heads.

Tanvi said, "Come on, Maddie. I'll take you home." She turned to Sylvie and Ava. "Enjoy the rest of your night, ladies. Behave yourselves."

In the car, Maddie was exceptionally quiet. Normally, she would have told Tanvi her reason for refusing Charlie's advances. Her pride stopped her. She felt too vulnerable and insecure. At her age, she was witnessing the waning of attention from the opposite sex. Her pool of available suitors had gone from a lake to a mud puddle, so when Charlie paid attention to her, it was indescribably gratifying. Tanvi was her good friend, but it didn't stop Maddie from feeling like a failure. After all, she had just been used in a bet. The women made small talk and she silently thanked her friend for not prying. All she wanted to do was go to sleep and pretend it never happened.

2

By the time Maddie was finished recounting the night, Priscilla was wide awake. She had made a cup of tea and was sipping it while eating a chocolate chip cookie.

"What a schmuck. What a gorgeous, sexy schmuck. So what are you going to do if he calls? He is going to call, you know."

"I know," Maddie said as she lay back on her bed. Mick jumped up and lay beside her, sensing her malaise. "I should have known that a movie star who dates beautiful, young women wouldn't be interested in me."

"That's true."

"Priscilla!"

"Sorry, kiddo, but that's the honest truth. Let's face it, the man thinks a woman in her thirties is over the hill. You're like Grandma Moses. No offense."

"Offense totally taken. My ego is plummeting faster than my heart."

Priscilla finished off the cookie and washed it down with the last gulp of tea. As she put the mug down, she said, "I know a way to buoy your ego. Go out with him. Have a blast."

Maddie was insulted. "The man is a jerk. Why would I want to spend time with him?"

"Uh, what's going on in your life right now?"

"I'm on my bed and it's..."

"M&M, you know what I mean. You're in a lull. More like a coma. Take advantage of the hiccup in activity and let go. Have fun."

"That doesn't seem right. I'd be using him."

"Honey, he's using you."

"Yeah, but two wrongs don't make a right."

Priscilla got up off the couch and started pacing. The conversation got her totally energized. "Sure they do. If Charlie gets the part in the movie, he has you to thank for it. That's worth something, isn't it? Don't you deserve a commission? Maddie, the guy's loaded. USE HIM!"

"I don't know."

"Don't overthink it. Just do it."

Maddie smiled. "It could be fun, huh?"

"Duh. It's movie premieres and hanging out with Robert De Niro and Julia Roberts and vacationing on the Riviera. It's eating at the most expensive restaurants and getting fabulous gifts, like jewelry and clothes. It's..."

"I don't know if he'll buy me gifts."

"Make him! Sweetie, this is a once-in-a-lifetime experience. I'm drooling again!"

Maddie was starting to get excited. Up until now, her dating life had been dismal. She could be doing a lot worse than going out with Charlie Evans. As she sat up, her shirt rose above her waist and she caught sight of her stomach slightly hanging out. She groaned.

"I can't do this. My body's starting to look like a tube steak." She grabbed her stomach and massaged it. "My belly feels like warm dough. Let's get real, Priscilla. The man is used to stellar bodies and large, fake breasts. I look like Mama June compared to them. It'll be humiliating."

"First of all, you're exaggerating. You look great. You know you're in better shape than most thirty-year-olds. But if it bothers you that much, don't let him see you naked. Don't sleep with him."

Maddie thought about it. "That could work. It will also drive him crazy. I'll be the only woman he's never slept with." She got up and put the phone on speaker, then started taking off her jewelry. "You're a good friend. A brutally honest friend, but a good one. Give Mr. Peepers a hug for me and one for yourself. I'll let you know when Charlie calls. Goodnight, dear."

"Goodnight, M&M. I can't wait for an update. This is so exciting."

As soon as she hung up, Ray knocked on her bedroom door.

Maddie said, "Come in."

With very red eyes, Maddie's son walked into her room. "Were you talking to Priscilla?"

"Yeah. Were you smoking a ton of pot?"

"Yeah. So, how was dancing?"

"It was fun. You'll never guess who asked me out tonight."

Ray scratched his head. "I don't know. Brad Pitt?"

"Nope."

"Daniel Craig?"

"Would have been nice, but no."

"Charlie Evans?"

"How'd you know?"

Ray just laughed. "I'm going to bed."

"He really did ask me out. I even danced with him." Maddie pretended to dance with an invisible partner.

"Now who's the stoned one? Goodnight, crazy lady."

"I'm serious."

Ray just shook his head and went to his room, leaving Maddie alone with her thoughts. The situation felt surreal. When she was talking to Priscilla, the plan to date Charlie made sense. He uses her. She uses him. The wrongs cancel each other out. Simple. It didn't feel simple, though. Maddie put her hands over her heart and closed her eyes. She silently asked herself if this was the right thing to do. Almost immediately, the answer came back, clear and without room for interpretation. She opened her eyes and looked in the mirror. "It could have been fun."

Back at the nightclub, Charlie had talked Donna into staying a little longer. They shared a bottle of champagne to celebrate his latest challenge. He and Donna made a bet of their own. She thought Maddie would sleep with him on the first date.

"I know her a little better than you and I think she's going to make me wait until date number three."

"She seemed pretty smitten to me."

"I don't know. I had to pull out the charm gun to get her to give me her number. I was getting nervous."

Donna looked shocked. "You pulled out what? With all these people around?"

"Hell no! It's an expression, like pulling out the big guns. I pull out the charm gun when I need help talking someone into something I want. Come on, let's dance."

"Only under the condition that you keep the charm gun under wraps. I'm impervious to you actors and your charms, gun or no gun."

Between dancing and drinking, Charlie had to refuse the advances of no fewer than six women and two men. He had no problem telling the men to get lost, but it took all his will power to tell at least three of the women that he had to decline their invitations of guaranteed intimacy. Playing the role of Madeleine Mozart's boyfriend was going to be tougher than he thought. Charlie tried to remember what she looked like. She had small crow's feet around her eyes and her two front teeth just barely crossed over each other. The rest of her face was a blur.

3

Sunday night at the Mozart house found Maddie watching the tail end of *Dateline*. Ray was in his room finishing up homework. After Maddie asked him to turn down the stereo twice, he relented and the volume was no longer competing with Erin Moriarty's interview with a woman who allegedly murdered her husband for the insurance money. Mick's snore was becoming increasingly loud as he drifted deeper into slumber. Maddie gently nudged him with her foot. He snorted a few times, looked up at her with his soft, wet eyes, and then lay his head back down on her foot. Shortly after, the snoring started up again. Maddie sighed and turned up the volume. When her cell rang, she paused the program and looked at the number. It had a 310 area code. She didn't recognize it.

"Hello?"

"Madeleine Mozart?"

"That's me."

"I thought you might have given me a wrong number. I'm so glad you didn't."

"Hello Charlie." It's Showtime, she thought. Time to tell the man who rarely hears the word 'no' that she's refusing his invitation to go out. She was astronomically nervous. She began to perspire, first on her forehead. Then her upper lip. She steeled herself, then continued. "The thought crossed my mind, then I realized that I could have set you upon an unsuspecting person."

Surprised by the rebuff, he forged forward. "I'm enjoying a glass of wine on my hotel room veranda overlooking the Golden Gate Bridge and I thought of you."

What a crock of shit, she thought. "The bridge is quite a sight, isn't it?"

Charlie stood up and went over to the railing. "It would be if the fog hadn't set in and partially ruined my view. It's also very chilly. Too bad you're not here to warm me up."

Maddie almost laughed out loud. On the corny scale of one to ten, that was a solid nine. Did he really think she'd fall for that?

"I guess you're just going to have to drink more wine. That'll heat you up. Have you started shooting the film yet?"

Feeling a bit deflated by her snub, he tried again. "I'll answer your question after you pour yourself a glass of vino. It will be like sitting with you."

Creative, Maddie thought. No harm in enjoying their first and last conversation. "Okay, I'll play along." She got up off the couch and went into the kitchen. Luckily, she had an opened bottle of pinot noir from her dinner last night with Priscilla. "Can you hear me pouring?"

"I can. Don't tell me. I bet you're having a zinfandel."

"Wrong. I'll give you a hint. It's fruit forward with an aroma like roses and black cherry."

"That's easy. It's a pinot noir. My stepfather is into wines. He taught me well."

"He certainly did. I love reds. Zinfandel is actually my favorite. I love the peppery overtones."

"I agree. So, Ms. Mozart. You're into fine wines and I bet your favorite music is classical. Very chic."

Maddie took a sip of her wine and lay back on the couch, resting her feet on Mick. "You would have lost the bet. I'm a huge country music fan. Years ago, I was a sales rep for a country radio station. I never cared for the music until I really started listening to the words. They tell such great stories. Before I knew it, I was buying Vince Gill and Shania Twain CDs."

"There's nothing wrong with country." Charlie grimaced. He hated country music.

"So, when do you start shooting or have you already begun? Wait, you told me Friday night. You're at the Japanese Tea Garden in Golden Gate Park, right?"

"Yup. Do you want to come to the set and watch?"

"Thanks for the offer. I already have plans."

"You have a standing invitation."

For the next half hour, Charlie and Maddie talked like they were old friends. He asked her about her childhood, her marriage to Tommy. Even her children. She couldn't believe how attentive he was and how easily the conversation flowed. One more glass of wine and Maddie's resolve to reject his advances began to weaken. Instead of feeling antipathy, she was fantasizing about being in his arms.

"What are you doing Friday night?" Charlie asked.

"I think I have plans," she said unconvincingly.

Charlie didn't see that coming. He could have sworn she was going to ask him out first. Undeterred and with a slightly bruised ego, he tried again. "I'll make you a deal: let me take you out to dinner this Friday and if you never want to see me again, I shall slink away into the night, lick my wounds and move on. Deal?"

Maddie now knew what it was like to have an angel on one shoulder and a devil on the other. In her case, it was her intuition whispering in her right ear that she must politely decline the enticing invitation. A mini-Priscilla stood tall on her left shoulder, yelling in her ear that she'll never, ever have an opportunity like this again. *It's one date, M&M. Just do it!*

Maddie dusted off her right shoulder and said, "Deal."

Charlie was ecstatic. "Wonderful! How about I take you to the best restaurant in San Rafael?"

"I'm in."

"Great. What's your address?"

Maddie recited it. Before she could give him directions, Charlie said he'd let GPS find it. "I'm looking forward to seeing you."

"Me, too."

"Enjoy your evening. Talk to you soon."

"You, too. Good night."

Maddie hung up the phone and finished her wine. She stared at the empty glass. "You made me do this. Fie on you, killer of intuitive action." She called Priscilla. While waiting for her to pick up, she turned off the television, no longer interested in watching.

"I just got off the phone with Mr. Evans. He was turning on the charm, big time. Or at least was trying to."

"You didn't get too sarcastic with him, did you? I know how you can get."

"Don't worry. I played into his corniness, to a degree. He's trying too hard to win me over. If he only knew that I knew."

"But he won't. Ever. Right?"

"No, dear. Don't worry, okay?"

Priscilla said, "Okay."

It was close to 11:00 when their conversation ended. Maddie was exhausted and excited and confused as to why she would be excited going out with a man who was using her. She washed her face and brushed her teeth, then looked more closely at her teeth. They didn't look white enough. She would go to the drug store and pick up one of those whitening pens. She used the magnifying mirror to check out the part in her hair. The grays were starting their assault, easily overtaking the dwindling chestnut brown hairs. She made a mental note to call her stylist and make an appointment.

"Come on over, Ms. Mozart." Angie gave the chair one more slap with the towel, removing any traces of her last client's curly auburn hair. Her spike heels made little clickety sounds as she walked around to the front of the chair and gave Maddie a hug before she sat down.

"Where the hell have you been, woman? I thought you went and found another hairdresser to harass."

Maddie placed herself in the plush, sky blue chair, her destination for the next two hours. "You know you're my favorite snipper and dyer. I'm between jobs. Pretty hair is a luxury right now."

Angie smirked. "Okay, who's the guy and when are you seeing him?"

"How do you know it's not a job interview?"

"You use that 'Tween Time coloring crayon for interviews. You spend the bucks for a special date. So tell me, is he local?"

Maddie wondered if she should tell Angie, the human megaphone, whom she was dating. Once told, the city of San Rafael would be buzzing with the news. Then again, stepping out in public with Charlie Evans would alert the paparazzi and then the whole world would know.

"If you must know, I have a date this Friday with Charlie Evans."

Angie stared at Maddie in the mirror. Finally, she said, "So how short do you want it and are we keeping the same color?"

"Did you hear what I said?"

"Listen, if you don't want to tell me who you're going out with, that's your choice. It's not my place to pry." Angie put her hand about two inches above the bottom of Maddie's hair. "I think that would be a good length for you. You like?"

Maddie played along. Angie would find out soon enough. "Yeah, and let's stick with the chestnut brown."

While Angie went into the other room to prepare the hair color solution, Maddie picked up the latest *People* magazine. She started reading about supposed marriage troubles between Ryan Gosling and Eva Mendes. In the chair to her left, a very chatty client was talking about her recent trip to San Francisco. Maddie only half listened until she started talking about Charlie Evans.

"I couldn't believe it. Here I am walking through Golden Gate Park and all of a sudden the Japanese Tea Garden is closed to the public. There were police cars everywhere and all these people were standing around. Then I noticed the cameras and big Klieg lights. They were filming a movie. It was so exciting. I got as close as I could and then I saw him. Charlie Evans! He is so handsome. Even more so in person. Rachel Swanson is also in the movie except she wasn't at the location. I would have loved to see what she really looks like. I heard she's not nearly as beautiful in person."

Angie's head popped out of the doorway. "You weren't kidding, were you?"

Maddie shook her head and as soon as she did, she regretted it. She loved the attention and she hated the attention because she knew Charlie's attraction wasn't genuine. The adulation was based on a lie.

Angie pointed to Maddie and then said loud enough for the

entire salon to hear, "She's going out with Charlie Evans! I'm so jealous!" With a bowl of chestnut brown hair paste, Angie came back to Maddie and said, "Where did you meet him? When? How? Talk, woman!"

The salon was aflutter with shouts of congratulations. There were more than a few mouths agape. Some women looked like they wanted to come up and high-five Maddie and others looked downright envious. A few others weren't convinced and looked at Maddie as if she were delusional. They held those images of a lithe, young beauty with her arms wrapped around Charlie's willing body, not a woman slightly older than he sitting in a San Rafael salon like themselves, getting her gray hair dyed. That was the look Maddie was most expecting to see for the duration of her relationship with Charlie Evans.

While Angie applied the coloring paste, Maddie regaled her with the story of how she went to the city to dance and came away with the promise of a date. There was no mention of the wager between actor and director.

Maddie had to admit that the two hours flew by, fielding questions, some of them intimate from people she didn't know. Peripherally, she understood how celebrities felt, violated by the press and by strangers who approached them, asking for an autograph or a photo op. She had automatically had become public property. If this was a small taste of what was to come, Maddie realized that she better mentally brace herself. She was stepping into uncharted territory. It reminded her of Cher's young boyfriend of twenty or so years ago, dubbed Bagel Boy. The poor guy lasted about two months in the spotlight. He could barely take a step without being hounded. Maddie wondered if she would be given a nickname. They'd probably call her the Marin County MILF or the San Francisco Forty-Sixer. She prayed that no one coined a nickname with the word 'old' in it.

When Maddie walked through the front door, Ray was sitting on the couch watching television. He was munching on what looked like a cross between a Hostess snowball and a huge dandelion. He looked up and Maddie moved her head from side to side, giving her son the full impact of her new hairdo. He whistled.

"Looking hot, mom. I was wondering when you were going to delete the line of cocaine from the top of your head."

"I beg your pardon. It wasn't that bad."

"My teenage eyes outplay your old lady eyes. It wasn't pretty." Ray held up his snack. "Check it out. My latest munchie sensation. I call it the S'morb. Inside the marshmallow covering is a ball of raspberry fudge and crushed graham crackers."

Maddie got closer to inspect her son's latest creation. Only cooking when she absolutely had to, she was in awe of how creative his culinary skills were. "This looks like one big marshmallow."

Ray smiled broadly, feeling very pleased with himself. "It's not. I gently toasted each mallow and stuck them together. The result is an orb of pleasure. Here's the coup de grace." He took a lighter out of his pocket and swept it back and forth under the S'morb. "Now try it."

Maddie took a bite and closed her eyes. The fudge was rich and crunchy from the graham crackers, the marshmallow warm and gooey. "Someday, in the not-too-distant future, I'm going to be bragging to my friends that my son is the owner of a snack company extraordinaire. Keep up the great work, kiddo."

"Thanks, Mom. So, what's for dinner?"

Maddie put down her purse and took off her sweater. "After I check out what's in the fridge, I'll let you know."

4

It was Friday night. Charlie Evans would be picking Maddie up in an hour. Her outfit chosen, she went into the bathroom to touch up her make-up. As she grabbed her make-up bag, Mick ran into the bathroom and bumped her, sending mascara, eye shadow and a few lip pencils flying.

"I'm sorry, Mick, did you want something?" she said as she picked everything up off the floor before the boxer had a chance to drool on it. "Sit."

Dutifully, Mick did as he was told, then lay down on the bathroom mat, resting his head on his paws.

Maddie stood in front of the floor length mirror and inspected her image as Eric Church serenaded her with *Smoke A Little Smoke*. She began to dance and sing along. "Break out that old rock and roll. Drink a little drink, smoke a little smoke. Yeah."

From the kitchen, Ray yelled, "Turn it up, Ma! Sick song."

Maddie danced over to the stereo on her dresser and increased the volume. She wore a teal sweater over her light yellow tank top. Her skinny jeans hit the strap of the teal high-heeled sandals. She chose a pink quartz heart necklace with matching earrings. Never one to fawn over precious or semi-precious stones, Maddie idly wondered if she would be adding more expensive items to her jewelry collection via Charlie.

The theme from *A Summer Place* chirped to life. Maddie grabbed her cell. Priscilla. She smiled as she answered. "Hallo."

"Hallo you lucky thing, you. Are you ready for the date of the century?"

Maddie turned to look at her back in the mirror. "I believe so.

This is going to be fun."

"Wait a minute. You don't sound like the slightly hyper Maddie I know and love. What's up?"

"I can't be poised and cool under pressure?"

"Nope."

"I'm offended."

You're lying."

Maddie giggled. "I had a glass of wine. It deleted the freaked out emoji in me and replaced it with the half-lidded smiley face. I feel soft and fluffy."

"Not too fluffy, dear. You have to remember why Charlie is going out with you. You need a little edge, otherwise there's nothing in your emotional arsenal to fend off his advances. No more wine, okay?"

"Yes, Ms. P."

The doorbell rang. Maddie yelled, "Get the door Ray, please." Back on the phone. "Got to go. My date has arrived. Later."

Ray walked out of his room, followed by a plume of marijuana smoke. When he opened the front door, he was eye to eye with Charlie Evans. Charlie put out his hand. "Hi. I'm Charlie. Are you Madeleine's son?"

Ray poked his head around the door, first to one side, then the other. "Am I being punk'd?"

Charlie said, "Don't you have to be famous to be punk'd?"

"Are *you* being punk'd?"

Charlie laughed. "No. I'm here to pick up your mother. She is your mother, right?"

"Uh, yeah, I guess. I mean, yes." He continued to stare at Charlie.

"Can I come in?"

"Sorry, dude. I'm usually not this rude. Come on in. I'll get my mom."

Charlie watched as the last remnants of smoke settled on the furniture, then evaporated. He went over to a wall of photos. Most of the pictures were of Kenzie and Ray at various stages of childhood. He lingered on Kenzie's high school graduation picture, then sat down on the sofa next to *Tatted Up* magazine. He picked it up and leafed through it while waiting for a very stoned Ray to get his mother.

Slightly above a whisper, Ray said, "I can't believe Charlie Evans is in our house!"

"I told you he asked me out."

"I thought you were joking. You are so much cooler than I thought."

"Thanks?" Maddie turned off the stereo, glanced in the mirror one more time, reapplied her lipstick, fluffed her hair, sucked in her stomach and walked out of her room to greet her date.

Charlie stood when he saw Maddie. He had to admit it. She looked very pretty. Sexy even. And not just for an older woman. "Don't you look beautiful, Ms. Mozart."

Brace yourself, Maddie, she said to herself. This man is dangerous. She gave him the once over, from the very expensive-looking shoes to his pleated jeans and pinstriped pink and white button-down long-sleeved shirt. He looked like he just came off a photo shoot for J. Crew. Despite his compliment, she didn't feel nearly as beautiful as he looked.

"Thank you," she said. "I see you met Ray."

"I certainly did." Charlie picked up the magazine. "Do you have any tattoos?"

Ray walked over to where Charlie was standing and pulled up his left pant leg to reveal a skull with a bottle bursting out of its head, the contents splashing out onto his knee.

"I designed this one."

"That's quite a tattoo. You're a talented artist." Charlie pointed to the rattlesnake wrapped around a gold carrot, its forked tongue licking the top. "Did you design that one, too?"

"Sure did. And this one." Ray pulled up his right pant leg and Charlie was staring at a wolf, its tail wrapped around his shin.

"Wow. Very nice."

"Thanks. Do you have any tats?"

"No. Not my style." Charlie turned to Maddie. "Shall we go? A friend told me about this great steakhouse. The Tinderbox. He said they have the best cuts of sirloin he's ever tasted. I made reservations."

Ray shook his head. "Bad move, dude."

Maddie said, "I'm a vegan. Not a fan of steakhouses."

"I thought you loved country music."

Maddie laughed. "I do, but that doesn't make me a redneck or a carnivore. Dwight Yoakum and Kellie Pickler are vegetarians and Carrie Underwood is vegan."

"Well, I stand corrected. Okay, you pick the restaurant."

"Already did. Shall we?"

Charlie nodded. They said good-bye to Ray as Charlie attempted to put his arm around Maddie. She shifted, deliberately avoiding the move. Charlie rolled with it, not wanting to look like a jerk in front of her son.

As soon as they closed the door, Ray called his sister. Kenzie was three years older than her brother, in her third year at UC Berkeley. She picked up on the second ring.

"Ray-man. What's up?"

"Mom's dating Charlie Evans. That's what's up."

Kenzie sighed. "I told you that if you keep smoking so much pot, you'll start hallucinating."

"Yes, I'm stoned. No, I'm not hallucinating. It's him, Kenzie. I heard the words come out of his mouth. 'Hi, I'm Charlie. You must be Madeleine's son.' She told me that he asked her out, but I didn't believe her."

"Unreal. Our mother is dating a celebrity." Kenzie was proud of her mom. It was common knowledge that Charlie preferred women younger closer to her age than her mother's. "Do me a favor and tell her to call me when she has a chance."

Ray said, "Why don't you just text her?"

"I'm not going to bother her when she's on a date, especially one with a movie star. Please just write her a note or something."

"Fine. Later."

"Later."

"Turn right at the stop sign. Nice car," said Maddie as they pulled away from the curb. The late model Porsche had a new-car scent. "Except for the leather seats, I wouldn't mind owning one of these babies."

Charlie mentally rolled his eyes. "What's wrong with leather?"

"Think about it. If I don't eat the cow, why would I wear or use its skin? In addition, the hide tanning industry is an environmental disaster. Turn left at the light."

"Are you going to tell me where we're going?"

"Sorry. The Veggie Grill in Corte Madera. Have you heard of it?"

"No. Should I have?"

"They have restaurants all over. There's one in Los Angeles. You live there, right?"

"Malibu." He turned left at the light. "You picked a restaurant chain for our first date? Not very romantic, Ms. Mozart."

Maddie turned to face Charlie. His profile was flawless. She marveled at how his hair was styled perfectly. His nose was not a pug or a hook, but straight with a slight dip at the end. Even his eyebrows looked manicured. She had an urge to touch his cheek to make sure he was real.

Charlie said, "Were you going to say something or just stare at me?"

"Don't flatter yourself. I was going to say that the Veggie Grill has great food and that takes precedence over ambience. Oh, turn right onto the freeway. In about five minutes you'll exit at the Madera off-ramp." As an afterthought, she said, "You do have a nice profile."

"Thanks." Charlie sped up the freeway ramp and raced ahead of the traffic, going about eighty miles an hour. Maddie wasn't sure if he was showing off or he normally drove recklessly. She ignored it for now.

Bright orange umbrellas surrounded the front of Veggie Grill as if beckoning diners to come inside the festive restaurant. The orange and lime-green color scheme greeted its guests. One wall was covered with photos of their plant-based dishes. The décor reminded Charlie of the commissary at 20th Century Fox. It was almost utilitarian. Even though the restaurant was nearly full of patrons seemingly enjoying their vegan meals, Charlie was confused by Maddie's choice of restaurant. He was prepared to spend hundreds of dollars. Instead, he could pay for the entire meal with cash. He had been counting on the steakhouse to assist in his seduction. He was told the soft lighting and plush booths made for an amorous dining experience. Instead, he was going to have to improvise or find a cozy bar to cap off the evening before he took Maddie home. Or back to his hotel suite.

Maddie handed Charlie the menu and they took their place in the order line. Heads were turning. People were pointing and cellphone cameras were clicking. Most of the women had goofy smiles on their faces. The only people not gawking at the couple were children and more than a few men.

Charlie returned some of the smiles and willingly gave autographs. Maddie knew this would happen and she was fully prepared. She mentally calmed her mind and physically blocked out the attention by concentrating on the menu.

"So, what do you recommend?" Charlie said as he looked at the menu.

"My favorite is the breaded chick'n with cauliflower mashed potatoes, sautéed kale, and mushroom gravy."

"Sounds great," he said as convincingly as possible. What he was craving was a sirloin steak smothered in grilled onions and steak sauce with a baked potato dripping in butter, topped with sour cream and chives, and a nice glass of cabernet sauvignon.

When they reached the counter, the young cashier blushed. She grabbed her ponytail and nervously twirled it. "Oh my God. You're Charlie Evans. I didn't know you're vegan."

He smiled. "I'm not, but my date is and where she goes, I go."

After they ordered and were given a number, they picked a booth in the back of the restaurant, hoping it would give them a modicum of privacy. Maddie slid into the booth and, to her surprise, Charlie sat right next to her. She wanted to say something, but felt that the evening so far was being dictated by her, so she let it go. About a minute later, Charlie excused himself and went to the restroom.

Maddie tried to look busy. It wasn't easy. She took a sip of water and then checked her email on her phone. She felt people eyeing her, judging her. It was unnerving. Maybe she wasn't cut out for this kind of scrutiny and it had only just begun.

Charlie returned at the same time their meal was brought to the table.

"So tell me. What do you do in San Rafael besides looking lovely?"

"Nothing else. Looking lovely is a full-time endeavor." She took a bite of the meal. "So good!"

Charlie cut into the chick'n and took a bite. "It really is good. No, it's great."

"You sound surprised."

"This type of food is new to me, but I could definitely get used to it."

"Getting back to your question about work, I was laid off a few months ago and am living off unemployment. How sexy is that?"

Rarely was Charlie stymied. When it came to seducing women, he seemed to have an answer for every situation. When he discovered that a hand model he ended up in bed with had a prosthetic leg, he seamlessly switched his compliments from her beautiful hands to admitting that she had the most beautiful leg he'd ever seen. If she had two legs, he would have been overwhelmed. The model was flattered, the sex was interesting and he never asked her out again. How was he supposed to turn living off the government with a measly check every month into a compliment? He stuffed a forkful of kale into his mouth while he thought about it. Suddenly, he said, "There's nothing sexier than a woman who's available all the time. It will give you a chance to visit me on the set. Would you like to?"

"That sounds like fun. Sure." She took another bite of mashed potatoes. "So tell me. What is the movie about?"

"It's a romantic thriller. I play a high-powered executive who falls for an associate's wife. They begin an affair that ends very, very badly for me."

"What happens?"

"I can't tell you. You're going to have to see the movie."

"I knew you'd say that. Is Rachel Swanson the femme fatale?"

"How'd you know?"

"I saw it on TV. She's so beautiful."

Charlie glanced over at the door, then said, "You're just as beautiful."

"Please. She is so hot."

"It's not natural. She's had a lot of work done."

"I still say she looks great and if I had the money, I'd gussy myself up, too."

Charlie chuckled. "Gussy?"

"That really dates me, doesn't it?"

"Yeah, like early 20th century. That's okay. It's one of my favorite eras." Again, Charlie looked over at the entrance. "So, are you ready for dessert?"

"I thought you'd never ask. The carrot cake is unbelievable. It's moist and sweet and I love it."

Charlie stood up. "Don't go anywhere. I'll be right back."

It took him three times longer to reach the counter than normal. He was stopped by no fewer than five other diners. Autographs, fawning, words of adulation. Maddie marveled at his patience and grace. People did everything but paw him.

When Charlie returned to their booth, he slid in next to her and planted a big kiss right on her mouth. Too stunned to refuse, Maddie leaned into him and enjoyed the experience. Flashes of light appeared suddenly, distracting her. When she looked up, two men with cameras were shooting away. One of them sat across from the couple and continued to shoot. Charlie looked clearly upset.

"Well if isn't the puppy squad."

The chubby, unkempt paparazzo smiled at Maddie. It verged on a leer. "How's it going, Charlie? Is this your new girlfriend?"

"Ms. Mozart and I are trying to have a nice dinner. If you don't mind, we'd like a little privacy."

Undeterred, the chubby one continued to badger the couple. "Mozart? Is that your real name?"

Maddie said, "No. I only use it when I date celebrities. My real name is Doe. Jane Doe."

The thinner paparazzo who was sitting at their booth, stood. "She's funny. It's nice to see you dating someone your own age. Come on Phil. Enjoy your dinner." The men were gone as quickly as they showed up.

Maddie said, "I certainly didn't need to hear that."

"Me, neither. What an asshole."

"Totally."

The waiter arrived with their carrot cakes. As they ate, Maddie said, "So tell me. What's your favorite movie?"

"Let me see. *Angels of Truth* used to be my favorite, but now I think it's *Roughing it in Detroit* because I won an Oscar for best actor."

"Not one of yours. I'm talking about a movie you've seen so many times that you've lost track. A movie that you could pop in the DVD tonight and watch it like it was for the first time."

Without even thinking, he said, "That's easy. *The Great Race*."

"Are you serious? That's my favorite movie!"

"No way."

"Yes way. 'Push the button, Max'."

They continued to eat their dessert, talking about the Blake Edwards movie made in 1965 starring Jack Lemmon, Natalie Wood, Peter Falk, and Tony Curtis.

Charlie said, "What's your favorite scene?"

"There are so many. If I had to pick my very favorite, that would have to be the pie fight. It's a classic. Is that your favorite, too?"

"Nope. It's when they're stuck in the snowstorm and the polar bear climbs into Professor Fate's car. The look on Jack Lemmon and Peter Falk's faces is classic. I have a good idea. Why don't we go back to your place and watch it?"

"You won't believe this, but I used to have the video. When I got rid of my VCR and got a DVD player, I never bought the DVD. Can I still be part of the fan club?"

Charlie shook his head in disbelief. "Granted, it's not easy to find on DVD and I have to admit that Jack Lemmon gave me a copy when I told him it was my favorite movie, but still, you should have it in your library. If the actors who played major roles weren't all dead, and the director, too, I would have had to report you."

"It's hard to believe they're all gone. How sad."

"You know what they say: Old actors never die, they just get digitized."

Maddie laughed. She picked up her water and lifted it high. "A toast. To the Great Leslie, Professor Fate, and Maggie DuBois."

"And Max." Charlie held up his water glass, clinking it to hers, letting it linger. She pulled away first and took a sip. Charlie finished the last bite of carrot cake. "Why don't we go get a drink?"

Maddie wanted to say something. Instead, she held her tongue. Charlie was trying way too hard and she knew why. The kiss was exclusively for the tabloids and having a cocktail was the perfect scene to set his trap and have her walk right into it. She didn't care for the subterfuge, yet she did sign up for the game, so she relented.

"I have the perfect spot. Have you heard of the Pelican Inn?"

Charlie took out his iPhone and asked Siri to find it. Seconds later, an image of a country cottage appeared on his screen. Directions followed. "It looks exactly like what I had in mind. Let's go."

Twenty minutes later, the Porsche roared into the parking lot. If Beatrix Potter had lived in Muir Beach, her home would have been a replica of the Pelican Inn. The only thing missing from the English country inn was a thatched roof. Charlie was ecstatic. He pictured them having a few drinks, then retiring to one of the rooms for the night. Or maybe for just a few hours.

Maddie could feel the sexual energy coming off the determined actor. She made it her objective to be the one woman who wouldn't turn to flubber in his arms, in his bed, or in his car. The resolution made her walk a little taller and a lot prouder.

The hostess greeted them, dressed in Renaissance garb. Her white flouncy shirt, covered by a patchwork corset, accentuated her breasts. The striped skirt partially hid knee-high boots. She walked them past the massive stone fireplace where a fully engaged fire heated up the bar. The imposing oak mantel was inscribed with a parable in gold lettering. It read, "Fear Knocked at the Door. Faith answered. No one was there."

They were seated at a window table, looking out over the English garden. It was dark, but small, white lights illuminated the path that wound its way through the trees and shrubs. Charlie exchanged looks with the waitress and said in a British accent, "What's in a name? That which we call a rose by any other name would smell as sweet."

The waitress said, "Shakespeare ala Jude Law!"

Maddie countered, "I believe that was Sir Lawrence Olivier."

Charlie pointed to Maddie. "Correct."

"Who?" the twenty-something barmaid said.

"One of the best Shakespearean actors of all time. Now, if you would be so kind, I would like your best single malt scotch on the rocks." He turned to Maddie. "And for you, milady?"

"Your finest cosmopolitan, if you please." Once the waitress left, Maddie said, "Have you ever been in a Shakespeare play?"

Still channeling Olivier, Charlie said, "Oh, how you jest. From Garber High School's drama class to Ye Olde Avon Theatre in Burbank, I've been in many a Shakespeare play. Too many to count, milady." Then Charlie proceeded to list the plays and his roles in them. Nearly an hour and two drinks later, Charlie was more than amorous and Maddie was less than willing. Every time Charlie attempted to hold her hand or put his arm around her, she deflected his touch. By the third failed try, Charlie looked exasperated.

Maddie said, "You're going to feel a whole better if you realize that I'm not comfortable with your advances. I told you that back at the Veggie Grill and I mean it. Can I please enjoy myself without wondering if you're going to try something?"

She sounded like she was admonishing a child, but she felt he was acting like one, not to mention being completely disrespectful of her wishes.

Charlie's first instinct was to lash out. He was mad. His plan wasn't working. Then he recalibrated his emotions. He talked himself down. Maddie wasn't the helpless prey he had believed her to be. It reminded him of his breakthrough role, where he played a starving artist in love with a reporter from the Los Angeles Times. She was beautiful and talented and engaged to the publisher. The odds were against him, but he slowly and patiently wooed her and she was his in the end. He loved Hollywood endings.

Charlie did his best to look sincere and humble as he simmered just beneath the surface. "You are so right and I'm sorry. I'm very much attracted to you, Maddie, and it feels natural to want to hold your hand or have my arm around your shoulders. I have to respect your wishes, so I do solemnly swear to let you make the first move. Is that a deal?"

"It's a deal and a great one. You've just given me the power and I gleefully accept it."

"Does that mean we won't be capping off this perfect date by spending the night in a room resembling an Elizabethan bedroom, making love for hours and hours?"

Maddie downed the last of her cosmo, looked into Charlie's bedroom eyes and said, "That's exactly what it means, Bucko. This is our first date. Did you really think I was that easy?"

"Of course not!"

"Don't you mean, of course?"

Charlie cleared his throat. "Can we change the subject?"

"Since we're on the subject of dates, why don't you tell me about the worst date you've ever been on?"

"Come on," said Charlie. "Isn't that cliché for a first date?"

"No. Cliché for a first date is if we went down to the beach and walked along the shore, hand in hand, looking longingly into each other's eyes."

"True." Using his fingers, Charlie ticked off a number of past dates until he grabbed his thumb and said, "It's definitely this one. I was an extra in a film about pawn shops. I spent a lot of time with another extra and finally got the courage to ask her out. I was nervous because she was very exotic looking and I felt very white and plain, like Wonder Bread." He downed the rest of his scotch and held it up until the bartender noticed. Charlie looked back at Maddie. "Another Cosmo?"

She shook her head. "Continue," she said.

"I didn't have a lot of money at the time, but I wanted to take Elena someplace special, so I borrowed two hundred dollars from my mom and took her to Spago, one of the classier restaurants in L.A. She looked amazing. Men, women, even children watched her as she seemed to glide down the aisle to our table. I felt like the luckiest man alive. We ordered drinks and talked about how much we were both in love with the movies. She said she wanted to be the next Meryl Streep and I told her that she totally could do that. At some point, I think after we finished a bottle of champagne, Elena kissed me and grabbed my leg. I returned the gesture. Instead of feeling a woman's soft thigh, I felt something hard and small and…"

"Get out!" Maddie threw her head back and let out a very loud laugh. A few people turned in her direction.

"I couldn't make this stuff up. I pulled my hand away so quickly, it hit the underside of the table, knocking it over. The candle lit the side of the tablecloth and after our waiter doused it with water from the champagne bucket, Elena and I were personally escorted out of Spago and asked never to return. We barely said a word to each other on the ride home. She got out of my car and flipped me off. We kept our distance on the set. After my stint in the movie, I never saw her again. Afterwards, I did have to admit that her voice was kind of deep. I just thought it was sexy. Okay, it's your turn. I want to hear about your horrible date."

"Oh, there are so many. Let me think." Maddie closed her eyes for a moment. When she opened them, she said, "I believe this one stands out as being one of the worst. I also think I went out with him due to my state of mind at the time. I had broken up with a man whom I had been going out with for over a year. I was feeling very lonely and then along came Kippy…"

"You went out with someone named Kippy? That was your first mistake."

Maddie nodded. "You may be right. Can I continue, man who dates transvestites?" Charlie gave her a dirty look. "As I was saying, Kippy was friends with one of my clients. I was selling ad space for the Yellow Pages." Maddie waited for Charlie to make a snide remark. He didn't. "Anyway, I'm talking ad rates while Kippy's standing off to the side, wearing overalls and a dirty T-shirt. His golden blonde hair was to his shoulders and he had these beautiful green eyes, which he was using to stare alluringly at me. He worked for a sheet metal company and was taking his lunch break visiting my client. When I was finished soaking his friend for a full-page ad, Kippy asked for my business card. He told me that he used to be a stripper and he could show me a really good time. Thinking back, I want to slap myself because he was such a player, but like I said, I was feeling very vulnerable. We went out a week later."

"Did he change his shirt?" Charlie said.

"Very funny. He cleaned up nice. He looked good and smelled good. He was a perfect gentleman through dinner and I was having a nice time. Then he suggested we go to Traxx, a biker bar in the city. Reluctantly, I said yes. What a mistake. We walked through those doors and his eyes were on every woman there. He danced with me while looking at other women. He even danced with a couple of other women. It was horrible. I asked him to take me home. He agreed and when we got to the door, he asked if he could spend the night. I almost laughed, it was so absurd. I told him I don't sleep with a man on a first date and he said -- I swear I'm not making this up -- I'll only put it in halfway."

Charlie was dumbfounded. "Please tell me you didn't go out with him again."

Maddie gave him a sideways look. "I may have been desperate, but I'm not brain dead. The next time I saw Kippy, he was on the front page of the Marin Independent Journal. He was arrested for trying to sell meth to an undercover cop. His mug shot closely resembled what he looked like when I first met him, trying to look alluring with a stained T-shirt and ill-fitting overalls. Quite the cheesecake shot."

"I bet it was a woman who took his picture." Charlie finished his drink. He wasn't wasted, but he was lit. He took his keys off the table and handed them to Maddie. "Looks like you're driving us home. You can, right?"

"I'll admit that I'm not completely sober. I do feel, however, that I'm capable of driving responsibly. I know I'm within the legal limit." Maddie glanced at the clock on the wall. It was almost 11:00. She didn't have to worry about traffic. "The last time I drove a Porsche, the owner dared me to push one twenty. I won. This is going to be fun." Maddie stood up and dangled the keys in front of Charlie's slightly red eyes. "Let's go, buddy."

Reluctantly Charlie stood up, then steadied himself against the chair.

"Are you okay?" said Maddie.

"I just gave you the keys to my rented 2015 Porsche Carrera and I don't even know if you can drive a stick. How do you think I'm doing?"

"I'd say you're drunk and snippy. Let's go before I leave you here."

The drive home consisted of Charlie lowering his window for fresh air, while Maddie had the radio tuned in to KBLL, 103 Bull Country. He protested, but Maddie reminded him that the driver has music rights. She enjoyed watching him scrunch up his face while Kenny Cheney sang about drinkin' and smokin' and dancing in the moonlight to his pickup's radio. After driving a Honda Accord for years, Maddie felt like she was on a ride at Disneyland without the track. She took corners a little too fast and stopped at lights a little too late. She was having a blast.

5

Twenty-five minutes later, Maddie pulled up to the curb in front of her house. As they got out of the car, they heard a quick succession of clicks, shaking branches, and then a thunk and an 'oomph!' On the ground, under the large magnolia tree in front of Maddie's home, lay a man in a semi-fetal position, his camera a few feet away. He was gingerly holding his right arm.

"I'd like to leave you here to rot, but that wouldn't be very humane of me, would it?" Charlie glared at the paparazzo.

"My arm's killing me. I think I broke it."

Maddie said, "Let's bring him in the house. We can call an ambulance if we need to."

Together, they helped the man up and into the house. Once he was on the sofa, Maddie was able to get a good look at him. She was surprised at how old he was. She always thought following celebrities was a young person's job. They seemed to be constantly moving, jumping in and out of their cars, staying up late or getting up early to catch the famous or not-so-famous person off guard. This man was in his fifties with thinning hair, large ears and pockmarked skin. He was on the heavy-set side. Maddie wondered how he got up in the tree. He looked neither athletic nor agile.

Charlie placed the camera on the coffee table. "What's your name?"

"Conrad," he said as he lay back, cradling his arm.

"Well, Conrad. You're not going to be very happy when I tell you that your camera lens is shattered. It serves you right. A decent person wouldn't be hiding in a tree, waiting to take photos."

Maddie looked crossly at Charlie, then turned to Conrad.

"How's your arm? Can you move it at all?"

Conrad slowly took his left hand away and tried stretching his right arm. He let out a yell and quickly cradled it again. Maddie picked up her phone and called 911.

While they waited for the ambulance to arrive, Maddie brought Conrad and Charlie each a glass of water. She thought it was the polite thing to do for the impaired stranger on her couch and a necessity for Charlie, who needed to sober up so he didn't have to sleep over.

Conrad took a long drink of water. "It would be a lot less expensive for me if one of you just drove me to the emergency room."

Charlie said, "I know. I'm not driving you. Maddie?"

"Nope."

Conrad was about to say something, then stopped. He knew it was useless. He looked around the room. It was a modest home. Tastefully decorated. It was also a far cry from the mansions he was used to hiding around. He wasn't the only paparazzo wondering what Charlie Evans was doing with an older, middle-class woman. Unemployed and unknown, she was truly the mystery woman.

The ambulance took Conrad to Marin General, thankfully without the siren blaring.

Charlie fell back on the couch. "That was fun."

"A regular yuck fest. Does this happen often with you?"

"Being followed, yes. People dropping out of the sky? Not really."

Maddie sat down next to him. When he tried to put his arm around her, she moved away. Charlie looked behind him. "Is your son here?"

She would have loved to lie and tell him yes. It would have been easier than deflecting his persistent advances. Instead, she told him he was at his father's for the weekend. Charlie rubbed his eyes and moved his head right to left. He stretched his arms over his head. "Do you think Ray would mind if I spent the night in his room? I really shouldn't drive and I'm tired."

Relieved, Maddie said, "I have a guest room. It's a lot cleaner and there's no chance of getting a contact high from the furniture, curtains, walls, or carpet."

"Why do you let him smoke pot in his room? I could never get away with that when I was a kid."

"So you didn't smoke pot?"

"Of course I did. Everywhere but my house. Oh, I see where you're going with this. What's the point, right?"

Maddie nodded. "Ray is a great kid. He gets stoned way too much. He's also kept up a 3.5 GPA. And, to top it off, the guy's got a talent for cooking. His snacks are off the chart amazing." Maddie got up and went to the kitchen. Charlie heard her opening the refrigerator and moving things around. She came back with a white ball the size of a softball. She handed it to Charlie. "Try it."

Tentatively, he took a bite. "It's really good. It tastes like a s'more."

"Ray calls it a S'morb. And it's all vegan, from the marshmallows to the graham crackers to the chocolate. Ideally, it belongs on a stick, roasted over a campfire. Or a stove."

Charlie handed it back to Maddie. "Fire it up!"

Smiling, she took the tasty snack dutifully to the kitchen and toasted it to perfection. They spent the next hour sharing the S'morb and watching Thursday's Late Late Night with Craig Ferguson. Maddie taped it since she never stayed up until 12:30 to watch the show. Turns out Charlie was a Ferguson fan, too.

They never made it to their respective rooms. Both fell asleep on the couch, Charlie on one end and Maddie on the other, Mick in the middle. Charlie was the first to awaken. His head didn't hurt nearly as much as he thought it would. Still, he was desperately seeking coffee. He lightly shook Maddie on her shoulder. She slowly opened her eyes. Even with small bags under his eyes, bed hair, and rumpled clothes, Charlie looked every bit the movie star. It was unnerving. She wiped her mouth and slowly sat up. "Good morning," she said.

"I need coffee."

"And?"

Charlie was clueless. Maddie said, "Good morning."

"Oh, yeah. Good morning. Will you make me some coffee?"

"And?"

"Now?"

Exasperated, Maddie stood up and looked Charlie right in the eyes. "Would it kill you to say please?"

"Jesus Christ! All I want is a cup of coffee. Is that too much to ask?"

"If I'm not your housekeeper, waitress, or one of your bubble-headed girlfriends, then yes, it is too much to ask. What happened to being polite?"

Charlie rubbed his face. "I have a hangover. I spent the night on a couch and coffee would make it better. Why can't you just do what I say?"

"Rewind the previous answer."

"Shit. I'll make a goddamn pot of coffee myself." Charlie started to go to the kitchen. Maddie grabbed him by the sleeve.

"I'd like you to leave."

Charlie stepped back.

"Come on. Just make me a cup of coffee and we're good. Okay?"

Maddie went to the front door and opened it. "No, we're not okay. You're demanding and rude and I want you to leave. Now."

"Fine! I bet you make lousy coffee, anyway. Some weird vegan concoction."

Charlie stomped out. Maddie slammed the door behind him, then went to the window and watched as he stepped on her newspaper, then got into his car.

After going to the bathroom, she glanced at herself in the mirror and nearly fainted. Mascara had pooled under her eyes, giving her an eerie resemblance to Benicio del Toro. Her foundation smudged, she looked like she was in the beginning stages of leprosy. She was surprised Charlie didn't tiptoe out of the house, never to return. She washed her face, then went into the kitchen to make a cup of coffee and toast. Part of her felt great that she told Mr. 'I'm going to boss you around' how she felt. She also regretted it because the fun ended before it could begin. She wouldn't get to go to premieres or hang out with famous people. She had lost out on being wined and dined and bejeweled. But for a few hours Maddie had spoken her mind. She hadn't caved to a man's advances and she had done what she wanted to do.

Reading the paper, enjoying the last sip of coffee and bite of sourdough toast, Maddie picked up her cell and dialed Priscilla.

"Good morning. Let me tell you about my first and last date with Charlie Evans."

6

"**M**s. Brockner will see you now." The secretary walked Charlie into Gretchen's office. It was in the financial district in downtown San Francisco. Her two Oscars sat on a credenza against the wall. Photos of Gretchen with various celebrities flanked the golden statues that she had won for best director and best original screenplay. She was hoping to nab another soon. She looked at Charlie like she would a spoiled child.

"Can I help you?" She motioned to the chair in front of her desk. Charlie stood.

"I don't think I can do this."

"Do what?" She loved playing dumb.

"Romancing the crone. Going out with an older woman who loves country music. Her last name is Mozart and she's into George Strait and all that other twangy stuff. Did you know she's a vegan? Not even fish or cheese! Her son's a stoner whose goal is to cover his body with tattoos. This is ridiculous. What am I doing dating a woman who lives in the suburbs and drives a Honda?"

Gretchen was ecstatic. She hadn't thought Charlie would be able to sustain the relationship, but she had no idea it would end so quickly. "She didn't sleep with you, did she?"

Charlie shook his head.

"I'm shocked. She's not smitten by the sexy Charlie Evans?" Gretchen picked up The National Enquirer. On the cover was a photograph of Charlie and Maddie kissing in Veggie Grill. She showed it to him. "You called them, didn't you?"

"You said you wanted it public."

"Don't worry, Charlie. It was a stupid bet. I spoke to Depp this morning and he's very interested in playing Danny."

Charlie said, "Johnny Depp?"

"No, Horace Depp."

Charlie was about to respond when the secretary popped her head in the office. "Brad Pitt's on line one."

"Are we done here?" Gretchen said. "I have to set up a meeting with Brad. He wants to read for the part, too."

The thought of another actor nabbing his role infused Charlie with a sense of entitlement. His mind went into turbo drive. "The bet is back on. Don't write me off, Gretchen."

"What about this old woman being a country western vegan and possibly wearing Depends?"

"I'm in and I'm going to get this part. You're looking at the next Danny Jensen. Tell Pitt and Depp to back off."

Charlie strode out of the office, winked at the secretary as he walked past her desk and practically ran to his car. He had some apologizing to do.

Maddie watched the robin on the branch of the apple tree. She studied it as the bird pecked at the bark, its rust-colored breast moving slightly as it attempted to lift a bug from the branch. After a few more minutes, it flew away, bug in beak. She continued to stare at the branch, studying its form, texture, and design. She dipped her brush in the water and then in the brown watercolor paint. She closed her eyes and gracefully put brush to paper. First, long strokes, then short, punctuated stabs.

Painting was the perfect antidote for the way Maddie was feeling. She needed to release the tension she'd experienced after seeing the shot of her and Charlie kissing at the restaurant. There was an inset photo of the two walking out of the restaurant. It wasn't the kiss that bothered her. It was the headline: "The Movie Star and The Suburban Mom." That's how she was perceived? The Somebody and the nobody. It was embarrassing. It was humiliating. After forty-six years of living on the planet, this is how a tabloid depicted her.

She opened her eyes, cleaned off the brush and dabbed it in the dollop of vermillion paint. Again, she closed her eyes and sent the brush on a journey of long vertical strokes.

Maddie was so engrossed in painting that she didn't hear the car pull up in her driveway. When the gate opened, she swung around and saw Charlie close the gate behind him. He was holding a bouquet of flowers.

"What are you doing here?"

"I want to apologize for how rudely I behaved this morning. I was hung over and impatient and…"

"A total dick."

"That, too. A complete moron." Charlie held out the long-stemmed red and white roses. "Forgive me."

Maddie was back in the game, the potentially lucrative game. She was also going to have to contend with the lack of privacy, extreme exposure to her every move, and continued lying to friends and family. She was amazed and disappointed at how easily she was able to trade in her integrity for material gain.

She accepted the flowers. "I forgive you as long as you never behave that way again. You made me feel like one of your gofers."

"Yes, ma'am."

"And don't EVER call me ma'am again. I just went from my forties to my seventies."

Charlie plastered a smile on his face. "Anything else?"

Maddie thought for a minute. "I think that's it. The flowers are beautiful. Thank you."

"You're welcome." Charlie walked over to the easel and looked at the partially finished painting. He didn't like it. "This is really good!"

"Liar. I'm experimenting with instinctual painting and it looks like a bird took a dump on my canvas. You want to try painting?"

Charlie backed away from the easel. "Me? No. My stepdad is the artist in the family. I'm no good with a brush. Besides, I was hoping that I could take you to lunch."

"That's sounds good."

"Where would you like to go? Any place you want."

Without thinking, Maddie said, "Portofino."

"Perfect. I love Italian food. Is it in San Rafael?"

"Last time I checked, it was a city in Italy." Maddie's expression was blank. She loved testing him. Pushing the envelope. Seeing how malleable it was or if she'd tear it.

"That's funny. You're funny." Maddie continued to stare at him, not saying a word. "Sure. Let's do it."

Maddie broke into a big smile. "Really?"

"Why not? Of course, not today, but let's plan it for next weekend. Lunch, dinner, breakfast. Tutta la baracca."

Maddie gave Charlie a big hug, nearly stabbing him with one of the rose stems. "I am so excited! I've never been to Italy before. Thanks."

"You're very welcome." Charlie kissed her. "I still want to go to lunch. Anything closer than six thousand miles?"

Maddie laughed. "There's a great Italian restaurant downtown. Il Locatorre. They make a killer pasta primavera. I'll put the flowers in a vase and then we can go."

Charlie nodded and watched Maddie leave. When she disappeared into the house, he took out his cell. "It's Charlie. Do you know where Il Locatorre is? That's where we'll be in about fifteen minutes...sure. I told you that you'd get the exclusives...later."

Charlie was glad that he decided to reinstate the bet. It hadn't occurred to him that he could have fun with this romance. It didn't matter if it wasn't authentic. It was never his intent to get serious about any of his relationships. His ultimate goal was having sex and, up until Maddie, he never had to work at achieving it. It simply happened. Changing the venue, especially to Italy, would bring her crashing into his bed. One of the most romantic countries in the world was going to be Charlie's accomplice. And he had Maddie to thank for it.

Ten minutes later, Maddie reappeared. Her hair was in a ponytail and she changed into black jeans and a light blue T-shirt. She was wearing dark blue wedge sandals, elevating her height. Being nearly as tall as her date bolstered her confidence by four inches.

Charlie put his hand to his heart. "Be still, my heart."

"Be still, the compliments. Too much too soon."

"You're such a killjoy."

Maddie gave him a big smile. "I'm a realist. Now let's go. I'm starving."

Charlie looked down at her shoes. "I thought vegans didn't wear leather?"

"They don't. These are synthetic. I also don't wear wool, silk or, need I say it, fur."

"I don't know how you do it. I couldn't live without my leather jackets and belts and shoes."

"What if the only leather you could buy was made from dog skin? Would you wear it?"

"Hell, no!" The thought made Charlie cringe.

"I look at cows and pigs the same way I look at dogs. They don't give their skin willingly. It's brutally taken from them. Why should I feel less sympathy for these animals? And I hate to tell you, but some of the leather coming from China is dog. Besides, they now make realistic looking vegan leather. It's durable, too." To prove her point, Maddie took her purse off her shoulder and held it up to Charlie. He gave it a cursory feel. If he didn't know it was synthetic, he would have thought it was leather.

"Okay. I got it. Vegan leather is cool. Check. Let's go eat."

7

A-list movie stars had many perks. One of them was being put up in the nicest hotels while on location, in the cushiest suites. While the lesser-known actors grabbed their morning coffee at the local Starbuck's after emerging from standard motels, Charlie Evans had his favorite coffee delivered to his room, along with a blueberry scone from Pinkie's Pastries, San Francisco's iconic bakery. He had a dining room, living room, separate bedroom, and luxury bathroom complete with a bidet and sauna. It was a far cry from twenty years ago. When he had played a small role as the murderous husband in *Enter Slashing*, accommodations verged on abuse. Filming in Needles, California, their only choice of hotels were two broken-down hovels, both badly in need of repair. Since the film's budget had been practically non-existent, the cast and crew had reluctantly bedded down at the Needless Inn. For three weeks, the movie people endured its saggy mattresses and poor quality water. The plumbing leaked and closing the windows didn't stop the dust from entering the rooms, permeating every living and inert object and covering it all with a film of light brown dirt. Veronica Waters, the actress portraying the doomed wife, had joked that she was getting free microdermabrasion sessions while she slept. And ate and showered. More than a few of the crew had suspiciously eyed the sky as buzzards seemed to endlessly circle the motel and set location. They'd even spotted a couple of coyotes, looking healthy and well-fed, hanging around the outskirts of town.

Despite a few years more of slightly better lodging, Charlie was glad he'd endured the discomfort, the B movies, and the forgettable roles. As he poured himself a glass of wine, there was a knock at the door. "Donna?"

"That would be me."

Charlie greeted his agent with an air kiss. She was wearing a Calvin Klein pantsuit and Jimmy Choo sandals, a sharp contrast to Charlie's Harvard sweatshirt and jeans. "How's my money machine doing?"

"Please don't mince words. How do I really fit into your life? Friend? Associate? Client? Prostitute?"

"The last one, unless that makes me a pimp. Then it's the one before that." Donna eyed the glass of wine on the table. "Where's the second glass?"

Charlie grabbed another wine glass from the credenza and poured Donna a generous helping. He handed it to her. "I have to make a quick call."

"Take your time. I'll go out on the balcony and enjoy the fabulous view of the bay."

Charlie grabbed his cell and dialed. "Hey Dad, I have to change our plans for next weekend. I'm going to Portofino. No, not the restaurant, the city...Yes, it's with a woman...Trust me, she is NOT like the women I usually date. Check out the tabloids. You'll see. I'll call you when I get back and we can set something up...okay...The film's going well...Thanks. You, too."

Donna was standing just inside the balcony door. She shook her head. "I can't believe you're taking this woman to Italy. Can't you romance her right here in Sausalito, Tiburon, or Napa Valley? You have to travel over six thousand miles to do it? What's gotten into you?"

"It sounds like fun. She suggested it and I thought, why not?"

"Hold it. She asked you to take her to Italy? Who's using who?"

Charlie downed his wine and refilled his glass. "It's not like that, Donna. Maddie was joking when she said she'd like to go to Portofino for lunch. It was my decision, not hers. Besides, what better place for me to play up my affection for her?"

Donna held up her hands. "Uh. Here? San Francisco? Where Tony Bennett left his heart?"

"I disagree. Think about it. Maddie and I will be sipping espressos at sidewalk cafes, walking on the ancient sidewalks of

Portofino, holding hands, looking longingly into each other's eyes. The paparazzi will eat it up. I would love to see Gretchen's face when she reads the tabloids and catches photos of the two lovebirds."

"I hope you're right." Donna sat down on the sofa and kicked off her shoes. She picked up the remote and turned on the 65-inch flat screen television mounted on the wall. Charlie's face filled the screen alongside Gwyneth Paltrow's. Donna laughed. "I can't get away from you, can I?"

"Nope."

"I bet there's a Charlie Evans blow-up doll in the bathroom."

Charlie nodded. "And he's anatomically correct. You may just get lucky."

"Very funny." Donna muted the sound as the two onscreen actors made out. "Doesn't it bother you a little bit, exploiting Madeleine for a part in a movie?"

Charlie sat down next to Donna. "Maddie is unemployed, living in San Rafael. She's a divorced mother of two. Now, she's dating a famous actor and going to Italy next week."

"So that's a no?"

"I bet she's the envy of all her friends. I'm doing her a big favor."

"And she's doing you a bigger one."

"True."

Donna said, "I trust in your ability to win her over. Just in case this affair doesn't pan out, I set up an appointment for you to talk to Marty Scorsese about his next movie."

Charlie rolled his eyes. "I don't want to do another thriller."

"Please?"

He sighed. "Fine. When?"

"Next Thursday at ten. He'll be in San Francisco."

Charlie went over to the gilded mirror on the wall. He studied himself, turning his head right, then left. "I look good for my age, don't I?"

Without looking up, Donna said, "Very. You're delicious."

Charlie smiled at himself in the mirror, then got closer, examining the part in his hair. He moved the hair around, looking closely at the roots. "Damn it. I just dyed my hair."

"It's a bitch, isn't it?"

"Yeah. By the way, I need you to run damage control for me on the set. Vicente said I wasn't needed Wednesday through next Tuesday, but just in case…"

"Will do. That's what agents are for, right?"

"You don't get the big bucks for sitting around looking pretty."

Donna laughed. "No, I don't. That's your job."

Shortly after Donna left, Charlie stood on the balcony. To his left was the Golden Gate Bridge. To his right, in the distance, he could see the Bay Bridge. The night air was brisk and the wind gave him a chill, but at the moment he felt blessed. Charlie knew he was part of a minority. The privileged few who had an infinite number of choices. He took it for granted more often than not. It was half past nine and he had to get up early, expected on the set at 5:30. He wondered if it was too late to call Maddie.

The phone rang and on the fifth ring, the machine picked up. "You've reached the Mozarts. Leave a message after the bum, bum, bum, BUM. Wait, that's Beethoven." Before it beeped, Charlie hung up. He turned on the television and ended up falling asleep, only to awaken at three a.m. He surveyed the room, disoriented. Once he remembered where he was, he also remembered he was alone. He didn't like being alone. It wasn't his natural state. Since he had been a teenager, living with his mother in Los Angeles, then rooming with a fellow actor, Charlie liked having other bodies around. He'd had a dog like that, Roger, an Airedale with an appetite for chocolate cake, a habit of barking at anything that moved, and hot spots galore on his back side. He became manic if he was by himself. As soon as he saw another being, he was fine. He didn't want the affection, just the company. Charlie joked that he could put a corpse in the room and Roger would be happy.

Instead of going back to sleep, he dragged himself to the shower. It wouldn't be long before he had to be on the set. He smiled as he thought about the impending trip to Italy. He hadn't been to

Portofino in a few years. He was going to make sure that Maddie would have a most memorable time. And, hopefully, so would he.

8

This was not a conversation Maddie wanted to have. She and Tommy got along famously for a divorced couple. Until they split up the first time, their children never saw them fight or fling derogatory remarks at each other. They were civil because they genuinely liked and respected each other. Tommy completely understood why Maddie divorced him. His drinking was excessive and near constant. Despite his downright pleasant demeanor when he was intoxicated, hanging out with an alcoholic wasn't preferred. He was so passive when he drank that Maddie could practically predict when he would fall into a deep sleep, to the minute. And Tommy was an equal opportunity sleeper. It didn't matter where he was at the time of his departure from the waking world. He could be at a party, a wedding, even Ray's soccer game, when his eyes would lightly flutter, his speech would become less coherent, and he would drift off to slumberland, leaving Maddie in charge of explanations. When her husband wasn't drinking, he was a delight. Tommy was attentive, affectionate, and a wonderful father. Unfortunately, that was forty percent of his waking life. The other sixty percent was booze-filled and forgettable.

Tommy was still in love with Maddie. Everyone knew it. Even his mail carrier. That's how transparent and open he was. He also knew that his ex-wife dated. His objections were minimal. At least on the outside. Internally, he felt the pain. He still had visions of the family being united once again, for the third time.

When Tommy found out that Maddie was dating Charlie Evans and, a mere week into their relationship, she was vacationing with him in Italy, he lost it.

It was the day before Maddie was to leave. She believed she had everything in order. Ray and Mick would be staying with Tommy, a friend would come by the house and water the plants, and the girls were coming over in a couple of hours to help her with her self-control. She was determined not to sleep with Charlie. She thought she could use some pointers to fortify her resolve.

She hadn't expected to be standing on her front porch, arguing with Tommy over what he called her lack of judgment. After he'd raised his voice more than once, Maddie talked him into continuing the conversation inside. The last thing she wanted was to appear on the front page of a tabloid, facial expression twisted into disgust, exchanging barbs with her ex. Before she shut the door, she glanced up at the magnolia tree to make sure it wasn't growing any more paparazzi.

Tommy stood over Maddie, deliberately trying to intimidate her into capitulating and cancelling her trip. It wasn't working. Maddie stood stick straight, arms crossed. Defiant.

"I would say that I appreciate your concern, but I don't. At all."

"Maddie, you don't even know this guy. Sure, he's handsome and charming…"

"And very rich," added Maddie.

Tommy gave her a dirty look. "Filthy rich. He could also be a psychopath. For all you know, he's plotting to wine and dine and kill you. Look what Robert Blake did to his girlfriend. You're taking a big risk."

Maddie softened her stance. She knew exactly why Tommy was adamant. She lightly touched his arm. "I know what I'm doing, Tommy. Charlie Evans, if anything, will kill me with kindness. Trust me on this one. I'm absolutely positive that he's not a loon bucket. Besides, the two of us can't go anywhere without a crowd of admirers or exploiters. Privacy is one thing he does not have. Now, please take good care of our son and our dog. Do you want me to bring you something back?"

Ray walked in with Mick on his leash and said, "How about a T-shirt that says, 'My ex-wife went to Portofino with the most famous actor in the world and all I got was this lousy shirt'?"

Maddie and Tommy started laughing. He hugged his ex hard

and said, "Promise me you'll be careful."

Maddie saluted him. "Sir, yes, sir!"

Ray hugged and kissed his mom. "Have fun. Do everything I'm not allowed to do."

She was about to answer when, once again, she got the 'Tommy look.'

As they walked to the car, Tommy said to Ray, "You don't mind if I drop you off at the house and go to an AA meeting, do you?"

"Not at all. It will give me a chance to make a new snack I've been formulating in my head. I'm calling it Nachichis." Ray looked back at his mom, who was standing in the doorway. "I hope you don't mind. I took the bag of chia seeds from the cupboard."

"Knock yourself out, kiddo. Love you."

"I love you, too."

Tomorrow, Charlie was picking Maddie up at 6:00 a.m. Not a morning person, she made sure that she packed before she went to bed. She wanted to sleep in as late as possible. Ava, Sylvie, Tanvi, and Priscilla were coming over in an hour. It was a combination bon voyage party and therapy session. She made it clear to Charlie that she wouldn't be sleeping with him. After he got over the shock, he said he understood and respected her decision. She knew he didn't mean it and could almost hear the wheels turning in his macho brain, devising ways to break her down.

Priscilla was the first to arrive. She handed Maddie a chocolate bar and pulled a bottle of wine out of her tote bag.

"Chocolate. Cabernet. My life is complete. Who needs men?"

"I couldn't agree more," said Priscilla and followed Maddie into the kitchen. She opened one of the drawers and pulled out the corkscrew. "Did Ray leave any of his creations? I'm hankering for one of his snacks."

"Check the fridge. There might be some popcorn balls in the crisper. He mixed popcorn with brewer's yeast, coconut oil and caramel. He calls them sticky stinky balls."

Priscilla made a face. Maddie laughed. "His friends think it's hilarious."

"I keep forgetting Ray's a teenage boy."

"My son is stoned ninety percent of the time and overuses the word 'dude.' I can't forget that he's not a teenager."

Priscilla opened the crisper and found two balls. She grabbed one and bit into it. "This is delicious. Who would have thought to put these flavors together? I'm telling you, this boy's your ticket to that big house on the hill."

"I think you're right. And if I keep eating his snacks, I'll be the big lady in the big house on the hill."

Priscilla eyed her friend's petite figure. "Dear, you know you'll never let yourself get an ounce over your ideal weight. I don't know how you do it, but you look great."

"Thanks. It's discipline." Maddie took the crudités out of the fridge, along with a chive and garlic spread. She put it on the counter. "Sylvie, Tanvi, and Ava will be here soon. If there's anything you want to ask me about my fake boyfriend, let loose."

Priscilla dipped the celery stick in the spread and took a bite. "Mm. This is delicious. It tastes like a cheese spread but I know that can't be. Another Ray creation?"

"I made it with cashews, garlic, brewer's yeast and some other stuff. I'll give you the recipe, if you like. It's super easy to make."

"Email it to me." After one more swipe she continued. "I think he's going to be very determined to bed you, so you're going to have to be super determined to resist. Aside from what we're going to do tonight, you should always have the conversation that his agent had with her client in your head. Always. I'm telling you right now, there's no way I could resist Charlie Evans. The man is a walking sex toy."

"Now why would you put that image in my head? All I can see is a six-foot dildo. Wait, maybe that's a good thing." Maddie uncorked the bottle of red wine. "You're good, Ms. P."

Just then, the doorbell rang. "We're coming in!" Tanvi yelled. She and Sylvie walked into the kitchen, each holding a dish for their feast. Tanvi set the plate of stuffed zucchini boats next to Sylvie's bowl of roasted root vegetables. Maddie eyed the food.

"Thanks for bringing these, you two. They look delicious. Who wants wine?" Three hands went up.

Tanvi helped herself to a carrot stick. "I can't believe that at the same time tomorrow, you're going to be in Portofino. I'm beyond envious."

Sylvie nodded. "I know. It's like a dream come true. You lucky dog."

"I am a lucky dog, aren't I?" She glanced at the clock over the breakfast table and handed the women their glasses of wine. "I hope Ava gets here soon. I'm starving and this won't do." She held up a celery stick and slid it through the spread.

Tanvi raised her wine glass and the others followed. "To Maddie and Charlie." The women repeated the toast, then sipped the pinot noir.

A knock on the door interrupted their chatter. Soon after, Ava walked in, carrying her offering for the evening. She handed the covered bowl to Maddie. "My famous fettucine mushrooms and capers, sautéed first in a homemade chicken stock." Before Maddie could say anything, Ava shook her head. "I don't believe it. I'm so sorry, Maddie. I even bought a vegetable stock to use and then defaulted to my recipe. Shit."

Maddie did an internal eye roll. Ava seemed to be negligent a little too often when it came to preparing vegan food. From baking scones with butter to creating a veggie lasagna with ricotta cheese, her mistakes were forgiven. There was always something else Maddie could eat; however she was beginning to wonder if these indiscretions were intentional. Ava never verbally questioned her veganism, yet she wondered if it was a subconscious dig, Ava's passive-aggressive way of disrespecting Maddie's lifestyle.

Maddie gave Ava a hug. "Don't worry about it. There's plenty here for me to eat." She looked at Tanvi and Sylvie. "Right, guys? I can eat what you brought?"

"Of course," said Tanvi. "I cook vegetarian, anyway. If it weren't for Sanjay, I'd be a vegan, too."

Sylvie said, "All I put on the veggies was olive oil and balsamic vinegar, salt and pepper. Not a drop of animal anything."

Priscilla added, "Chocolate bars are vegan and raw. Even the wine is vegan and organic. I always check everything so I know you can have it, M&M." She looked over at Ava. It wasn't an accusatory glance, but she still wanted the woman to feel guilty. She wasn't a fan. Priscilla had a feeling that Ava knew exactly what she was doing.

After dinner, the women got down to the task at hand. All four were there to help Maddie stave off any advances from Charlie. Under normal circumstances, their friend could hold her own, deftly deflecting a man's genuine or quasi-genuine proposition. This situation wasn't normal. If a regular date represented a bullet from a .45, Charlie was a torpedo. He had more charm, grace, money, looks, and pizazz.

Ava said, "Just to be clear, you want us to help toughen you up so you can resist Charlie's advances, right?"

"Exactly."

"Next question: What the hell is the matter with you? I'd be tapping that man every chance I got. He'd have to use a crowbar to get me off him."

Maddie said, "I really would like to get to know him before I sleep with him. He's probably never had to worry about getting a woman in his bed. I want to be the first. Besides, I have the upper hand right now. I like the feeling. It's empowering."

"I think it's wonderful, Maddie," said Tanvi. "I made Sanjay wait almost two months. It drove him crazy and I really wanted to have sex with him. After we got married, he told me that he respected me for it."

Ava clapped. "Nice story, Tanvi. Don't take this the wrong way, but Sanjay is no Charlie Evans, and if he can't get some booty, Maddie's booty is going to get booted."

"I think you're wrong, Ava," said Tanvi. "And I think Sanjay is every bit as sexy as Charlie."

The other women agreed, all to Ava's chagrin. Priscilla was next. "It doesn't matter what anyone thinks. It's Maddie's choice and we're here to help. We want her coming back from Portofino a 'Charlie Virgin,' so let's get started." She turned to face Maddie and pulled a fake moustache out of her pocket and put it on. This got the women laughing, which delayed the intervention by a good five minutes.

Sylvie insisted that she get a photo of Priscilla, then she wanted to try it on. The 'stache' was passed around. The photos were posted on Facebook. By the time it landed back on Priscilla's upper lip, the adhesive was worn on one side, so the sad little black tuft of fake hair drooped.

"I can't concentrate with that thing on your face. I think it served its purpose. It's time to say bye-bye." Maddie removed it from her friend's face and placed the moustache on the table, sticky side up.

Priscilla took Maddie's hands in hers and peered lovingly into her eyes. "You look beautiful tonight, Ms. Mozart."

"Thank you, Charlie."

"I would love to slowly undress you and give you the best sex you've ever had in your life."

"That sounds great, but I can't."

"Why not?"

Maddie hesitated, then said, "I have chlamydia."

Priscilla dropped Maddie's hands. "You do?"

Sylvie said, "Really?"

Maddie said, "No, but what a great way to get out of having sex, right?"

Priscilla said, "M&M, our goal is to help you become a stronger person, not a diseased liar."

"Besides," said Sylvie, "you can treat chlamydia with antibiotics and then what excuse are you going to use?"

Maddie sighed. "I didn't realize how hard this was going to be. If I say no, he's going to get mad at me and it's really going to hurt his ego. His very big ego."

"You're absolutely right," said Ava. "Give in to his needs and yours, Maddie. For God's sake, you're not getting any younger. This could be the last time you have sex." Ava finished off her wine and put the glass down on the coffee table a little too hard. The stem broke and the glass fell off the table and shattered.

Tanvi immediately went into the kitchen to retrieve the dustpan and brush. "Everyone, leave it alone. I'll sweep it up."

Priscilla looked at Ava. "I think someone needs sex more than Mr. Evans."

Embarrassed, Ava recovered quickly. "No offense, Maddie, but your wine glasses aren't very well made. I'll buy you another one."

Maddie said, "Don't worry about it. Most of them are from Ross. I've got plenty more."

Tanvi swept up all the glass, deposited it in the trash can and came back in time for Priscilla's second attempt at wooing Maddie. Once again, Priscilla took Maddie's hands in hers and said, "Maddie, darling, I really like you a lot. Let's go into the bedroom and I'll make this a night to remember."

"I'm sure making love to you would be wonderful Charlie, but I'm not ready."

Priscilla looked offended. "I don't get it. Why not?"

"Well," Maddie hesitated. "I want to get to know you first."

"But we're in Italy. I paid for the first class flight over here and this is a five-star hotel. You owe me."

All of a sudden it hit her. That's exactly what Charlie would say. He doesn't respect her. If he did, he wouldn't have bet Gretchen that he'd convince her that he was in love with her, then dump her. She released her hands from Priscilla's and stood over her.

"I owe you nothing. If anything, you owe me big time. Without me, you don't have a chance in hell of getting that…"

Priscilla broke in. "Okay. Calm down there, missy. You're right. I owe you. Let's call it a night. I get the couch, right?"

"Yeah…right."

Priscilla and Maddie looked at their friends. All three were clearly befuddled. Tanvi said, "Did I miss something?"

Sylvie agreed. "Where did that come from?"

Ava nodded. "Yeah."

Maddie quickly recovered. She looked at Priscilla. "If you would have let me finish, all I was going to say is that, without me Charlie wouldn't be able to get that," Maddie pointed to Priscilla's crotch, "in here." She grabbed her crotch.

Tanvi said, "Since when have you become so crude?"

"Dating Charlie Evans can do that to a respectable woman."

"I wouldn't go that far," replied Tanvi. Then she laughed. "Just kidding. Shall we continue or do you think you can ward off his advances? If not, I would like to be Charlie."

Priscilla got up and offered Tanvi her seat. "She's all yours. Good luck."

Maddie said, "You know how much I love your accent. I may not be able to resist you. Just sayin'. You're going to have to be pretty obnoxious. Can you do that?"

"According to my family, I can be very hard to take. By the way, are you and Charlie sharing a bed in Italy?"

"I hope not," said Maddie. "The man has enough money to pay for two suites in the best hotel in Portofino. I guess I should be prepared in case we're staying together."

"Just sleep with him already!" cried Ava.

Priscilla wanted to grab Ava by the throat. She caught her temper and instead said, "We all know what you'd do, Ava. This isn't about you. It's about Maddie's decision to stay chaste and it's our duty as her friend to support her, okay?"

Ava threw up her hands in defeat. "Fine. I'm going to get another glass. Where do you keep your wine glasses?"

"In the cupboard next to the fridge."

For the next half hour, Maddie was thrown every line the women thought Charlie would fling at her. She deflected them like a pro. They proclaimed that she was ready to travel across the continent to the boot-shaped country and hold her own. Maddie certainly hoped so.

9

Maddie watched in anticipation as the black stretch limo pulled up in front of her modest home. She wondered if the driver found it odd that he was picking someone up in her neighborhood to sit alongside a famous star.

On the opposite side of the street, she noticed a hunter green Chevy truck. Its driver was sitting low in the seat. Aviator sunglasses covered his eyes. She could just make out the top of a telephoto lens near the window. Was he always there or did someone alert him to Charlie's impending arrival?

She checked the house one more time for any lights left on or unlocked doors. She chuckled as she took the little baggie of pot that Ray left for her and put it in the kitchen drawer. He attached a note: 'Frayed nerves? Not anymore. Enjoy Italy with a little chronic from your son.' Ray had no idea that marijuana would have disabled her defense mechanism and unceremoniously ended her celibacy.

Her cellphone was in her purse, as was her passport, driver's license, and melatonin. She needed the supplement to regulate her sleep when she changed time zones. She had three different shades of lipstick and one gloss, generic ibuprofen in a teeny Tupperware container, a ponytail band, and her vintage hankie. She was set.

The doorbell rang and she yelled, "Come on in!"

As Maddie grabbed her suitcase and slung her purse over her shoulder, the limo driver greeted her just inside the door. "Let me get your suitcase, ma'am."

"I'll give it to you as long as you never call me ma'am again. Call me Maddie, please."

The driver nodded.

Maddie reached the limo door just as it opened. Charlie stepped out and greeted her with a hug and kiss. Through the corner of her eye, she watched the camera lens pop into view and silently photograph them. The fact that the truck was parked in the perfect spot to take snapshots was not lost on her. Get used to it, kid, she said mentally. Charlie may not be the brightest bulb on the tree, but he certainly is the most ambitious.

"You look lovely, Ms. Mozart."

"Thanks, Mr. Evans. You don't look too shabby, yourself."

Maddie had been in limousines before. Some were rather cheesy, like mini-Las Vegases with small white lights around the foot of the seats and neon ceilings, lights pulsating to the beat of disco music emanating from ceiling speakers. The one Tommy had surprised her with on her fortieth birthday had been more tasteful, refined. He'd invited four other couples and they had spent the day wine tasting in Napa Valley. In the evening they'd dined at Mustard's Grill in Yountville. Tommy had even called the restaurant in advance, requesting a vegan feast for the party. It was a memorable birthday. Maddie didn't even mind when Tommy fell asleep on the way to the restaurant and on the ride home. It was one of the few times she'd excused his drinking to unconsciousness.

This limo was different. It had been designed and blessed by gilded winged angels. Maddie was convinced that she would never have experienced a vehicle so extravagant without knowing a multi-millionaire. She felt like she had stepped into someone's smoking study. The seats were dark brown and plush. Recessed lights cast a soft glow on hardwood floors and the bar was trimmed in oak. The crystal decanters were filled with top-shelf spirits. Charlie watched in delight as she continued to scan the elegant interior. Classical music played in the background.

"You like?" said Charlie.

"Except for the leather seats, I love it. It's gorgeous."

"Look again. These aren't leather. I specifically requested a limo with Naugahyde. You'd be surprised how many celebrities are vegan."

"I'm very touched. Thank you, Charlie."

He smiled, then grabbed a bottle of champagne from the cooler and placed it in the ice bucket. He took two champagne flutes from the sink. They were frosted. Charlie deftly popped the cork and poured generous portions into the glasses. He handed one to Maddie. She took it just as the limo turned onto the freeway. Maddie checked out the label. It was Bollinger Blanc de Noir. She wasn't a big champagne drinker. She did, however, know that Bollinger was a respected and expensive bubbly. She was about to take a sip, when Charlie said, "A toast to us."

They lightly touched glasses and took a sip. Maddie closed her eyes and smiled. "Wow. This is the best champagne I've ever had."

"Can you describe it?"

She took another sip. "It's very intense in a good way and...I don't know, bright, like I'm drinking liquid sunshine. Does that make sense?"

Charlie raised an eyebrow. "I get intense, but bright? As long as you like it. Speaking of liking, what do you think of the music? I'll give you a hint. It's not country."

"Very funny. It's one of my favorite concertos by Mozart. Number 23 in A major. You thought of everything, didn't you?"

Charlie picked up a piece of paper from the seat. "I've put together a little game to test your knowledge of Mozart. I'll play five to ten seconds of each piece and you have to give me the title. If you can't, you take a sip of champagne. If you get it right, I have to take a drink."

"And the point is?"

"To find out how much Mozart you know and who can get smashed first."

"I know you're younger than I, but now I'm guessing eighteen, nineteen?"

"Come on. It'll be fun and I bet that listening to too much country twang has destroyed your taste for real music."

Maddie kicked off her shoes and got comfortable on the bench seat. "Sir, I will rise to the challenge. Let's hope the chauffeur won't have to fling your sotted body over his shoulder to take you to the airplane."

"It certainly wouldn't be the first time. Are you ready to play, 'Name that symphony, concerto, etude, and sonata'?"

"Bring it on."

Charlie rolled up his shirtsleeves. He replaced the current CD with his Mozart mix and was about to hit play, when he said, "I almost forgot." He picked up a small gold box and lifted the lid. In it, were ten dark chocolate truffles. Each one had a different color flower on top. They looked like multi-colored sugar daisies. "I hope you like raw vegan chocolate."

"If you meet a woman who doesn't love chocolate, I'll bet you anything she's an alien or an android. Or a guy." Maddie picked the truffle with the dark purple flower. She bit into it. The soft center tasted like mocha. "Delicious. Are you going to have one?"

"Of course. Let's see. This one looks good." He picked the truffle with the dark blue flower and popped it into his mouth. "Raspberry. Not my favorite berry, but it will do." He finished the chocolate, turned up the volume and pressed play. For ten seconds, the sound enveloped the limo. The quality was so superior, they well could have been in a concert hall. Charlie hit the stop button and looked quizzically at Maddie. "Well?"

"Die Zauberflote."

"Wrong! It's the Magic Flute. Take a sip."

"Die Zauberflote is German for the Magic Flute. Bottoms up."

Obligingly, Charlie finished the champagne and refilled his glass. He hit play and gave Maddie a seven-second taste of her distant relative's creation.

"Symphony number 41 in C, otherwise known as the Jupiter Symphony. Are they all this easy?"

Charlie took a smaller sip. "I'm starting with the easy ones. Just wait."

"I am allowed to take small sips, aren't I? It doesn't seem fair to pour me an amazing glass of champagne and make me watch you drink."

"You could intentionally get one of the answers wrong."

"Never! I would be a disgrace to my family."

Charlie did a combo eye roll and head shake. "Whatever. If you want to take some sips, you may. Now, are you ready to take it up a notch?" His hand was poised to press the button. Maddie nodded. She looked out the window as they drove by a car full of teenagers.

With the exception of the driver, all of them were trying to look through the darkened windows of the limo to catch a glimpse of the passengers.

"Before we start, do those kids a favor and let them see you. It will be the highlight of their day."

Charlie replied, "I'll wave and give them a megawatt smile only if I can also give you a much-needed kiss."

"Charlie..."

"Maddie..."

"Okay, but hurry. We're starting to lose them." She rolled down the window and, as promised, Charlie flashed the shocked teens a big smile, then he leaned over and gave Maddie a very long and sensuous kiss. It literally made her knees wobbly. He tasted like expensive champagne and he smelled like triple milled soap: soft and clean and élite. She wanted it to last. She also knew that the longer they kissed, the weaker her resolve, so she reluctantly pulled away. Through the sound of the traffic and the air whipping through the window, she could still hear the whooping and hollering of the delighted teens. She smiled at the starstruck group as she rolled up the window.

Charlie had a silly grin on his face. "What do you say we make a lot more people happy and do it for the rest of the trip?"

"Let's continue with the game, please."

"You are one tough cookie." Charlie combed his hands through his hair, then pressed the play button.

After Maddie heard the oboes, French horns, and violins for six seconds, she said, "Violin Concerto number five in A."

"Damn. What did your parents do, lock you away in a tower until you memorized all of Mozart's music?"

Maddie nodded. "I was released two months ago. How much more, Mr. Evans? I'm getting bored."

"A few more and then we can stop. It took me a long time to put this together."

"Right. You compiled the music? This isn't the hard, laborious work of your assistant?"

Charlie looked offended. "First of all, Miss Smarty Pants and Mozart savant, my assistant is not with me in San Francisco. Secondly, and most importantly – that's a word, right?" Maddie nodded. He continued. "Even if she were, I would have wanted to do this myself. It was fun and it didn't take that long. A couple of hours, tops." Charlie waited for Maddie to applaud him. She simply sat there and smiled, so he took a big sip from the flute and offered up the second to last entry.

He played it for no more than five seconds when Maddie blurted out, "Sinfonia Concertante in E flat for Four Winds. As they say in Vienna, 'down the hatch!'"

Charlie obliged. With an empty flute held high, he said, "I give up. You win. This time."

"What's that supposed to mean?" Maddie said, knowing exactly what it meant.

"Nothing. Forget I said it." Charlie pushed the button to the window separating them from the driver. As it slid down, he said, "How long before we're at the airport?"

"About thirty minutes, Mr. Evans."

"Thanks." The window went up. Charlie filled their glasses. "A toast to the smartest woman I've ever dated."

"I'll drink to that." Maddie watched as her 'boyfriend' downed his champagne. She was feeling light-headed and loving it. She wasn't thinking about being unemployed or about Ray and Kenzie's futures. San Rafael was worlds away. Life as she knew it didn't exist and it felt divine. She wanted to sit next to Charlie and wrap her arms around his beautiful body and kiss his soft, sweet lips. She would have if Charlie didn't start taking his shirt off. Maddie panicked.

"What are you doing?"

"I wanted to show you my abs. Nice, huh?"

"Lovely. You have beautiful abs."

"You can touch them, if you like."

Any amorous feelings she had for Charlie dissipated. She was confident that any time she had a moment of weakness, his ego and bravado would whisk her back into reality. It was her goal that he fail in his attempt to nab the part in *Julia's Love Affair*. She was now ready to strike.

"Is it true that you've had ab implants?"

Charlie's shirt dropped back down faster than his face fell. His veneer was beginning to crack. "Where did you hear that?"

"I read it online. So?"

"Is nothing sacred?" After finishing off his glass, Charlie looked at Maddie. His eyes were glassy. "Did you see the movie, *Men, Gods and Mortals?*"

Maddie shook her head.

"Of course you didn't. Anyway, I played the god of darkness and it required that I have a six-pack. There wasn't enough time to get my body in shape, so I had implants. Is that so terrible?"

"No. It's a result of the industry that you're in, demanding that you movie stars have flawless bodies and beautiful faces and that your teeth are perfectly straight and stunningly white. A fifty-year-old actress looks thirty, making mere mortals like me look like flabby, wrinkled trolls."

Charlie squinted. "I don't see any wrinkles on your face." He felt her bicep. "And your arms are toned."

Maddie glanced up at the diffused ceiling lights. "The lighting in this limo was designed to soften features and diminish, if not eliminate, any wrinkles. I'm thinking of having it installed in my house."

Charlie lifted up his shirt again, oblivious to Maddie's reply. "You want to touch them? You're going to sooner or later."

"Later is more like it."

For the second time in less than five minutes, Charlie took another blow to his ego. The shirt slipped over his natural pecs and fell past his $15,000 abs. "Do you know how many women approach me on a weekly basis, wanting to have sex with me?"

"Two, three hundred?" Internally, Maddie was grinning ear to ear.

"No. About four to seven, maybe ten. That's not the point. The point is that I was looking forward to making love to you."

Maddie softened her stance. She actually felt sorry for the guy. He was trying so hard to be desirable. Under normal circumstances, she would have succumbed to his charms. If he only knew...if he only knew, this wouldn't be happening: the limo, the champagne, the trip to Italy. She wouldn't have even been noticed by the famous actor in the nightclub filled with young, desirable women.

"Charlie, I find you attractive and I enjoy your company. I want to get to know you before we jump in the sack. I told you that when we planned the trip, remember?"

"No...yeah, I do. I was hoping you'd change your mind. Portofino is one of the most romantic..."

"I know. You remind me frequently. Maybe our next trip."

The limousine came to a stop. The chauffeur opened the door and Maddie got out and was accosted by a horde of paparazzi. Oblivious to the scene, Charlie yelled at her from the back seat, "How many trips do you have planned? Who's in charge here?"

Charlie stumbled out of the limo and into the gleeful 'arms' of the freelance photographers. They couldn't get enough of the inebriated star. Maddie gave them her best exasperated look, hoping Gretchen Brockner would catch the photo on the cover of one or all of the gossip rags.

The limousine driver shielded them from the cameras as he ushered the couple through the airport and to the gate. Another delicious perk of being with a celebrity. They were even excused from going through the security line. While the rest of the passengers boarded flight 247 bound for Genoa Airport, Maddie and Charlie were settled into their first class seats, enjoying the accommodations. Maddie played with the electric seat adjustments, thrilled that she might actually get comfortable enough to fall asleep for part of the nine-hour flight. She took off her shoes and was getting cozy when the flight attendant came up with a chilled bottle of champagne and two iced flutes. Maddie declined and requested water instead. She'd had her fill of alcohol two champagne glasses ago. Charlie willingly accepted a glass from the flight attendant. As the young attendant poured him a generous amount, Charlie said, "I certainly hope that you'll be in first class for our flight."

"I will indeed, Mr. Evans." She blushed, giving an already flawless complexion a rosy tint.

When she left, Charlie turned to Maddie and said, "She wants me."

Maddie rolled her eyes, then picked up a copy of *Vanity Fair* magazine and started reading, trying to block her view of the self-proclaimed Adonis.

Two hours into the flight, Maddie settled back to watch the

movie, *Men, Gods and Mortals*. As Charlie Evans' chiseled abs filled the screen, she looked to her left. The mere mortal was soundly sleeping; every once in a while he'd make a snorting sound. His hair was rumpled, his shirt slightly wrinkled, his head drooped down, and there was a tiny rivulet of drool on his chin. Maddie grabbed her phone and snapped a picture, then wiped his chin with her handkerchief. The photo was texted to Priscilla with the caption, *That's Amore?*

10

Maddie had stayed in three-star and four-star hotels before, but the closest she'd ever gotten to a five-star hotel room was a visit to the lobby. When she and Tommy were on their honeymoon, they'd stayed in Paris. Their hotel, Le Belmonte Chateau, was a four-star establishment and was far nicer than any place either of them had ever been. Tommy surprised Maddie by taking her to L'Oiseau Blanc, the restaurant on the sixth floor of The Peninsula Paris, a five-star hotel in the heart of the city. Glass walls afforded magnificent views and Tommy had made sure that their table was looking directly at the Eiffel Tower. After they had become vegans, they laughed about how they would have gotten the Parisian boot if they had requested vegan fare. The only thing they could have eaten was the bread. And that was doubtful, as the French are known for using butter in almost everything.

For Maddie, the anticipation of finally staying in a five-star hotel was exhilarating. As they walked into the lobby, she was tempted to take out her phone and start snapping photos. She thought better of it. Tacky was not something she wanted Charlie to affix to her personality. Prude, crazy vegan, and country music fan were enough. Still, the entryway of Belmond Hotel Splendido was beyond splendido. They walked through the arched doorway, stepping onto the black and white marble tiled floor. Potted palms sat strategically between doorways and next to the windows, which were framed in dark, polished wood. She suddenly felt frumpy. Her eyes were red-rimmed, her hair in need of washing and her jeans were less-than-snug, stretched out from being worn since yesterday morning.

Maddie looked over at Charlie and she wanted to punch him. On the limo ride over to the hotel, he had changed into fresh clothes, combed back his hair, and even washed his face. He covered his bloodshot eyes with Ray Bans. When he stepped out of the limo, he looked refreshed and refined. It was reprehensible. Maddie was thankful that there were no telescopic lenses being thrust into their faces. It would have been catastrophic if the paparazzi had caught the couple as they registered at the hotel. She could only imagine the headline: *Suave Star sighted with Hideous Hag. What was he thinking?*

Once they reached their room, Charlie took off his sunglasses, revealing very bloodshot eyes. He walked into the Presidential Suite like he belonged. Maddie's first instinct was to take off her shoes so she didn't soil the plush white carpet with her Payless ShoeSource faux leather boots.

"What do you think?" Charlie said as he made a beeline for the balcony. Pale yellow roses crawled up a trellis on the right side of the very private terrace. Terra cotta planters overflowed with flowers in every color and shape. They even had a small fountain near the railing. Each of the three tiers were different shells: a scallop shell on the bottom, an abalone in the middle and a conch on top, water flowing up through the middle and cascading over the top.

As they looked out at the harbor, Maddie said, "I've never stayed in a hotel this exquisite. And this view. Well, I'm speechless. I know this is second nature to you, but I'm in culture shock."

Charlie watched a yacht pull out of its slip. A couple was dining on the upper deck. In the early evening light, it looked like a Maxfield Parrish painting. The water glistened against the very white boat and liquid sun seemed to fill the couple's wine glasses. "It wasn't always like this. When I visited Italy as a child, we would stay with my nonna and nonnino in Santa Margherita Ligure. It's less than four miles north of here. They lived in a modest apartment. It had one bedroom. I would sleep on a cot and my parents got the couch bed. Nonna would take me to Portofino for lunch at her favorite café. Later, she'd buy me a gelato and we'd walk around town pretending that we were staying at one of these fancy hotels. We'd walk into the lobby like we owned it."

"Sounds like you have good memories of your grandparents. Evans doesn't sound Italian at all."

"It's not. I changed my name when I became an actor. It was Torregrossa."

"That's not so bad," said Maddie

"In Italian it means big tower."

She laughed. "Just think, if you hadn't made it big in Hollywood, you could have been an Italian porn star."

"Nonna would have been proud. If you think that's bad, my mother's maiden name is Barbagelata."

"Don't tell me. Does it mean beautiful beaver?"

"Close. Frozen beard."

Maddie doubled over laughing. "You are making this up!"

Charlie smiled. "I'm not that good." He grabbed her hand. "Let me show you the rest of the suite."

From the balcony, they once again stepped onto the plush white carpet, their feet sinking into what looked like whipped cream. All the furniture resembled eighteenth century pieces. Many of them were antiques. The others were authentic-looking reproductions. Maddie felt like she was in a baron's castle. It reeked of affluence. The décor was not her style, but she very much appreciated it as a guest.

In between the two sets of French doors leading out to the balcony sat a small, antique-style writing desk. The stationery had the hotel's crest embossed in gold. A feathered pen was positioned diagonally across it. The lamp base resembled an urn. Maddie made a mental note to write Ray and Kenzie letters on the cream-colored paper.

They walked under the high arched doorway to the bedroom. Even though she was determined, Maddie at once regretted her decision to stay chaste. The bedroom was every woman's fantasy location to engage in prolonged, passionate, and memorable lovemaking.

"Are you okay?" Charlie looked quizzically at Maddie.

"Yes. Why?"

"Your breathing got pretty heavy. Are you sleepy?"

Maddie wanted to say, 'No, you thimble-headed gherkin. I want you to ravage me on that amazing four-poster bed in this spectacular room dripping with lust. Why the hell did I have to overhear your agent? I could have probably had the best sex of my life. Instead, we're both getting jack shit.' Instead, she replied, "I am a little tired, but I'm also starving. Are you hungry?"

"Very. Why don't we freshen up and go grab dinner?"

"Sounds like a plan."

The bellboy had put their suitcases in the bedroom. Maddie grabbed her toiletries bag and went to the bathroom. "We're not staying with anyone else, like a family of four, are we? This bathroom is huge. I mean, bigger than my house huge." A few seconds later. "There are two toilets. Not one, but two!"

"Are you sure one isn't a bidet?"

"Yes, Charlie. I may not be a world traveler, but I ain't no hillbilly neither. There are two water closets. I suppose that's so any undesirable odors from the first user don't have to be smelled by the second. But then again, I thought rich people's shit didn't stink."

Charlie came up behind Maddie and put his arms around her. He gently kissed her on top of her head. "You're very sexy when you're funny."

Before she melted into his arms, Maddie turned to face Charlie. She put her hands on his shoulders. "Thank you, sir. Now please let me get gussied up so I don't embarrass you in front of your fellow Italians. I won't be long."

Reluctantly, Charlie closed the bathroom door behind him. He placed his suitcase on the bed and began unpacking. He had totally underestimated his date's reluctance to sleep with him. As he unfolded his shirts and hung them up, he thought about what he had planned for the evening. He was almost positive that Maddie would buckle and beg him to sleep with her. If not, Gretchen had unknowingly picked the one woman Charlie Evans couldn't seduce.

The night was warm and the scent of lilacs, acacias, and roses permeated the air as they strolled past the ancient buildings in pastel colors of peach, lemon yellow, pale pink and mint green. They reminded Maddie of pop-up greeting cards – two-dimensional and way too charming to be real.

They decided to dine al fresco at a small restaurant called Il Libertore. The requisite Campari umbrellas hovered over oak tables covered with white tablecloths. Since the menu was in Italian and the waiter spoke broken English, Maddie let Charlie order for her. She made sure he asked about ingredients that omnivores wouldn't even think of, like chicken, fish, or beef broth as a soup base or cream in a seemingly non-dairy sauce. As a show of unity, Charlie ate vegan fare. He vowed to follow her diet when they were together. Maddie was sure that this gesture was to further garner her adoration, but she appreciated it nonetheless.

If Charlie weren't famous, Maddie was certain the waiter would have refused his request for meat-free and dairy-free dishes. Yet another perk of being with a celebrity. From the salad to the appetizer to the main dish, the food was exquisite. They shared a bottle of pinot grigio and by the time the meal was over, the bottle was empty. For every glass that Maddie had, Charlie had two.

The conversation throughout dinner was light. Both wanted to avoid any discord. Charlie didn't once bring up sex, nor did he regale her with his Hollywood exploits. He got the feeling that name dropping wasn't going to impress her, anyway. Instead, they talked about what they planned to do for the next couple of days.

As they sipped espressos, the waiter came up and placed the bill on the table. Before he could leave, Maddie said, "Can you tell me what barbagelata means in English?"

"Si. It mean, uh, like..." he touched his chin.

Maddie said, "Beard?"

"Si, but frozen one." And with that translation, the waiter walked away.

Charlie said, "You didn't believe me!"

"I'm sorry, but it sounded too bad to be true. Forgive me."

"Done."

"Thank you and thank you for this amazing dinner. It's a perfect way to end this evening."

Charlie took out his credit card and placed it on top of the bill. "The night has just begun."

A young girl, around seventeen, came up to Charlie. She was

holding a cloth napkin. "I'm so sorry to interrupt, but I'd be so pissed at myself if I didn't at least try to get your autograph. I'm from Missouri and I know I'll never have this chance again. So…" She extended the napkin with a pen to Charlie. He graciously accepted it.

"What's your name, young lady?"

"Charlotte."

Charlie wrote, 'To Charlotte, it was a pleasure meeting you. Charlie Evans.' He handed the pen and coveted napkin back to the very excited girl.

"Thank you so much! My friends are going to freak. Thank you!"

Maddie said, "You're so patient with people. With your fans. You must have been mobbed when *People* magazine declared you the Sexiest Man Alive."

Charlie put his hand to his chest. "Tell me, Ms. Mozart, who do you think is the sexiest man alive?"

Without thinking, Maddie blurted out, "That's easy. Adam Lambert."

"The guy from American Idol?"

"Yeah."

"He's gay."

"I know."

"He wears black nail polish and eyeliner."

"I think he's very sexy, eyeliner and all."

"He dyes his hair jet black."

Maddie looked at Charlie's hair and cocked her head.

He said, "At least it's close to my natural color."

"Adam also has an amazing voice. Have you heard his version of *Mad World*?"

Charlie shook his head. Maddie took out her iPhone and was about to find it on YouTube, when Charlie said, "Don't bother. I don't want to hear it."

Maddie forgot whom she was dealing with. Perhaps she could have appeased his ego and told him what he wanted to hear. She put her hand on his. "You're very sexy, too."

Charlie took his hand away and leaned back in the chair. "Gee, thanks. I just wish I was as sexy as Mister 'I'm gay and glam and…and gay."

"Come on now. You were the sexiest man alive in 2013."

"Whatever."

A wonderful dinner. Great conversation. The espresso was perfect. Then the question that brought awkward silence. Finally, Charlie spoke.

"I'm sorry. That was a really stupid question. I set you up and you didn't fall for it. You're a better person than I am, Maddie."

Maddie put her hand back on top of Charlie's. "No, I'm not, but thanks."

As they walked back to the hotel, Charlie put his arm around Maddie. She didn't protest. He said, "Adam Lambert is only thirty-three."

"So?"

"You're nearly old enough to be his mother."

"And the Victoria's Secret model you last dated was how old?"

Charlie looked up at the moon and pointed. "I think it's a full moon. Pretty cool, huh?"

Maddie laughed.

As they approached a large open area off the marina, Maddie noticed a makeshift theater. "This reminds me of the movie, *Cinema Paradiso*, where the young Italian boy…"

"It does, doesn't it? Great movie, by the way."

A large screen was facing about two hundred chairs. Almost every seat was taken, except for two in the front and smack dab in the center. Charlie led a very confused Maddie to the front.

"Have a seat. I'll be right back."

"What's going on?" said Maddie.

Charlie just smiled and walked over to where a man was setting up the projector. They hugged and began speaking in Italian. Maddie watched as the animated conversation seemed to drag on. She was beginning to get impatient when Charlie returned and sat next to her. "Sit back and enjoy the show."

"What is this, the Charlie Evans Film Festival?"

"You're funny."

"I know."

The screen began to flicker and The Warner Bros. logo

appeared. As it faded, it was replaced with a placard that read, 'For Mr. Laurel and Mr. Hardy.' Maddie knew exactly what she was about to watch and couldn't believe it. She knew the planning that went into this and was beyond impressed.

"You're good," she said and squeezed Charlie's hand.

"I know."

Charlie had hired a few of the local teenagers to hand out drinks and popcorn to anyone who wanted them, free of charge. Maddie was full from dinner, but couldn't resist eating popcorn while watching her favorite movie. She glanced over at Charlie, bathed in the light from the screen. He was completely engaged in the film. He looked like a little boy, anticipating what would happen next. Maddie had a mad urge to kiss him. She wanted to take him right there, front and center, while The Great Leslie was wooing Maggie DuBois. She was aware of his motives and she knew it was wrong, yet she was having a difficult time convincing her body to simmer down. Instead of thinking about ravaging the second sexiest man alive, she put her full attention into watching the film.

In the warm, balmy evening, eating popcorn from a red and white striped box and washing it down with Pellegrino, Maddie reveled in the outdoor theater in the picturesque seaside town. For the next two and a half hours, she and Charlie, along with the rest of audience, laughed, groaned, cheered on the Great Leslie and booed Professor Fate. They both recited their favorite lines along with the actors and were doubled over watching the pie fight. Even though both had seen *The Great Race* at least twenty times each, this time would be the most memorable.

As the credits rolled, moviegoers began to leave. It was past 11:00 p.m. Some parents were carrying sleeping children. Light blankets covered their small frames. Maddie and Charlie walked back to the projectionist, the man Charlie had spoken to earlier.

"Maddie, I'd like you to meet Carlos, an old friend. And a damned good projectionist."

Carlos offered his hand and Maddie shook it. "So nice to meet you." His English was a little broken, but understandable.

"You, too," said Maddie. "Was this the first time you saw The Great Race?"

"Si. Very funny movie. I like it very much, especially the pie fight." Carlos turned to Charlie and said, "La vostra amica è stata?" *Was your girlfriend impressed?*

"Molto." *Very much*, Charlie replied.

Carlos patted him on the back. "Missione comiuta, eh?" *Mission accomplished, eh?*

"Lo lascerò sapere domani." *I'll let you know tomorrow.*

"Charlie Evans, siete ua canaglia!" *You are a rogue!* Carlo turned to Maddie, "A pleasure to meet you. Buona sera."

"Buona sera," said Maddie.

As they walked back to their hotel, Maddie turned to Charlie and said, "What were you two talking about? And why in Italian? Obviously, I wasn't supposed to know."

"Not at all. Carlos is more comfortable speaking in his native tongue. It was just idle chat."

"Between two Italian men? I don't think so, but you know what? It doesn't matter. This was a great evening. No, this was a fabulous evening."

Charlie was beaming. "On a scale of one to ten, how great was it?"

"Ten point seven five."

"That's what I was hoping for." Charlie put his arm around Maddie and pulled her close to him. She hoped he didn't feel her heart beating a little bit faster. If his objective was to turn her into putty, then he succeeded. She would have to employ every restraint molecule in her possession to fight the urge to completely give in. Then again, what was the big deal? As a single woman, Maddie didn't wait for the third date to sleep with a man. She had no problem ending the first date in bed. She loved the spontaneity of it all, not having to count dates and worry if the man would call her again. She started to question her stand on staying chaste. She was with Charlie Evans, one of *People's* sexiest men alive. She began to believe that she was crazy *not* to sleep with him. She could see the headline in the National Enquirer screaming, *Madeleine Mozart says no to Charlie Evans' advances. What an idiot!*

The hotel walkway was empty as they meandered their way through the covered arbor, teeming with ivy and miniature pink roses. Charlie picked one of the roses, smelled it, and put it in Maddie's hair. It was cheesy, but very romantic. She was beginning to anticipate touching his naked body and her heart beat faster.

Before they could make it to the bedroom, Charlie brought her to the couch and began kissing her. Unlike some men who used absolutely no finesse, Charlie was a master. His technique was flawless. When he started to unbutton her blouse, her heart soared. He lightly nibbled her ear, then kissed the nape of her neck. Then she heard it. And it wasn't a little voice telling her to stop. It was Priscilla's booming invective, reminding her that she was a bet, nothing more. If she gave in, he won and she would lose her dignity. Her libido went into lockdown. Her eyes popped open and she said, "Charlie, I can't do this."

"Do what?" he asked as he kissed her neck, then lightly bit it.

She gently pushed him away and began buttoning her blouse. "I'm not ready to have sex with you."

Undaunted, Charlie kicked off his shoes and started taking off his shirt, revealing his broad chest and surgically-enhanced abs.

"Stop. Please." She finished buttoning her shirt. "I want to get to know you first."

Slowly, Charlie got up from the couch. He started to dress. "You know me. I'm the one who brought you to Italy, first class, took you to one of the most expensive restaurants in Portofino, no, make that one of the most expensive restaurants in Italy and then went to enormous pains and expense to set up your favorite movie under the Italian stars."

"So I owe you?" Maddie glared at him.

"You owe me big time."

"I didn't ask you to do any of this. I owe you nothing and I resent you for implying that I do!"

"I put filming on hold for you!" he said, knowing it was a lie.

"Now why would you go through all that trouble for me? I'm not young. I'm not gorgeous. Hell, I'm not even employed. What's the angle, Charlie? Why are you really doing this?"

"What's that supposed to mean?"

"You tell me."

Charlie laughed. "You think I'm using you for sex? That's a

laugh. To further my career? I'm already at the top."

"Are you?" Maddie stood there, her arms crossed, thoroughly disgusted with the man opposite her. Every bit of allure and sexuality was absent from his chauvinistic body.

Charlie slid into his shoes and grabbed his jacket. "I'm out of here. Enjoy the Presidential Suite, which, by the way, is the most expensive suite in the hotel. You're welcome." He slammed the door behind him, leaving Maddie in such an agitated state, she wasn't sure what to do next. She grabbed one of the embroidered satin pillows on the couch and threw it at the door. "Good riddance, you egotistical jerk!"

By the time Charlie returned to the theater site, the only sound was that of folding chairs being flattened and loaded onto the truck. Behind the screen, Carlos was initiating its breakdown. When he was able to collapse it, he saw Charlie sitting in the front row on one of two seats left standing.

"This is not a good sign. Why are you not with your girlfriend?"

Charlie leaned back in the chair, balancing it on two legs. "That's a very good question, Carlos, and one that I'd love to answer. The truth is, I don't know. Physically, I know exactly where she is: alone in the Presidential Suite. Mentally, your guess is as good as mine. My friend, the night is full of surprises."

Carlos laid the screen on the ground and sat next to Charlie. He pulled out a small amber bottle. "Surprise!" He handed it to his morose friend who immediately uncapped it and took a swig. He made a face and handed it back to Carlos, who also took a generous gulp.

"Is this homemade grappa?"

"Si. You like it?"

"You know I think you make the best grappa. Give it here." Carlos handed it back to Charlie who practically downed the bottle. He wiped his mouth on his sleeve. "How did life get so complicated?

I planned this trip right down to unbuttoning Maddie's blouse on the sofa. It should have been a slam dunk. Now I'm in Italy with a woman who won't let me touch her." He shook his head. "I envy you, Carlos, with your clothing store and wife of twenty years."

Carlos regarded his friend with incredulity. The retail owner looked older than his forty-five years, with pronounced laugh lines and deep crow's feet. He was slightly bow-legged from years of riding motorcycles across Italy in his youth.

"You envy me?"

Charlie replied, "Not really."

"Now that's the Charlie I know." He reached into his jacket.

"How much stuff do you have in there?"

Carlos pulled out two black licorice vines and handed one to Charlie. He stared at it. "Licorice with grappa?"

"Oh, sure. They go great together. Try it."

Charlie took a bite. "Who would have thought? It's really good."

The two sat in silence, alone with their thoughts. Finally, Carlos spoke.

"Quando il gioco degli scacchi è finita, le pedine, torri, cavalieri, alfieri, re e regine tutti vanno nella stessa scatola."

Charlie gave Carlos a perplexed look. "My Italian's not that good."

"When the chess game is over, the pawns, rooks, knights, bishops, kings, and queens all go back into the same box."

"Ain't that the disgusting truth. Whoever said money can't buy you love was right." Charlie ripped off another piece of licorice.

Carlos took another gulp of grappa. "I think it was the Beatles."

For the first half hour after Charlie left, Maddie sat outside on the balcony. The lights from the yachts on the bay sparkled brighter than the stars. The streets were empty, save one or two cars. It was still warm. She wondered if she did the right thing, refusing a man who nearly roped the moon for her. Did she owe him? Did he have a right to be angry? She knew he was sexually frustrated and that was part of her ploy. Did she go too far? She asked her gut and the answer came back so fast it nearly knocked her over. 'Hell no! You don't owe that man anything.'

If she did the right thing, why did she feel so lousy? Maddie imagined Charlie getting smashed at one of the local bars. Before he could plop his ass onto the bar stool, Maddie could already see women coming up to him, flirting with him, yearning to take him back to their place. She prayed he wouldn't disgrace her by having a one-night stand. She turned and surveyed the hotel room. "Where are you, Charlie Evans?" she said aloud.

After changing out of her clothes and into a T-shirt and sweats, Maddie had a mad urge to run around the suite and touch everything in it. It was totally irrational and very childish, yet it was exactly what she wanted to do.

She popped her iPhone into the speaker pod conveniently positioned on the nightstand. It looked completely out of place in the Victorian-era décor. She figured that some wealthy twenty-somethings had requested it and the hotel decided to leave it for future guests. She turned the volume up as Carrie Underwood sang, *Before He Cheats*. Standing barefoot on the king-sized bed, her back to the highly ornate headboard, she jumped up and down until she felt ready to do the 'deed.' She landed on the floor and made a dash for the armoire, tickling the side of it with her fingers. She darted in and out of the furniture and smacked it or touched it or brushed it with her hand. It very well may be the last time Madeleine Mozart would grace a room this prestigious with her presence. She wanted to leave her mark and have a little elegance rub off on her.

Carrie Underwood segued into Bruno Mars' *Uptown Funk*. She had worked up a sweat by this time, plinking urn-shaped lamps and sliding her finger down the gilded frame of a landscape painting. Ending with Shania Twain's *Honey, I'm Home*, Maddie felt completely vindicated. She had pawed nearly every item in the suite. The walls inside the shower stall and Jacuzzi were all touched. She lay spread-eagle on the floor, relishing the unflattering posture. She didn't owe the great Charlie Evans a damn thing. The money spent on the trip was chump change for him. Even though it was a capital idea, he probably got his assistant to work out the logistics and timing of the movie.

Maddie closed her eyes and took some deep breaths. Every time she exhaled, her concern for Charlie's attitude lessened. If he wanted her to leave Portofino tomorrow, she would do it with pleasure. The rug was starting to get itchy. Maddie scratched her back and arms and sat on the couch. She turned on the television and found a rerun of *Modern Family* with Italian subtitles. Twenty minutes later, she fell asleep.

She slowly opened her eyes. Sun filtered through the thick brocaded curtains. In her peripheral vision, she could see Charlie. As she turned toward him, she noticed that he was staring in horror at the foot of the bed. She followed his gaze and, to her revulsion, she found herself looking at her butt. It was large and doughy and dimpled and seemed to have melted onto the sheets. She tried to cover it up with the blanket, but she couldn't pull it over her body. The more she tried, the bigger her butt got. With all her effort, she pulled really hard. The next thing she knew, she awakened. Another episode of *Modern Family* was on the television. She checked to make sure her ass wasn't a melted mess. Relieved that it was only a dream, Maddie turned off the TV and went into the bedroom, expecting to find Charlie.

The bed was empty. So was the bathroom. By the time she washed her face and brushed her teeth, it was 3:10 in the morning. She got into bed, wondering where and with whom Charlie was sleeping.

It was almost 9:00 in the morning when Maddie awoke. Despite the tumultuous night, she felt rested. Still wearing her sweats and T-shirt, she walked into the living room. On the couch, snoring soundly, was her quasi-boyfriend. She could smell liquor from where she was standing. He had shed his pants and jacket. They were lying on the ground next to his shoes. Far from glamorous, Charlie was curled up in the corner of the sofa. He looked like a human pillow. Maddie figured he'd be awake when she finished showering. She was wrong.

Disgusted with his absence last night, Maddie deftly slipped Charlie's wallet out of his pants, perused his credit cards and grabbed one. As she closed the hotel door behind her, she waved the credit card at the inert body on the couch and said, "Arrivederci and grazie."

After having an espresso and grilled bread at a corner café, Maddie walked into Signore Austen, a boutique clothing store. The clothes were slightly edgier than Maddie's taste. It was exactly what she was looking for. In a foreign land, she didn't want to be predictable. She was greeted at once by a young woman who introduced herself as Ashley. "You are the girlfriend of the famous Charlie Evans. You are very lucky, yes?"

Maddie smiled and produced the credit card, waving it in front of the salesgirl. "Right now, I'm very lucky. I was instructed to buy whatever I wanted. Money is no object. You need to help me find beautiful clothes. He's going to be so surprised. And by the way, his real name isn't Evans. It's Torregrossa."

Ashley put her hand over her mouth. "No lie?"

"Nope and you can tell everyone you know. He won't mind." Maddie started looking at the rack closest to her. She pulled one of the dresses off and held it up to her body. "What do you think…"

"Ashley."

"Right. That doesn't sound very Italian."

"My mother loved watching the Olsen twins. I was named after Ashley."

Maddie raised her eyebrows.

Ashley said, "I feel the same way." She looked over the dress Maddie was holding, nodded, and then extended her hand. "I'll put it in the dressing room."

Maddie continued to check out the clothes. She went from one end of the store to the other, making sure she didn't miss anything. Once she had amassed a number of shirts, pants, dresses, and even a couple of jackets, Maddie went into the dressing room to begin the ritual of trying them on. Normally, she didn't like clothes shopping. The dressing and undressing was too labor intensive. Today, however, the purpose of the event made the experience fun, exhilarating.

Two and a half hours later, Maddie walked out of Signore Austen's a little taller and a lot more confident in her appearance. The

3-inch tan sandals made her legs look slender and long. The peach and teal patterned dress, cinched at the waist with a wide belt, flowed graciously as Maddie strolled down the street. She made a few more purchases, then decided to have lunch. Como del Lago had an outdoor patio near the harbor. Seated at a table next to the water, Maddie watched the seagulls flying over and between the boats. It was another warm day in Portofino and the sailboats were out in force, sharing the inlet with yachts. Some were leaving the port, heading out to the Ligurian Sea, making their way to another of the Italian Riviera's picturesque towns, like Camogli or Genoa. Others were docking. Maddie took off her new sweater and placed it in one of the two shopping bags. She removed her new sunglasses, revealing a professional make-up job. Upon learning that she was Charlie Evans' girlfriend, the saleswoman at L'Occitanato Portofino, a beauty store, insisted on re-doing Maddie's make-up and even gave her a free lip gloss: Lavanda Tramonto.

"It means lavender sunset," the saleswoman told her.

The waiter came over and handed Maddie a menu.

"Make that two menus, Signore."

Charlie was wearing a baseball cap and sunglasses. Instead of meeting her gaze with critical eyes, he smiled and said, "I've been looking all over for you."

"Apparently, you weren't looking in the right places." Maddie put her sunglasses back on. Her attempt at keeping an air of confidence and entitlement was made easier in her new, edgier ensemble.

Charlie took in the shopping bags surrounding his girlfriend. "Apparently not." He sat down on the other side of the table, facing Maddie.

"I'm sorry about the way I behaved last night."

"You were an asshole."

"I know."

Maddie leaned over the table. "I appreciate this trip more than you can imagine. Up until you stormed out of the room, I was having the time of my life. The dinner was wonderful and The Great Race, well, you know that was inimitable. I didn't think I had to further prove my gratitude by having sex with you."

Charlie leaned across the table and put Maddie's hands in his. "You're right. I behaved very badly."

"Thank you."

They both decided to get salad and pasta primavera. The requisite bottle of Pellegrino graced the table.

Once the waiter took their order, Charlie got up and moved next to Maddie. "I like your new look. It's very sexy. Capolavoro di Mozart."

"What does that mean?"

"Mozart's masterpiece." Charlie leaned over and kissed Maddie on her lavanda tramonto lips. "Mm. You even taste sexy. Don't worry, I promise I will behave. Scout's honor." Charlie held up two fingers. "Can I have my credit card back, please?"

"I thought you'd never ask." Maddie dug into her new purse and handed the well-used Visa card back to its owner.

Charlie pulled out his wallet. "What do you say we go hiking after lunch? There's a great trail in the hills behind the hotel. It's a favorite spot for the locals. The tourists have yet to discover it."

"Sounds great."

"Did you bring tennis shoes or do I need to keep this out?" His held his card over the wallet.

"I brought a pair. I wonder if they're appropriate for hiking, though." She flashed a big smile.

"For someone who's vegan, you sure know how to milk it."

Maddie laughed. "You're not only rich and famous, but funny, too. Who knew?"

Before Charlie could answer, the waiter returned with their salads. They were topped with mozzarella, so Charlie asked him to take them both back and bring the non-cheese version. Maddie watched with a renewed respect as Charlie explained to the waiter that they were vegan. She wondered how long before the tabloids would begin calling him a vegan.

11

The hike was a challenge, but Maddie and her tennis shoes made it effortlessly up and down the mountain trail. She was convinced that Charlie paid the weather to put on a perfect show of brilliant sunshine with a cool ocean breeze. Even the wildflowers performed flawlessly, displaying their rich reds, blues, and yellows to a receptive audience. Whether he wasn't used to hiking or suffered from the effects of his hangover, Charlie tripped, stumbled and stopped to catch his breath more than a few times. Maddie had to fight the urge to take out her iPhone and surreptitiously take shots of his blundering. If nothing else, dating Charlie Evans opened her eyes to the fact that celebrities were like everyone else. They couldn't pay for eternal grace and poise. When they were out in public, their coiffed persona was financed. She knew they paid dearly for it, too. There were plenty of documented celebrity gaffes, but the majority presented a flawless, serene exterior.

Maintaining his gentlemanly behavior, Charlie insisted that Maddie shower first. She stepped into the gold and white tiled shower stall and turned on all three, vertically positioned shower heads. The first one sent a steady stream of hot water on top of her head. The second sprayed her torso and the third tickled the backs of her knees. As she soaped up her body, she imagined for a moment Charlie in the shower with her, lathering her hair with the hotel's fragrant shampoo. She could practically feel his strong hands massaging her head. Then he moved down to her neck. She closed her eyes and started to feel Charlie's hands wandering down her back. Once they reached her ass, she opened her eyes and yelled, "Get a grip, M&M!"

From the bedroom, Charlie called, "Did you say something?"

"No. I got some soap in my eyes. I'm fine." Maddie muttered, "More like stars in my eyes."

Once Charlie showered, they decided to order in and have dinner on the veranda. While they were waiting, Maddie excused herself so Charlie could have some privacy taking a call from his agent.

"Yes, things are going great...why would The Globe say I was vegan? Unbelievable. Well, worse things could be said about me, right?"

They spoke for a few minutes longer, then Charlie wandered into the bedroom. After putting on his jeans, he opened the door to the bathroom and found Maddie holding her right breast in one hand and tweezers in the other, positioned in front of the magnifying mirror. She saw Charlie and immediately grabbed her shirt.

"I locked the door!" she yelled.

"Don't think so."

Maddie finished buttoning the top. "I'm so embarrassed."

"Don't worry about it. I've only been temporarily blinded. Why are you doing that anyway? You have no intention of sleeping with me."

"It was a precautionary measure. In case one, you know, accidentally slipped out."

"Does this happen to you often? Migrating breasts?"

"Very funny. Now you're going to tell all your friends that I have hairy breasts. This is horrible."

Charlie walked over to where she was standing. "I would never do that."

"I could have sworn I locked the door. Don't the Italians know how to make locks?"

"Maddie, calm down. If it makes you feel any better, I'll do something embarrassing, okay?"

She thought about it, then said, "Like what?"

"Well, I have to go to the bathroom."

Maddie rolled her eyes. "Do you know how many men I've seen pee?"

"No, and I don't want to know. I wasn't talking about peeing."

"Oh. That's a good trade." Maddie sat down on the edge of the tub facing the water closet.

"You can listen only. No watching."

"Of course. Yuck, I wouldn't want to watch, anyway. What was I thinking?" Maddie got up and walked out of the bathroom, closing the door behind her.

Leaning against the door, Maddie waited. After a long silence, she said, "I don't hear anything."

"Jesus, I'm not on stage. Give me a minute."

About ten seconds later, a plop was heard and then another. Maddie started laughing. "I think that was your best performance yet."

"Show's over. You can leave now."

"Don't you find it odd that all other bodily functions are acceptable, like coughing and sneezing, but sounds 'down below' always get a good laugh?"

"Can we talk about this when I'm not sitting on the toilet?"

"Sure. Sorry. I'll be in the living room." She snickered as she walked away, "Portofino *is* the most romantic spot in the world."

When Charlie reappeared in the living room, Maddie was on the couch watching television. "Modern Family reruns. How cool is that?"

"Very cool. We can watch until our food arrives." He sat down next to Maddie, then pointed to one of the actors. "Ty Burrell, the husband. Very nice guy. I worked with him on a film. He's really down to earth."

"That's good to know. I bet a lot of actors are jerks, though. Huge egos and most would probably do anything for a part." She kept her eyes on the TV. Peripherally, she watched his reaction. He didn't waver. Not even a glance in her direction.

"I would say that's a fair assessment." Charlie ran his hands through his still damp hair. There was a knock on the door. "It must be our dinner. Go to the bedroom and don't come out until I say so. Oh, and put on the outfit lying on the bed."

Reluctantly, Maddie turned off the TV. "Did you order a slab of meat that you're going to devour before our dinner?"

"No! Actually, though, that's a good idea." Charlie got up. "Go on now and no peeking."

Ten minutes later, Maddie was summoned to the veranda. She was dressed in an emerald green sleeveless dress, circa 1940s. It fit perfectly, gently outlining her slim figure, falling two inches above her knee. The three-inch heels matched the dress. The dimmed lights draped the suite in a soft, dreamy ambience. Out on the deck, the table was set with a white linen cloth. Two long tapered candles sat in pewter holders in the middle of the table. On the side of the table was an ice bucket. A bottle of Veuvet Clos Chardonnay chilled. Darkness had fallen and Maddie could see the yachts on the water. Their masts sparkled with tiny lights. Planters filled with red roses covered the balcony. For privacy, Charlie had drawn the white gossamer curtains on either side of the patio. It reminded her of a scene out of *To Rome with Love*.

Maddie almost said, 'Where are the rose petals and violins?' She stopped herself because she wanted to savor the moment. Charlie was standing next to her seat, dressed in a black suit with a slim emerald green and black tie, beckoning her to sit down. She complied and said, "You make me feel very special. Thank you."

"My pleasure. Would you like a glass of wine?"

She nodded.

Charlie raised his glass and Maddie did the same. "Here's to our relationship, but more important, to our friendship."

"To friendship."

They dined on polenta with porcini mushrooms and garlic, grilled eggplant, focaccia, and a tomato, basil, garbanzo bean and parsley salad. Dessert was strawberries swimming in brandy. The conversation was effortless. Charlie wasn't overly complimentary. He wasn't trying to impress her by name dropping or name calling. He was silly and funny and unpretentious. She wondered how many people got to see this side of him.

When they were finished eating, Maddie got up. "Another amazing meal, brought to you by the amazing Mr. Evans. Now, if you don't mind, I'm going to change back into my sweats."

"Not just yet. I have one more request. Don't move."

Charlie disappeared into the living room. A few minutes later, Frank Sinatra's rendition of *The Way You Look Tonight* filled the veranda.

"May I have this dance?" Charlie held out his hand and Maddie willingly accepted it. She put her head on his shoulder as he placed his hand on her back and imperceptibly rubbed it. Her heart beat a little faster, the air felt a little warmer and heavier. Maddie realized that this was as close as she was going to get to being intimate, so she let go. She relished Charlie's touch, his sensuality, and his grace.

Charlie finished the third dance off with an expertly executed dip.

"I am so impressed. I didn't know you could dance, too." Maddie pulled her hair off her neck and began fanning it with her hand.

"Dancing lessons and singing lessons when I was nineteen."

"You sing, too?"

"Let's just say that all my talent lies in acting and dancing, leaving nothing left over for my vocal chords."

"Damn. I was looking forward to being serenaded."

Charlie shook his head. "Not going to happen." He kicked off his shoes. "What do you say we slip into something more comfortable, like…"

"Sweats?"

"Sure."

Back in the living room, Charlie sat down next to Maddie. She kept her make-up on, but all traces of evening wear disappeared and were replaced with sweatpants and a T-shirt that said, 'Go Vegan and No Body Gets Hurt.' She held up a deck of cards. "Look what I found in the credenza. You want to play?"

"How about gin rummy?"

"I love that game. I used to play it with my mom all the time. She was a master."

"Well, my dear. You're looking at a gin rummy champion." Charlie grabbed the pad of paper from the coffee table and a pencil. He drew a line down the middle of the paper and wrote their names on either side.

Sinatra sang *My Funny Valentine* as Maddie dealt the cards.

Charlie said, "I bet Adam Lambert doesn't even know how to play gin rummy."

"That's a real deal breaker. I better cancel my date with him next week."

Charlie's eyes got big. "You have a date with…wait, that's a joke, right?"

"Sweetie, the sarcasm is going to start coming fast and furious. You gotta catch up, 'kay?"

"Yes, darling," he said dripping with equal sarcasm.

Maddie picked up a card and put it down near the pile. "I know I'm going to regret asking this, but you never told me who you think the sexiest woman alive is."

"Are you trying to distract me?" Charlie picked up Maddie's discarded ace of spades and displayed three aces on the coffee table. "I'm going to tell you my choice and why only if you give me the chance to explain. Don't interrupt. Can you do that?"

"I shall zip my big fat lip." She pulled an imaginary zipper across her lips and nodded for Charlie to continue.

"You're the sexiest woman alive and here's why. You're very smart and funny. You're not afraid to speak your mind. You got class and you're the most honest person I know. You also happen to be beautiful."

"About the hones…"

"I said no interruptions." Charlie threw down the seven of diamonds.

"I thought you were done."

"I am. I just don't want to hear you break down the pedestal that I erected for you. Can you please let it be?"

"Even if I don't feel I deserve the accolades?"

Charlie nodded, then said, "Wait, what does accolades mean?"

"Compliments," Maddie answered with a lump in her throat. Her deception felt like a suit of armor. The weight of her lie made her bones ache. Do two wrongs make a right? Priscilla convinced her they do. Despite his charade, she didn't feel good about her duplicity. She had a sudden urge to tell Charlie the truth.

"It's your turn and yes, please keep the accolades, the compliments. You do deserve them for putting up with me."

Maddie picked a card from the pile and discarded it. She repositioned herself on the couch and when she did, her shirt lifted just enough to expose her belly fat. She pulled her shirt down quickly, hoping Charlie didn't see. He did.

"You want to re-think the sexiest woman alive?"

"It's not that bad."

"That's because you only saw a portion of my jelly belly."

Charlie displayed another grouping: the seven, eight, and nine of hearts. "Why don't you go to a gym? Work out?"

"I can't afford it right now and getting up the incentive to exercise at home is really tough." Finally, Maddie put down three twos.

"How's this for motivation? At the end of the shoot, we're having a wrap party at the Mark Hopkins. It's in about five weeks. I'll buy you a membership at a local gym, even throw in a personal trainer."

Maddie was thrilled. "Thanks, Charlie."

Charlie smiled, picked up the card that Maddie discarded, threw a card face down and said, "Gin."

Nearly an hour later, the game was over and Charlie was the victor.

"You want to play another game?" he said as he prepared a blank sheet of paper for keeping score."

Maddie yawned. "I'm pretty tired. It's been a long day of shopping, dancing, and of course, we can't forget your performance in the bathroom."

"Or yours."

She smiled, then stretched her arms over her head. "So, who gets the bed?"

"We both do."

"Charlie…"

"I promise I won't try to maul you. We'll have some serious cuddling. That's all."

"No funny business."

Charlie crossed his heart. "None whatsoever."

They both got into bed at the same time. Reluctantly, Maddie pressed her back against Charlie Evans. She could feel his abs on her spine. Her body temperature started to rise as he draped his arm over her waist. He smelled of lilac soap. It was faint but intoxicating.

"How are you doing back there?" Maddie said as nonchalantly as possible.

"Fine. You?"

"Just dandy." Maddie readjusted her body. "Well, then. Good night."

"Good night." Charlie lightly kissed her on the back of the head. She thought she was going to lose it. She had to dip into her reservoir of self-discipline, which was precariously low, and stave off the desire to turn around and ravage him.

Charlie's light snoring brought her libido back into standby mode. The man isn't the least bit interested in having sex with me, she realized. There was no final appeal for foreplay. His hands didn't move. It was like sleeping with a corpse. Then it hit her: he must have gotten turned off by her stomach. She should have been grateful for her jelly belly. It kept the man at bay, yet she was still offended that he didn't seem tempted at all. Her inner dialogue continued for a few more minutes until, exhausted by its fervor, she fell asleep.

Their flight was leaving in less than three hours. Already packed, Maddie made a quick run to the local pharmacy to pick up some last minute items. Waiting in the checkout line, she spotted an Italian newspaper. The cover displayed a color photo of Maddie and Charlie kissing in the park after the movie. The caption read, *Un Grande Romance!* She grabbed two copies as she reached the front of the line. After paying, Maddie was leaving when she was approached by a middle-aged British couple. The woman said, "Would you mind terribly if my husband took a photo of us? I'm such a huge fan of Charlie Evans."

Flattered, Maddie replied, "Of course."

Like they were old friends, the woman put her arm around Maddie. Her husband snapped two pictures and thanked her.

The woman said, "You two look so sweet together, not like those tarts he's usually with. Thank you, dear, and do give that man a big hug and kiss for me."

"I'll do that."

When she returned to the room, Charlie was closing his suitcase.

He looked up and saw Maddie holding the newspaper. He said, "A Great Romance, eh?"

"Yeah, if they only knew." Maddie went over to Charlie and gave him a hug and kiss. "That's from a very sweet British woman who wanted her picture taken with me. Me! I'm going to end up on someone's picture wall because I'm dating you. How strange is that?"

"It feels odd at first and then you get used to it. Can I have one of the newspapers?"

"Sure."

The bellboy arrived and brought their luggage downstairs. Maddie walked through the suite one more time while Charlie waited at the door. He found it endearing that she was so enamored of the hotel room. He couldn't count the number of suites he'd stayed in around the world. He watched as she snapped photos of the rooms. She ended up on the balcony, looking out at Portofino's famed harbor.

Charlie came up behind Maddie and put his arms around her waist. "We can come back any time you want after I finish filming."

If the invitation took Maddie by surprise, it absolutely floored Charlie. He liked Maddie, yet he honestly hadn't felt that the relationship would last longer than it took to film the movie in San Francisco. He was clueless as to why he had the urge to offer his girlfriend another trip to the city where everyone was getting laid but him.

Maddie turned to face Charlie. She gave him a kiss and said, "That's very sweet of you."

As they walked out the door, Maddie said, "However, I've always wanted to go to the south of France."

12

The flight home was thankfully uneventful. A few fans approached Charlie and, as always, he was gracious and patient. He didn't even complain when two teenage girls took turns taking their picture with him. He did take a stand when one tried to sit on his lap. Maddie had no idea what he was like when she wasn't present, but she doubted that she could maintain her composure if people treated her like an object to be used for their photo ops.

As they waited for their luggage, Charlie checked his messages. He listened intently to one, then pressed call back.

"Hi Jackson…Italy was wonderful…Hamlet? Shit. Yes, I would. We're only about forty-five, fifty minutes away…Yeah, I'll see you soon." Charlie turned to Maddie. "That was my stepfather. One of his dogs, my mother's dog actually, is dying. I hope you don't mind if we go there. I want to see him before…"

Maddie put her hand on his arm. "I don't mind at all. I'm so sorry, Charlie."

"Yeah, me, too."

Before they left the airport, Charlie went to the restroom. Maddie took the opportunity to call Priscilla.

"Hey gal."

"Are you home?" Priscilla said as she prepared a salad while listening to Mumford & Sons' *I Will Wait*.

"At the airport. Listen, Charlie will be back soon so I need to talk fast. We had a great time and I'm discovering a very beautiful side to him. I'm going to tell him that I know about the bet."

Priscilla stopped in the middle of cutting up a tomato. "Don't you dare, M&M. Let's talk about this first. Please!"

"I've made up my mind. I don't like deceiving him."

"Listen to me. You still have the magic of Portofino clouding your decision. Promise me you won't say anything until after you get…"

"Here he comes. I got to go. I'll call you when I get home." Maddie hung up the cell despite hearing her friend yelling as she pressed the end button.

As the cab left the airport and got onto the freeway, the driver slowly merged into the heavy traffic. Maddie took a deep breath. She was fully prepared to deal with any verbal lashing she might receive. She also knew that Charlie wasn't in much of a moral position to defend his actions, either.

"Can I talk to you about something?"

Charlie glanced at his watch. "Shit. It's going to take at least an hour."

He took out his phone. As he texted Jackson, Maddie's phone beeped. It was a text from Priscilla. 'PLEASE wait until we talk before you say anything.'

Maddie texted back. 'Why?'

'Trust me. PLEASE!'

'Fine'

'TY TY TY TY!'

Maddie laughed.

"What's so funny?" Charlie asked.

"Priscilla. She's a nut."

"Did you want to tell me something?"

"It can wait." She looked out the window at the wall-to-wall cars. It didn't seem that long ago that she riled her Los Angeles friends over the horrendous freeway traffic they had to fight. Now, the Bay Area was no different.

An hour and a half later, the cab pulled into the circular drive in front of a Mediterranean-style home in Palo Alto. Maddie felt like she was back in Italy. The two-story estate was exquisitely landscaped. Bright pink azaleas and white rose bushes hugged the three-tiered fountain in the middle of the driveway. As they walked up the steps to the front door, Maddie inhaled the sweet smell of gardenias. The bushes were interspersed with yellow and orange nasturtiums.

It sounded like there were at least two dogs barking at the door. Maddie could hear a man telling them to be quiet and sit. The barking stopped and a man Maddie assumed was Charlie's stepfather opened the door. He was in his early fifties and reminded Maddie of a cross between a younger Gene Hackman and Joseph Gordon Levitt. Maddie knew Charlie was in his early forties, but his stepfather looked a mere eight years older, if that. She looked from father to son and back to father. He smiled broadly and extended his hand.

"I'm Jackson. You must be Maddie."

Maddie shook his hand. It was strong but not bone-crushing. "I am indeed. Nice to meet you."

"You, too. Please, come inside." He gave Charlie a big hug while the dogs leapt up at the guests, no longer able to stay seated. They weren't sure whom to go to first. They knew Charlie and wanted to welcome him back, but Maddie was new and fresh and they were compelled to investigate.

Charlie squatted next to the dogs, petting them and letting them lick his face. "Hey there, Bubbles. Hi, Georgie. It's been a while."

After a few minutes, he got up and followed Jackson and Maddie into the living room. Underneath the black baby grand piano, in a well-padded doggie bed, lay Hamlet. The fifteen-year-old mixed breed barely lifted his head when he saw Charlie. He did manage to weakly wag his tail. Charlie sat down on the floor and gently petted the ailing dog. He was visibly shaken by Hamlet's condition.

"How you doing, boy? Did you miss me? I missed you. Yes I did." Charlie turned to Jackson. "What's the matter with him?"

"Renal failure. His appetite has been waning for months. A few days ago, he stopped eating. The poor guy can barely stand."

Charlie said, "He's fifteen. That's like seventy-six in human years. He's not that old."

"One hundred five. Fifteen times seven," Maddie said.

As if Hamlet knew he didn't have long to live, he made an effort to get closer to Charlie, whimpering as he moved. Not wanting the dog to expend any more energy than he had to, Charlie lay down next to him and continued to pet him. Jackson looked at Maddie and signaled for her to follow him. As they walked to the kitchen, Maddie marveled at the décor. Jackson's taste was impeccable. Large Aztec-patterned rugs covered the Mexican tile floor. The furniture was oversized and colorful. Paintings and prints by Maynard Dixon, Georgia O'Keefe, and Diego Rivera hung on the walls.

Maddie knew it was inappropriate, but she couldn't help admire Jackson's physique. He was average in height with broad shoulders, a slim waist and long legs. His black T-shirt hugged his frame and his faded blue jeans were on the snug side. He turned around as she was admiring another part of his anatomy.

"Were you staring at my ass?"

Shocked by his bluntness, she blurted out, "Absolutely...not!"

He smiled. "Just checking."

As they reached the kitchen, Jackson said, "Would you like something to drink?"

"Water would be great, thanks."

Jackson handed her a glass of water. "I know what you're thinking. How come Charlie and I are so close in age."

Maddie took a sip of water. "That did cross my mind."

"I married Charlie's mother when he was eighteen. I was only twenty-six."

"May I ask how old your wife was or is that rude? But then again, how rude could it be when you asked me if I was checking out your backside?"

"Touché. When I married Jackie, she was forty-two. She died five years ago of cancer. What an amazing woman she was." Jackson looked away.

"I'm sorry." Maddie got up and went over to the window. The backyard was expansive and, from what she could see, a large garden was thriving. Next to one of the raised beds, a rooster perched on an overturned bucket. "What a beautiful bird."

Jackson said, "That's Sherlock. I adopted him from the animal shelter. He was rescued from a cock fighting ring." Jackson pointed to the rooster's left. "See the small pitched roof? That's the chicken coop. I have six hens. They keep Sherlock busy and I have all the eggs I can use and then some. I give the extra to my neighbors. After I adopted them, I stopped eating chicken."

"In that case, I'll have to buy you a cow, sheep, some pigs, and a couple of fish. You certainly have the room."

Jackson laughed. It reminded her of her father's laugh: unbridled and natural, not forced. "Charlie told me you were a vegetarian."

"Vegan."

"Isn't that no animal products at all, even honey?"

"Yup."

"That must be tough."

"It's not at all. I don't think about what I can't eat, but what I can and it's a lot."

The oil painting above the kitchen table caught Maddie's eye. It was of a pond with large, multi-colored koi. Instead of the typical orange, black, white, yellow, and red fish, they were brilliant blues, purples, and tans with splashes of green and turquoise. She looked at the signature. "Jugsy Daff?"

"Close. Jackson Danoff."

"Whoops."

"No problem. I've been told my paintings are better than my signature."

"It's true. This is beautiful."

"Thanks."

Maddie scanned the room. "Do you have any of your other paintings on display?"

"I do." Water glass in hand, Maddie followed Jackson down the hallway to the bedroom. Over his bed was a four-foot by three-foot painting of his three dogs. Jackson changed the dogs' coats so that they wore each other's. It was an interesting concept, one that fascinated Maddie.

"I love how you enjoy changing reality just enough so the subjects are still realistic. Do you ever cross over into abstract?"

Jackson smiled and said, "Follow me."

"How about I walk in front of you, lest you accuse me of leering again?"

"Good idea."

They went downstairs and entered a large, sunlit room. Two of the four walls were glass. Three easels stood in various positions in the room. One of them held a canvas, its paint nearly dry. Maddie studied the painting. It reminded her of Van Gogh's *Starry Night*. Bursts of bright yellow and white exploded in the black sky. Jagged mountains were barely visible. After a few minutes, she said, "It's mesmerizing and I'm not saying it because you're standing right here. It really is beautiful. You're extremely talented."

"Thank you."

"And your studio is to die for. What I wouldn't give to have this kind of space and freedom to work on multiple projects and to paint on a large canvas. A really large canvas."

Jackson walked over to an antique cabinet. He swung open the large, double doors and pulled out a stretched canvas. "This baby is seven square feet. Are you jonesing to paint on it?"

"Totally!" Maddie eyed the large canvas like it was an original DaVinci.

From upstairs, they heard Charlie yell, "Where are you two?"

"Down in the studio," Jackson replied.

Charlie tried to hide it, but it was apparent that he had been crying. His eyes were red-rimmed and he sniffed a few times. "Trying to impress my girl with your big canvas?"

"I believe I succeeded." He turned to Maddie and she nodded.

"You've got a very talented father."

"I agree," said Charlie. He took a tissue out of his pocket and blew his nose. "My mom loved his work. You should show Maddie the portrait you did of her. Is it still in the guest room?"

Jackson nodded.

"I'd love to see it," Maddie said.

If the painting was any indication of what Jackie Danoff looked like, she was beautiful. She had short blonde hair, big brown eyes and a warm, inviting smile. It was obvious that she was completely in love with the artist painting her portrait.

"How old was Mom when you painted this?"

"Fifty-three."

Maddie said, "She was a beauty. I can see the resemblance, especially in your smile."

"Thanks," said Charlie. He turned to Jackson. "Would you like me to go to the vet's with you when you take Hamlet in?"

"No. I'll do it. I'm glad you had a chance to say good-bye."

Charlie got on his phone to call a cab. Jackson stopped him.

"Take the Prius. I can use my truck."

"Are you sure?" said Charlie.

"Absolutely, but only if you promise me that you'll bring your girlfriend back so she can paint on the big canvas. Deal?"

"Deal."

Maddie's eyes lit up. "Really? Those canvases are expensive."

Jackson shrugged. "I think I can spare one for you."

"Wow! Thanks!"

"My pleasure."

Before they left, Maddie excused herself and went into the living room. She sat beside Hamlet as the ailing dog slept, his chest imperceptibly rising and falling, and gently stroked his back. She kissed his head and said, "Good-night, sweet boy. I'm glad I met you."

Jackson stood on the porch with Georgie and Bubbles and watched as the car turned onto the street. He looked down at the dogs. "What'd you think of Maddie? Yeah, I liked her, too. I wonder if Charlie knows how lucky he is."

Charlie drove in silence. He turned on the radio so he wouldn't have to talk. His thoughts were devoured by Hamlet. It was devastating to see this once energetic dog reduced to a silent, shrunken body of skin and bones.

Maddie turned off the radio. "Tell me about Hamlet."

"What do you want to know?"

"How old was he when your mom got him?"

The tension in Charlie's shoulders eased and he smiled. "I could hold that little guy in the palm of my hand. I don't think he was even three weeks old when I found him and his siblings on a lot at Universal Studios. We had just finished up a scene from the movie, *Tell Me Your Destiny*. It was about an out-of-work actor who finally gets a part in a local production of *Hamlet*. We had broken for lunch and I was wandering around, eating a sandwich. I heard a noise behind one of the sets. There she was, a mutt with four crying puppies. She was obviously homeless and starving. I swear, within an hour, we had them moved into one of the office buildings and fed. When they were old enough, we adopted out the puppies and the mother. I was working so much that I knew a dog would be lonely living with me, so I gave Hamlet to my mother as a present. He was so smart. And loyal. When my mom was sick, he wouldn't leave her side. She even took him with her to the oncologist. He was lying next to her when she died."

Charlie wiped his eyes.

"He lived a long life, Charlie, and it sounds like he lived a good life."

"He did. I'm still going to miss him."

"Of course." Maddie repositioned herself on the seat so that she was facing Charlie. "When I was six, we got our first dog. He was a black and white sheltie terrier. He had freckles on his nose and legs. He was adorable. We named him Dickey after Dickey Darling." Maddie waited for a reaction. She got none. "You know, the Kurt Russell movie?"

"Before my time, babe."

"I'm not that much older than you, babe."

Charlie looked over at Maddie and raised his eyebrow.

"Anyway…" Maddie continued, "Dickey was a great family dog, but he had one big problem: He didn't like other dogs. I took him to the beach with a friend of mine and as soon as we let him off his leash, he made a beeline for this little corgi and attacked him right in front of the family. It was horrible. After that, we had to make sure that he was always on a leash."

"That was a fun story."

"I just thought you'd like to hear a dog story. My dog story."

Charlie softened. "I'm sorry. That was rude of me." He put his hand on Maddie's leg and lightly squeezed it. She laid her hand on top of his.

"It's okay. I know how you feel."

The first thing Maddie wanted to do when she got home was take a nap. She didn't expect to find Tommy fixing himself a sandwich in the kitchen.

"Welcome home, world traveler," Tommy said as placed his meal on a plate and went into the living room. He wasn't in his usual attire. Instead of a worn sweatshirt and shorts, he was wearing what looked like a new pin-striped shirt tucked into his jeans. His hair was newly shorn and styled. "Did you have a good time with the movie star?"

Too tired to object to her ex-husband's presence, Maddie abandoned her luggage and went over to the sofa.

"I had an amazing time with the movie star. Have you been here long?"

"About an hour. Ray wanted to come home, so I thought I'd keep him company until you got here. So, is this serious?"

At warp speed, Maddie's mind filled with visions of Jackson. She shook her head to dispel the images. "I don't know. We haven't been going out for long. Why?"

"Because I was going to ask you out."

"Tommy, don't you think getting divorced twice from me would nip this fantasy of us getting back together in the bud?"

"They say three's a charm." He flashed a big smile, not realizing that a piece of lettuce was hanging from his front tooth.

"I don't know who 'they' are, but they're wrong. One was a charm, two was a dud, and three would be a nightmare."

Tommy replied, "I think *you're* wrong. I've been sober for over three years and I have no intention of changing. If you let me, I'll..."

"Listen. I've been on a plane for nine hours and in a car for two and a half. Right now, sleep sounds better than a Will Ferrell movie marathon and you know how much I would love that. If I don't lie down, pink matter will be seeping out of my ears. Stay as long as you want, Tommy. I want to hug Ray and Mick and then my pillow."

"I hear you. Go rest and we can talk about this later."

"Tommy..."

"Go on now. I'll let myself out after I finish eating. And a Will Ferrell movie marathon sounds great. We could make it a family event."

Maddie didn't have the energy to reply. She poked her head in Ray's room and was pounced on by a very excited boxer. Mick wanted badly to kiss her. As much as Maddie adored dogs, her aversion to slobber was acute. It activated her gag reflex. Mick reached for Maddie's face and she deftly deflected his advances. Ray came over and gave her a big hug.

"I heard you tell Dad that you're going to nap. When you wake up you have got to try my latest chron snack. I call it swirling delish. It's a take-off on whirling dervish."

"Very clever, son. Give me a couple of hours and I'll be ready to regale you with tales of Italy while swirling a delicious dervish."

Ray rolled his eyes. "You *are* tired. Go to sleep, Mom."

Maddie drew the shades, stripped off her clothes and slid into bed. Two minutes later, her cell rang. She tried to ignore it, but whoever it was called again. And again. Digging the phone out of her purse, she saw the number and touched the number. It was immediately answered.

"You said you'd call me." Priscilla was irritated.

"Sorry about that. I was having a problem staying awake and forgot. I guess you want to hear what happened in the car with Charlie, right?"

"I'm waiting."

"Tell you what. Give me two hours to sleep and return to normalcy, then come on over for dinner and I'll tell you all about it."

"Maddie, did you spill the beans?"

"I did not spill said beans." She could hear Priscilla exhale.

"Thank God. Go back to sleep and I'll see you soon."

She hung up before Maddie could say good-bye. After she turned off the phone, she dove back under the covers and slept without interruption.

Priscilla's loud, raucous laugh woke Maddie up and cut her dream short. In it, she was back at Jackson's house and they were painting together on one canvas.

Her head was still a little fuzzy as she managed to throw on some clothes and join her friend and son in the living room. Priscilla held up a half-eaten swirling delish.

"Your kid is a genius. This is delicious stuff!"

Ray was beaming. Of all his mom's friends, Priscilla was his favorite. Getting a compliment from her meant a lot.

Maddie took the snack out of her friend's hand and took a bite. "Mm! I taste cinnamon, ginger, cloves, lemon cream, and cookies. You're a compassionate Guy Fieri."

Ray got up from the couch and took a bow. "Thank you, fans. And now, I must go meet Jack and Colin and share the swirling delishes with them. I will leave one for each of you."

He gave the women a hug and left. As soon as she heard his car take off, Priscilla said, "Before you tell me everything, what possessed you to want to tell Charlie that you knew why he was dating you? I love you, M&M, but that's plain nuts."

"His mom's dog is dying."

"Well, that explains everything," she said in a sarcastic tone. "You met his mom?"

"No. His mother died five years ago." Maddie eyed the snack Ray left her. "Should we have dinner before eating Ray's creation?"

Exasperated, Priscilla said, "I feel like I'm in a maze and I'm not sure how I got there. Focus, Ms. Mozart."

"Fine. Let me start from the beginning and when I'm done, you'll understand why I was going to tell Charlie the truth. You don't mind if we talk while I fix dinner, do you?"

"Not at all."

Maddie recounted her journey with Charlie starting with the limo ride and ending with the Jackson Danoff experience. When she finished, a very large salad was on the kitchen table. Maddie handed the tongs to her friend. "Guests first."

Priscilla piled the salad on her plate, then sat down and pointed her fork at Maddie. "I want to give you major kudos for standing your ground. I know that took a lot of self-control to resist someone as hot as Charlie Evans, especially while being spooned by him." Maddie agreed. "I'm also thrilled that it was my voice of reason that gave you the strength. Way to go, me!"

"Go ahead. Pat yourself on the back. You deserve it. Now I have a new dilemma: I'm kind of liking his stepfather. The man is so sexy.

Did I mention that he caught me staring at his ass? While Charlie's pining over Hamlet, I'm checking out the bod on dear old dad."

Priscilla dug her fork into a cucumber and avocado, then took a bite. "A couple of months ago, I could have sworn that you were bemoaning the pathetic choices you had in menfolk. Now, you can't decide if you want to be with the superstar or the sweet cheeks stepfather. I really want your dilemma. My last date through match.com ended in the emergency room. The idiot was so intent on copping a feel while kissing me goodnight that he fell forward when I sidestepped him and hit his head on the brick wall behind me."

Maddie laughed. "When was that?"

"Three nights ago. While you were in Italy deflecting the advances of a hunk, I was avoiding being pawed by Sasquatch."

"Life is funny that way, isn't it?" said Maddie.

"Yeah, unless you're the one on a date with the missing link." Priscilla got up and went to the cupboard. "Did you bring back any Italian chocolate?"

"It's still in my suitcase. I'll get it in a sec. What do you think I should do?"

Priscilla sat down. "Right now, I'd just sit back and enjoy the ride. Continue to play hard to get and whatever you do don't tell Charlie that you know about his little bet. Now go get the chocolate. Please."

Obediently, Maddie went into her bedroom. She emerged a few minutes later with six bars of chocolate and her laptop. She laid the bars side by side on the table. Priscilla picked one up and marveled at its packaging: a painting of cacao pods on a brick background.

"I've never heard of Amedei Chocolate before. Don't tell me. It's really expensive, right? Only the best for Charlie Evans' girlfriend."

"In the States, it's $18.50 a bar."

"Get out! It better be fair trade."

"It is." Maddie took the Porcelana chocolate bar from Priscilla and opened it, gently peeling back the wrapper so she wouldn't tear it. She broke off a square for each of them.

Priscilla took a bite. "This is amazing. I mean it. It's the best chocolate I've ever had."

Maddie agreed. "Wait until you try Chuao. It's made from cacao beans grown in Venezuela."

As they broke into the Chuao chocolate bar, Priscilla said, "You'll be getting a call soon from Ava. She wants to have a party, but she won't set a date until she knows when you and Charlie can come."

"How sweet."

"Sweet, my ass. She wants to show him off to her friends. You know what a name dropper she is. Her association with him will bump her up a couple of social notches."

Maddie thought about it. "Don't be so hard on her. Ever since her divorce, she's been kind of down. If Charlie can bring a little sunshine into her life, what's the harm?"

Priscilla shook her head, then popped another square of chocolate into her mouth. "Hon Bun, you are so naïve. The woman is totally self-serving. If I were you, I'd be careful." She eyed the laptop. "Were you going to show me something?"

Maddie turned on the computer. After a few minutes of typing and scrolling, she motioned for her friend to take a look. On the screen was a photo of Jackson Danoff standing in front of one his paintings. He was wearing his signature faded blue jeans and a black T-shirt. Priscilla looked confused.

"This is Jackson," she said. "Isn't he adorable?"

"You know, we have very different taste."

"Not impressed?"

"He's okay. He's definitely sexier than he is attractive."

"To each his own, right?"

"Totally."

13

Gretchen stared at the photo of her late husband. Until his fatal heart attack nearly ten years ago, she and Bentley had been inseparable. In the middle of directing her first film, she'd gotten the call; Bentley had been found unconscious on his law office floor. He had suffered a massive coronary as a result of hypertrophic cardiomyopathy. In many cases the disease, in which the heart muscle becomes abnormally thick, isn't fatal and can be treated. Unfortunately, Bentley had been unaware of his condition. Their marriage of eight years had thrived on a healthy diet of mutual respect, a love of golf, jogging, and tennis, and sarcasm that both could deliver with ease. In her grief, she had sequestered herself in their home for months and written *Julia's Love Affair* as an homage to their marriage. After she'd finished the screenplay, she had tucked it away in her desk, only to pull it out a decade later. Gretchen had felt it was time to bring their love story to the public. She'd made a few edits, then began shopping it around. After Warner Bros. declined, she went to Harmony Films. A multi-million-dollar deal was agreed upon and shooting was to begin in three months.

A few years after Bentley's death, Gretchen had been directing *Cotton Candy*, a romantic comedy, in England. She and the leading man, Roger Halstad, had begun an affair that lasted the length of the filming. When she had returned to the States, he'd promised to come and visit within the month. A number of excuses and delays hadn't deterred her from believing that Roger loved her and she would be seeing him again. Then she'd picked up a copy of *US* magazine while waiting in line at the grocery store. On the cover, the headline screamed, *Heading for the Altar!* In the photo, Roger was in a fierce embrace with Lange Stroppford, England's latest singing sensation. Crushed, Gretchen had vowed never to date a celebrity again. She loved the movie industry, but abhorred the monster egos it created. Gretchen had to acknowledge that she, too, had changed as she became more prominent as a director and screenwriter. She worked hard at keeping her ego in check and not exploiting her power. However, there were a few occasions when she'd used her celebrity status to get her way. Her bet with Charlie was an example of abusing her position. Her justification was her distaste for Charlie Evans. He was arrogant and entitled. He also reminded her of Roger.

"Cecily, has the mail arrived?" she said to her assistant as she stood to stretch her legs.

No sooner had she asked than the mail carrier walked into the office and handed Cecily a thick bundle of mail. She thanked him and brought her boss five legal-size envelopes, two oversized manila envelopes, *The National Enquirer*, *The Star*, and *The Globe*. Gretchen picked up The Globe. Surprisingly, Charlie and Maddie weren't on the cover. She found them on page three. Charlie's hand was up, shielding his girlfriend from the spray of flashbulbs. No mention of the couple in the other two rags. Satisfied that the tabloids were not announcing a love fest between the ill-suited pair, Gretchen was free to believe that Charlie was going to lose his bet.

"You hungry?" Gretchen said to Cecily as she grabbed her coat. "I'd like to treat you to lunch."

"Starving. What's the occasion?"

"A celebration of sorts."

Maddie checked the clock on her cell and grimaced. Ava was late. Normally, it wouldn't bother her as much, but she was volunteering at the Marin Center for Women and couldn't be late. Five minutes later, Ava strolled over to where Maddie was seated.

"Sorry. I was showing a house to this mega-rich couple and they took their sweet time. I even told them I had a meeting. What are you going to do? When you work, you have to take the bitter with the sweet, right?" Ava eyed Maddie's drink. "That looks good. What is it?"

"Almond milk mocha with extra foam."

"Yum. I'm going to get that. Be right back."

Maddie watched her leave. For a woman with a pear-shaped body, Ava moved gracefully. It must be her clothes, Maddie thought. The woman spent thousands of dollars on her wardrobe. Considering she was one of the top realtors in Marin County, the investment in her couture paid off.

Ava returned to the table with a drink and a croissant. She offered Maddie some.

"I'm vegan, remember?"

"Croissants just have flour and butter in them, right?"

"Butter. Dairy. Vegan no-no."

"Sorry." She took a bite of the flaky dessert. Little flat crumbs fell onto her dark blue Ralph Lauren jacket. She flicked them off. "Did Priscilla tell you about my party?"

"Yes, she did."

"It's going to be great. I've already got Robinson & Sons to cater. I didn't want to set the date until I knew that you and Charlie could come."

"Good for business, Ava?"

"Honestly, yeah. I'm dying to get Sid and Violet Freize as clients. You know them, right? They're the power couple in Corte Madera. She's a divorce lawyer and he's an investment banker. I heard they're selling their estate and I'd love to be their realtor. And then there's Miriam Honeywell. She's such a bitch, but she owns the old Gilden mansion in Tiburon. Another realtor said he believes she'll be putting it on the market soon. She'd be turned upside down if she could meet Charlie Evans. What do you say?"

"I'll see when Charlie's available. I'm assuming you prefer a Saturday?"

"That would be super. Thanks so much, Maddie."

"No problem. I'll give him a call tonight and get back to you."

Ava sipped her mocha. "So, tell me all about your trip to Italy."

While Maddie described the highlights of her vacation, Ava

nodded and smiled as if she were fully engrossed in the travelogue. She was barely listening. Instead, Ava was envisioning the upcoming party. She saw herself introducing Charlie to her friends and clients. She relished the looks on their faces as they met the mega star. And Ava could barely contain her anticipation of getting Charlie alone.

Ava was still lost in thought when Maddie stood to leave. They hugged good-bye and each went her separate way. Maddie was off to volunteer and Ava went back to fantasizing.

Every time Maddie pulled into the parking lot of the Marin Women's Center, she circled the area, scanning for any untoward activity or someone who didn't fit in with the regular clientele. The building was intentionally bland and unadorned. It sported small letters on the front, next to the door, claiming to be a nail salon. As she circled back around, she noticed a man sitting low in the driver's seat of an old Toyota Camry. He was unshaven and his hair was greasy and long. Her heart began to pound. She rarely saw men in or near the center.

Maddie parked in one of the front stalls, even though those spots were reserved for clients. She did her best to look nonchalant as she stepped out of her car and into the center. As always, there was a line in front of the receptionist window.

Apologizing to the women as she made her way to the front, she was about to tell Jeannette about the man in the parking lot when the front door crashed open, the door knob cracking the wall. Some of the women screamed as the long-haired, unshaven man pushed his way up to the front of the line. Jeannette reached under the desk and pressed the emergency button. The door to the therapists' offices, phone room, and sleeping quarters automatically locked. It also sent a silent alarm to the police department. She looked the man straight in the eyes and in a steady voice said, "Can I help you?"

Eyes unfocused, left hand in his pocket, right hand shaking, he said, "Where's my fucking wife? I know she's here. I followed the slut."

"What's her name?"

"Lanie Gleason."

"Sir, if you'll have a seat, I'll…"

"Bring her out here now, bitch!" He took a gun out of his pocket and slammed it against the receptionist's window. It shattered, sending safety glass flying. Instinctively, Maddie shielded her face. Her arms took the brunt of the assault, glass slapping her like tiny marbles. She looked over at Jeannette and could see the fear in her eyes. The woman had worked at the shelter for years. She had encountered angry women, disobedient children, and an irate husband or two. She'd never seen a gun up close and personal.

A few of the women ran out of the building. Others were too scared to move. They sat there, some passively as if this were an everyday occurrence: one more angry, violent man interrupting their lives. But for others, the presence of a gun scared them into paralysis. A few women were crying. When sirens could be heard in the distance, the man panicked and ran out the door. Instinctively, Maddie followed him. As he jumped into his car, she memorized the car's license plate, the make, model and color. The man gunned the engine and exited the parking lot on a side street, avoiding the approaching squad cars. When the police arrived, Maddie was the first person Officer Mercer questioned. Before her memory failed her, she rattled off the information: 4DNJ924, faded blue Toyota Camry. When she finished, the officer said, "You know you're bleeding?"

Maddie looked down at her arms. Small pinpoints of blood had soaked through the sleeves and the front of her shirt. In her heightened state, she hadn't even thought to check her body for glass. Suddenly, her arms and torso stung. She felt faint and started to collapse. Officer Mercer caught her and sat her down on the curb. He instructed her to put her head between her legs. She obeyed.

"Is Jeannette okay?" she mumbled.

"Let's worry about you right now, okay? Officers are in the building, checking on the occupants."

Feeling better, Maddie lifted her head. "Damn. I loved this shirt."

The officer read the front of Maddie's shirt. "*Go Vegan and No Body Gets Hurt*. Don't tell me. You're vegan."

"I can see why you became a cop. Very perceptive."

The officer smiled. "Top of the class at the police academy."

"God help us." Maddie slowly stood up. She pushed up the sleeve on her right arm and was relieved to find very little damage. The glass had just broken the skin, enough to cause light bleeding. Same with the other arm. She turned away from the officer and lifted her shirt. The wounds on her abdomen were more severe, perhaps because the skin had been shielded from the sun for decades. It was soft and tender. After her daughter, Kenzie, was born, bikinis became extinct in her wardrobe. While most of her body enjoyed a gentle bronzing from the sun, her midriff looked like it belonged to an albino.

"I'm calling an ambulance," Officer Mercer said as he walked to his squad car.

"It's not that bad," Maddie yelled to him. He ignored her.

The scene inside the waiting room was more civilized than Maddie had expected. Turned out, she and Jeannette were the biggest recipients of the broken glass. The other women had moved away from the receptionist's window when the man pushed his way to the front. They didn't hesitate to give him all the room he needed.

Ellen Nolan, the nurse from the center, was dabbing the wounds on Jeannette's face with hydrogen peroxide. Instructed to tilt her head up, she saw Maddie out of the corner of her eye. "I hope you got that bastard's license plate. Ouch. That stings."

"Sorry, dear. I want to keep you infection-free." Ellen continued her procedure, gently applying the antiseptic.

Maddie said, "I did get his license number. It looks like you took the brunt of the assault. I'm so sorry. Does his wife know?"

"Yeah, and she feels horrible. She's been living at a friend's house and we've already had the police pay them a visit. She'll definitely be staying here for the night." Jeannette looked briefly at Maddie. The blood on her shirt had started to dry. The fabric's pattern hid the dark red blotches. "I'm glad you didn't get hurt."

Maddie lifted up her shirt. There were twelve pebble-sized wounds. Jeannette gasped. "Oh, honey!"

"They look worse than they are. I'm fine. Really. I wish we had better security."

"Maybe you should tell your boyfriend about what happened and we'll get some publicity. It's amazing how attentive the media is when there's a celebrity involved," Ellen said. She put the bottle of hydrogen peroxide down. "I think we're done here. You need to go home and rest. You, too, Maddie."

Officer Mercer walked in and agreed. "Once the shock wears off, you're both going to be emotional wrecks."

Jeannette went over to the policeman. "Would you say that if we were men?"

Taken aback, he said, "I would say it to anyone under these circumstances. Male or female. Having a gun waved in your face and exploding glass hitting you are cause for concern. As a matter of fact, I've witnessed men in less stressful situations breaking down. Do yourselves a favor. Go home and lie down."

"I thought you called an ambulance."

Officer Mercer said, "I did, but it looks like rest is all you need and some Neosporin."

Jeannette softened her stance. She looked at Maddie and nodded. "I will if you will."

Maddie said, "Who's going to take over the reception desk? And I was relieving Rhonda on the hotline."

Ellen practically pushed them out the door. "Don't worry about it. We'll handle it."

Reluctantly, they left. On the ride home, Maddie called Priscilla and told her about the incident. She offered to come over. Maddie said she wanted to be alone.

By the time she walked through the door, the severity of the attack hit her. She felt like she weighed three hundred pounds and her head was throbbing. She dropped to the sofa and immediately lay back. Mick came over and started licking her face. For the first time, she didn't protest. It felt comforting to have someone give her his full attention. Dogs were masters at unconditional love.

When Maddie woke up, it was dark. Mick was wedged between the sofa and her legs. When she moved, he opened his eyes and seemed to say, "Are you feeling better?"

"I'm feeling much better. Thanks, Micky." She gave the boxer a head rub, then got up and went to the kitchen. She was suddenly famished. It wasn't until she opened the refrigerator that she noticed she was still wearing the blood-soaked shirt. Without thinking, she took it off. Some of the skin from the scabs came with it, eliciting a cry of pain. Mick came running in. He got up on his hind legs and went over to the shirt sitting on the kitchen table and began furiously sniffing it.

Despite her hunger, Maddie grabbed a washcloth and slowly cleaned the cuts. She took the officer's advice and dabbed Neosporin on each wound. As she tended to her body, she thought about the fear that must pervade battered women's lives every day. The physical toll was bad, but emotionally it must be hell. She had never been in an abusive relationship. True, Tommy was an alcoholic, but he wasn't a mean drunk. There were no threats, physical or otherwise. Still, it wasn't a healthy relationship. Suddenly, she had a strong desire to talk to Jackson.

After fixing herself a sandwich, Maddie sat down in the living room and turned on the television. Not more than five minutes into *Dateline*, her cell rang. She didn't recognize the number. She paused the program and answered the phone.

"Hello?"

"Hi, it's Jackson, Charlie's dad."

Her heart involuntarily leapt. "Hi."

"I hope I'm not disturbing you."

"I'm watching Dateline with Keith Morrison. The man reminds me of an old Macaulay Culkin."

Jackson laughed. "Really old!"

"True. So, what's up?"

"I just got off the phone with Charlie. I want you two to come and paint and then stay for dinner. He said that this Saturday works for him, around three o'clock. He asked me to call you to confirm."

"That sounds like a blast. I'd love to come. Did you have a nice day?"

"I did. I spent it in my studio working on a new piece. I'm exhausted and energized at the same time, if that makes sense. How about you? Was your day special?"

"It was terrifying." Maddie recounted the drama at the women's center for the second time. Jackson's reaction was exactly what Maddie hoped for.

"You poor thing. If you need someone to talk to or be with, I could come over."

Maddie wanted to tell Jackson to jump in his Prius and hightail it over the Golden Gate Bridge and into San Rafael. She also knew her self-control would be non-existent and, despite his noble intentions, he'd have to fight her off.

"That's so sweet of you and I really appreciate it, but I'll be okay. Before I took a nap, I flashed on something that happened to me when I was nine. I was at a pool party. Our host, Robbie, asked me if I wanted play a game to see who could hold their breath underwater the longest. I said sure. We jumped into the pool and Robbie put his legs around my waist. We both held our breath and went under water for the count. Turned out his lung capacity was better than mine. When I ran out of breath, I tried to go to the surface, but Robbie wouldn't release me. I began to panic. He could see that I was trying to get out of his grasp. He had a smile on his face. As I was beginning to take in water one of the kids, Sally Lang, jumped in the pool and forcibly removed me from Robbie's grasp. I felt the same helplessness today."

"Where did you say the shelter is located?"

"It's in northeast San Rafael. Not the best part of town."

"How many beds does it have?"

"Twenty. It's a great center. I wish it had better security and was more aesthetically pleasing. It looks like your typical shelter. It reminds me of a bunker. I think if it was surrounded by a garden or was on a large piece of land it would make for a more peaceful and nurturing environment."

"I agree. Right now, they'd better be focusing on tighter security, like a camera outside a locked door so they can buzz people in."

"I'm sure that's at the top of their agenda. Tell me, Jackson, have you ever experienced a traumatic event. One where your life was in danger?"

Jackson refilled his wine glass. He was beginning to feel a soft buzz. Just enough to loosen his muscles. He had been in roughly the same position for hours. His shoulders felt rigid. That wasn't the only reason he needed a libation. He was nervous calling Maddie. The woman was more his type than Charlie's. When he was asked to call her and solidify dinner arrangements, he hesitated. Charlie didn't have a clue that his feelings for her were more than platonic. He was sure it wasn't reciprocal. Competing with Charlie Evans was like offering a woman turquoise when she could have the Hope Diamond.

He took a generous sip. The merlot meandered through his veins and tickled his bones, willing his body to relax. "I honestly can't think of a situation where I was in danger or felt threatened. I will say that when my wife was dying of cancer, I was rendered helpless. I watched her slowly leave me. It was devastating. Just devastating."

"I'm so sorry. How long were you married?"

"Twenty years."

As she was racking her brain to say something sympathetic, Jackson said, "Enough morose talk. We'll have plenty of time for that on Saturday, right? Get some sleep and promise me you won't volunteer at the center until they install a camera and lock their front door."

"We'll see."

"Maddie…"

"Jackson…"

He laughed. "Sorry. I don't mean to tell you what to do. I'm just worried about you."

"That's very sweet of you. I'll be fine. I should bring a change of clothes to paint in, right?"

"Definitely. I almost forgot. Charlie said that he'll meet you here since he'll be coming from the set."

"Sounds good. Well, good-night."

"Good-night." Jackson hung up the phone and finished off his glass of wine. Fifty miles away, north of the Golden Gate Bridge, Madeleine Mozart all but forgot about the drama that had unfolded earlier in the day. She couldn't wait for Saturday when she'd be painting with Jackson Danoff. Oh, and Charlie would be there, too.

14

Nervous and excited, Maddie pulled into Jackson's driveway and parked next to his Prius. She grabbed her tote bag containing her painting clothes and a bottle of wine.

The barking of the dogs announced her arrival. Jackson opened the door before she had a chance to knock. Bubbles and Georgie came out to greet her. Wearing faded Levi's jeans and a long-sleeved, V-neck T-shirt, Jackson welcomed her into his home. Maddie held out the bottle of wine.

As Jackson took it from her, he read the label. "How did you know this is one of my favorite merlots?"

"I asked Charlie."

"Well, thank you. Speaking of Charlie, he's not going to be able to make it. They have to re-shoot a scene. I hope my company alone is not too much of a letdown."

"Absolutely not," Maddie said as she internally let out a gleeful shout. So far, the day was going better than expected. She also made a mental note to stay sober. Last time she'd checked, flirtatious activity with one's boyfriend's father was an Emily Post no-no.

After handing Maddie a glass of wine, he took the appetizer plate out of the refrigerator and suggested they sit out on the patio.

Jackson pushed up his sleeves and sat back in the chair. He pointed to the cheeses on the platter. "The vegan cheese expert at Whole Foods assured me that you would love these. This one is chive and garlic and the other is a smoked brie. Allow me." He cut her a slice and put it on a cracker, then handed it to his guest. She popped it into her mouth.

"Mm! Delicious."

Jackson made one for himself. "Wow, this is good. Who would have thought?"

Maddie jumped up. "I totally forgot to give you something. I'll be right back." She went into the house and came back moments later. She handed an envelope to Jackson. On the back was an illustration of a farm house. Curious, he opened it up. A photo of a black and white calf fell onto his lap. Across the bottom of the photo, it said, 'Clive the calf has been adopted by Jackson Danoff.' He turned the picture over and read the back aloud.

"At only seven days old, Clive was brought to Midlands Auction Yard. Alone and scared, he was pushed into the bidding area to be sold and sent to a veal farm. Instead, a good Samaritan bought Clive and brought him to Sycamore Sanctuary where he now lives and cavorts with the other rescue animals."

Jackson was about to say something, when Maddie handed him another envelope. "This is your pet pig, Darla."

Laughing, Jackson said, "Guests have brought me flowers and even dessert, but farm animals? This is a first."

"I figured that if you stopped eating chicken because you have them as pets, you're going to have to give up dining on cows and pigs since they've joined the fold at the Danoff menagerie. Of course, they live away from home. Boarding school, so to speak."

As if on cue, Sherlock flew up to the patio and walked over to Jackson. He stroked the rooster's back. "Where is this sanctuary?"

"North of Sacramento in a town called Hinton."

"I may have to take a trip up there and visit my kids. You'll come, too?"

"Sounds like fun."

"With Charlie, of course."

"Of course," said Maddie.

Jackson sliced off a wedge of cheese and put it on a cracker. "I've never met an ethical vegan before. A few friends became vegan after having heart attacks. It was for their health, not the welfare of the animals. What prompted you to become vegan?"

"About nineteen years ago, I read a book called *Animal Liberation* by Peter Singer, an Australian philosopher. Up until that point, I never looked at non-human animals as having their own value. It was always in relation to how they could serve me. Did they taste good? Could wearing their hide keep me warm or make me look stylish? Even pets served my desire to have a companion. I didn't think about what their life was like under my domain. I never mistreated them, but they lived in unnatural conditions and I know that my pet turtles and fish died prematurely as a result of their captivity.

"I'd go to the circus as a kid and be in awe of lions jumping through hoops of fire and elephants standing on their hind legs with performers cradled in their trunks. It never occurred to me that they were miserable, forced to perform ridiculous tricks that they'd never do in their natural habitat. Same with the zoo. I got so excited seeing the gorillas and the orangutans in person that I looked past the bars on their cages or the moat around their simulated jungle home.

"There are approximately 16 million vegetarians and vegans in the United States but there are over 302 million who aren't. There is no way you can humanely raise food animals, egg- layers and dairy cows for that many people. And that, sir, is why I'm vegan."

Jackson gave Maddie a sympathetic smile. "That was quite an explanation. Thank you for sharing it. I'm totally guilty of exploiting animals. I eat them. I wear them."

"If you'd like to read *Animal Liberation*, I can lend you my copy."

"Sure. I think it's time my compassion for all beings was expanded. It's funny that you're dating Charlie, the biggest meat eater I know. Really."

"He's been very respectful of my diet. He eats only vegan when he's with me and I really appreciate it. I've become increasingly uncomfortable around people eating meat. I went to a friend's fortieth birthday party where they boiled live lobsters. I was the only one who didn't partake of the feeding frenzy. Can you imagine being boiled alive?"

"That's a big no. But they taste so good."

"Should our taste buds dictate our needs or should our compassion?"

"Is this a trick question?"

Maddie laughed. "To a lot of people, it's not. Everything on this planet is for us to use and abuse. Might equals right."

"When you put it that way, we humans sound like bullies."

"We are." Maddie knew when it was time to step down from the soapbox. "So, are we going to paint or not?"

"Nice segue, Ms. Mozart. Grab your wine and let's go to the studio. You can change down there."

As promised, Jackson set Maddie up with a monster canvas. It was a good foot taller than she and five feet wide. Without thinking, she grabbed a one inch wide brush, mixed the oils on the palette, closed her eyes, and began to paint. The elation she felt at having such a large surface to paint on was palpable. Jackson hadn't yet begun to work when he got caught up in Maddie's enthusiasm. He stood behind her and watched with delight as she created with abandon. She even dipped her brush back in the paint without opening her eyes. When she did look at the palette, she turned to see Jackson behind her with a big smile on his face.

"What?" she said.

"I love your style. Are you having as much fun as I think you are?"

She nodded. "I took a freestyle painting class a few years ago. The instructor was this young, very talented hippie. She taught us a lot of unique techniques. My favorite was what she called, spirit painting. It's meditation with paints. Even with our eyes closed, we knew when she was near us because she wore patchouli-scented lotion. It reminded me of high school where half the student body smelled like that."

"I'll have to try it. Any pointers before I begin?"

Maddie put her brush down and followed Jackson to his easel. "Don't have any preconceived notion of what you want to paint. Clear your head."

Jackson stared at the canvas, absorbing its whiteness.

Maddie continued. "Let your brush go to the oils. No prompting. No choosing. Once you've prepared the brush, close your eyes and start painting. Remember to keep your mind open."

Jackson grabbed a tube of M. Graham Cadmium Red and squeezed out a generous amount in one of the palette wells. Then he took the Hansa Yellow and Permanent Green Light and did the same. He chose a wide brush, mixed the paints together, closed his eyes, and with one fluid stroke, he swept the brush onto the virgin canvas.

He opened his eyes and, without looking at the canvas, replenished his brush. Once again, with eyes closed, Jackson let his arm do whatever it wanted. "This is so liberating. Even if I didn't like the painting, I really dig the process."

"It's groovy, man."

"Are you making fun of me?"

"Yup."

Jackson laughed. "Go back to your easel."

The two artists continued to paint for a couple of hours. With the exception of classical music playing in the background, it was quiet.

Maddie wiped her hands on the towel provided and went over to Jackson. He was finishing up, as well.

"Did you intend to paint a horse with your eyes closed or is that your mad, crazy talent showing?"

Jackson stepped back to examine his art. "It does resemble a horse, but that wasn't what I was trying for. Actually, I was more concerned with the colors than the content. Not bad, eh?"

"Jackson, it's stunning. Mine looks like something a cat would do...blindfolded. It's obvious who makes a living off their paintings."

"Don't be so hard on yourself. Let's see what you've done." He went over to Maddie's easel. Vibrant colors competed for attention as they seemed to leap off the canvas. "The energy in this piece is amazing. I can feel it radiating. These red and green swirls are moving." He saw the look on Maddie's face, as if she didn't believe him, so he tried again. "I'm serious. Put your hand right here."

Maddie put out her arm, palm about a foot from the painting. Jackson moved it six inches closer, leaving his hand on her arm. She felt energy, but it wasn't coming from her work.

"Can you feel it?" he said.

"I can. I also feel like eating. I'm famished." Maddie put her hand down and pushed up her sleeves, revealing the small scabs covering her arms.

Jackson's eyes widened. "Does it still hurt?"

She had completely forgotten about the sores. She looked down at her mottled skin and lightly touched her left forearm. "No. It just looks hideous. I got off easy. Poor Jeannette got hit in the face and neck."

"In a week or two your skin will be all healed."

"In the meantime, I get a lot of sympathetic looks. Like the one you're giving me now."

"Dare I ask if they installed a security camera and are locking the front door?"

"I haven't been back since the incident, so I don't know. I hope so."

"Me, too." Jackson shook his head. "They'd better not wait until something worse happens."

Once they were in the kitchen, Jackson gave Maddie the task of setting the dining room table while he put the casserole in the oven. The conversation was casual. Jackson asked about her children. Maddie asked about his stepson.

"You two seem to get along great," Maddie said as she lit the tapered candles.

Jackson placed the salad next to the casserole dish on the table. "We do, as long as he keeps his ego in check. His mother spoiled him, but she also taught him strong values."

Maddie wanted to say, 'Like telling the truth about why you're dating someone? Failed there, I'm afraid.' Instead, she nodded.

"Can I pour you some more wine?" Jackson said as he positioned the bottle over Maddie's glass.

"Sure." Maddie watched as the dark red liquid fell into her wine glass. She was approaching her limit.

"I'm having a great time," she said and raised her glass. "To the master painter and, hopefully, master chef. Thank you."

Jackson's glass met hers. "My pleasure." He spooned out a generous helping of the macaroni and cheese casserole and put it on Maddie's plate. "I found this recipe for vegan mac and cheese online. I hope you like it."

Maddie took a bite. "You multi-talented son of a bitch. This is delicious. And I bet you made the salad dressing, too."

"Of course I did. I'm glad you like the casserole. I'm impressed myself. I grew up on Kraft Macaroni and Cheese and thought it was best meal ever. When I got older, I was really curious how they got the cheese that color. It practically glows in the dark."

"Yellow 5 and 6 food coloring. They're banned from use in a number of countries because…"

"Children were starting to glow in the dark?"

Maddie laughed. "That and they may be carcinogenic and cause allergies and hyperactivity in children. The good old U S of A continues to use them like they're going out of style. Yellow 5 is used in candy corn, potato chips, Mountain Dew. Tons of stuff."

"And you know about this because?"

"When I had kids, I became more vigilant about what I ate. I grew up on the standard American diet and I was determined not to do that to my children. I didn't want to support Hostess and all the other companies that turned children into sugar, salt, and fat addicts. Besides, I was vegan before Kenzie was born. By the time Ray was born, I was a nutrition whiz." Maddie took another bite of the savory dish. "I wish I could put all that knowledge to use."

They ate in silence for a short time, both lost in thought. Strangely, it didn't feel awkward at all. Jackson broke the quiet. "I don't know if this is the wine talking, but I think I just had an excellent idea. What if there were an animal sanctuary that doubled as a safe house for battered women and children? They could live there temporarily and help take care of the animals and the land."

Maddie stopped eating mid-bite. Jackson was putting into words her two favorite causes: farm animal welfare and empowering women. "That's a brilliant idea! It would have to be a vegan sanctuary."

"Of course. We can't have some of the residents eating the other residents now, can we?"

"And security would have to be tight. I can just see some of these crazy abusers sneaking into the sanctuary and taking their frustrations out on the animals."

Jackson got up and went into the kitchen. Maddie couldn't help but watch him leave the room. She hoped *he* didn't have any security cameras.

"I'm going to make some coffee. You want some?"

"Sure."

From the kitchen, he said, "Why don't we take a trip up to Sycamore Sanctuary? It's not too far from here and we could call them in advance and tell them our plan."

"I'd love to." She hesitated. "Do you think Charlie would mind?"

"Hell, no. I'm no threat...am I?"

Jackson was a good eight years older and a few inches shorter than his stepson. His grey hair was thick and rested just above his ears. He wasn't nearly as good looking as Charlie, but Jackson's charisma and charm made him very sexy.

"Don't underestimate your sex appeal, Mr. Danoff. Now let's change the subject before I get myself into hot water, okay?"

"I'll just say thank you. And now, would you like dessert?"

"Yes, please."

Jackson pulled a plate of multi-colored cupcakes out of the refrigerator and placed them in front of Maddie. She pointed to one with mocha-colored frosting and chocolate jimmies.

"They're all gorgeous. What flavor is this one?"

"That's bourbon coffee. This one is peach. The yellow one is butterscotch and this charming little pink one is peppermint coconut. I'll give you first choice, but I'm eyeballing the yellow fellow."

"Perfect, because I want the bourbon coffee."

He poured them both a healthy mug of coffee and offered Maddie the carton of coconut creamer.

Maddie took a large bite of the cupcake and closed her eyes as she savored the flavor. "Unbelievable. I've never had a cupcake this good." She watched as Jackson bit into the butterscotch dessert.

"Wow. These are vegan? Delicious."

Once they finished dessert, they took their coffee and went into the living room. Jackson opened up his laptop and googled 'Rural land for sale in the Bay Area.' Maddie sat close as they perused the various available lots. Without warning, an orange and white cat jumped up on the couch and sat on Maddie's lap.

"Where did he come from? I thought you only had dogs."

Jackson said, "That's Butch. I have two more cats. Tupelo is an Abyssinian and there's Velcro. She's a Persian. They all adopted me."

Butch purred as Maddie stroked his back and continued to check out the properties. Some had existing structures and were fenced in. Others were on hilly terrain and the property lines were barely visible. The prices ranged from $900,000 to over $3,000,000. One piece of land appealed to both of them. It was a sixteen-acre site located in the hills above the city of Woodside. It used to be a goat farm. A ranch-style house was the only residential structure. Two barns, a silo, and a water tower were interspersed throughout the property.

Maddie said, "Unless we have the money, state and federal funding are almost non-existent. The shelter I volunteer for has a full-time grant writer."

"I'm not that concerned with the purchase of the land and the start-up costs. The challenge will lie in keeping the doors open. That's where we'll need support. We could have annual fundraisers. We could even auction off our paintings."

"Yeah. They'll be clamoring to buy mine, 'the artist formerly known as Charlie Evans' older girlfriend.' I didn't know there were people more naïve than myself."

"I've been called many things, but naïve has never been one of them. First of all, you're underestimating your ability. Whether you choose to accept it or not, you're very talented. Secondly, by the time we need to have a fundraiser, you will have had the opportunity to create a nice body of work."

Maddie looked at Jackson like he was made of pure gold. Then she had a question. "You embraced this idea awfully quickly. Why? I mean, we began talking about it less than two hours ago. What's up?"

Jackson closed the laptop and sat back on the sofa. "I have two brothers and one sister. I used to have two sisters. Lydia was the baby of the family. She was funny and beautiful and had a heart so big, it could accept all kinds of misfits and miscreants. When she was twenty-two, she met Geoff Hudson. The man was almost ten years older than she. If he had any potential as a kind, decent human being, only she saw it. We all hated him. He had a drinking problem and a nasty temper and who knows what else. Despite all our efforts to convince her to leave him, she married the guy. They eloped, actually. Lydia withdrew from the family and ended up moving with Geoff to Portland. Three years later, my parents got a call from the Portland Police."

Jackson's voice cracked. He stared off into space, then continued. "Lydia was found in her bed, shot to death. Geoff was arrested and convicted of manslaughter. May he continue to rot in jail for the rest of his life."

Maddie wiped tears from her eyes. "I'm so sorry. I had no idea."

"Of course you didn't, or maybe subconsciously you did. I've been donating to transitional housing for women and women's shelters ever since Lydia's death. When I spoke to you the night of the attack at the women's center, it infuriated me that someone could so easily breach a safe spot for women who have been physically and emotionally abused. They gather the strength to get help, only to feel terrorized again. When you adopted the farm animals for me, something clicked. The pig and cow. They were abused, too. This is my chance to really make a difference.

"Plus, living at a sanctuary can help educate the residents about farm animals. We could even have a vegetable garden. Can you imagine how healing this could be? I bet some of these women and their children haven't had fresh, organic vegetables...ever."

Maddie glanced over at the clock. It was close to 11:00. "It's late. I should be going, but we have to continue this conversation. Are you serious about going to Sycamore Sanctuary?"

"Definitely. I'm free any time. You?"

"I'm unemployed. Any day. Any time."

"What do you mean, unemployed? I do believe you just found a job."

Maddie looked at Jackson, surprised. "You want me to run the sanctuary?"

He nodded. "Who better?"

"Maybe someone with experience? I don't know the first thing about running a women's shelter or an animal sanctuary. I bet the learning curve is very high. And would I have to live there? I love my home. I don't know if that's something I'd like to do. And what about my son? Would he have to live there, too?"

Jackson gave Maddie a big hug. "Calm down, dear. We have plenty of time to work out the details. Let's take the first step. Call Sycamore and set up an appointment...or do you want me to do it?"

Maddie wanted to say, 'Can we stand here and hug for about an hour?' Instead, she said, "You can call, then let me know the day and time."

Jackson walked her out to her car, the dogs in tow. He watched Maddie drive away until the car's taillights disappeared down the street. He really enjoyed Maddie's company and it was clear that she was comfortable with him. And she did make that comment about him being sexy.

As he got ready for bed, he studied his face in the bathroom mirror. Almost fifty-one, he thought he looked good for his age. He had most of his hair. It was thick with a slight wave. His laugh lines were pronounced but not dramatically. He had been told by more than a few people that he looked like a cross between Gene Hackman and Joseph Gordon Levitt. A most strange combination, but they were right. His nose and mouth looked more like Joseph's and his eyes twinkled like Gene's. He moved the medicine cabinet mirror towards the wall mirror until he saw his profile. He touched the top of his nose and followed it down the straight edge to the tip. Satisfied, he brushed his teeth, washed his face, and joined the dogs and cats in his king-size bed.

"Move over, Georgie. I keep telling you that's my pillow, not yours. Go lie next to Velcro at the foot of the bed."

Georgie picked her head up and moved it off the pillow, then rolled over and fell back asleep. Bubbles got up from the other side of the bed and plopped himself down on Jackson's right side. He snuggled up under his right arm and let out a satisfied groan. The cats stayed put, all three intertwined like a 3-D puzzle. Jackson surveyed the scene and shook his head. If he ever did live with a woman again, she would have to be an animal lover and a very tolerant one at that. As if on cue, Bubbles let out a loud yawn. Tupelo jerked awake, disrupting her sleeping partners, knocking Butch off the bed. That sent Velcro running out of the room. Jackson laughed.

"Welcome to my animal sanctuary."

He picked up his laptop and clicked on the bookmark for Sycamore Sanctuary. He wanted to learn more about the animals and the lay of the land before visiting. He went to the resident animal page and scrolled down to check on the status of his pig, Darla. She was a large sow, lying in a bed of straw while one of the volunteers rubbed her belly. Jackson swore she had a big smile on her face. He knew that food animals had a bad, no, a horrible life, yet the only change he'd made in his diet was eliminating chicken. And that wasn't too long ago. Once he visited the sanctuary, he was sure that he'd be cutting meat and dairy out of his diet. He also knew that he would be getting flak for it from his friends. He wondered how Charlie would react. Maybe he'd be pleased that his girlfriend was making an impression on his stepfather.

Jackson closed his laptop, his elbow accidentally hitting Bubbles in the head. He turned and looked at him as if to say, 'Can you please be more careful?' Jackson patted the dog's head and apologized, then said goodnight to his bedmates and turned out the light.

They wrapped up the scene shortly after 11:00 p.m. Instead of feeling exhausted, working that late put the cast and crew into overdrive. A few of them went back to their respective hotels for the night. Others opted for a late, late dinner. The rest descended on a small bar close to Pier 13 where they had been filming. Club Foot was already crowded. Add thirty people, mostly out-of-towners, and you have a mob scene without a reason. Charlie was chosen to procure the beverages for the group. He pushed his way through the crowd to the amusement of those he was pushing. Once he got up to the bar, he requested thirty bottles of Anchor Steam beer. He was positive they'd have an ample supply since the rich, distinctively flavored brew was made in San Francisco. A few of the waitresses helped pass the beers out to a very receptive crowd.

Charlie turned to the director and said, "Vicente, I've said it before and I'll say it again, you're the best director I've worked with to date. Can we all raise our beers to *the man*?"

A resounding cheer went up from the group. They clinked their bottles together and all took a big slug. As the cast and crew mingled, some went over to the pool tables and others waited for a chance to play darts. Charlie grabbed a bar stool and Rachel quickly nabbed the one next to his before anyone else could. She had been on the set performing for hours, yet she looked beautiful, nary a golden blonde hair out of place. Of course, half a can of hairspray didn't hurt.

"Do you really think John is the best director you've ever worked with?" Rachel asked Charlie, trying not to notice some of the local men ferociously eyeing her. She loved being attractive. She also knew the price she paid for it – caught without makeup or looking exhausted in public wasn't an option.

"I do," Charlie replied. "He has a great eye for detail and style and he respects actors. He also keeps his ego in check. You don't agree?"

"I guess." She nonchalantly took out her lip gloss and applied it, slowly. "I thought the shoot went really well. I'm usually uncomfortable with sex scenes. With you, I was very relaxed."

Charlie immediately tensed up. He knew what was coming and as sensual as his co-star was, he wasn't interested. Rachel had a reputation for sleeping with her leading men and, from what he was told, she was a dynamo in bed. If he wasn't dating Maddie, he would have propositioned her weeks ago, but his desire for the role of Danny in *Julia's Love Affair* superseded his libido and he didn't want any misstep to sabotage his efforts.

"I'm glad you were comfortable."

"Were you, too?" Rachel said as she leaned in closer, their shoulders touching.

"I think our personalities are well-suited." Charlie looked over toward the pool tables and saw Phil, the production assistant, chalking up his pool cue. "I'm going to play some pool with Phil. Enjoy your beer."

Rachel grabbed his arm as he slid off the barstool. "You want to come over to my hotel room later? We could continue the scene, for real."

"As much as I'd like to, Rachel, I'm dating someone."

"You're not serious, are you? The woman is old enough to be my mother." Rachel flipped her hair back and struck a seductive pose. Charlie almost laughed out loud.

"Aren't you twenty-three?"

She nodded.

"Honey, I'm old enough to be your father."

Rachel put her face an inch from Charlie's. "Honey, if my daddy looked like you, I'd have a real problem controlling myself."

Temporarily stunned, Charlie wasn't sure what to say. Finally, he stepped back and said, "I appreciate the compliment, Rachel, but I'm dating Maddie and until that changes, I don't play around." With that, he turned and walked over to the pool tables. Phil gave him a sideways glance. He had watched the exchange between the two stars.

"You'd rather play pool with me than hit that?"

Charlie grabbed a pool cue from the wall rack. "I'm dating someone."

"And…"

"What do you mean, and?"

"I've worked with you before, Charlie. Having a girlfriend never stopped you from getting some on the side."

Charlie grabbed the chalk cube. "Well, it does now." To prove his point, he took out his cell and made a call. Maddie picked up on the second ring. "Hi."

"Hey babe. You miss me?"

"*Babe*? Are you still in character?"

"Yes, I miss you, too. How was dinner at Jackson's?"

Ignoring the disconnect in the conversation, Maddie said, "I had a great time. We painted and then, get this, Jackson and I want to open an animal sanctuary and…"

"It's hard to hear you in this place, so I'm going to sign off…See you soon. Miss you, too." Charlie turned to Phil. "You want to break or shall I?"

Stunned, Maddie hung up the phone. She knew something was amiss. Charlie's call was to prove a point to someone. Was it his co-star? She was no doubt hitting on him. The assumption didn't bother her. Maddie's emotional attachment to Charlie was never that strong to begin with. After meeting Jackson, it was virtually non-existent, but she had to continue to play the game to its eventual end. If she quit now, she could jeopardize her relationship with Jackson. The aroma from the kitchen disrupted her thoughts. "What are you concocting now, son?"

Ray was arranging pineapple slices in a frying pan on the stove. He held up a bag of coconut bacon, a vegan version made with seasoned, smoked, and baked coconut flakes. "Making magic. I call it Smokin' the Pineapple. You want to try it? It's almost done."

"It smells amazing, but I don't like to eat before I go to bed. Save me some, okay?" She went over and kissed Ray on his forehead. "I predict that you're going to be the next Emeril, vegan-style."

"I could live with that."

15

Maddie heard the Porsche pull up to the curb. She looked at the clock. He was right on time. One more mirror check and she was ready. Tonight was Ava's party. Her friends hadn't seen her with Charlie since the Purple Umbrella.

"Come in!" she yelled after he rang the bell. As a precaution, she had Ray keep Mick in his room until they left. The boxer had a tendency to transfer his drool onto clothes and the last thing Maddie wanted was any deviation from looking her best. She knew Charlie wouldn't appreciate getting slobbered on, either.

Charlie grabbed Maddie around the waist and gave her a kiss. "You look amazing. How come you haven't worn skinny jeans before?"

Maddie looked down at her pants. She had to admit they looked great. Tucked into her cowboy boots, she felt sexy. "I wore them on our first date, Mr. Observant."

Charlie was embarrassed. He faltered, trying to find the right thing to say. Maddie interrupted his thoughts. "Don't worry about it. I don't remember what you wore that night, either."

Twenty minutes later, Maddie and Charlie were being embraced by one extremely happy hostess. In her quest for perceived perfection, Ava over-accessorized. If Maddie didn't know that her friend's jewelry sported real gems, she would have sworn she'd seen the gaudy pieces on the QVC, the home shopping channel. Ava's hair had been professionally coiffed and her dress was two inches shorter than it should have been, exposing too much of her ample legs. Ava personified Marin County's nouveau riche.

She grabbed Charlie's hand and said to Maddie, "I hope you

don't mind, but there are more than a few people who would like to meet your boyfriend. May I?"

"It's not up to me. Charlie?"

"It would be my pleasure. Ava, show away."

Maddie noticed more than a few cellphones pointed in their direction, flashes going off like fireflies. She could also feel the energy in the room change. Women began primping, hoping they would catch Charlie's eye. And men, feeling threatened by someone rich and famous and painfully handsome, exhibited more bravado than normal. Maddie remembered initially feeling the unease and desire to live up to an unrealistic expectation. After going out several times with Charlie, his supersized appearance began to shrink as his very flawed human qualities bled through. With more street sense than scholastic smarts, the mega star wasn't going to win any scholastic competitions. Maddie learned to dumb down their conversations without him catching on. It wasn't that difficult. She employed a simpler, more pedestrian vocabulary. Once, she accidentally described one of their meals as delectable. Charlie looked at her and said, 'So...you liked it?'

Someone tapped Maddie on the shoulder. She turned to find Priscilla.

"So, where's Romeo?"

"Ava's showing him off like a prize bull at the state fair," Maddie said.

"What a shocker. The only reason I'm here is because I wanted to see you and Tanvi and Sylvie. Oh, and I was a little curious about meeting your boyfriend. What's his name again?"

"The dashing and over-the-top sexy, liar and cheat."

"What's that supposed to mean? Did he cheat on you?" Tanvi looked like she was ready to hunt down Charlie and pummel him into Ava's Oaxacan area rug. Her husband patted her on the back and told her to calm down.

Maddie laughed. "Not at all. I was just being silly. Silly and a little too loud. Charlie's been great. He's meeting Ava's friends and associates and everyone Ava's ever met who happens to be at the party. Let's go find the bar, shall we?"

After securing a glass of wine, Maddie nonchalantly scanned the crowd for Ava and Charlie. There must have been at least seventy-five guests, so it took a concerted effort to check them all out.

Priscilla said, "They're on the deck." She pointed to the redwood patio with her bottle of beer. "You ask me, Ava's getting a little too chummy. I'm going to bust up the dynamic duo."

Before Maddie could protest, Priscilla made a beeline for the couple. She held out her hand to Charlie and introduced herself, then grabbed his arm and brought him back inside.

"I wish I had that girl's guts," Tanvi said. "I would have to be really drunk or offered a lot of money to do what she just did."

"Believe me, dear," her husband said. "You have no trouble speaking your mind. Just ask my parents or our children."

Tanvi was about to counter when Charlie and Priscilla joined the group. He went over to Maddie and gave her a kiss. "Your friend is a lifesaver. If I had to meet one more of Ava's friends or clients…" He shook his head.

"She can definitely be aggressive. Isn't that the sign of a good realtor?" Maddie took Charlie's hand and he looked at her with genuine affection.

It felt good to be envied by almost every woman in the room. She knew the circumstances were ephemeral, so she made sure that she inhaled every bit of attention. More cellphone photos were taken as the group chatted. They eventually made their way over to the buffet table. Ava let everyone know the food was provided by Robinson & Sons, the prestigious and very expensive catering company out of San Francisco. For 99% of the guests, they didn't disappoint. Exotic meats and cheeses were enthusiastically devoured along with platters of crudités and roasted vegetables. As desperately as Charlie would have liked to sample all the food, he stuck by his resolution to eat vegan around Maddie. When questioned about his eating habits, he put on a stellar performance and told her friends that it was easy eliminating meat and dairy. He didn't miss it at all. He wasn't a big cheese lover anyway, he claimed as he surreptitiously looked longingly at the melted brie covered in candied walnuts.

He and Maddie, along with vegetarians Tanvi and Sanjay, piled their plates high with the grilled asparagus, eggplant, padrone peppers and tomatoes stuffed with shitake mushrooms and rice. They also grabbed the avocado maki, cucumber rolls and green bean tempura rolls.

"I've noticed that after I eat with Maddie, even if I'm full, I feel lighter. Healthier," Charlie said as he placed a slice of pickled ginger on top of the tempura roll, then dunked it in wasabi-laced soy sauce.

Sanjay said, "I was raised vegetarian and I've never eaten meat, but I know what you mean. Maddie's definitely the healthiest person I know."

"Thanks, Sanjay."

Priscilla rolled her eyes. "Knock it off with the veggie talk. I'm pretty damn healthy, too, and I'm not vegan."

Maddie pointed her fork at Priscilla. "Just wait." She was expecting a sarcastic retort when Sylvie walked up to the group with her date in tow.

"We only had to park about five blocks away, but we made it." Sylvie put her arm around Garrett and gave him a quick squeeze. He was tall and thin with snow-white hair and a goatee to match. He had a pleasant face but when he smiled, he exposed a set of yellowish, slightly crooked teeth. "Everyone, this is Garrett. Garrett, that's Tanvi, Sanjay, Priscilla, Maddie and Charlie."

The group resumed eating while Garrett and Sylvie went to the buffet. They had to practically shout, since the music coming from the adjoining room was so loud. Ava turned her spacious family room into a mini-disco and a DJ was playing hip hop, funk, and rock. Except for a few couples, the dance floor was empty. Priscilla groaned when she saw Ava approaching them.

"How was the food? You like?" Ava directed the question to the group even though her gaze was on Charlie.

All nodded their approval. Ava clapped in delight. Priscilla rolled her eyes and wanted badly to say something, but knew it was inappropriate. Not that it ever stopped her before. She wasn't ready to be derisive. Yet.

As soon as she heard *Uptown Funk*, Ava practically yanked Charlie out of the chair. "I love this song. Please dance with me."

Charlie's first inclination was to decline, less than gracefully. He stopped himself because Ava was Maddie's friend and Maddie was his girlfriend. He needed to show the world what an amazing boyfriend he was, so he let the pushy, obnoxious Ava lead him onto the dance floor. Ava mouthed 'thank you' to Maddie.

Priscilla laughed. "I actually feel sorry for the guy. She doesn't really have any boundaries, does she?"

Maddie said, "Ava's harmless. It's not every day she can hold court for a movie star. Let her have her glory."

Tanvi glared at Ava as she danced with Charlie. "She is acting most inappropriately."

Sanjay took his wife's hand in his. "You're not jealous, are you?"

"Hell, no! Sylvie, help me out here."

Sylvie took the last bite of grilled asparagus dunked in hollandaise sauce, dabbed her mouth with a napkin and said, "I never liked Ava and now I like her even less. I came to the party because I wanted you to meet Garrett and I always love seeing you three, no offense, Sanjay."

"No offense taken."

Sylvie continued. "Ava is a spoiled woman who likes to get her way and if I were you, Maddie, I'd be watching her like a hawk. Now, I'm going to get another glass of vino. Anyone else?"

Charlie had to stifle his laughter. Ava's dancing style reminded him of someone being electrocuted. Her arms and legs shot out from her body in bursts. Occasionally a hand or two would land on his waist or thigh. They were halfway through the song when Ava pulled him off the dance floor. "I totally forgot to give you a tour of the house." She could tell he was about to protest, so she added, "Maddie made me swear to show you my place. She loves it and wanted your opinion. Please?"

Charlie said, "If Maddie made you swear, I can't refuse." He was sure Maddie could care less about what he thought of her friend's decor.

She walked him over to the kitchen where the caterers were busy preparing dessert. The countertops were covered with platters of petit fours and chocolate truffles. "I had the kitchen remodeled a few years ago. The refrigerator, stove, and dishwasher were all chrome. It was so 'yesterday,' you know?"

She waited for a response from the man whose Malibu mansion had a kitchen equipped with chrome appliances down to the electric can opener. He was tempted to tell her. "It looks great. You did a wonderful job."

"Thanks, Charlie. That means so much coming from you. Of course, I had a decorator design it. Wait until you see what she did with the upstairs."

Ava's jewelry jangled as she bounded up the stairs. She quickly guided Charlie through the guest room, office, and guest bathroom. Pausing for dramatic effect, Ava opened the double doors to the master bedroom. The room was tastefully decorated in pastels with a king-size bed covered in pillows from large to small. The thick pile white carpet was spotless.

"What do you think? Does it look like Rachel Swanson's bedroom?"

"I wouldn't know, Ava. I'm not friends with her. We just happen to be in a movie together. It's very nice, though."

"Thanks."

Ava unlocked the French doors to the balcony and went over to the railing. She saw Maddie talking to Priscilla in the back yard. She sighed. "I love Maddie. She's a great gal, but don't you think she's just a tad too old for you? I mean, I'm in my thirties and that's pushing it by your usual standards, right?"

She moved closer to Charlie. "Plus, she's unemployed and has two kids. We're talking some serious baggage here. Oh, and she's got an ex-husband who wants her back. She intimated that she misses him, too."

Charlie put his hands up, but not before Ava planted a kiss on his lips. He gently pushed her away. "This tour has officially ended."

As Charlie left the room he turned back to a very flustered Ava and said, "You're a lousy tour guide, and an even worse friend. And every appliance in my house is chrome." He practically sprinted down the stairs. He went over Maddie and Priscilla. "I have a great idea. Let's ditch this party and start another one at my hotel room. All your friends are invited."

Priscilla said, "It's close to 9:00. By the time we get into the city and park, won't it be too late?"

Maddie looked around her, then circled her friend and scratched her head. "Funny, I don't see your walker."

Charlie laughed. "Come on. It's Saturday night. The home will let you stay out a little later, won't they?"

"Ha, ha. You two are so funny. Fine, let's do it. I'll find Tanvi and Sanjay. You two nab Sylvie and Garrett. We'll meet you at the door."

As they wound their way through the crowd, Maddie watched Ava slowly descend the staircase. She had a befuddled look on her face as she eyed her guests, like she had no idea why all these people were in her home.

"What happened?" Maddie yelled over the noise.

"I'll tell you in the car."

They found Sylvie and Garrett conversing on the couch. When told of the plan, they practically leapt off the sofa as if it was on fire. Earlier, they tried talking to some of the other guests and realized that the only thing they had in common was Ava.

At the entrance, Charlie intimated that Ava exhibited highly inappropriate behavior. He promised to tell them about it at the hotel. All agreed to leave without saying goodbye to the hostess. Emily Post would have been aghast.

Since they'd left the party before dessert was served, Charlie ordered a variety of vegan treats from room service, along with three bottles of Cristal Champagne. In the car, Maddie heard all about Ava's attempted seduction. When Charlie retold the story to the group, she got even madder.

"I never liked that woman," said Priscilla. "She has this air about her, like she's better than everyone else. She's nothing but a skank." She poured herself another glass of champagne. "This is really good shit."

Maddie said, "I just thought of something. That bitch tried to sabotage my first date with you."

Charlie said, "How so?"

"The day of our first date, Ava dropped by. She told me she had just come from Whole Foods and they were handing out samples of dried blueberries. They were so good, she bought a bag for herself and one for me. I thanked her and was going to put it in the cupboard, but she insisted that I try them. I did. They were delicious. I ended up eating the whole bag. Later, I was talking to Ray while getting ready for the date. He said something funny and I laughed. He gave me the weirdest look and told me to look in the mirror. Blue teeth and blue tongue! I mean, really blue. I brushed my teeth three times. It looked like I ate a Smurf."

Charlie said, "For the record. I still would have asked you out again, blue mouth and all." He leaned over and kissed Maddie.

That got a big aww! from the group.

Tanvi was clearly buzzed. The mother of two rarely drank. She liked being in control at all times. Tonight was different. She and her husband were sipping champagne in Charlie Evans' luxurious suite on Nob Hill. She tried not to stare at the actor. She'd never known a celebrity before. Aside from his looks, she was struck by how charismatic he was.

"Let's play a game!" Tanvi said.

"Let's!" Sylvie chimed in. "How about truth or dare?"

Priscilla, Charlie, and Maddie all shouted at the same time, "No!"

Tanvi said, "Are we hiding something?"

Sylvie rubbed her hands together. "I think so. Now we really have to play."

The mood in the room became playful, tense, light, and fearful. Garrett said, "How do you play?"

Tanvi gave Maddie a sly, little glance, then she turned to Garrett. "A person is asked to choose truth or dare. If they pick truth, they are asked a question that they have to answer truthfully. If they pick dare, they have to do what they are told. I'll start. Charlie, truth or dare?"

Charlie's initial reaction to playing the game came from his gut. *No* came out without even thinking. He wondered why Priscilla and Maddie were also opposed to playing. It didn't matter. It was a stupid game. He could lie if he wanted to and if he had to.

"Truth," said Charlie.

Tanvi rubbed her hands together. "This is going to be good. Hold on. I have to think of a...wait. I got it. I read in *People* magazine that all movie stars cheat on their significant others. Have you cheated on every girlfriend or woman you've ever dated?"

"Tanvi, that's not nice," Sanjay said. "Don't answer that, Charlie."

"No, it's okay. I don't mind. The truth is that I have cheated on every girlfriend and woman I've dated until I met Maddie."

Without thinking, Maddie blurted out, "I don't count." The champagne had dulled her brain. She mentally slapped herself upside the head. She didn't notice Priscilla's glare.

"What's that supposed to mean?" Charlie said.

"It means that we haven't gone out long enough for you to make that statement. Three months is the measurement of time."

"Says who?" said Sylvie, clearly bemused by her friend's outburst.

"Google it. You'll see."

"That's ridiculous," said Charlie. "I've played around on women I've been with for one month, two months. You name it."

"I wouldn't be shouting that from the rooftops if I were you." Maddie said.

Charlie gave Maddie a dirty look. "Excuse me." He got up and went into the bedroom, closing the door a little harder than he needed to.

The room was quiet. "Sorry, guys. I was out of line."

"Apologize to him," Tanvi said. "Go."

"Fine. Please continue drinking, eating, dancing, whatever."

Maddie knocked on the bedroom door, then let herself in. Charlie was in the bathroom.

"Are you okay?" she said, timidly.

"I'd like to go to the bathroom in private, if you don't mind."

Maddie ignored his request and waited until he returned to the bedroom.

"What is it with you?" Charlie said as he sat her down on the bed. "It seems like every time I try to give you a compliment, you throw it back in my face. What am I doing wrong? I don't mean to sound vain, but you're the first woman I've ever met, let alone dated, who has no interest in even sleeping with me."

Maddie felt sorry for the egotistical dolt. He was generous and even-tempered. He enjoyed her friends and they seemed to really like him, too. Perhaps she carried on the lie longer than she should have and it was time to tell the truth. After all, that was her goal in dating him. She wanted to be able to speak her mind and no longer defer to a significant other. She looked Charlie in the eye and was about to end the charade when he said, "Does menopause make you frigid?"

There it was. The big neon sign flashing over Charlie's head: He's using you. He thinks you're ancient. She snapped back into survival mode, into 'you're going to lose that bet, you asshole' mode. In a performance worthy of accolades, she smiled sweetly and said, 'I have been harsh with you and I'm sorry. I find you attractive and no, I'm not frigid or close to approaching menopause. I need a little more time, okay?"

"Sure." Charlie gently pulled her to him and kissed her passionately. Despite her brain instructing her to conjure up libido-deadening images, like Donald Trump or Ted Cruz, Maddie felt a wave of warmth and desire from her pedicured toes to the part in her freshly dyed hair. If it weren't for her friends in the next room, Charlie would have gotten lucky.

"Shall we join the party?" Charlie asked. He held out his hand. She stood on unsteady legs.

She was going to say yes, but it came out as, "Uhhhh."

When they finally emerged from the bedroom, Sylvie said, "One more minute and we were taking off. You two okay?"

In a German accent, Charlie said, "When you court trouble, you have to be prepared for it. If not, then why did you court it in the first place?" He looked expectantly at his guests. Garrett became animated.

"I know that line! It's from...don't tell me. You played opposite Blake Lively. It was a romantic comedy, right?"

Charlie nodded.

"Cashing the...no wait. *Catching It All!*"

"Close. *Cashing It In.*"

"That's right. Good movie."

"Thanks." Charlie grabbed the last champagne bottle from the ice bucket. "Are we done with Truth or Dare?"

Priscilla said, "I think that ship has sailed. How about charades?"

"I'd love to play. Everyone okay with that?" Maddie smiled appreciatively at Priscilla.

The vote was unanimous. For the next few hours, a very animated group of friends played the age-old game while dining on truffles and mini-fruit tarts and washing them down with champagne.

During a break in the game, Priscilla said, "I should go. These old bones are tired and are begging me to put them to bed." She turned to Charlie. "Thank you for throwing a better party than our whore friend. Excuse me, ex-friend."

"My pleasure." Charlie gave her a hug.

Maddie said, "Are you okay to drive?"

"Fine. I didn't have that much to drink. Really. Anyone else leaving or am I the only party pooper?"

Everyone in the room looked at each other. No one budged. Tanvi said, "You seem to be the only one."

Maddie said, "Come on, Grandma. I'll walk you out."

Once they were down the hall, waiting for the elevator, Priscilla said, "What happened in the bedroom?"

"Let's just say that if you all weren't in the next room, I might have totally succumbed to Mr. Evans' undeniable allure."

"AND, he is such a scum bag. Please remember why you're dating him."

The elevator door opened and a well-dressed elderly couple exited.

Maddie sighed. "I'd like to see you do better at refusing McDreamy's advances."

The elderly woman turned to Maddie and said, "If my husband doesn't mind, can I give it a whirl?"

It was nearly two o'clock in the morning when Charlie's guests left. His attempt at convincing Maddie to spend the night failed. She hitched a ride home with Tanvi and Sanjay.

Charlie stood out on the balcony and admired the Golden Gate Bridge. It looked like a deep orange trail across the Bay. He always wondered why it was called golden because it was anything but. Orange Gate Bridge sounded bland. He'd have to ask Maddie the next time he spoke to her. He was almost positive she would know. She was by the far the smartest woman he had ever dated. She might have been the *only* smart woman he'd ever dated. His past relationships hadn't been filled with witty repartee or deep thoughts. They hadn't expanded his mind, only titillated his body. Maddie forced him to think, to re-examine his values and his vocabulary. He would have preferred her fifteen or even twenty years younger, but for a woman in her mid-forties, he had to admit that he found her attractive. His need to sleep with her was no longer a challenge. It was a desire.

16

Ray knocked on the bedroom door. "Mom, are you up?"
He heard the rustling of bedsheets. "Mom?"
"What is it?" Maddie barely croaked out the words. Her
head lightly throbbed, the result of too much champagne. The tiny
bubbles tickled her blood and bruised her brain, but she never
refused a flute-full.

"You have a guest."

Maddie groaned. She looked at her alarm clock. It was 10:00
a.m. "Give me a sec."

After about five minutes, dressed in shorts and a T-shirt, her hair
and teeth brushed, face washed, Maddie walked into the living room.
Ava stood up when she saw her friend. "I've been trying to reach you
since last night. Why won't you answer my calls or texts?"

Maddie crossed her arms and glared at Ava. "Why the hell
should I?"

She was about to answer when she noticed Ray standing in the
doorway. "Do you mind if I talk to your mom in private?"

"He may not, but I do." She turned to her son. "You can stay.
Talk, Ava."

"Fine. I'm sure Charlie told you some ridiculous story about how
I came on to him. Whatever he said, it's total bullshit."

"I see. What really happened, Ava?"

"I'll tell you what really happened. Here I am being a gracious
hostess, giving him a tour of the house. We get to my bedroom." She
stopped at looked at Ray. His facial expression hadn't changed one
bit. If anything, he was enjoying the story. She continued. "As I'm
walking out on the balcony, the jerk grabs me and says, 'I've always

liked younger women' – sorry Maddie – and he tried to kiss me. I told him that you're my good friend and pushed him away. He hit his head on the French door. You must have seen a bump or something."

Maddie shook her head.

"Well, I'm sure he had one. I was so upset that I lay down for a few minutes, locking the door, of course. When I came downstairs, you were all gone. I've been trying to reach you ever since." Ava nervously tucked her hair behind her ears.

Maddie said, "Are you done?"

She nodded.

"Do you want to hear Charlie's side of the story?"

She nodded again. "This should be rich."

"It is." Despite a headache that was making its way down her neck, Maddie recounted the event almost exactly as Charlie told it. She enjoyed watching Ava's face change from smug to incredulous to disgusted.

"That's unbelievable. I would never say those things about you. You're my friend!"

"Funny. That's what I told him. Then he pulled a mini recorder out of his pocket and played back the unbelievable truth. The thing is, Ava, Charlie's been involved too many times in situations where women will accuse him of all sorts of horrible things: sexual assault, even rape. He carries that handy little recorder everywhere he goes to protect himself against liars and opportunists. Like you."

Ava's face took on the pallor of wet clay. She looked as though she might throw up. Before she turned to leave, Ray took a picture of her with his phone.

Maddie said, "I'd like you to go now."

Ava practically sprinted out the door. Ray went over to his mom and patted her on the back. "That was classic. Do you think Charlie will let me hear the tape?"

Maddie said, "Do you really think Charlie's smart enough to carry a tape recorder around? Unless you have a snack that cures a hangover, I'm going back to bed."

"Sorry. I'll work on it."

"You do that, son. Before you do, text me the photo. I know some people who would love to see Ava looking like she's about to hurl."

Maddie closed the bedroom door and crawled back into bed.

Two hours later, Maddie woke up to the sound of muted voices coming from the kitchen. Headache-free, she bounded out of bed, splashed water on her face and went to join the company. She suspected it was Ray and his friend, Louis. It was Tommy. They were drinking iced tea.

"Hey there, Miss Sunshine. Drank too much expensive champagne with Mr. Wonderyucks last night?"

"Yup. I feel great now."

"Ray told me what happened earlier. I love the tape recorder ploy and the picture of Ava is priceless. I never did like her."

"Yeah. I had my doubts about her sincerity. So, what brings you here? Ray isn't supposed to stay with you until next weekend."

"I was in the neighborhood and thought it would be nice to take you two out to lunch. What do you say?"

Maddie stretched. She was hungry, but didn't feel like spending time with her ex. "I'm going to pass. Thanks, anyway."

Tommy looked disappointed. "Are you sure? I wanted to go to the new vegan restaurant in Fairfax. What's it called again?"

Ray said, "Viva Las Vegan. I'm going to change into shorts." Ray took off, leaving his mom and dad alone in the kitchen.

Tommy got up from the table and went over to Maddie. He put his arm around her shoulder. "If you'd been with me last night, you wouldn't have had a hangover and you wouldn't have wasted the whole day sleeping."

Maddie wiggled out from under her ex-husband's grasp. Whenever Maddie was involved in a relationship, Tommy pushed hard for a reconciliation. It never failed, despite her insistence that she was no longer interested. Twice divorced from the same man was her limit. She sincerely hoped that Tommy would remain sober, if not for his own health then at least for his children. In her heart, she loved Tommy as a friend. Nothing more.

"Sleeping half the day was a small price to pay for a fantastic evening. Besides, I'm dating Charlie exclusively and have no intention of ending the relationship. I'm going to ask you again and for the last time…Are you listening?"

"Yes, dear."

"Don't 'yes dear' me. This is my life, too, Tommy. I've told you countless times that we're not getting back together, but you keep trying. In order to have a reconciliation, you need two willing adults and I'm not willing. Period. Don't ask me again."

Ray walked in, oblivious to the conversation. "Ready, Dad?"

"As I'll ever be." Without saying good-bye, he left, Ray in tow.

With the house to herself and no plans for the afternoon, Maddie fixed herself lunch and read the newspaper. Mick came in from the backyard and sat at her side, hoping a piece of vegan meat would drop to the floor. He was used to Phoney Baloney and Tofurky turkey. His kibble was vegetarian, too. Maddie had started feeding him V-Dog a few years ago. It felt great not having to buy meat. Even Mick's treats were vegan. His favorites were Sam's Yams Veggie Rawhide Sweet Potato Dog Treats and Zuke's Mini Naturals Dog Treats. At first, her friends chided her for turning a carnivore into a vegan. After witnessing his transformation from a neurotic boxer to a mellow and healthy canine, they'd stopped their riling. Some had even started their dogs on vegan diets.

Maddie was out back gardening when Ray returned from lunch. He found his mom in the far corner of the backyard pulling weeds. Mick was lying next to her, soaking up the sun. He squatted next to Mick and rubbed his belly. "Lunch was bomb, except Dad was in a foul mood. I shouldn't have left you two alone. What happened?"

"No offense, but your dad is a big baby." She sat down and took off her gloves. "I told him for the zillionth time that I'm not interested in getting back together with him. Maybe this time it will sink in. I hope being in his company wasn't too uncomfortable."

"It was fine. I rolled a blunt and skated through unscathed."

"Your dad lets you smoke in front of him?"

"Totally. He told me a while ago that he could care less about ever getting high. Crazy, huh? It's the alcohol that he craves every day. That must suck."

"Yeah, it would. I hope your dad stays sober. It's not knowing if he'll slip again and start drinking that killed the relationship for me. Too much information?"

"It's cool. When I was having lunch, I got this great idea for a snack. I'm going to mad professor it in the kitchen. Is that okay?"

"Of course, sweetie."

Ray got up to leave. "I forgot to tell you that Kenzie's coming over tonight."

"Time?"

"She said around six."

Tired and sweaty, Maddie was greeted at the back door with the strong aroma of roasted garlic and charred peppers. She guessed chipotle. Ray was sautéing thinly sliced celery, artichoke hearts, and Kalamata olives.

"Whatever you're cooking, it smells amazing. It doesn't look like your typical snacks."

Ray began spooning the mixture into the sliced, hollowed-out peppers. "I finished making the snack a while ago." He pointed to the other side of the counter with the spatula. "Dad and I had this for lunch and I wanted to put my spin on it."

Maddie walked over to a stack of thin, red and tan striped wafers. She picked one up and took a bite. "I don't know how you manage to create the most incredible-tasting food, but I must warn you that I'll never let you move out of this house. I like having a personal chef. So tell me, what do you call these wafers of love?"

"Wafers of love."

"Really?"

"No! I'm a dude, not some hippie chick. They're called Frisbeets. They look like a Frisbee and they're made with chickpea flour, maca, hemp seeds, and beets."

"How do you come up with these concoctions?"

Ray pulled a large joint out of his shirt pocket and held it out. "Voila. Want some?"

"I'm not in the mood to be in an altered state. Could you please feed Mick? I'm going to jump in the shower."

Ray nodded as he finished filling the peppers with the sautéed mixture, then spooned cashew cheese sauce on top. Once they were in the oven, he lit up the joint and took a deep drag.

Kenzie knocked, then let herself in. Ray was watching television in the living room, munching on Frisbeets.

Kenzie said, "I don't want to freak you out, but there's a man sitting in his car across the street. He looks really shady, like a hit man or something. And get this: on the passenger seat, he has what looks like some sort of assault rifle. I'm calling 911."

Maddie walked into the room, her hair still damp. "Put the phone down, dear. The police know who he is. He's worse than a hit man. He's a paparazzo. He's waiting for a Charlie Evans photo op and he'll be getting one in about an hour."

"Charlie Evans is coming over tonight?"

"Uh-huh. You'll finally get to meet him."

Kenzie sat down on the couch next to her brother. "You know I'm not into the idolization of celebrities. His claim to fame is acting. Has the man done anything to help the impoverished, the environment, or the animals? Probably not. He's just like everybody else."

Maddie rolled her eyes. "I'm well aware of your attitude. It's just that I've been dating him for a while and I thought you'd like to meet him."

"You'll like him, Kenz. He's sick." Ray picked up the half-smoked joint and re-lit it. "I bet he gets stoned."

"Whatever. What's for dinner, Ray?" said Kenzie.

"Get thee to the kitchen and you'll see."

Maddie grabbed her daughter's hand and pulled her off the couch. "Come on. Let's chow down before the thespian arrives and ruins your appetite."

"You can say that again."

Kenzie was waxing poetic about Ray's latest snack when she heard the roar of an engine settle in front of the house.

"Is that your jerk neighbor with his testosterone muscle car?"

Maddie laughed. "No. That's my rich boyfriend with his very expensive Porsche Carrera. Promise me you'll be nice to him."

"Cross my heart." Kenzie made an X across her chest, then turned to Ray and mouthed, 'No.'

As the photographer snapped away at his prey, they could hear

Charlie cussing him out.

Despite the fatigue he felt from being on the set since five that morning, Charlie looked good. Very good. Dressed in jeans and a pin-striped, long-sleeved shirt, his hair was impeccable and his tanned skin was flawless. He gave Maddie a hug and kiss, gave Mick a nice head rub, said hi to Ray, and then introduced himself to Kenzie.

"Nice to meet you," she squeaked. Charlie Evans wasn't like everyone else. Normal people looked like cardboard cutouts compared to him. He sizzled. She swore she could see his aura. With all her talk about celebrities being just like your average, yet attractive, Joe, she didn't have a leg to stand on, especially since hers felt like Play-Doh.

"Your mom tells me that you're going to UC Berkeley. What are you studying?"

"I'm a poli sci major. I want to be an animal rights lawyer."

"A theme definitely runs in this family." He saw the Frisbeets on the coffee table. "Is that your latest snack, Ray?"

Without looking up from the TV, Ray said, "Try one, dude."

Charlie picked one off the plate. The delicacy was crisp with a sweet and salty flavor. After eating one, he turned to Maddie and said, "Your kid is really talented. You know that, right?"

"I do."

He turned to Ray. "Are you serious about pursuing a career in cooking?"

Ray paused the TV show. "I prefer to call it culinary artistry and yes, I'm totally going to make this my vocation."

Charlie turned to Maddie and said, "For a stoner, he's really good with words."

"He was born articulate," Maddie replied. "I swear his first word was caramelize."

Charlie sat down next to Ray. "I have a friend who runs a venture capital firm in San Jose. He normally funds computer start-ups, electronics companies, like that. I think he'd be blown away by your talent. How would you feel about making some of your snacks and presenting them to Floyd?"

"Dude, are you serious? That would be so sick!"

Charlie said, "Sick is a good thing, right?"

Maddie nodded. "Charlie, that's really nice of you. I mean, really nice."

Charlie wasn't sure, but he thought he detected a glimmer in Maddie's eye when she looked at him. Was she finally falling in love with him?

"I think you've got what it takes, Ray. You seem to really enjoy cook…culinary artistry and you have a natural talent for making phenomenal food. I'm glad I can help. Of course, ultimately it's up to Floyd." Charlie then assumed a boxer's pose, his head down and his hands in fists in front of his stomach. "I know I got what it takes. I just need to convince you, Sam. I need you to believe in me. Do you, Samantha? Do you?"

Kenzie shouted out, "*Boxing in the Dark*!"

Charlie said, "Bingo."

"Huh?" Ray looked at both of them questioningly.

"My latest movie, B*oxing in the Dark*."

"I saw it with my girlfriends. We all loved it," said Kenzie.

"Thank you." Charlie bowed. Kenzie blushed.

Intent on getting the conversation back to him, Ray said, "Dude, you just tell me when and I'll have a shitload of snacks to present to Floyd. Seriously."

"I'll call him tomorrow. Wait, I have to be on the set at five in the morning. I'll call him now."

Maddie said, "While you're doing that, can I get you something to drink? Coffee, tea?"

"Do you have any beer?"

"Beer it is. Kenzie, Ray, anything besides beer?"

They both shook their heads. Kenzie followed Maddie into the kitchen. She shut the door.

Maddie was about to ask Kenzie what she thought of Charlie, when her daughter grabbed her by the shoulders and said with hushed enthusiasm, "I can't believe you're going out with him! He is so hot and those eyes. It's like you're the only person in the room. Mom, you are so lucky!"

At that moment, more than anything else in the world, Maddie wanted to tell her daughter the real reason she was being courted by the hunk in the next room. She felt like a fake. A cheap knockoff.

Kenzie saw her mother as someone worthy of his attention. Maddie also knew that she didn't want to burden her daughter with the truth, especially since she'd been playing along for almost two months. With feigned zeal, she tested her acting chops and became as animated as the smitten young woman before her.

"It is pretty cool, huh? At first, I was intimidated by his celebrity. Now, he's just Charlie. Of course, I'm still not used to being followed by those damn photographers and people staring and pointing at us. It could be worse, right?"

"Are you guys serious?"

"Sweetie, I'm having fun right now. Going to Italy was amazing and the man is a master at wining and dining. When he's done filming in San Francisco, I'm going to tell him it's over. Unless he breaks it to me first. There's no way I could sustain a relationship with an actor and maintain a healthy ego. I'd be a wreck. Once Charlie goes back to his home in L.A., I'm done."

"Seriously? You're not in love with him? You can just let *that* go?" She pointed to the living room.

"When you're my age you'll understand. I can't compete with all the young, beautiful women out there and honestly, I don't want to."

Kenzie's voice dropped to a whisper. "I get it. He's a lousy lay, huh?"

Without missing a beat, Maddie said, "I wouldn't know."

"Seriously?" Kenzie practically shouted.

"Is everything okay in there?" Charlie yelled.

"Fine." Maddie said to Kenzie. "We'll talk later."

"You bet we will."

Maddie handed the beer to Charlie. "Were you able to get in touch with your friend?"

"I left him a message." He took a swig. "So what does the Mozart family do for fun on a Sunday night?"

Ray said, "First of all, our last name is Dreadsky. Mom never changed her name. Do you blame her?" Without waiting for an answer, he continued. "Second, I'm leaving as soon as Rick picks me up. Kenzie came over for dinner and, if I'm correct, she'll be driving back over to the East Bay soon because she said she had a lot of homework."

Kenzie cut in. "I don't really have that much homework. I can stay longer, if that's okay with you guys."

"Of course it is," said Maddie.

"I'm fine with that, too," added Charlie. "Why don't I take you two out for dessert?"

Both nodded.

Charlie continued. "By the way, Dreadsky isn't so bad. My real last name is Torregrossa. It means 'big tower' in Italian."

"I think it's a sick name. It would be a lot worse if it was Torreteenie." Ray got up and went over to the window just as Rick pulled into the driveway. "Ride's here. Gotta go. Later, big tower." He hugged his mom and sister, grabbed a baggie full of weed and stuffed it in his pocket.

Once he left, Kenzie said, "Just think. If you didn't make it in Hollywood, you could have had a career in Italian porn."

Charlie and Maddie looked at each other and started laughing. "That's exactly what your mother said."

Maddie added, "Dirty minds think alike."

The three ended up going to Hijinks, a bakery that had a few vegan selections and cold brew coffee. Unlike her mother, Kenzie loved the attention garnered in the presence of a celebrity, especially a hot celebrity. After Kenzie left, Charlie and Maddie retired to the living room.

"You want to watch a movie?" she asked.

"Sure. Before we do, I wanted to talk to you about your trip up to that sanctuary with Jackson."

All of a sudden, Maddie got butterflies in her stomach. Charlie didn't seem mad, yet she had a feeling he might not approve. It might interfere with his bet, dilute his courting strategy. She said as nonchalantly as she could muster, "Go ahead."

"Jackson told me that you know about his sister, so I can imagine between the two of you, the passion runs deep."

"Passion for the women."

"Of course, and the animals for you, right?"

"Yup."

"I just wanted to say that I think putting together a combo animal sanctuary and women's shelter is a great idea. It reminds me of a movie I did back in 2008. Did you see *Blotterproof*?"

Maddie was so relieved, she didn't care that Charlie was directing the conversation back to himself. She was actually glad because it made her affections for his stepfather that much stronger.

"I did see *Blotterproof*. I don't see the connection though. What does an eighteenth-century man writing the quintessential novel have to do with animals and abused women?"

"Passion, M&M. Passion."

"Oh, yeah. I see." She didn't see at all.

17

Monday morning, Jackson picked Maddie up at the appointed time. With a big, warm smile, he handed her a mocha soy latte, the one he had promised her since he had insisted on getting to her house at 7:00. They were making small talk, driving up Highway 80, when Maddie's cell rang. She looked at the caller ID. It was Kenzie.

"Hey, sweetie. What's up?"

"Can you tell me now why you haven't slept with the sexiest man alive?"

She pushed the phone firmly against her ear. "Not a good time. I can call you later."

"When?"

"I don't know, Kenzie. I'm on my way up to the Sycamore Animal Sanctuary with Charlie's stepdad. We'll probably be gone all day."

"Is he hot, too, or an old dude?"

"I won't be able to answer that question right now. I'll call you later."

"You sure get around. Have fun, but not too much fun if you know what I mean."

"Bye, sweetie."

"Bye, Mom."

Maddie put the phone back in her purse. "That was my daughter, Kenzie."

"Uh-huh."

Both didn't speak for a while. Maddie thought it odd because in the short time that she knew Jackson, she found him to be a man of many words. Then it struck her and her cheeks turned schoolgirl pink.

"Did you hear what Kenzie asked me?"

"Uh-huh."

Not knowing how to respond, Maddie looked out the window, eyes unfocused, staring at the blur of scenery shooting by, too embarrassed to speak.

Jackson said, "Personally, I think you should get a medal. I think it's admirable."

When she looked at him, she could see that he was more happy than impressed by her abstinence. "I really want to get to know a man before I'm intimate with him. It sounds so prudish, but as I get older, trust and friendship are more important than sex."

"I hear you, not that I subscribe to that philosophy."

"Charlie doesn't either."

"I know. That's why he's the second person I'd give a medal to. I didn't think the guy had it in him to stick with an intelligent, funny, attractive woman who won't sleep with him. I don't give Charlie the credit he so rightfully deserves."

Maddie thought, *if you only knew*. "Thank you, Jackson."

An hour later, they arrived at Sycamore, a sanctuary dotting the northeastern Hinton hills. The main building and the various outbuildings looked new, as did the many fenced-in areas. Some held chickens; others, turkeys. A flock of sheep grazed in a meadow close to the parking lot. It reminded Maddie of a book her mother used to read to her when she was a young child. The depiction of serenity and love was on every page. Her mother would ask her to point to the chickens and cows and horses. All the while, Maddie thought that the animals lived there forever. Children's books never ended with Farmer John driving the animals to a slaughterhouse or using the cleaver himself on his beloved animals.

Maddie and Jackson walked into the main building. Its farm-style décor and atmosphere was homey and comfortable. To their left was the gift shop. The usual items were for sale: T-shirts with the sanctuary's logo, mugs, stuffed animals, keychains, books, and other assorted branded merchandise. They walked up to the front desk and asked for Trinity Travers. Moments later, they were greeted by an attractive woman in her late 20s with long blonde hair, an athletic body, and tanned skin. She was dressed in cargo shorts, a light blue crop top, and hiking boots. Maddie was intimidated. She saw the way Trinity's eyes got bigger when she introduced herself to Jackson.

"Your name sounds familiar. You adopted two of our animals, right?"

"Actually, they were adopted for me by this woman here."

Trinity tore her eyes away from Jackson and studied Maddie's face. "I recognize you from somewhere. Have you been here before?" Trinity looked quizzically at Maddie.

"No. This is my first time."

"I know! You're dating Charlie Evans, aren't you?"

Maddie nodded.

Jackson feigned surprise. "You are? You told me you were available. I'm crushed."

Trinity's mouth dropped open.

"Just kidding," Jackson said. "Charlie's my stepson. We're all one big, happy, non-biologically related family."

Trinity laughed. "This is going to be a fun tour. First off, I want to thank you for your interest in opening up your own sanctuary and women's shelter. I think it's an excellent idea. You'll see how much work there is to do here. We rely on volunteers, but you're going to have to have a live-in staff at your disposal. The opportunity for educating the women and their children on animal rights and human rights is astounding." Trinity grabbed her cellphone from the front desk and tucked it into one of her shorts pockets. "Shall we begin?"

They started at the storage barn. The enormous building housed the food, medication, supplies, and equipment for the fifteen-acre animal refuge. Trinity gave them a rundown on the sanctuary's monthly food bill, which appeared to be the bulk of their expenses. Some of it was donated, and some food was grown on the property.

Next stop was the vegetable garden. This was Trinity's baby. She went over to the string bean plants and checked the soil's moisture level. "I grew up in the suburbs of Sacramento. I never saw a vegetable garden before I went to college and took an ag class. The idea of growing my own tomatoes and green beans was thrilling." She picked three green beans and handed one to Maddie and one to

Jackson. "Eventually, I'd like to get a couple of greenhouses so we can grow summer vegetables all year long. They're on my wish list, which seems to be growing by the month."

Jackson said, "I like the idea of a greenhouse or two. We're planning on growing enough food to supplement the meals for the women and children. We're also going to plant fruit trees."

"That's our next stop. The orchard."

After strolling through the apple, peach, apricot, and lemon trees, Trinity took her visitors to the meadow. A pond was at the far end and a gaggle of geese mingled with the sanctuary's ducks. The scene was so peaceful, Maddie wanted to sit down near the water and enjoy the serenity.

In the distance, Jackson saw a cow lying on its side rolling back and forth. He asked Trinity, "Is that normal?"

Trinity followed Jackson gaze and made a face. "Not really. Shall we go help 'right' a cow? It's not the easiest thing to do. Good thing we have a nice, strong man to help." She gave Jackson a big, warm smile. A little too big and a lot warmer than Maddie cared for.

She walked behind Trinity and noticed her well-developed muscles. Her arms and legs were toned and her skin actually had a dewy quality to it, something Maddie thought only existed in magazine ads. The sanctuary owner's hair shone golden in the sun. Maddie self-consciously fluffed her hair in an attempt to make herself look more alluring. She glanced over at Jackson and to her displeasure, he was eyeing Trinity, as well. Maddie immediately flashed on a book she used to read to her children when they were young: The Berenstain Bears, *The Green-Eyed Monster*. Maddie bought the book after Kenzie came home from her best friend's birthday party, jealous of Bella's cache of presents, especially the hot pink bike she received from her parents. It took a few readings to change Kenzie's attitude. Perhaps, Maddie thought, she should fish the book out of the closet and read it again.

They reached the distressed bovine just as it righted itself, much to Maddie's relief. She looked over at Jackson and said, "I guess we won't need you to flex those big, strong muscles after all."

Maddie regretted saying it as soon as the words tumbled out of her green mouth. Trinity apparently didn't hear what she said. She was too busy talking to the clumsy bovine. Jackson gave Maddie a look that could have either meant, 'what the hell did you say that for?' or 'do I have big muscles?' Whatever the interpretation, she felt foolish.

"How many cows do you have?" Maddie asked in an attempt to change the subject.

"Forty-two, including this big lug." Trinity slapped the cow on its hindquarters. It didn't budge. "Come on. Let's go over the hill to where the horses hang out and then we can head back to the office and I'll give you a complete rundown on the operations from the birth of a calf to the treatment of Cushing's disease."

Maddie made a point to ask Trinity questions and compliment her on the sanctuary. She needed to make up for her 'green' behavior. She knew that she had no right to feel jealous. After all, she was dating Charlie and her relationship with Jackson was one of friendship and partnership. It could change in the future, but at the moment she needed to realign herself with the task at hand.

More than a few times, Trinity 'accidentally' brushed her arm against Jackson's or touched his shoulder for emphasis when explaining a routine. Maddie was sitting on Trinity's other side, yet she remained untouched. Deep breathing kept her from getting angry. Or jealous. She noticed that Jackson was thoroughly enjoying the attention from a woman at least two decades younger than himself. When Trinity finished her tutorial, she said, "I want you both to feel free to call me any time and ask for help. I would love to come down once you have the site for the sanctuary. My expertise will be gladly offered, free of charge."

Jackson said, "Thank you so much, Trinity. At the very least, you would be taken to dinner for your generosity."

"Now there's an offer I couldn't refuse."

Maddie added, "It would be our pleasure and I know just the place. Millennium in Oakland is vegan dining at its most exquisite."

Trinity's face showed just enough disappointment to make Maddie happy. She couldn't prevent Jackson from going out with the sanctuary beauty, but she vowed to make it difficult for them to be alone.

Maddie extended her hand to Trinity. "You've been a

tremendous help, and thank you so much for your time."

Trinity shook her hand and said, "You're very welcome. I know you two will create a wonderful haven for animals and people." As she turned to Jackson, he put out his hand. Trinity gave him a big hug instead. Maddie cringed.

Before Jackson had a chance to question Maddie's behavior, she suggested they grab lunch in Davis.

"I asked Siri if there were any vegan restaurants in Davis and she found one called Davis Dirt."

"That doesn't sound very appetizing."

"I thought the same thing, but when I looked it up on Yelp, it had great reviews. You want to try it?"

"Sure." Jackson readjusted the rear view mirror. "What did you think of the sanctuary?"

Maddie chose her words carefully. "I loved it and it's so organized. I think Trinity's done an amazing job. How about you?"

"I agree and I think our sanctuary is going to be as good, if not better than Sycamore. How many acres did she say they had?"

"Fifteen."

"That goat farm in Woodside is on sixteen acres. It may be the perfect spot. It's not centrally located on the peninsula, but it is close enough to be able to transport women and children to the location. It helps that it's far enough away from San Jose and San Francisco. It will be harder for the abusers to find the place. And it's isolated enough that anyone driving to the sanctuary will be noticed, not like what you experienced in the parking lot where you volunteer. I have a call in to the real estate agent selling the property. You want to look at it with me?"

"I'd love to. The sanctuary being so close to where you live is also a bonus. If you need to be there in a hurry it's only, what, ten minutes tops?"

"Without traffic or lights or stop signs. I'm about eight miles away from the site. It normally takes me twenty minutes to get to Woodside. How about you, though? San Rafael is a good forty to fifty miles away. Would you be willing to move closer to the sanctuary or live there?"

Maddie's heart lurched to the left when she thought about moving away from her friends and her home for the last ten years. Then it took a turn to the right when she thought about living closer to Jackson. "It's something I will definitely think about."

Jackson exited the freeway, following his GPS to Davis Dirt. "I've given it a lot of thought. I figured, if you're up for it, you could be the general manager. I think you would be perfect overseeing the sanctuary, making sure everything ran smoothly. You have the temperament and the personality." He glanced over at Maddie, who looked shell-shocked. "Have I upset you?"

"Not at all. I've never been in a position of power before. It sounds very intimidating."

"Why don't we hire Trinity as a consultant? She could show you the ropes, at least from the sanctuary point of view and you could get insight and direction about the women's center side from your boss."

Maddie wanted to yell, 'Absolutely not!' She didn't want Trinity around Jackson any more than she had to be.

"It's a consideration. What would your role be, Mr. Danoff?"

Jackson pulled into the restaurant's parking lot and turned off the car. "I would like to help run the animal side of the sanctuary and help with fundraising. I don't think it would be a good idea for me to be directly involved with the women's shelter for obvious reasons."

"Quite a few men have and do volunteer at the women's center. I know people think that men are the last beings that women want to see there, but it's worked out very well. Don't let being a man deter you from participating. I bet you'd find it very rewarding. You should come up to the Marin Women's Center and check it out. Talk to the director, Honor. She could answer a lot more questions than I can."

"Sounds like a plan."

The first thing that struck Jackson and Maddie about the small, deco-style restaurant was how many young people there were, but then the city was home to UC Davis, the area's premier ag school. The chatter was at a minimum because the majority were students on their laptops, busily typing away, headphones firmly planted around their heads, oblivious to their surroundings.

As they waited in line to order lunch, Jackson said, "I'm going to grab those seats over there before they're taken. Whatever you get, order two. I trust you." He handed her $40. At first she refused, but he stuffed the two twenties into her purse. Discussion over.

Ten minutes later, their food was delivered to their table. Jackson was looking at a map of the Woodside property and had drawn his vision of the sanctuary layout. He pushed it aside to make way for their meal.

"This looks delicious. What is it?" Jackson took his fork and poked at what appeared to be sautéed greens.

"It's the college special. You've got collard greens and kale sautéed with fake bacon. That there is grilled zucchini with a pesto sauce and lentil loaf topped with mushrooms."

Jackson speared all three dishes on his fork and took a bite. Maddie held her breath. Even when vegan food was good, omnivores enjoyed criticizing it.

"What do you think?"

Jackson said, "Very good."

"I'm so glad you approve."

"Why wouldn't I? The food is great."

"I still get flak from my meat-eating friends about vegan food. I sometimes think they do it just to rile me." Maddie took a bite of her meal. She watched a young college couple sharing a piece of apple pie a la mode. The boy was playfully teasing his girlfriend with a forkful of pie. After a few attempts, she bit down on the fork and claimed her prize. The boy gave her a kiss on the cheek. On one hand, she envied their youth, their naiveté. On the other hand, the thought of reliving her twenties and thirties put her into a mental tailspin.

"You could still get dessert," Jackson said, pulling her out of her reverie. When she turned to face him, Maddie had a melancholy look. Jackson blurted out, "Do you love him?"

"That kid? Ew. No."

"No, not him." He turned away and continued eating. "Never mind."

The light bulb went on. "Charlie? Do I love Charlie?"

"It's none of my business. Why don't we go over the sanctuary site?" He pulled out the map, but Maddie put her hand on his and stopped him.

"Are you asking as a concerned parent, or?"

Jackson quickly changed his tone. "Exactly. As an older woman, what are your intentions? I would hate to see my sweet, innocent son exploited."

Playing along, Maddie said, "Actually, I'm in it for defiling purposes only. I want to take him for all he's worth and let a gaggle of nubile, pretty girls assuage his bruised and broken heart when I leave him for an older man."

"I knew it."

"That's how I roll." She pulled the map over to her side of the table and pointed to what appeared to be a shed-like structure on the side of the hill. "Is this where you were going to have me live?"

"Nope." Jackson put his finger next to a lean-to near the cow barn. "This is. Only the best for the general manager."

After they finished lunch, they sipped soy lattes, split a piece of chocolate cake, and discussed the layout. In the back of her mind, Maddie held onto Jackson's question. *Do you love him?* Maybe she didn't need to be jealous of Trinity after all.

Jackson dropped Maddie off a little past 4:00 p.m. She was mentally and emotionally exhausted. Spending that much time together, Maddie was falling hard for her boyfriend's father. Stepfather. She needed to rest her overactive mind.

Before she reached the door, a cacophony of male voices spilled out of the open windows. It was louder when she stepped inside. Her home, her refuge, resembled a frat house for high school boys.

"M&M! Welcome to the home of Snackman, not to be confused with Smackman." Rafael was Ray's best friend. The tall, good-looking boy with long sandy blonde hair gave Maddie a big hug.

"Nice to see you, too, Rafael." Two boys playing video games grunted hello. Before she could ask what was going on, Ray shouted to her from the kitchen.

"Great news, Mom. Charlie's friend wants to meet me and check out my snacks! I thought I better create some more, pronto."

Normally, Ray was a neat chef. He took after Maddie that way. She liked putting items away after using them, frequently wiping down the counters and sequestering all dirty bowls, pots, and pans in the sink. Today was different. He must have been channeling the Tasmanian devil. Every counter was laden with ingredients. Spilled soymilk, crackers, and scattered chocolate jimmies sullied the floor. While three of Ray's friends sat at the table sampling his latest creations, two others helped him whip them up. Mick sat underneath the kitchen table, happily eating whatever fell or dripped from above.

As badly as Maddie wanted to admonish her son for temporarily destroying her kitchen, she silenced the scolding mother and channeled the proud mother. "That's wonderful, Ray. Did you set up an appointment with...what was his name, Floyd?"

"Yeah. A week from Friday. Come here. Try this." Ray held out what looked like a fat oatmeal cookie. When Maddie took a bite, creamy caramel hidden inside oozed out, mixing with the hard cookie. It was divine.

"Amazing. Do you have a name for it yet?"

One of the boys sitting at the table said, "I think he should call it the lava cookie."

Ray replied, "And I said that's lame, dude."

"You'll think up something. You always do." As she turned to leave, she said, "Boys, stay as long as you like, but clean up after yourselves. Please."

Some of them mumbled 'sure' and others nodded. With that, Maddie went to her bedroom and closed the door in an attempt to distance herself from the arcade atmosphere throughout the rest of the house. She called Priscilla and told her about the day, including her intensified feelings for Jackson and her negative ones for Trinity. True to form, her best friend listened without interruption, then dispensed her advice, not knowing if Maddie would follow it or ignore it: *You'll have time to concentrate on Jackson when Charlie has returned to Southern California* and *Trinity is no match for your charm and intellect. Get over it.*

After changing into her sweats, Maddie went out back where the noise level was low, carrying the latest issue of *Vanity Fair*. She liked to complain to anyone who would listen about how the magazine's articles were the length of novellas, yet she loved reading the in-depth stories. Currently, the trees were getting an earful.

A few minutes into an article on a newly discovered manuscript by Flaubert, she heard the kitchen door open slightly. Mick trotted over and jumped up on the chaise. From the look on his face, he had reached his limit with Ray and the gang. After a sigh and slight snort, he put his head on Maddie's lap and closed his eyes.

"Micky, I couldn't have said it better."

18

A sharp knock on the back gate almost caused Ray to gag. Holding in his breath, he said, "Who is it?"

"Charlie. Can I come in?"

"Sure," Ray replied while blowing out a thick plume of marijuana smoke. "You scared the shit out of me. I thought it was the cops or that loony paparazzi dude who practically lives in his car across the street."

"Sorry about that. I should have known that you're almost always in the stoned zone."

Charlie came up to the patio table where Ray had on display a stoner's paradise: A plate of his latest snack creation was piled six deep, a mason jar full of marijuana buds the size of small plums sat next to the plate and, in a class by itself, was a three-foot tall, marbled glass bong. Charlie picked up the bong.

"Isn't this overkill, Ray?"

Ray chuckled. "On a scale of one to ten, this is an eleven. Trust me. It's the difference between driving a Prius and cruising in a Jag." He took a bud out of the jar and started picking off sections of it, then packed it into the bowl. He checked the water level. Satisfied, he handed it to Charlie.

"I don't know if I should. Your mom and I are going to a party tonight and I haven't smoked pot in a long time. I think I'll just have one of these instead." Charlie reached for a triangular cookie. Ray stopped him.

"Come on. One small toke. It will make the Trijungle taste so much better."

"The what?"

"Take a hit and I'll tell you what's in it."

After a small hesitation, Charlie took the bong from Ray. "Light her up."

With Charlie's mouth firmly over the opening, Ray lit the bowl of weed and Charlie took a deep breath. He then released his finger from the tiny hole in the middle of the bong. A torrent of smoke rushed into his mouth. At first, he felt fine. When the smoke hit his lungs, he began to cough furiously and had to sit down.

Ray looked concerned. "Are you okay?"

When the coughing subsided, Charlie looked up at Ray. His eyes resembled tiny sunsets, the whites tainted cotton candy pink, the irises a deep blue sun. "Who grew this weed, Lucifer?"

"A buddy of mine. It's called Devil's Breath." Ray grabbed the bong from the table and took a hit. "I can't believe I'm getting stoned with Charlie Evans."

"Please don't post this on your Facebook page or tell anyone."

"Don't worry, I don't have a Facebook page and I'm not on Instagram or Twitter. They take up too much time and I'd rather be cooking, which brings me to this." Ray held up one of his cookies. "I call it a Trijungle because it's made with three superfoods from the Amazon: Acai, Camu Camu, and Cupuacu."

"Are you speaking in another language? Because I didn't understand a word you said." Charlie rolled his head around, then from left to right. "I am so high. That Devil's Tongue is super strong."

"Breath."

Charlie put his hand up to his mouth and blew on it. "Is it bad?"

"It's called Devil's Breath and yeah, it's strong."

"I just remembered why I stopped getting stoned. It makes me really stupid. I mean really dumb."

Ray laughed. "You don't need to convince me. Try the cookie. Tell me what you think. Honestly."

Charlie took a bite. "Oh my god. Ray, you're like a vegan Rachael Ray. I could eat a million of these puppies."

"Thanks, but if you're going to compare me to a chef, would you mind making it a dude, like Emeril or Bobby Flay?"

"Yeah. Sorry about that. Blame it on the Devil's Breath." Charlie finished the cookie and grabbed another one. "Floyd is going to love these. I heard you're seeing him next Friday."

"I am totally stoked. I really appreciate the opportunity."

Charlie got down on one knee, looked up at Ray and in a British accent said, "Everything I have, I give to you, my one true guiding force in this crazy world."

Ray looked at the famous actor like he was nuts. "What the fuck?"

Charlie jumped up and said, "What movie is that from?"

"Hell if I know."

Charlie looked hurt. "Didn't you see *Calypso Sunrise?*"

"That would be a big no."

"Why not?"

"What's it rated?"

Charlie said, "PG-13."

"I only watch R-rated movies."

"Because?"

"PG-13 movies don't have enough sex, violence, and drugs." Charlie gave him a look of concern. "Just because I'm vegan doesn't mean I don't like my entertainment raunchy, full of blood and guts and drugs. I am a teenage boy, you know?"

"Got it."

Ray could see that Charlie was hurt. "My mom and dad like your movies. And I'm sure the girls at school do, too." Ray broke off a piece of Trijungle and devoured it.

"The women do love my movies." Charlie leaned over the table to grab another Trijungle. His elbow knocked the bong. He watched it fall, mesmerized by the colors in the marbled glass. Before it hit the table, Ray grabbed it, but not before it belched out some water, splashing a few drops on Ray's pants. He wiped them off, then moved the plate of snacks in front of Charlie.

"Knock yourself out, dude. Just don't knock the bong."

"Sorry."

"I can't believe I'm admonishing Charlie Evans. What a trip."

"You certainly are your mother's son, using big words like she does. Is it a vegan thing?" Charlie stuffed half a Trijungle in his mouth. The usually suave Mr. Evans looked like a child grabbing the last cookie before anyone else could claim it.

Ray shook his head as he observed the man sitting next to him. He was good-looking, a multi-millionaire, talented…and possessed the vocabulary of a pre-teen. Even with his brain floating on a cloud of purple haze, Ray appreciated his command of the English language more than superficial or material possessions. "Yeah, Charlie, it's a vegan thing."

"I thought so." As he finished chewing, he said, "Is it hard being a vegan teenager? I bet kids make fun of you because you don't eat meat."

"It's not difficult at all being vegan and sure, there are the unenlightened boneheads who thinks it's funny that I don't consume animal flesh or animal secretions. You know, milk and cheese. I tell them to watch *Indigestible*, a documentary about factory farming, and then justify how they can be complicit in industries that turn animals into machines. That either silences them or…" Charlie stared at Ray with an expression of complete incomprehension, like he was just whacked with a mallet. "They give me that look."

Ray took another hit off the bong. "The thing is, dude, I was raised vegan and I silently thank my parents every day for teaching me compassion and respect for all beings, human and non-human. I may be a primo stoner, but I've never ingested the flesh of a being that was raised in brutal conditions and died a violent death. The thought sickens me."

"Wow. That was well said. And you're stoned. What was the name of the movie again?"

"*Indigestible*. Look it up on YouTube."

"I will."

For a while, the two sat in silence. One was lost in deep thought, the other simply lost.

"So, why are you dating my mom? I love her and everything, but you have a reputation for going out with hot chicks. Young, hot chicks."

"Your mom is beautiful and she's smart. Really smart. And she's funny."

"Dude, she's old."

"Come on, Ray. She's not that old."

"Yeah, she is."

This was not a conversation Charlie wanted to have with Maddie's teenage son, especially when both of them were baked. He tried to focus, but it was difficult when his mind kept jumping all over the place. His brain felt like it was in a hot frying pan being flipped over and over again.

"You should be sticking up for your mother. I'd be proud of her. You know, my mom married a much younger guy and I was fine with it."

Ray's eyes got wide. "Are you going to marry her?"

"No! I'm just saying that you should be happy for her." Charlie looked over at the front gate. "Where is she, by the way? I told her I was going to be here at six."

Ray picked up his cellphone. "It's 5:30."

"Whoa. How did that happen? I wasn't even stoned when I left the hotel." Charlie sat back in the chair and closed his eyes.

Ray looked over at the megastar sitting in his backyard, chatting like old friends. "You could have any woman you want."

"I know," he said with a smile on his face.

"I bet you could date Megan Fox if you wanted to."

Charlie's smile broadened. "I have."

"No way!"

"Oh yeah."

"I am so jealous! What was she like?"

Charlie leaned forward, about six inches from Ray's face. "Have you ever had a hot fudge sundae with two large, luscious scoops of Ben & Jerry's vanilla ice cream cov..."

"Soy vanilla ice cream. Go on."

"Soy vanilla ice cream covered with whipped...soy whipped cream, toasted nuts and warm, gooey, rich fudge...soy fudge?"

"Dude. Just fudge."

"Okay. I want to be politically correct, vegan-wise. Where was I?"

"Two large mounds of vanilla soy ice cream dripping with hot fudge, covered in..." Ray looked up. Maddie was standing next to the table. "How long have you been there?"

Charlie said, "Wow, you must be higher than me. I've been here the whole time."

Ray physically turned Charlie's head around. "Not you. Her."

Dressed in sweats and a T-shirt, her hair up in a ponytail and no make-up, Maddie looked a lot younger than her age. "Having fun, boys?"

Charlie shot up and gave her a big hug and kiss. "You look so pretty."

"Hot fudge sundae pretty?"

"Definitely. Speaking of hot fudge sundaes, can we make one?"

Maddie looked down at her son's legs. He was wearing shorts for the first time in a while and now Maddie knew why. "What's on your leg?"

"Hair. Skin."

"Ray…"

"I couldn't resist, Mom. The artist at Tit for Tat gave me a great deal." He looked down at the eagle, its talons gripping his ankle.

Maddie took a closer look. The detail was striking. Each feather was delicately drawn. It almost looked like a photograph. The talons were sharp, clutching her son's lightly hairy ankle. "He did do a good job."

"She. Her name is Madeleine. Pretty cool, huh?"

"Has your dad seen it?"

"Not yet."

"Let me know what he says." She turned to Charlie. "Are you going to be okay to drive to the party?"

"First things first. Do you have any ice cream? Soy ice cream?"

"Follow me, stoner."

Maddie opened up the freezer and removed a pint of So Delicious Cookie Dough ice cream made with soymilk. She handed it to him with a spoon "Knock yourself out. I'm going to get dressed."

Charlie read the front, then turned it around and perused the ingredients. Popping the lid off, he took a big spoonful. "This stuff is great. Are you sure it doesn't have any milk in it?"

Maddie yelled from her bedroom, "You don't think a soy product can be good on its own?"

"Nope. Does that make me a soyist?"

"No. Just an idiot. Speaking of which, did you have to get stoned with my son? What if he puts it up on Facebook?"

"He's not on Facebook. Or Instagram. Or Twitter. So there. Besides, I wanted to bond with him. We're officially buds." He laughed. "Get it? Buds?"

Maddie slipped into a retro-style red, sleeveless dress, then proceeded to the bathroom to put on her make-up. "Very funny. You're a regular yuck fest."

Charlie was spooning the frozen dessert into his mouth at record speed. He couldn't eat it fast enough. "Do you mind if I finish this?"

"Knock yourself out, soyist."

"Now that you're going to the gym, you wouldn't want to eat it, anyway."

Maddie said, "That's right, because if you gain weight you can have plastic surgery…again."

Charlie stopped mid-bite, wanting desperately to eat the large scoop of soft, creamy soy ice cream mixed with chunks of chocolate and cinnamon-flavored cookie dough. He looked down at his stomach. It was slightly distended. One more bite wouldn't hurt. He savored the spoonful like it was his last meal.

After licking the spoon clean, he put the lid back on the pint and set it in the freezer. He then quietly sneaked into Maddie's room and walked softly to the bathroom door. It was open wide enough so that he could see her posing in front of a full-length mirror. She pretended to meet Charlie's co-workers, coyly smiling at one and offering her hand to another. Through bloodshot eyes, Charlie watched for a full minute, hand over mouth, before he broke the silence with a snicker. Maddie whipped around and gave him a dirty look. "You snoop!"

Charlie grabbed Maddie by the waist and pulled her to him. "That was adorable. You'll be a hit at the party as long as you do what, you know, you were doing in the mirror." Taking advantage of the bed being in close proximity, he fell onto it and tried to bring Maddie with him. She resisted.

"I don't believe it. I'm on Madeleine Mozart's bed. And it only took me two months. This is a Kodak moment." Charlie took out his cellphone and snapped a number of selfies in a variety of poses. When he was done, he said, "Come on, let's play."

She was tempted. Stoned, Charlie was even more endearing. He wasn't posturing or trying to impress her. Her anger over the bet stopped her from sleeping with him before. Now, it was her attraction for Jackson that helped her resist pouncing on him, red dress and all.

"Wouldn't you rather have a nice glass of ice water?"

Suddenly, Charlie was parched. He sat up and smacked his lips. "That sounds so good."

"Go into the living room and I'll get it for you."

Dutifully, he went and sat down on the sofa. He started bouncing up and down. "This is really a comfortable couch. Wow. Where'd you get it?"

Maddie started laughing. "The next time my son asks you if you want to take a hit off of a three-foot bong, just say no." She handed Charlie a cold glass of water. He drank it all.

"But I'm having fun. You should get stoned, too. Then we can be stoned together. Ray!"

From the backyard, Ray yelled back, "What?"

Before Charlie could answer, Maddie yelled back, "Nothing, dear. Ignore the man with kaleidoscope eyes."

"Whatever," Ray said.

Maddie said, "I don't want to get stoned and I also don't want you to drive to the party in the condition you're in. Why don't we blow it off and stay here instead? We can watch a movie. I'll even make popcorn."

Charlie's eyes widened. "Make it a big bowl."

"Yes, sir. While I do that, pick out a movie for us to watch. The DVDs are in the cabinet below the TV."

Once the popcorn was made, Maddie put a large bowl on the coffee table. "What did you choose?"

"It's a surprise."

Charlie grabbed a handful of popcorn and pressed 'play.' About three seconds later, he paused it and looked at Maddie. Before making the popcorn, she changed into her comfy clothes. She looked soft and vulnerable. Charlie was suddenly ashamed of the bet. He could feel it from his toes to his hair follicles on the top of his head. The guilt entombed him. "Do you like me?"

Maddie raised her eyebrows and gave Charlie a sideways glance. The emotionally stable man looked apprehensive. As much as she wanted to give him a sarcastic answer, she refrained. "Yes. I like you."

"A lot?"

"What's going on?"

"Answer me."

"I'll tell you what," Maddie said as she took the remote from him, "Let's watch the movie and then we can have a marathon conversation about my feelings for you. Deal?"

As suddenly as Charlie was struck with guilt, the insane grip Devil's Breath had on his brain rerouted his train of thought, directing him back to the movie.

"That sounds like a plan. I like it. A lot." He gave her a goofy smile.

Mimicking his smile, she hit 'play.' After a few moments, the title came on the screen: *Sense and Sensibility*. Maddie paused the movie. "Is this a joke?"

Clueless, Charlie said, "What do you mean?"

"You picked *Sense and Sensibility*?"

"I may be incredibly stoned, but I'm not blind. I'm a huge fan of period films. Jane Austin movies are my favorites."

Her mouth dropped open. "Does anybody know about this? If not, mum's the word. You realize if people found out, it could sink your reputation as a macho man."

"No way. My fan base is solid. They love me no matter what." Again, the goofy smile. This time, there was popcorn in his teeth.

"Dating me has definitely secured your place in the hearts of middle-aged women everywhere. I wouldn't be too sure about middle-aged men." She watched as Charlie continued to shovel the popcorn into his mouth. "Save some for me."

He looked down at the half-empty bowl. "Maybe you should make more. Wait, I have a better idea. Ray should make us a snack and he can call it the Torregrossa."

Ray happened to be walking through the living room to his bedroom and overheard the conversation. "As challenging as that sounds, I'm not in a creative mood right now. If you want, eat the rest of the Trijungles."

"Done. Thanks, *dude*." Still holding the bowl of popcorn, Charlie retrieved the remaining treats and returned to his place on the couch.

He appeared to be burrowing in.

Maddie said, "If you could play any Jane Austen character, who would it be?"

Charlie looked at Maddie like she had just asked him what two plus two was. "Fitzwilliam Darcy. Duh."

"I never knew his first name. In the movies, he's always referred to as Mr. Darcy."

"Which do you prefer, the one with Colin Firth or Matthew Macfadyen?"

"Macfadyen, because I really loved Keira Knightley as Elizabeth Bennet. I find Colin Firth better looking, but Matthew's looks grew on me. By the time he walked through the mist in the long coat, his hair rumpled, looking hopelessly in love, I was his."

"I could play Mr. Darcy better than both of them."

"Aren't you cocky?"

"Confident." He grabbed the Trijungle. "And cocky. Shall we watch the movie?"

Maddie nodded and hit 'play.' Charlie put his head on Maddie's shoulder. "This is nice," he said.

"It is, Mr. Darcy."

19

The Marin Women's Center, or, as it was often called, MWC, was packed, as if the disruption a little over two weeks ago had never happened. It was a combination of people's short attention span and the sad fact that the center was the only one within a ten-mile radius. Abused and battered women didn't have a choice. Besides, the receptionist's glass window had been replaced the day after the incident and Jeannette's wounds were all but healed. A camera was positioned outside the locked front door and in order to enter, one had to be buzzed in. Employees and volunteers were asked to use the side entrance. They were given card keys to go along with the new security lock.

It was the second time Maddie had come to the center since the incident. She let herself in through the side door and was heading to the office to relieve Jamie Lowe on the abuse hotline when the director of the center stopped her.

Honor Rosten was a no-nonsense woman. Ten years ago, she had been a victim of spousal abuse. MWC had saved her life by giving her a safe place to live. Months of therapy had increased her self-esteem and soon after, she began volunteering, first on the phones, then as a therapist's assistant. Over the years, she had worked her way up to director. The staff loved her. She ran the center with love and respect for all those who worked under her and all those who walked through MWC's door with the courage to seek help.

When she approached Maddie, she seemed nervous. "Do you have a moment? I'd like to talk to you about something."

"Sure. I'll tell Jamie to man the phones a little longer."

"No need," said Honor. "I already let her know that we were

going to meet for a few minutes."

Honor closed the door to her office. She took a seat next to Maddie instead of behind her desk. "I'm not sure how to put this without sounding like I'm pandering, so I'll just come out and say it. It's common knowledge that you're dating Charlie Evans, which I think is wonderful. You're the envy of millions of women, myself included. I was wondering, no, I was hoping that you could use your influence and talk him into doing a fundraiser for the center. Suzy, our grant writer, is having a really hard time procuring funds. I don't know if it's the time of year or we're competing with a plethora of other non-profits, but our future is looking bleak. Under the current circumstances, we have enough funds to last us another year."

"Funny you should ask me about this, Honor. I'm working with Charlie's stepfather to open a combination animal sanctuary and women's refuge in Woodside. I don't see why we couldn't raise funds for both facilities. We hadn't asked Charlie yet about helping us out financially, but I can't imagine him objecting."

Maddie went on to tell Honor how the idea came about. She was thrilled that Maddie was so open to the idea. They decided to meet later in the week after Maddie had a chance to talk to Charlie.

Jackson stood in front of the massive canvas. The memory of Maddie's enthusiasm and delight working on a similar-sized canvas made him smile and gave him pause. The last time a woman mesmerized him, he was in his early twenties, practically a kid. Jackie Torregrossa was forty-two and a knockout. Not just in looks. In personality, kindness, and compassion. They had met at a Pink Floyd concert. Their respective dates for the evening had both been unable to attend. Jackie had said it was meant to be and pointed to their identical Dark Side of the Moon black T-shirts with the prism and rainbow. After the show, they'd ended up going to an all-night diner. When she'd told him that she had a teenage son, he didn't care. He'd been that smitten. They would still be together now if she hadn't died.

She would have been sixty-seven.

To the panoramic sounds of Mozart's Jupiter Symphony, he plunged his paintbrush into the Brilliant Blue oil paint. Then he closed his eyes and let the brush lead the way. His hand traveled slowly up the canvas in short dabs until he was on his toes, then it veered right, then left. Swipes of red crossed the blue. Then Highland Green jumped into the mix and played in the left corner. Yellow #33 raced through the painting, bisecting it in delight. Jackson had developed his own rules to painting 'blind.' For every three strokes with his eyes closed, he would paint one with eyes open. He didn't rush and, at times, let the symphony's rhythm dictate his moves. When he finished, he studied his composition. To the naked eye, it was an abstract painting. To Jackson, it was Madeleine Mozart. He decided to call her. She beat him to the punch. Delighted, he answered on the first ring.

"Hi."

"Hi there. What are you doing?"

Jackson looked at his painting. "Just finished doing something very satisfying."

"Oh. Is it something you can talk about?" As soon as she said it, she wanted to retract the question. She was speaking to her boyfriend's father. Her inappropriate comment made her blush. "I'm sorry. That was uncalled for."

"Don't worry. You'd have to do a lot more to upset me. I was painting and employed a version of your blind practice. I think this piece is going to be spectacular."

"I can't wait to see it." Maddie was standing outside the MWC. "I was talking to the director of the women's center and she had an idea. I wanted to run it by you."

Maddie went on to tell Jackson about Honor's proposal. He not only thought it was a great idea, but suggested that he and Charlie visit the center with her and discuss the details with Honor. It was more than Maddie had hoped for. Back inside, she told a very excited director and added that, as soon as they could decide on a date and time, she'd let her know.

On the ride home, Maddie turned off the radio and reflected on the current events. It was hard to believe that a few months ago, she'd wondered if she would ever meet a man who shared her passion for painting and had a good heart, a compassionate heart. She knew that man wasn't Charlie Evans. But his stepfather? Also, it had never occurred to her to use her newfound status to help mistreated animals and abused women. Her mind didn't operate that way. Maddie had never been a schemer or an exploiter. It wasn't in her make-up. Using Charlie was a novel experience. A part of her found it exciting. She wasn't inhibited by fear. She wasn't deterred by insecurity. Her moral side still found it uncomfortable and deceptive. She found solace in the fact that soon the farce would be over.

Twenty-five miles away, Charlie was dealing with his own problems. His leading lady's insistence on getting into his pants was escalating to a point where he would have to request assistance from the director if his own efforts proved ineffective. Rachel Swanson had been in a highly successful television series. Part of an ensemble cast, she had played a pediatric doctor in the hospital drama, *St. Hope Emergency*. Until the show became wildly popular, Rachel had been an unknown. Her ego, buoyed by the fame, outgrew the small-screen drama. She forced her agent to break her contract with the studio so she could pursue movies full-time. The romantic thriller was Rachel's third feature film. She had no problem seducing her male co-stars, if they didn't pursue her first. Married or single, it didn't matter. When she found out that she'd be playing opposite Charlie Evans, she was thrilled. As a teenager, she had had a crush on the movie star and now it was her chance to fulfill a dream. She had assumed he would seduce her. After all, he had a reputation for sleeping around, finding his leading ladies particularly easy to bed. A few weeks into the shooting, Rachel realized that Charlie wasn't going to approach her. For reasons unfathomable, he began dating an older woman. Rachel was half her age, yet Charlie seemed smitten by this Madeleine Mozart. Undeterred, Rachel invited her co-star to her room, to dinner, for drinks. Every request was declined. The only time she'd heard 'no' from a man was when she had asked him, 'Should I stop?' The more Charlie refused, the more determined she was to have him.

Before they wrapped for the night, the scene they were shooting took an unexpected turn when Rachel tripped while running through a park with her co-star. The injury wasn't bad. Still, the director decided to call it a night and resume early the next day. Rachel lightly hobbled over to Charlie who was chatting with Larry, the production assistant. She waited impatiently for a few minutes, then interrupted their conversation.

"Charlie Bug, can I talk to you for a minute?"

Charlie said, "Please don't call me Charlie Bug."

"I thought you liked it."

"I don't. What is it, Rachel?"

Rachel slathered on the sex appeal until it oozed out her pores. She moved closer to him as Larry walked away, acutely aware that his presence was unwanted. "Since we're knocking off early, I thought you'd like to grab a bite to eat. I found the sweetest little café on Nob Hill. My treat." She lightly squeezed his arm.

Charlie inwardly groaned. He still had a few more weeks of shooting and, up until this point, had done an exemplary job of keeping his co-star at arm's length. "Thanks for the invite, but I'm going to have to pass. Maddie is coming down to the city as we speak."

"Really?"

"Yes."

"That's interesting because we were supposed to work late tonight. If I hadn't hurt my ankle, we'd still be shooting. I've been with you since John shut down the set. When did you call her?"

Charlie didn't know what to say. He had no problem lying. He simply needed more time to create a story. She caught him.

"Come on. Have dinner with me just this once."

A continuous stream of Rachel Swansons jammed the pipeline into Hollywood. Every state in the nation birthed its share of young girls dreaming, hoping that they would be the next Kristen Stewart or Jennifer Lawrence. Most were statuesque beauties with flawless complexions and ripe libidos, either waiting to be discovered or already working their way up the Hollywood ladder. Charlie would have plenty of opportunities to meet up with as many gorgeous, vapid women as he wanted for as long as he wanted. The problem at hand was how he could extricate himself from Rachel's talons without upsetting her inflated ego. He'd heard stories about her tantrums on the set and he didn't want to witness one.

"Rachel, I'm in a relationship right now, so having dinner with you isn't such a good idea."

"Jesus Christ! I'm not asking you to sleep with me. It's dinner, Charlie. Is your girlfriend, or should I call her your grannyfriend, that insecure?"

Charlie kept his temper in check. He wanted to verbally berate her, but he knew he would pay for it when they filmed, so he remained calm. "My decision has nothing to do with my *girl*friend. I'm not comfortable having dinner with you, so let's leave it at that, okay? I'm going back to the hotel. Have a nice night." As Charlie was leaving, his cell rang. He took it out of his pocket and looked at the caller ID. "She must have known we were talking about her." Before he could answer it, Rachel grabbed the phone from his hand. "Rachel!"

In a sultry, throaty voice she said, "Charlie can't talk right now. He's very busy. Bu-bye." She threw the phone to him. "You have a nice night, too."

The limp gone, Rachel sashayed off the set. Charlie quickly got back on his cell. "Maddie, are you there?"

"Not anymore." She hung up.

"Shit!" Charlie yelled. He redialed and waited as the phone rang, then went into voice mail.

"Why do I feel like I'm on a reality show, a bad reality show?" Maddie said to Mick, who was sleeping next to her on the couch. He answered with a snort, then a loud snore. "You're right. Sleeping with the leading lady is so cliché." Maddie was relaxing from a day of volunteering at MWC. It had been particularly rough. More than a few of the callers had been hysterical. One of them had threatened suicide and Maddie had had to talk her out of it. The call had lasted an hour. When it was over, she was mentally exhausted. One of the other volunteers had covered for her so she could go home early. Once she poured herself a glass of wine and relaxed, she was ready to tell Charlie about her conversation with Honor and his possible involvement in a fundraising effort.

She took a larger than usual sip of the Stag's Leap Merlot. It went down smooth and warmed her from the inside out. "Why would he take the chance of blowing the bet? I don't get it."

Mick opened his round, dark brown eyes, gave her the same look he always flashed her when she spoke gibberish to him, groaned, and went back to sleep.

Maddie tried reading, yet her thoughts circled back to Rachel's voice. She imagined Charlie lying naked next to the beautiful actress. She saw him kissing her hungrily and practically pawing her body, so desperate was he for what Maddie had been denying him for months.

She put the book down and dialed Priscilla.

"What's up, famous lady?"

"The jerk slept with Rachel Swanson."

"How do you know?"

"I called him and she picked up. Said Charlie couldn't talk because he was busy. She said it in a voice dripping with sex. He did it with her."

Priscilla turned off the TV. She needed to focus all her attention on the crisis at hand. "Are you upset because you're jealous? I thought you had a thing for his dad. Why does it matter that he's with another woman?"

"It's a matter of respect. He's telling the whole world that I'm his girlfriend. Our faces are plastered all over the tabloids on a weekly basis. If this bitch tells anyone that she slept with Charlie, and I'm sure she will, then I look like a chump. Plus, it confirms what probably everyone's been thinking: 'She's so old, of course he's going to fall for a younger, prettier woman.' It makes me feel like shit."

"First of all, M&M, you're not old. You're only forty-six."

"Wrong. I am old. I could be Rachel Swanson's mother. Her mother!"

Maddie was getting herself so worked up, she jumped when someone knocked on the door. "Maddie, open up."

From a deep sleep, Mick jumped off the couch and ran to the door, barking.

"Gotta go, Priscilla. Charlie's at the door."

"Good luck, sweetie. If you can, call later and let me know what happened."

"Okay. Bye."

Maddie opened the door. In front of her was a very distraught Charlie Evans. He was dressed in a dark blue suit and tie. His wingtips shoes were scuffed. She swore she could smell Rachel on him.

"What do you want?" Maddie stared into his intense blue eyes. She wondered why he looked so desirable when she was so mad at him.

"Can I come in?"

Maddie opened the door wider and he stood in front of her. "You need to believe me when I tell you that Rachel and I were standing on the set when you called. I haven't done a thing with that woman except when the script calls for it."

"She didn't sound like she was on the set."

"Maddie, I swear we had just finished shooting for the night and…"

"And you were the only two left, so you did it on the set. That's rich, Charlie. That's really rich." She could see the front page of *The Globe, Sex on the set with Swanson, Charlie Evans no longer playing Mozart.*

Charlie ran his fingers through his hair. He looked like he was going to cry. "I am going to be completely honest with you. If we weren't dating, I would have had sex with Rachel. But we are together and I wouldn't betray your trust. Rachel invited me to dinner tonight and I refused. I was leaving when you called and she grabbed the phone from me. I swear that's the truth."

The truth. It was coming from a man who lied about being attracted to her to get a movie role, so Maddie was reluctant to believe him; yet she also knew how important that role was to Charlie. "Why would Rachel want me to believe that you were in bed with her?"

Charlie laughed. "Here's a truth that you can easily believe. We actors are a bunch of egotistical, insecure people. Rachel doesn't like being rejected. The woman has a reputation for sleeping with all her leading men. When you called, it was a perfect opportunity for her to get me in trouble. It looks like she almost succeeded. Right?" He went to put his arms around Maddie. She let him. He was warm and for some inexplicable reason, he smelled like Charlie again: a hint of cologne mixed with his unique, masculine scent.

He kissed the top of her head, then reached into his pocket. "I brought you something." He took her hand and placed in it a miniature cow. "It's your first sanctuary resident."

Maddie looked at the small porcelain black and white cow standing on her palm. That did it. She hit the tipping point. She kissed Charlie. He kissed her back with such intensity, her knees buckled. She always thought that it was just an expression. How could a mere kiss disable a person? Sitting impatiently in the back seat for over two months, her libido was at last able to climb into the driver's seat. It was the first time in a while she didn't think of Jackson.

Maddie awoke at three in the morning. Her body felt like her mind: satisfied and tender. She looked at Charlie sleeping next to her, lightly snoring. His body was partially covered by the paisley and striped sheets. She was about to stroke his leg when Jackson popped into her head. He was sitting across from her at the café in Davis. She heard him ask, 'Do you love him?' She groaned, "Why now?"

Charlie opened his eyes. He smiled as he pulled her to him and kissed her forehead. "Do you know what I want?"

Before she could answer, she was lying under him and the vision of Jackson evaporated in the sexually charged air.

The next time Maddie looked at her alarm clock, it was 8:30 in the morning and Charlie was gone. She was surprised that she didn't hear him get up and leave. She shuffled into the kitchen and there, on the kitchen table, was a note explaining that he had to be on the set at 6:00 a.m. He'd call her later. He signed it with an x and an o. Her heart jumped. What was she getting herself into?

20

"Well?" Priscilla waited for her best friend to say it.

"Well, what?"

"Don't toy with me, woman. I know you would have called me right back the minute Charlie left, which means he didn't."

"Which means we did it. Boy, did we do it."

"Before I ask the million-dollar question, I want to say that you did an admirable job of holding out. You lasted longer than any able-bodied or physically impaired woman could have. So what made you give in?"

Maddie sat at the kitchen table finishing off the remaining soy ice cream. She licked the spoon and stared at the small object that made her cave. "A teeny cow."

"Say what?"

"After a very convincing denial that he was cavorting with his co-star, Charlie reached into his pocket and gave me a small porcelain cow. He said it was the first resident of the animal sanctuary. He shot me in my Achilles' Heel."

"And we didn't think he was very smart."

"Scholastically, he's not. But the man is a genius when it comes to women. I actually swooned. Not once but twice!"

"You're talking to a woman who hasn't had sex in a while. Don't turn me into another Ava, lusting after your man. Speaking of men, what are you going to do about Jackson?"

Maddie glanced up at the kitchen clock. It was almost 9:00. "Shit! I'm supposed to meet Jackson at the property in an hour. Gotta go. I'll call you later."

"Oh, what a tangled web we weave."

"Yeah. Whatever."

By the time Maddie got to the property, she was thirty-five minutes late. Getting lost didn't help. She parked next to Jackson's truck. As she briskly walked toward the barn, she heard laughter. Perhaps it was the realtor, Maddie thought. She turned the corner and there was Jackson standing next to Trinity. They were looking at a map of the property spread out on a makeshift table.

"I'm sorry I'm late. I got lost."

Jackson went up to her and gave her a hug. Maddie felt a shiver of guilt run through her body. "I should have warned you about this area. It's confusing. You remember Trinity? She graciously agreed to give the property her expert eye."

"We haven't been here that long, but from what I can tell, it's a perfect piece of land." Trinity went back to perusing the map, leaning over it in her crop top and short shorts, exposing every inch of her long, lean legs up to and past the frayed hem. Maddie tried not to stare. Jackson was much more obvious.

"Why don't we go up to the top of that hill and check out the property from there?" Jackson said. The women agreed. When they reached the top, they all marveled at the view. They could easily see the main house, both barns, and the silo. The water tower was partially hidden by a hill.

Trinity stood close to Jackson and pointed to a ridge of mountains.

"Do you know the name of that range? It's beautiful."

"Those are the Santa Cruz Mountains." He turned toward town. "Here's a fact you two may not be aware of. The San Andreas Fault runs through the center of Woodside."

"That's comforting," Maddie said. "Were you expecting someone?"

Jackson looked in the direction of Maddie's gaze and saw a small figure standing by the main house. He began waving his hands and yelling, "Up here! Come on up!"

As the figure got closer, Maddie realized it was Charlie. He was in shorts and a polo shirt. His tennis shoes were brand new. For someone who got little sleep the night before and arose very early, he looked refreshed and enormously handsome.

"Hey there, Ms. Mozart. Don't you look outdoorsy and, dare I say, glowing?" Before she could say anything, he gave her a big kiss. Peripherally, Maddie noticed Jackson glance downward. It was almost as if he knew that they had consummated their relationship.

"And this must be Trinity. Nice to meet you. I'm…"

"I know who you are. The famous Charlie Evans. I'm thrilled you're part of this project. The animals need someone of your stature. Thanks for helping them." She held out her hand and Charlie shook it.

"I'm glad to do it." He turned to Jackson. "I didn't think I'd be able to get away this early. Since I'm not in the next couple of scenes, I'm all yours." Charlie grew serious and said, "The seasons come, go, and come again. Turn from the bare tree and I will be there. Turn around again and I'm all yours."

Jackson looked sideways at Maddie and she rolled her eyes. Trinity was smitten. *The Map of the World*. That's what it's from, right? I loved that movie!"

"You got it. One of my favorite roles, Lawrence Gotsland, drifter and adventurer." Charlie put his arm around Maddie and kissed the top of her head. Jackson looked away.

Trinity said, "Before we head down the hill, do y'all mind if I talk to Maddie for a sec?"

The men look bemused. "Go right ahead," said Jackson.

Once the guys left and Trinity was sure they were out of earshot, she said, "I can't believe you're dating Charlie Evans! Dang, you're so frickin' lucky!" She watched as the men walked away, then she continued. "I know he's quite a bit older than me, but I have a huge crush on Jackson. I mean, how many sexy, hot vegans are there? I'll tell you. Not many at all." She lowered her voice, even though the men were hundreds of feet away. "Do you know if he's seeing anyone?"

Before she had asked the question, Maddie knew what Trinity was going to say and she dreaded answering. She didn't want to tell her the truth. And she certainly didn't want to compete for Jackson's affections with a woman a good twenty years younger than she. On the other hand, she didn't want to get caught in a lie. The internal grappling lasted longer than Maddie realized. Trinity tapped her on the shoulder, startling her. "Are you okay?"

"Sorry. My mind seized up."

"I totally know what you mean. It happens to my mom all the time. So, is the stud available or what?"

"I'm not positive, but I think he might be seeing a woman long distance. Also, he's not quite a vegan yet. I suspect by the time the sanctuary is up and running, he will be."

"Hmm. Is there any way you can find out if there is another woman? I'd really appreciate it. Maybe you could ask Charlie."

She lied. "Sure. Shall we join them?"

Trinity nodded and started down the hill. Maddie rushed ahead of her so she wouldn't have to look at the woman's amazing body.

The troupe spent another hour inspecting buildings, walking the property lines, deciding how much work they'd be putting into the land. They ended at the parking lot, Charlie suggesting they meet at the Railway Diner for lunch. Twenty minutes later, they sat down in the crowded restaurant, more than three-quarters of the patrons mesmerized by the star sighting. Maddie was used to it and Jackson had been dealing with it for decades. Trinity ate it up. She loved the attention and she didn't hide it. She made sure she sat between the two men. Maddie ended up on the other side of Charlie. With his hand on her thigh, she put her hand on his, appreciating his attentiveness and apparent apathy toward Trinity. This was a different Charlie. His affection seemed genuine, not rote or strained. Then again, he was an accomplished actor. She had to remind herself that when the movie was done shooting, Charlie would be going back to his home in Malibu. She couldn't wait, despite the new intimacy in their relationship.

After they ordered, Trinity skootched a little closer to Jackson and said, "Are you going to make an offer on the property?"

"You're the expert. What do you think?" he replied.

Trinity placed her hand on his. "Thank you, Jackson. I'm flattered. I think it's a great piece of land. It's flat enough for the women's housing and additional buildings. The existing barns are solid and well-built and can be used for the animals. Grazing sites, check. Mature trees for shelter and shade, check. Oh, and the silo is in great condition. If you can get it for a good price, I'd say you got yourself a future animal sanctuary and women's center."

"Great. I'll make an offer after lunch."

Charlie said, "Aren't you going to ask Maddie's opinion? You know, the woman who is going to be running it with you?"

"Chill out, Charlie. Maddie gave me her blessing already. When we were inspecting the main house, she told me how much she loved it. I'm not that insensitive."

Maddie nodded. "I did say that. Thanks for being my advocate, though." She kissed Charlie on the cheek and was once again struck by his thoughtfulness. She wondered if she was *that* good in bed or if Charlie was deprived of sex for much too long.

Largely, the lunch conversation revolved around plans for the sanctuary. Maddie noticed Jackson spending more time talking to Trinity than to anyone else at the table. Much to her dismay, Trinity offered her services to the project unconditionally. She knew that a sanctuary expert's experience would be useful. She also knew that Trinity would endear herself to Jackson at every turn. She imagined them feeding the animals together, hiking together, creating flow charts and budgets. Together. When she thought of Charlie, he appeared as a noose around her neck, separating her from Jackson. She was finding it hard to breathe and excused herself from the table, saying she had to call Ray. She went outside and took out her cell, but she didn't dial. Instead, she put the phone up to her ear in case anyone was watching and took some deep breaths in an attempt to steady her mind. Maddie was starting to feel better when a woman pulled out her cellphone and took pictures of her. She offered the woman a tight smile and went back into the restaurant.

Charlie stood up when she arrived and sat down after she was seated. "We're all going back to Jackson's. You don't have other plans, do you?"

"I'm all yours."

After Jackson called the realtor and left her a message, he fixed margaritas and turned five ripe avocados, a bunch of cilantro, salt, pepper, and lemon juice into guacamole. The foursome sat outside on the deck, relishing the festivities and warm weather. Sherlock perched himself on the patio railing.

"I have a question for the animal rights women." Charlie paused for emphasis and took a sip of his drink. He licked the salt off his lips. "Let me set the scenario. You're walking on the beach and you hear yelling in the water. To your horror, you discover that a woman and a dog are drowning…"

Both Trinity and Maddie groaned at the same time. Trinity said, "You can't be serious. You're throwing that question at us? Do you know how many times I've answered it and I bet Maddie has, too?"

Maddie nodded and gave Charlie a look of exasperation. "Who would we save, right?" she turned to Trinity. "May I answer first?"

"Be my guest," she replied and scooped an extra-large dollop of guacamole onto her tortilla chip.

Maddie rubbed her hands together. "If the dog and the woman are both good beings, I would save the woman first and then go back and save the dog but, and this is a big but, if the woman was a pedophile, I would save the dog and tell the woman to have a nice life…under the sea!"

"Fair enough. What if the dog was a pedophile?" Charlie realized what he had just said and started laughing. The others joined in and soon all four were laughing so hard, they found it hard to breathe. The noise was too much for Sherlock. He flapped his wings, then left for the solitude of the chicken coop.

Charlie said, "I'm sure you're both against experimenting on animals." Both women nodded. "So here's the million-dollar question. If experimenting on an animal could save your child's life, would you be for it?"

Trinity raised her hand and Maddie said, "Be my guest."

"Thank you. I don't have any children, but if I did, anybody, including you, would be experimented on to save my child's life, so that's not a fair question. The question should be: do we have the right to incarcerate and inflict intense pain and suffering on other species and murder them for the benefit of our own species? I say no. Maddie?"

"I would have said the same thing and would like to add that if humans had never considered exploiting non-human animals in the first place, how much further would medicine be in the cures for diseases that continue to plague our species? The anatomical, physiological, immunological, histological, and even psychological differences between humans and non-humans are too great to overcome. Unfortunately, vivisection is an industry, a lucrative business, and there are too many universities, researchers, and companies that profit from it."

Charlie looked dumbfounded. He had no idea his girlfriend was that knowledgeable on the subject. Jackson clapped. "Bravo, M&M. I can call you that, right?"

"Only my good friends call me by that moniker, so by all means, use away."

With heightened awareness, probably from the margarita, Trinity watched the brief exchange. She detected a sexual energy between them, which was confusing because Maddie was dating Charlie and what woman in her right mind would give him up for any other man? Even Jackson, who was attractive in his own right, wasn't Charlie Evans. Trinity downed her drink, refilled her glass and said, "I've got an animal rights conundrum for you boys. Most people place the lives of humans over those of animals no matter what the circumstances. What if you were asked to pick your neighbor? You're given the choice of a family of pigs or a serial rapist and his meth head girlfriend. The ones you don't choose die."

Jackson spoke first. "That's a no-brainer. Do pigs prefer cabbage or apples as a housewarming gift?"

"Definitely apples. They hate cabbage." Trinity turned to Charlie. "Who's your neighbor?"

"Can the rapist be rehabilitated and the meth head cleaned up?"

Maddie and Trinity both said, "No!"

Charlie replied, "Fine. I now have pigs for neighbors. I have to say, you both have strong feelings about animals and you have the facts to back them up. Can we change the subject and talk about something else?"

Maddie held up her hand. She had never asked anyone this question before, but she thought about it on a daily basis. It was one of many moral soundtracks that played in her mind. Before she lost her nerve, she cleared her throat and said, "I have a question. We can all concede that there are millions, if not billions, of people who are impoverished. There may be just as many, like ourselves, who can help those people, whether financially or by volunteering our time.

What if we did? What if we used our free time gladly and lovingly to help others? Would there be poverty? Would there be people living in cardboard boxes or mud huts? Could poverty exist if every able-bodied human wanted nothing more than to eradicate it? Could we?"

Charlie pointed to the pitcher of margaritas. "What did you put in this, Jackson?" He held Maddie's hands in his. "Sweetie, that's way too heavy a topic right now. It will totally burst my mellow."

Trinity agreed. "We totally need to lighten this conversation up. Can we talk about it later?"

Somewhat deflated, Maddie conceded. "Sure."

Jackson turned his attention to Trinity. "Would you like to see my art studio? You had expressed an interest in painting before."

"That would be wonderful. Please show me." Trinity demurely held out her hand. Jackson took it and helped her up.

Before Maddie could say anything, Charlie said, "Been there. Done that. Have fun you two."

When Charlie heard Jackson and Trinity walking down the steps to the studio, he said, "I think Jackson is smitten."

"With whom?"

"What do you mean? Trinity, of course."

Maddie tried not to sound disappointed, so she spiked her voice with false enthusiasm. "You think so? I think he's being himself: attentive and respectful. Besides, she's too young for him."

"There may be a twenty-five-year difference, but Jackson's in great shape. Yeah, I think he's hot on her."

"If you're right, I hope he's not too let down because I think she's seeing someone."

It was Charlie's turn to be disappointed. "Too bad. It's been a while since he's dated. I think having some girl action would be good for him. Speaking of which, you were amazing last night. It was definitely worth the wait." He leaned over and kissed Maddie. As much as she was enjoying the new Charlie, her thoughts were downstairs in the studio.

"You were pretty amazing, too. How was Rachel on the set? She hasn't sent a hitman after me, has she?"

Charlie stood up and pointed toward the back of the property. "So that's who that guy is with the semi-automatic rifle." He quickly added, "Just kidding. Rachel was nasty until I told the director what happened last night. He spoke to her and made it clear that he'd ruin her reputation if she didn't shape up. Vicente has connections in the industry and Rachel is still making them. She can't afford to piss him off. So, all is well in the land of celluloid. Personally, I can't wait to get away from the bitch. Two more weeks of shooting and we're done."

Maddie wondered if Charlie wanted her to ask him what would happen after they wrapped up. She knew the romance would be finished and she didn't feel like listening to him lie and tell her otherwise. She stood and stretched her arms. "I'll be right back. Have to go to the bathroom."

She walked past the door to the studio and paused. Any attempts to overhear their conversation were fruitless. Faint mumblings and then Trinity giggling was all that emanated from the studio, infusing Maddie once again with the green-eyed monster.

After finishing off a pitcher of margaritas, the group decided they were in no shape to drive, so they decided to stay for dinner. Jackson was thrilled. He didn't entertain often and relished the company. He also insisted on making the meal himself.

Maddie slipped away from the living room while Charlie regaled Trinity with more movie quotes. She watched Jackson as he stood in front of the sink, washing the dirt off the zucchini from his garden.

"Are you staring at my butt again?" Jackson turned around and smiled. He looked irresistible. "I can see you in the window's reflection. Were you going to sneak up on me?"

"There's no getting by you, is there?" Maddie stood beside him. "Charlie and Trinity are playing 'guess what movie this line is from?' Played the game too many times. Let me chop or dice or do something. Put me to work."

"Ah yes, the Charlie show. I feel your pain." Jackson grabbed three washed zucchini and handed them to Maddie. She tried to hold them in one hand but they were too large. One fell on the ground and when Maddie bent down to pick it up, Jackson did, too. Their heads bumped together, making a soft thud. It knocked Maddie to the ground.

"Are you okay?" Jackson pulled Maddie's hand away from the

small, red bump above her left eye. "It's not too bad." He held on to her hand and, for a moment, they stared at each other.

"I'm fine, really." She stood and shook off her feelings of lust. "Who would have thought we could so easily channel Laurel and Hardy?"

"Are you sure you don't want some ice?"

Maddie shook her head. "Where's your cutting board?"

"It's in the drawer to the right of the stove. The knives are next to it."

After the zucchini, Maddie chopped red peppers, chives, kale and broccoli, garlic and onions. She placed it all in the large skillet on the stove and added coconut oil. The rice in the saucepan began to boil, so she turned it to low and placed the lid on top. "What should I set the timer to?"

"Twenty minutes. Thanks for helping."

"My pleasure."

"Is dinner ready?" Charlie said as he held up an empty bottle of wine. Trinity was behind him, her wine glass nearly empty. They were both clearly lit. "And do you mind if I open up another bottle of vino?"

"Dinner will be done in about twenty minutes and of course you can have more wine. Grab a nice cab from the wine cellar. It will go really well with the main course."

"Thanks, Pop," replied Charlie, then he took Maddie by the hand. "Come down with me. You've got to see this wine cellar. It's very cool."

Trinity gave Charlie a sad look. "Can I come, too?"

"Of course. I didn't mean to leave you out. All vegans are welcome. Follow me, ladies."

When they returned, the table was set. The veggies and rice sat side by side. A salad took center stage and Jackson topped it with yellow and orange nasturtiums and candied violets. Heated rolls were in a basket.

After Maddie regaled her host with flattery, she turned her attention to Trinity. The woman was clearly toasted and had just accepted another glass of wine. She lived a couple of hours away and was in no condition to drive home. That meant she might spend the night. Maddie glanced at the clock on the wall. It was 7:50.

"I don't mean to be a fuddy duddy, but you have a long drive ahead of you. Maybe you shouldn't be drinking anymore." Maddie wasn't sure if she was out of line, but the thought of Trinity spending the night at Jackson's was more than she could bear. She was sure they'd share a bed, especially with Trinity's inhibitions drowned in wine.

Trinity looked at Maddie like she was Mother Theresa. "I appreciate your concern, Mom, but I have a feeling if I can't drive home, that man right there will let me stay over. I'm sure there's a guest room or two in this spacious homestead."

Jackson smiled. "Trinity, if you don't feel comfortable driving home, you are welcome to spend the night."

Internal cheers and jeers filled the room.

Charlie was clueless. "That's so sweet of you to be concerned, M&M. We all might be staying at Casa de Jackson. Would you like a glass of," Charlie read the label, "2000 Running Wolf Cabernet Sauvignon?"

Defeated, Maddie said, "Sure. Fill 'er up."

During the meal, Jackson would catch himself staring at Maddie. He had to be discreet and even as he was doing it, he felt tiny stabs of guilt. On the other side of the table was a woman who was available, attractive, and very willing. But she wasn't Maddie.

Charlie suggested he and Trinity clean up since they didn't help with the preparation. Jackson and Maddie were only too happy to comply. In the living room, Jackson put on a George Strait CD. The singer's smooth voice crooned, *All My Exes Live in Texas.* Maddie sang along. From the kitchen, Charlie yelled,

"You, too, Jackson? All is lost!"

"Who doesn't love George Strait?" Jackson yelled back.

"Me!"

"Me, too!" Trinity added.

Maddie sang louder.

With the dishes done and the leftovers put away, Charlie and Trinity walked in on Maddie teaching Jackson how to do the two-step. Despite stepping on her toes a few times, he was a quick learner. He even dipped her a few times.

The two-steppers offered to teach Charlie and Trinity, but they less-than-delicately declined, opting for a movie instead. When the song was over, dancing shoes retired, Jackson turned on the television and they perused the Netflix selections. It took a while for the four of them to decide on a movie. In the end, they settled on *Casablanca*.

Trinity fell asleep, her head resting on Charlie's shoulder. He could barely keep his eyes open. They fluttered, shutting for moments, then opened briefly only to close again.

Jackson and Maddie watched the movie, wide-awake and drinking water. As the credits rolled, Charlie opened his eyes. He stretched his arms and said, "Guess how many times Humphrey Bogart says, 'Here's looking at you, kid.' I always thought he said it once."

"Me, too, but I could have sworn he said it at least three times," Jackson turned to Maddie.

"I'm going to say five. After the third time, it was getting annoying and I never thought I'd say that about *Casablanca*. It's still a classic. We could ask Trinity, but I have a feeling if we wake her, she won't remember where she is, let alone what she watched."

"Four times," said Charlie.

Jackson stood and stretched. "You must have known that already because I swear you nodded off quite a bit." He looked over at Trinity. Charlie repositioned her so she was lying on the sofa. Curled up in a ball, she lightly snored. "I know Trinity's going to spend the night. How about you two? You're more than welcome to stay."

Maddie felt fine. Her wine buzz was long gone and she wasn't sleepy. She also wasn't going to leave Trinity alone with Jackson for the night. "I'm still a little buzzed and don't feel comfortable driving home. Charlie?"

In a dead-on impersonation of Humphrey Bogart, Charlie said, "I'd be looking at a DUI, kid, so staying here is my only option."

"Alright, then. I'm going to get a blanket for Trinity. She can sleep there. Let's get your bed ready. I have extra toothbrushes in the guest bathroom and even pajamas in the bedroom drawer."

"Thanks, Pop, but we won't be needing PJs." Charlie winked, then said to Maddie, "Let's go make up that bed."

Jackson internally sighed. Maddie could have sworn she heard it.

And Charlie couldn't wait to close the guest room door.

The morning light softly filtered through the closed blinds. She wanted to sleep in, snug and warm in Charlie's arms, but Maddie was determined to wake up before Trinity so she could monitor the woman's time with Jackson. After a few unsuccessful attempts, Maddie managed to extricate herself from Charlie's arms.

When Maddie came into the kitchen, Jackson was by the sink, scooping coffee out of a canister and placing it in the coffeemaker. He was dressed in his faded 501s and a white tee. Even with the bags under his eyes, he looked very sexy. Maddie resisted the urge to wrap her arms around his waist.

"Good morning."

Without looking up, Jackson replied, "Morning. Did you sleep well or should I ask, did you sleep at all?" As soon as he said it, he regretted it. "I'm sorry. That was rather rude of me."

Maddie patted him on the back. "Apology accepted. Has Trinity awakened from her alcohol-induced semi-coma?" She looked out the window and waved to Sherlock who was sitting on the roof of the chicken coop.

"Someone stumbled into the bathroom earlier this morning, made some grotesque noises, flushed the toilet twice and then, after falling and cursing, went back to sleep. If it wasn't you or Charlie, I'm guessing it was our young guest."

"Isn't that attractive?"

"I think she was star-struck and went a little overboard. Trinity doesn't impress me as someone who over-indulges."

Maddie countered, "You may be right, but I don't think it was Charlie she was in awe of."

"I beg to differ." Charlie stood at the doorway. He had bed hair and looked tired as he rubbed his eyes and yawned. He was wearing jeans. No shirt or shoes. "I think drinking was the only way she could cope with being next to this." He brushed his hands over his chest.

Jackson and Maddie looked at each other, then at Charlie. Before they could say anything, Charlie said, "Just kidding. She's totally got the hots for you, Jackson." He went to the refrigerator and grabbed a bottle of tomato juice. "If I were you, I'd put the moves on her."

Maddie added, "After she wipes the puke from her mouth."

Charlie made a face. "I'm going to take a shower." He gave Maddie a lecherous look. "You coming with?"

"I'll take one after breakfast."

Charlie looked disappointed, so she added, "I would, but I'm hungry. Ravenous."

"That means really, really hungry, right?"

Maddie nodded.

"I knew it." He grinned and left.

Jackson said, "So, two pieces of sourdough in the toaster?"

"Yes, please."

Three minutes later, Maddie was spreading margarine on her toast. She smiled.

"What are you thinking?" Jackson had been watching her.

She took a sip of her coffee. "Every time I put margarine on my toast, and that's practically every morning, I remember a comment that this guy I used to date made. As he told me to lighten up on the spread, he took his knife and scraped off about half the margarine from his bread into the sink. That was a couple of years ago. The break-up was somewhat amicable, yet as long as I eat toast, he'll remain in my thoughts forever."

Jackson sat down next to Maddie at the table. "I know how you feel. When I pass the intersection at Twain and Manchester streets, I think of this homeless woman I saw waiting at the light. She was covered from head to toe in filthy, torn clothing. As I passed her, she looked up at me with the saddest eyes. It was heart-wrenching. I never saw her again, but she's always here." He pointed to his head.

"Any good recurring memory?"

Jackson thought about it. He got up and refilled his coffee cup. "Yes. Jackie would put stones, large stones, in the bird bath, then she'd fill it with water. She never told me why she did it, so I thought it was for aesthetic reasons. After she died, I kept up the tradition. It wasn't until a few years later that I read a column in the garden section of the paper. One of the ways to keep small birds from drowning in a bird bath is to place stones at the bottom so they have a place to rest while they bathe. Whenever I fill it with water, I look at those stones and think of Jackie."

"That's very nice. I have a bird bath in my back yard and guess what? I'm going to gather stones and do the same thing and then Jackie's memory will be in my heart, as well."

From the living room, Trinity moaned, "Too loud. Stop talking so loud."

Being the gracious host, Jackson poured a glass of water, grabbed a bottle of aspirin from the cupboard and brought it to his guest. Maddie followed. Trinity was sitting up, the blanket wrapped around her shoulders. She looked like the only survivor from a horror movie, set in the woods. Her blonde locks were tangled. Strands stuck to the side of her face. Her make-up didn't survive the night, mascara pooled under her eyes. A hint of peach lipstick was barely visible on her lips and the surrounding area. Maddie was thrilled.

Jackson set the water and two aspirin on the coffee table. He spoke softly. "Do you want to move to the guest room?"

Trinity slowly nodded, then put her hand up to her head and closed her eyes. Jackson helped her up and walked her to the second guest room, gently placing her on the bed. She curled up into a ball. Maddie brought in the water and aspirin. They closed the door behind them.

It wasn't until the three had finished eating that Trinity emerged. She had showered and, despite being make-up free, reminded Maddie of the 'farmer's daughter,' the one in the jokes who is fresh-faced, innocent, and completely tempting to the traveling salesman. She looked over at Jackson to catch his reaction. It was a non-issue. She might as well have been wearing a gunny sack. His expression was neutral. He pulled up a chair and motioned for her to sit down. "Feeling better?"

"Yes. Thanks. Sorry, y'all for my behavior. I rarely drink that much."

"Apology accepted. Would you like something to eat? I have toast and coffee."

"Toast and coffee sounds fine. Thanks."

Charlie walked into the kitchen looking all shiny and new. The bags were gone from under his eyes and his hair was perfectly slicked back. The man looked edible. "I see Trinity is alive and…well?"

Trinity replied, "Getting there. I didn't do anything stupid, did I?"

"Besides passing out last night and puking this morning?" Maddie smiled. The intentional dig wasn't lost on Jackson. Charlie barely noticed as he took a bite of someone else's leftover toast.

"I hate to eat and run but we're reshooting a scene in about an hour, so I have to jet. Thanks for the hospitality, Mr. Danoff. Trinity, it was a pleasure meeting you. This wasn't your toast, was it?" She shook her head. Relieved, he turned to Maddie. "Can you walk me out, M&M?"

Jackson watched as his stepson put his arm around Maddie. He could have sworn he heard his heart whisper, 'Don't give up.'

21

Satisfied that she and Trinity left at the same time, Maddie drove home feeling deceitful squared. She was lying to Charlie about her intentions and hiding her feelings for Jackson. She didn't have to ask herself how she slipped into this precarious emotional situation. She knew exactly how it had happened. Despite her dilemma, she couldn't help but smile when she relived last night. Sex with Charlie was exhilarating, like riding a roller coaster naked with plush velvet seats and unpredictable twists and turns. For a brief moment, she changed out Charlie for Jackson and became even more turned on by the memory.

Before Mick greeted Maddie with a slobbery kiss, she inhaled the sweet smell of licorice mixed with a scent she couldn't identify. "What are you cooking, Chef Ray, because whatever it is, I want some."

Maddie followed the aroma and found her son stirring a pot of thick, brown liquid on the stovetop. Ray pulled the spoon out of the pot and blew on it, then he held it out for his mother to sample. Maddie sipped the liquid.

"Where in God's name did you get such an incredible talent for cooking? I know not from me. And your father turns into a ten-thumbed goof when he's asked to prepare a meal. What's in this masterpiece?"

Ray beamed. His mother was one of his greatest fans. "I mixed caramel with licorice extract and…"

"Caramel is full of sugar, isn't it?"

"Yeah, so I'm using coconut palm sugar, which is healthier. I added coconut milk, vanilla extract and a pinch of Himalayan crystal salt. I'm going to throw in some cacao, then cool it off and pour it into these molds." Ray held up an ice tray, the cubes in the shape of marijuana leaves.

"That's my boy." She took the spoon from him and stole another taste. "Aren't you meeting with Charlie's friend this Friday?"

"I was. He called last night and re-scheduled for the following Friday. It's cool. It gives me more time to expand my selection."

"Good attitude." Maddie's cell rang. She fished it out of her purse and answered. "Hey Tanvi."

"Hello, stranger. Is this what happens when you become famous? Do your close friends fade from your memory?"

Maddie put her on speaker phone so she could change into fresh clothes. "Not at all. I talk to Priscilla and Sylvie all the time. It's you I've been ignoring."

The other end of the line was quiet. Maddie laughed. "Come on, Tanvi. I'm just funnin' with you. I've been busy planning the sanctuary with Jackson. Honestly, I'm not ignoring any of my amazing friends, especially you. What's going on?

"It pales in comparison to what you've been doing. According to *In Touch* Magazine, you and Charlie Evans are falling in love."

"Hold that thought." Maddie raced to her computer and turned it on. While it warmed up, she wondered what photo was plastered across the front page.

"Maddie, what are you doing?" Tanvi said.

"Going on to the magazine's website. I want to see what you're talking about."

The headline screamed, 'CHARLIE'S PART OF THE MOZART FAMILY!' The photo couldn't have exuded more sheer exuberance if they had tried. There was Kenzie with a big, starstruck smile on her face. She was watching Charlie give Maddie a bite of his vegan donut at the bakery. Even though her gaze was more playful, it could have easily been interpreted as one of adoration. The article went on to recount an evening with Maddie's children, the hunky star fitting right in with their family function and ending the night at a local bakery. They even quoted one of Charlie's friends: 'The man is giddy. I haven't seen him this happy and in love…ever!'

"I wonder how much he paid the reporter."

"What are you talking about?" Tanvi said.

Maddie had forgotten she was still on the phone. "I meant I wonder how much the tabloid paid the reporter to fabricate the story. Charlie's not in love with me. Believe me, I'd know. We're having fun. That's all."

"Are you sure about that? Charlie looks smitten."

"I'm positive. Do you and Sanjay and the kids want to come over for dinner this Friday? It will give us a chance to catch up."

"Sounds good. Let me check with the husband and I'll call you back. If we can get a sitter, I'd rather come without them. Okay?"

"Okay."

As soon as she hung up, she called Priscilla.

Ironically, Gretchen was at her desk eating a glazed donut when Charlie came in and dropped *In Touch* magazine in front of her. "If I didn't know any better, I'd say I was madly in love with Madeleine Mozart."

Gretchen glanced at the cover and smiled. "The only person who looks crazy in love is the daughter. With you." She perused the article. "How much did you pay the reporter to invent your friend?"

"Not a thing. I just told him that one of my close friends said he thought I was madly in love and had never seen me so happy. The reporter did the rest."

"Aren't you a clever little conniver? According to my sources, the word in Hollywood is that you're not in love with Ms. Mozart but it's simply a San Francisco fling and a way to completely miff Rachel Swanson."

Charlie was furious. He picked up the tabloid. "I put all this time and energy into creating the perfect rag cover and that's what people think, that this is a fling? Son of a bitch!"

Gretchen walked around the desk and stood next to the man whom she so enjoyed riling. "Doesn't the movie wrap up in a few weeks?"

Charlie nodded. He looked dejected. Gretchen smiled. "That doesn't give you much time, does it? If you want to call off the bet, I completely understand. It must take a lot of acting to spend so much time with the old lady. She's pretty, but she's no Victoria's Secret model. Know what I mean?"

"M&M is a…"

"That's what you call her? Cute. Continue."

"She's a great person. A lot smarter and funnier than those models. The bet is still on, Gretchen. And I'm going to win." Without saying good-bye, Charlie strode out of the office.

Gretchen sat back down and took another look at the tabloid cover. "What a putz."

Charlie slammed the car door. He sat there for a good five minutes trying to figure out what he had to do to convince the world that Maddie was the love of his life.

On the other side of the Golden Gate Bridge, Maddie was in a heated conversation with her ex. On his way out the door with Ray, Tommy suggested the two of them drive to the UC Berkeley lab protest together on Saturday. When she told him that she was unable to go because of a date with Charlie, Tommy lost it.

"Kenzie told you about this protest over a month ago. I can't believe how irresponsible you're being."

"I forgot, Tommy. She'll understand."

Tommy countered, "She shouldn't have to understand. You know she planned this by herself? She even got a reporter from the Oakland Tribune to cover it and the campus paper is putting her interview on the front page. We promised to support her fight against Gaston's research. The monster is using…" He looked over at Mick lying on the floor and lowered his voice, "dogs in a drug addiction study."

"I know, Tommy." Maddie let out a sigh. She found herself fighting more frequently with her ex since dating Charlie. At first, she could tolerate his jealousy. Now she found it annoying and immature.

While they were arguing, Ray took the liberty of calling his sister, believing she could settle the argument fairly. Once he got her on the phone, he handed his cell to Maddie. "I'd like to go have lunch with Dad, so please talk to Kenzie."

"Hi Mom. What's the problem?"

Maddie gave Tommy a dirty look and he responded by pointing to Ray and mouthing, 'I didn't do it.'

"Hi sweetie. It's not a big thing. I forgot about the protest on Saturday and made plans with Charlie to go to the opening of the Monet exhibit at the De Young. I'll call the university and lodge my protest and even write a letter to the dean."

"I've been planning this for a long time, Mom. It would mean a lot to me if you were there. Can't you go to the museum on Sunday?"

"Charlie goes on location. He's leaving Saturday night for a week."

"Oh." Kenzie thought about it. "If it means that much to you, go on. I'll have other protests."

"Sure you will. This is just the beginning. I'll be there in spirit, sweetie, and I'll be at your next one. Promise."

"I have to get to class. Talk to you later." Kenzie tried not to sound deflated, but her mother easily caught it.

"Okay. Love you, Kenzie."

"Love you, too."

Maddie handed the phone back to Ray. "Kenzie is fine with me not going. Go have lunch. Enjoy."

Tommy said, "She told you it was okay, but you know she wants you there. Who's more important, your daughter or a fling?"

"This conversation is over. See you later, Ray. Go to hell, Tommy." Maddie closed the door behind her and went into the kitchen to make herself a sandwich.

As she assembled the different layers of tomatoes, lettuce, Fakin' Bacon and pickles, she mentally replayed the conversation with her daughter. She knew Kenzie was disappointed. She also knew Charlie was going to be, too. It shouldn't matter that much to her, letting Charlie down. Kenzie was worth 1,000 Charlies, yet her comfort zone was invaded by feelings of rejection at the thought of cancelling plans with a man. She had to remind herself that Charlie couldn't break up with her or get upset with her decisions. By the time she finished her sandwich, she had made up her mind. With new resolve, Maddie dialed Charlie's cellphone.

"Hey there, M&M."

"Hi. What are you doing?"

"On my way back to the hotel."

"I totally forgot that I have a previous engagement on Saturday, so I'm not going to be able to get together. I'm sorry."

Charlie's face dropped. "You can't cancel. We made plans."

"It's complicated."

"Uncomplicate it. I'm leaving on location Saturday night for a week. Did you forget?"

"I didn't. It's just that Kenzie planned a big protest at UCB and she really wants me to be there."

"What kind of protest?"

"One of the researchers received a grant to addict dogs to cocaine. As if we don't have enough people who are addicted, Dr. Sadist is going to force dogs to ingest it. I had told her I'd be there and then spaced out."

"Do you really think you should be part of an animal rights protest?" Charlie was repulsed by the research, but he also didn't want bad publicity. He could see the headlines glaring, *'Charlie Evans' Girlfriend is an Animal Rights Nut!'*

"Yes, I do. And for your information, speaking out against gross injustice and needless animal suffering is very much part of who I am. Did you forget that?"

"No, I didn't. I thought I was more important to you."

"Than what, a protest or my daughter? Because you'll never be more important to me than Kenzie or Ray or for that matter, Mick!"

"You're putting a dog over me? Do you know how insulting that is?" Charlie was working hard at keeping his temper in check as he felt it spiraling out of control. "After all I've done for you and everything I've given you, it's obvious you don't give a shit about me. You're just a typical Marin princess, using me and expecting more without giving me a thing in return."

"Go to hell, Mr. Evans, and don't ever call me again!" Maddie hung up. Her heart was beating so hard she had to steady herself against the wall. Mick came over and put his face on her knee. He looked sad as he stared up at her with his caramel brown eyes. "That's the second person in less than an hour whom I directed to the underworld." She gave him a big kiss on his head and hugged him hard. "You are definitely more valuable than that egomaniac."

After she composed herself, Maddie turned off her cell. She then called Kenzie on the house phone and told her she'd be at the protest. She also apologized for her apparent dereliction of parental duty. Next, she called Tommy and asked if she could hitch a ride over to Berkeley. He was only too happy to pick her up. Once the two calls were out of the way, Maddie had time to contemplate the impact of her fight with Charlie. She wondered if he really meant what he said. No one had ever accused her of being a princess. In their nastiest arguments, Tommy had called her a lot of things, but he never implied she felt entitled.

She knew Charlie would try to reconcile. The man was driven by a need to succeed. He thrived on celebrity worship and he was convinced that the role of a lifetime was predicated on his relationship with her. It was a matter of time before he called or came by. As a precaution, Maddie kept her cellphone turned off. Then she went to the one place where she knew she'd be appreciated.

Once Maddie parked, she texted Priscilla, asking her if she wanted to go out to dinner after her stint at the Marin Women's Center. Her friend replied with a resounding yes.

"What did I just do?" Charlie was pacing back and forth in his hotel room. "I blew the part. Goddamn it, I just blew the goddamn part!" He poured himself another shot of scotch from the crystal decanter in the built-in bar. He added ice and then drank it down like water. It didn't deaden the pain. He was too worked up. Charlie continued to pace, going over the conversation for the umpteenth time. Maddie's cancellation wasn't that bad. In retrospect, she had every right to postpone their plans. If he hadn't crafted Saturday's events in flawless detail, he wouldn't have gotten so angry. He went over the doomed day in his head: A gourmet vegan breakfast at the Top of the Mark in San Francisco's premier hotel, followed by an exclusive tour of the Monet exhibit. The curator himself was going to accompany them. After the museum, a picnic at Golden Gate Park, catered by The Golden Horse, a four-star vegan restaurant. All the while, Charlie's favorite paparazzo was going to capture the romantic day and the many loving looks Charlie would have displayed. At dusk, they would be walking along Ocean Beach. Charlie knew it was corny, but he did miss the ocean and it gave him a chance to perform the piece de resistance: while walking hand in hand, he would take an object out of his pocket to show to Maddie. He would then drop it and on bended knee pick it up and show it to her. He knew the photographer would think he was proposing and the paparazzo would go into overtime, salivating while snapping every angle, every view. The next day, the tabloids would be flush with the photos and rumors would fly. No one would doubt that he was madly in love with Madeleine Mozart. Now, like a flash flood, the perfect scheme was gone. Washed away in a torrent of anger and bruised ego.

After the fifth call, he knew Maddie's phone was off. Even if she picked up, what would he say? A simple sorry wasn't going to cut it. He'd called her a Marin princess. What was he thinking? He knew she wasn't using him. For the second time in a week, Charlie Evans had to come up with another inventive plan. This time it was devising a foolproof way to get Maddie back. Normally, he was good under pressure. Not now. The alcohol dulled his ability to think clearly. He looked out the window. The sky was a vivid, crisp blue. He decided the best approach would be to sit out on his balcony and relax. Let the ideas come to him. He poured himself another scotch and opened the sliding glass door. A gust of cold wind pushed against him. He shivered, ducked back into the room to grab his jacket, and returned to the balcony, prepared to push back.

The Bay Bridge shimmered in the light and the Golden Gate rose gracefully out of the Bay. Charlie had traveled all over the world. He'd driven over London Bridge, the Rialto Bridge in Venice, even the Nanpu Bridge in Shanghai, but the Golden Gate was his favorite. Painted International Orange against the backdrop of the San Francisco Bay and the Pacific Ocean, the bridge's unique beauty and allure were among the things Charlie never grew tired of. As he continued to gaze at it, a flock of bright green parrots flew by, squawking. At first, he thought he was imagining it. Parrots in San

Francisco? Then they flew back towards the Bay Bridge and he got a closer look. Sure enough, they were parrots. Some were all green. Others had carnelian red heads. Without thinking, he speed dialed Maddie's cellphone. When it went straight to voicemail, he remembered that she had turned off her phone. With a heavy sigh, he sat down and stared out at the bay. He said, "Sometimes, you really are a putz, Charlie Evans."

He must have fallen asleep because a knock at the door startled him. With a foggy head, he went over to the door. "Who is it?"

"Your co-star."

Charlie inwardly groaned. The only person he felt like seeing was Maddie and he knew that wasn't possible. Rachel was a most unwelcome guest, but she knew he was there and turning her away wasn't an option. He opened the door expecting her to be dressed in a seductive outfit. Instead, she wore sweats and a UC Berkeley T-shirt. Charlie had to laugh at the irony.

Rachel said, "What's so funny?"

"What are you doing here?"

"The short answer is I'm bored. The long answer...wait, there is no long answer. I'm just bored and was hoping you wanted company. Don't worry, I won't try to ravage you. The last thing I want is some guy yelling rape." Once she walked inside, she got a good look at Charlie. "Are you okay? You look kind of ragged around the edges."

Charlie motioned for her to sit on the couch. He took a seat opposite her on the Queen Anne chair. He stood up again. "Where are my manners? Would you like a drink?"

"Water, please, and get yourself a glass. You look dehydrated."

Once the water was poured, Charlie sat back down and told Rachel about the fight he had with Maddie, omitting the real reason behind his anger.

"I found it odd that you were dating someone older than yourself. Now I find out that she's an animal rights activist and goes to protests at..." she looked down at her T-shirt, "UC Berkeley?"

"I know it sounds bizarre, but I'm crazy about her."

"Do you love her?"

Without thinking, he almost blurted out an emphatic *no*. Then he realized that Rachel handed him the ideal opportunity to spread the rumor. He looked up at her with eyes filled with despair. "Very much. Please help me get her back."

22

"**D**on't you see? Charlie has given you the perfect opportunity to end this charade. You can pursue the hot stepfather without any guilt whatsoever." Priscilla dipped a French fry into a pool of ketchup on her plate and ate it. She washed it down with a slug of beer. She was sitting across from Maddie at Kipler's Tavern and Inn. The waitress arrived with their veggie burgers. She placed the condiment basket in the center of the table.

"Thanks."

"My pleasure. Enjoy, ladies."

Priscilla continued. "Am I right or what?"

"I guess," Maddie said halfheartedly. The truth was, as much as she wanted to be with Jackson, she enjoyed Charlie's company. He was entertaining. She even got used to his impersonations and rattling off quotes from his movies. She dug into her purse and took out her iPhone's headphones. As she methodically folded them, she said, "You know how you can be so careful, folding the wires so they don't bunch up?" She unfurled the headphones and a few knots appeared. "They still get all tangled up." She stuck the jumbled mess back in her purse. "That's how I feel right now. I honestly believed that this whole charade with Charlie would be easy. Why does he have to have such a sexy stepfather?"

Priscilla picked up a French fry and pointed it at Maddie. "Don't blame it all on Jackson. It would have been easier, but you broke the cardinal rule. You slept with him. Tell me *that* didn't change everything."

"I wouldn't say it changed everything. It certainly didn't help my focus." Maddie leaned closer to her friend. "The man is an egotistical nightmare, but when he sheds his clothes and gets in bed, it's all about pleasing me. It's definitely an Oscar-worthy performance. Every time."

"Great orgasm?"

"Like experiencing an entire symphony in thirty seconds."

Priscilla said, "Cymbals, too?"

"Even the glockenspiel."

Priscilla sat back. "Well, Ms. Mozart, I must say that I wouldn't mind being entwined in your tangled mess. It sure beats my snoozer of a life." She took a bite of her burger. "Has Ray had the appointment with the venture capitalist yet?"

"It's this Friday. He's so excited. Every night the kid creates another masterpiece. I don't know how he does it. I'm jazzed when I successfully steam veggies. He made this one snack he calls, Slow Jammin'. He fills filo dough with chive and garlic soft vegan cheese and apricot jam, then sprinkles the top with crushed, toasted almonds. He bakes it until the cheese melts in your mouth."

After dinner, the two parted ways. When Maddie got home, she checked her phone for messages. There was one from Kenzie. She had tried her mom's cell first, then called home to give her the time of the protest. "I also emailed you and Dad with ideas for your signs. I can't wait to see you. Thanks again for coming. Love you."

Maddie had forgotten that she had turned off her cellphone. She activated it and noticed a few missed calls. Four from Charlie. He didn't leave a message. Good. She'd deal with him later.

Ray came out of his room. "Where have you been? I tried calling your cell, but it went straight to voicemail."

"I turned it off. Sorry. Everything okay?"

"Yeah. You want to check out the business plan Dad helped me put together for my meeting with Floyd?"

"Of course."

Ray went back into his room and reappeared with a manila envelope. He sat down next to his mom on the couch and pulled out a small stack of papers. The cover sheet had a photograph of three of Ray's favorite snacks: Chocolate Riptide, S'morb, and Wiffler.

"The cover looks great."

Ray jumped up. "Before we begin, I think it's only fitting that we munch on some Wifflers while reading the plan."

"Sounds good to me."

Ray returned with a plate full of mini-waffle sandwiches filled with mocha-flavored coconut milk whipped cream. Maddie popped one into her mouth.

"I hope you plan on serving these to Floyd."

"Of course, along with the S'morbs and Chocolate Riptides. The guy's going to be blown away."

"I think so, too."

23

"I knew Ray would ace the meeting," Tommy said as he drove over the Richmond-San Rafael Bridge. "You could tell Floyd was impressed. He even asked if he could take some of the snacks back with him for his associates."

Maddie turned to look at the signs on the back seat. Tommy's had a photo of a dog in a lab cage. Underneath it, it read, 'Don't Make Me an Addict.' Maddie's sign declared, 'DOGS DON'T SNORT COKE.'

Maddie said, "I haven't been to a protest in a long time. I'm a little nervous."

"It will be great. Kenzie's expecting at least one hundred fifty people."

Maddie stared out the window, not looking at anything in particular. She hadn't heard from Charlie since their fight. She did tell him not to call her again. Still, she assumed he would. As if he could her mind, Tommy said, "Have you heard from Mr. Holier-than-thou?"

"Who told you about the fight?"

"Ray."

"No, I haven't, and it's fine."

"It's over then?"

"I don't know."

"So…you want to go out to dinner sometime?"

Maddie could feel her blood pressure rising. She knew Tommy wasn't stupid. She also knew he was very aware that this conversation, albeit in different iterations, was one they'd had on numerous occasions. She had a desire to learn Spanish, French, and Italian so she could repeat her answer in multiple languages in the event Tommy no longer understood English. They were about fifteen minutes from the UC campus. The last thing she wanted was a fight, so she turned to her persistent ex and said, "Thomas Dreadsky, I am flattered that you're still interested in being with me. However, I have told you before and this is the last time I will say it. I do not wish to get back together. Not now. Not in the future. If you ask again, you will be met with silence because I've told you how I feel every time you ask. If I do change my mind, I will let you know. Is that clear?"

Tommy nodded and turned on the radio. He didn't speak to Maddie for the rest of the trip. The silence didn't bother her at all.

They were several blocks away when Tommy found a parking spot off Ashby. Still quiet, he grabbed the signs and handed Maddie hers. She thanked him. He gave her a tight smile.

As they approached the grassy area next to the research building that housed Dr. Gaston's lab, Maddie spotted Kenzie next to the dais set up at the far end of the building. She was holding a megaphone in her hand, talking to someone. Maddie began walking toward her. Tommy followed. As they got closer, Kenzie spotted her parents and waved excitedly. The person she was talking to turned around and Maddie's jaw dropped. Tommy tasted blood.

"What the hell?" Tommy said. "Is he trying to upstage our daughter?"

"Down, boy," Maddie responded.

Kenzie ran to meet them. She looked radiant. "You won't believe what Charlie has done. He is unbelievable. Please forgive him, Mom."

"Yes, Mom. Forgive me. I was a selfish idiot." Charlie was wearing sunglasses. His baseball cap was turned backwards. Even though his jeans were distressed, they looked expensive, as did his light blue polo shirt. Amazingly, he wasn't yet recognized by anyone in the crowd.

Tommy rolled his eyes.

"I'm Charlie." He held out his hand.

"Tommy Dreadsky."

"The ex-husband. Nice to meet you."

Maddie said, "What are you doing here, Charlie? I thought you had a reputation to uphold. You don't want your fans thinking you're an animal rights fanatic, do you?"

"Give me a hug first and then I'll tell you everything." He held out his arms and Maddie slid into them. She didn't realize how much she missed him until she felt his body against hers. And his scent. Like woodsy talcum powder. She inhaled deeply.

"They're here! Look!" Kenzie was pointing to the KABC Television van. "I'll be right back. Don't go away." As she headed over to the reporter exiting the van, Maddie turned to Charlie.

"You have thirty seconds."

"I googled the researcher, Gaston. The guy has a grant to…"

"I know that, Charlie. That's why we're here. Why are you here?"

"Because reading about what this asshole is going to do to dogs he got from the shelter made me sick. Bubbles and Georgie were shelter dogs. I wanted to help, so I called Channel 7 and told them I was going to be at a protest at UC Berkeley. And here they are."

He pulled out a piece of paper. "Kenzie asked if I would speak. I told her I couldn't wait."

Maddie wasn't sure if Charlie was an amazing actor or actually felt strongly about the research. His eyes were moist as he held out the paper for Maddie. She took it from him and perused his notes. "I'm really proud of you, Charlie."

Tommy said, "I hope you don't plan to upstage our daughter. She's worked hard on this."

"I don't want to take anything away from Kenzie. I'm here to help bring more awareness to the research. Maybe we can get this creep's grant revoked."

Maddie was about to respond when she saw Kenzie walking up to them with a reporter in tow. Sandra Bell was KABC's top newswoman. The tall, shapely redhead was dressed impeccably in a light gray suit and peach blouse. She was having a hard time keeping up with Kenzie, as her high heels kept sinking into the soft grass.

Kenzie made the introductions. Before she got to Charlie, he went over and gave the reporter a hug. "It's been a while, Sandra. Thank you for showing up."

"Thank you for giving me the exclusive and yes, it's been a very long while. Three years?"

"Three and a half." Charlie turned to Maddie and Tommy. "Sandra covered Jackson's first gallery opening. It was a big event since..." Charlie hesitated.

"Since Jackson Danoff is your stepfather. Your celebrity created the buzz and excitement. It didn't hurt that the man is an extraordinary artist. Will he be here, too?"

Charlie said, "No. He's finalizing the sale of a property that he and Maddie will be turning into an animal sanctuary and women's shelter. There's another exclusive story for you."

"I'm in. Thanks, Charlie." Sandra's cameraman joined the group. He handed the microphone to the reporter and she positioned herself in front of the camera. "Can you give me a summary of what's going to take place?"

Charlie deferred to Kenzie. The founder of Students and Others for Animal Rights, or SOAR, as she liked to call it, ran down the list of speakers and filled Sandra in on the researcher and his cocaine addiction study.

By noon, the protesters were almost two hundred strong. They covered the expansive lawn next to the R.K. Cooley Building. It not only accommodated Dr. Gaston's laboratory. It also housed the labs of other vivisectors. They, too, would eventually be targets of SOAR.

Kenzie nervously walked up to the microphone. She tapped it a couple of times to check if it was on. Looking out at the crowd, then the television camera, she was excited and anxious, praying she didn't forget her speech. After welcoming everyone, Kenzie recounted the nature of Gaston's research and vowed, with the public's help, to shut down his lab. Then she introduced Charlie. The crowd erupted into earnest applause as he walked over to the microphone.

"I'll be honest with you. This was not how I envisioned spending my Saturday. I have very few days off from filming and I wanted to take my girlfriend, Madeleine Mozart, to the opening of the Monet exhibit in the city. I had an amazing vegan lunch planned and our dinner was orchestrated down to the biodynamic wine. She cancelled on me because her daughter, Kenzie, coordinated this event to protest Dr. Neil Gaston's plans to addict twelve dogs to cocaine, then kill them and study their brains. I was angry. Not at the vivisectionist. At Madeleine! Why would she rather stand outside on this rather chilly day and hold up a sign for hours in an attempt to stop research that could help human addicts? I don't know about you, but that sounds anti-science to me. Human lives are worth more than animals' lives, right?

"Curious, I began looking up animal addiction studies. What I found sickened me. My belief about vivisection was blown apart. I had always been told that animal research was necessary. Why else would the government spend millions of dollars in grants so vivisectors could addict rats, monkey, dogs, cats, even sheep, to marijuana, cocaine, heroin, and methamphetamines? I'm sure I'm preaching to the choir, but I had no idea about the massive number of experiments involving the imprisonment, pain, and immense suffering and death of billions of animals that yield no usable results. These animals don't take drugs. They are forced to. Dr. Gaston's test subjects are shelter dogs. Some of these animals were pets. They lived in a home. They were cared for. Now they're sitting in small cages. They're scared. They're confused. And if we don't stop this, they're going to be carved up, their brains dissected. Their bodies discarded. For what? So Gaston can write up a paper on the effects of cocaine on dogs' brains?

"The office of National Drug Control Policy estimates the number of chronic cocaine users in the United States at 3.6 million. That's a hell of a lot of users. Do we really need to addict animals when we have so many human addicts? If Dr. Gaston is serious about helping humans, he should be conducting studies with them, not dogs. Not sucking up taxpayer money and disguising it as necessary research.

"My publicist split a gut when he found out that I was speaking at this protest. 'You're going to destroy your reputation,' he said. I told him if I have to turn a blind eye to needless animal suffering in the guise of research at one of the country's most prestigious universities, then my fans aren't the compassionate, caring people I thought they were. I am asking everyone here and everyone watching to please stop this research. Put Dr. Gaston and all the others out of a job and let's find homes for every one of those dogs. I will personally adopt two of them." Charlie looked over at Maddie. She was standing next to her daughter. Both were wiping their eyes.

"Maddie, thank you for choosing the animals over me today. You are an inspiration and I hope one day to be as kindhearted as you." He blew her a kiss.

As Charlie stepped away from the dais, the crowd erupted in wild applause. He paused and waved, silently thanking Rachel for writing the majority of his speech. He had always assumed that she was an airhead, like so many other young, gorgeous actresses. It was during their collaboration on his presentation that he realized the woman was smart *and* articulate.

Kenzie gave Charlie a big hug, then went up to announce the next speaker. Tommy had been watching Maddie as Charlie gave his speech, which made him dislike the man even more.

Maddie met Charlie as he walked toward her. "Well, knock me over with a feather. That was downright impressive."

Before he could respond, people began to converge on the couple. Some asked for his autograph. Others wanted to congratulate him on his speech and welcome him into the fold. Maddie tried to get away and let Charlie bask in the glory. He grabbed her hand and wouldn't let go. The gesture was touching. Once again, the lines were blurring between conniving Charlie and sincere Charlie.

Three hours later, the protest was nearly over. Two other major networks caught wind of Charlie Evans' presence and covered the last two hours of the event. Kenzie checked her emails throughout the protest and was overwhelmed by the inquiries she was receiving. She was certain the membership in SOAR would increase dramatically. A voice message she had anticipated and wasn't looking forward to returning was from Peter Van Leaves, the Vice Chancellor for Research. He requested a call back at her earliest convenience.

Tommy walked over to Maddie. "I'm going to take off. Did you want a ride home?"

"No, thanks. I'll get one with Charlie." She looked over her shoulder to where her daughter was packing up the electronic equipment. She was reeling up the wire while Charlie held the amp and microphone. They were chatting like old friends.

Tommy said, "Good luck. As much as I hate him, he seems like a good guy."

"Drive safely." She watched the father of her children walk away, his shoulders a little hunched. A tightness gripped her chest. She hoped he wouldn't break his sobriety to ease whatever pain he was feeling. She picked up her phone and dialed Ray.

"Hey, Mom. How'd the protest go?"

"Better than expected. Charlie showed up and wowed everyone with an amazing speech. Kenzie was fantastic. Three major networks covered it. Too bad you missed it. I have a favor to ask. Would you please go to your dad's? I don't think he should be alone tonight."

"Charlie envy?"

"I think so."

"Sure. I'll go over, but you know, Dad's not your responsibility. Or mine. We can't always monitor him and ultimately, he'll do what he wants."

"You're absolutely right. Checking up on him alleviates my guilt."

"Because you divorced him?"

"Yeah."

"Please don't feel guilty. You did the right thing. Dad's sobriety is in his hands, not ours. Still, I'll bring a movie and snacks."

"Thanks, kiddo. I love you."

"Love you, too."

Kenzie ran over to her mother. "Charlie's taking us to Five Four Three! I've been dying to go there ever since they opened, but it's so expensive. Is that cool or what?"

Five Four Three was vegan celebrity chef Dante Jance's new restaurant. It had opened the previous year on University Drive, two blocks from the campus. Northern California vegans felt like they won the lottery, since Jance had sold his Los Angeles restaurant to move up north and create his culinary masterpieces for Bay Area diners.

"Sounds great, but I've heard the waiting list is two weeks out."

"One of the waiters was at the protest. He called Dante and told him that Charlie was speaking. Dante personally invited us to dinner. In the meantime, Charlie asked me for a tour of the campus."

"I've always wanted to see the UC campus," Charlie said as he gave Maddie a light kiss. "You don't mind, do you?"

Maddie laughed. "Who are you and where have you stuffed

Charlie Evans?"

"Hey, now. What's so unusual about wanting to get a private tour of the campus by the president of SOAR?" Charlie said.

"Nothing. Sorry I said anything. Kenzie, lead on."

The university's grounds were fairly quiet. With the exception of the protest, not much was happening on campus. Kenzie took her guests on a two-hour walk, stopping along the way to rest their feet. When they arrived at Five Four Three, they were personally greeted by Dante Jance. He was tall, with an athletic build. Tattoos decorated his arms. If it weren't for a close-shaven beard, the thirty-five-year-old would have looked like a teenager. Having had a restaurant in Los Angeles frequented by celebrities, Jance administered the perfect amount of praise for Charlie without gushing. He did congratulate Kenzie for a well-organized protest and promised to lodge his own complaint over the research with the university.

In a private room, the three began their culinary journey with a grapefruit, kiwi and Campari aperitif. Kenzie's was alcohol-free. Three appetizers later, they were served seitan marinated in a white wine broth with chanterelle mushrooms over Himalayan red rice. Charlie had been eating vegan with Maddie since they met and he enjoyed and even raved about some of the food. Jance's dishes defied the ordinary. They were brilliant. His pairings were unique and the sauces transcendent.

A happy groan emanated from all three when they were served a vegan cheesecake topped with cherries jubilee. There was still half a bottle of Mount Helena Chardonnay on the table.

Maddie touched her stomach. "I am ready to pop, but I have to try that cheesecake."

Charlie agreed. "I heard it calling my name."

"The five women at that table in the next room are calling your name, not the cheesecake," said Maddie as she took a bite of the rich dessert. "I could live off this! It's so creamy and smooth."

Kenzie said, "Tell us the truth, Charlie, is it a thrill to have so many people – women – desire you, or does it get old and tedious?"

Charlie felt fantastic. He was back in Maddie's good graces, his speech was broadcast on all three networks speaking out for animals and singing the praises of his girlfriend, and he was coming to the close of one of the best dining experiences of his life. Normally, he had an insatiable craving for the acceptance of others. His fans fed his ego, an ego that needed massive amounts of fuel. Tonight, he sat in a private dining room with two people who made him forget that he was a megastar. He took a bite of cheesecake, closed his eyes, and savored the flavor.

"This can't be vegan," he said.

Kenzie persisted. "It is, and you're not answering my question."

"The truth?"

"No. Lie through your straight, white teeth."

He gave Kenzie a big smile. "There are times when I want to be able to go out and enjoy myself without being asked for my autograph or posing with a complete stranger for a picture. Then I remember the time my mom took me to the movies. I was twelve. We went to see *Back to the Future*. Afterwards, we had dinner at Cooper's Landing Bar & Grill. Sitting across the room was Harrison Ford. The restaurant wasn't crowded. Maybe four or five other tables were occupied. My mom talked me into asking him for his autograph. I remember thinking that I didn't want to disturb him. He was with a group of people and, believe it or not, I was a pretty shy kid. After some prodding, I reluctantly walked over to the table with a pen and paper and introduced myself. I said I would really love his autograph. I braced myself for a verbal lashing. Instead, Harrison asked me my name and then took the pen and paper from me and wrote, 'To Charlie, your friend, Harrison Ford.' I was stoked. Years later, I worked with Harrison on the movie, *A Stranger Vision*. He didn't remember me, but I'll always remember how he handled himself with grace and patience. If I can make someone happy with my signature or a photo, I'll gladly do it."

Kenzie said, "That was a lovely story. You still didn't answer my question. Do you get tired of being wanted by so many women or do you thrive on it?"

"It gets old, especially when you're happy and content with just one." He turned to Maddie and looked at her adoringly. Meanwhile, the table of women in the other room were getting more demonstrative in their quest to get Charlie's attention. Normally, Maddie would have found their behavior rude. Tonight, she found it amusing. She got up and went over to the table.

"Ladies, would you like me to get a picture of you with Charlie Evans?" A resounding 'Hell, yeah!' emanated from the five women. There was a blur of activity. Brushes, lipstick, and breath mints were grabbed out of purses and furiously used. One woman was so flustered, she flung a tampon, along with a lipstick and nail file, from her purse. The small, white 'bullet' fell into her wine glass. Fortunately, Charlie was still in the other room. When they were finished primping, Maddie motioned for Charlie to come over while she was handed five cellphones. Phone after phone, she snapped photos of her boyfriend as he posed with the women. A couple were bold, striking provocative positions, while the others simply beamed. After the last shot was taken, both were thanked profusely.

Kenzie said, "Harrison Ford would be so proud of you."

Charlie turned to Maddie. "She definitely inherited your sarcasm."

"I've heard that a lot, especially from her father."

Dante poked his head into the room. "So, how was it?"

"Amazing. If I lived up here, this would be my go-to restaurant."

"Thank you. I am honored. Ladies?"

Maddie said, "The best food I've ever had. As a matter of fact, the word food is too pedestrian a description for what you created."

"I agree one hundred percent," Kenzie added.

Dante took a bow. "You are too kind. Mr. Evans, if you have another chance to dine with us before you leave the Bay Area, dinner will be on me, again. You two are invited, as well."

Charlie said, "I insist on paying."

"Absolutely not. I invited you all here."

"At least let me leave a tip for the waiter." Charlie took out a $100 bill and placed it on the table. He shook Dante's hand. "Again, thank you for a fantastic meal. Are you sure the cheesecake was vegan?"

Dante laughed. "I get asked that a lot. I assure you it is. I loved cheesecake as a kid. I was determined to perfect the non-dairy version. It took a while, but it was worth it."

Charlie said, "Is it possible to buy one to take with me on location? We're shooting up in Mendocino for a week and I'd really like to wow the cast."

"That is entirely possible, but you're not paying for it. Let everyone know it's from Five Four Three. That's payment enough."

With cheesecake in hand, they walked back to the car. Charlie dropped Kenzie off at her apartment, then drove over the Richmond-San Rafael Bridge, back to Marin County.

"This is our last night together before I leave for a week." Charlie put his arms around Maddie's waist and pulled her to him. "Shall we make it memorable?"

"I hate to break the mood, but we're going to have to wait a while. I'm still so full that the night will be memorable for all the wrong reasons."

"Why don't we play gin rummy to pass the time? I'm in a winning mood."

"That's funny. I'm in a winning mood, too. Have a seat and I'll get the cards." Charlie sat on the couch and unbuttoned the top button of his jeans. He could hear Maddie opening and closing drawers in the kitchen. Then she went into Ray's room and came out with a deck of cards. "I couldn't find mine so we're going to have to use Ray's."

Confused, Charlie said, "Are they dirty?"

"Dirty? No. Juvenile, yes. Shuffle."

Charlie rifled through the cards. The design on the back was a psychedelic marijuana leaf. It looked like it was pulsating. The kings, queens, and jacks all sported red eyes and they wore silly grins. Instead of typical face card garb, the jacks were dressed like surfers, the queens wore flower wreaths in their long, flowing hair, peasant tops and patchwork skirts, and the kings looked like hippies. Their ripped jeans and T-shirts perfectly complemented Birkenstock sandals. Charlie put the cards up to his face and inhaled. "I don't believe it. They smell like pot. Are they made with marijuana?"

"No. I believe you're experiencing remnant fumes from the last time the cards were used. Ray and his friends like to get high and play poker."

"What a shocker." Charlie shuffled the cards. "Ready to lose?"

"For now."

24

It had been two days since Charlie had left with the cast and crew for Mendocino. His presence at the protest did more than highlight Dr. Gaston's research. It opened the innocent and naïve eyes of the general public, shining a harsh light on a sector of the research community, revealing the sterile living conditions of the dogs and the brutality of administering cocaine to unwilling participants. It forced the president of the university, who would have otherwise defended the researcher's work, to suspend the testing until further notice.

PETA, Last Chance for Animals, and other animal rights organizations took advantage of the publicity and urged their members to sign petitions to stop the research, call their congressperson to stop funding, and call the university president to pressure him into firing Neil Gaston. They knew that the public's attention span was short and their window of opportunity brief.

As Rachel predicted, and much to Gretchen's dismay, Charlie's vocal adoration of Maddie made headlines. A photo of the two of them was encapsulated in a big heart on the cover of *The Globe*. Not to be outdone, *The National Enquirer* created a montage of Charlie and Maddie in various romantic poses. The headline read, '*Love is in the Air*.'

Filming three hours northwest of San Francisco, Charlie was barely aware of the impact his speech had made. He was up at dawn and in bed late at night, and the television in his room sat cold and lifeless. His agent called him the second night of shooting and told him about the tabloids pushing the relationship to the next level. Charlie was thrilled. He was also interested in knowing what impact he had had at the protest. When Donna told him, it was the second best news he'd heard that night.

For Maddie, the tabloid photos were disturbing. Charlie Evans was speaking out against animal cruelty and they chose to cover their relationship. She knew the rags were only interested in scandal, celebrity gossip, and the latest from Hollywood's elite. Still, she hoped they would mention the protest. She also realized that Charlie was winning the bet. As wonderful as her time with Charlie had been, her resentment quivered just below the surface of her emotions. It was only when she was in bed with him that she turned off her antipathy and thoroughly enjoyed herself.

Maddie grabbed her easel and placed it under the mimosa tree in the yard. She had just finished setting up the paints and turned on the CD player when her cell rang. It was Jackson.

A big smile involuntarily appeared on her face. "Hey, stranger."

"Are my ears deceiving me or do I hear Percy Faith's *A Summer Place* in the background?"

Maddie laughed. "Don't judge me, but yes you do."

"My parents had all his albums."

"So did mine! His music helps me relax and it brings back really fond memories of growing up in suburban America. We were very white, very middle-class, and apparently very easy to please musically."

Jackson said, "Don't sell Percy short. They may play his musical arrangements in elevators and in retirement homes, but *A Summer Place* is a classic. My favorite is *Beautiful Obsession*. I get this flashback of clowning around in the pool with my friend, Steve Olsen. I think I was seven or eight. My parents and their best friends, the Levitts, were poolside, drinking mai tais, smoking Winston cigarettes, and playing bridge. Percy was playing on the stereo in the living room. My dad hooked up speakers outside. The quality wasn't very good, but then the stereo wasn't either. Still, it set the mood. Hearing it is like comfort food."

"It's comfort music."

"Exactly. So, do you feel like taking a drive up to Sycamore Animal Sanctuary? Trini said she'd give me some last minute pointers and tips, plus she wanted me to meet her latest resident, a calf she named after me."

Maddie wanted to unwind. She could feel the tension in her shoulders starting to creep up into her neck. The antidote was painting. She had been looking forward to it for days. The timing was ripe as Ray was at Tommy's and she had the house to herself. The last thing she felt like doing was sitting in a car for hours. She also didn't want 'Trini' to be alone with Jackson.

"Trini?"

"Trinity. She said all her friends call her Trini. Are you up for a road trip?"

Maddie could feel the green monster usurping her serene day. "You bet. I'll even bring some treats that Ray left for me. How do White Shrubs and S'morbs sound?"

"Really weird, but I trust you. Shall I pick you up in two hours?"

"Sure. Thanks for the invite."

"Of course. You're my partner."

It would take her twenty minutes, tops, to get dressed and dolled up, so Maddie figured she had at least an hour and a half to paint. She hit the 'back' arrow on the CD player so she could hear *A Summer Place* from the beginning. As Percy's orchestra lulled her into a calmer zone, she mixed the acrylics with water and thought about what she wanted to paint. She closed her eyes and let her mind decide. It shuffled through images, then stopped at one. Maddie opened her eyes and began.

Cleaning the brushes, Maddie glanced at the clock. She had ten minutes before Jackson showed up. Hastily, she packed up the easel and set it down in the dining room.

The painting clothes were pulled off and replaced with a pair of pants lying on the floor. She thought better of wearing the crumpled T-shirt on the chair and took a little bit more time to pick out a wrinkle-free and slightly sexy shirt. The Eat Your Ethics tee was just tight enough to accentuate her figure. Next stop: the bathroom. With less than five minutes to go, Maddie applied color to her freshly scrubbed face. Moisturizer was followed by concealer, then a light brush of blush on her cheekbones. Mascara, barely visible copper eye shadow, and a pencil-thin line of dark brown eyeliner transformed her eyes. Tinted lip balm finished off her new face. She brushed her hair, adjusted the bangs and declared to no one in particular that she was ready to go.

Maddie heard three sharp horn blasts. She grabbed her coat and went out the door. She was halfway down the walkway when she realized that she had forgotten the snacks. Maddie ran back and grabbed the bag in the refrigerator marked 'R' instead of 'M'.

"Sorry. I almost forgot to bring these." She held up the brown paper bag, then stuck it in her purse.

"No problem." Jackson was wearing jeans with a black pullover. He had on aviator sunglasses. Maddie swore he looked like he'd walked out of a *Vanity Fair* magazine ad. "Do you mind if I eat one now? I didn't have breakfast."

"Of course not." Maddie pulled a White Shrub out of the bag. She unwrapped it and handed it to Jackson. He regarded it as if it were an alien life form.

"Explain what it is before I eat it."

"Ray toasted white tea leaves, then poured raw almond butter on them to hold the leaves together. He added sliced bananas sprinkled with raw cacao. Finally, it was lightly dusted with pink Himalayan sea salt. He stuck them in the freezer for a couple of hours, then transferred them to the fridge."

Jackson took a bite. "Interesting. It's crunchy and sweet, slightly tart and salty. I never thought I'd be eating a tea leaf sandwich." He took another bite as he turned onto the freeway onramp. "I really like it. There's another taste that I can't put my finger on. Are you sure there's nothing else in it?"

"Tea leaves, cacao, almond butter, bananas, and salt. I think that's it." Maddie took another White Shrub out of the bag, unwrapped it and took a small bite. She looked at the bag and her face reddened. "Unless I'm wrong, the mystery flavor is marijuana. I grabbed Ray's bag instead of mine. I am so sorry!" Maddie expected to get verbally pummeled. Instead, Jackson finished the last of his leaf sandwich and licked his lips.

"I haven't gotten stoned in a long time. This should be interesting. Do you know how long it takes when you eat it?"

"About an hour to an hour and a half, but you ate it on an empty stomach, so you may start to feel altered within the next fifteen to twenty minutes. Let me know if you want me to drive. I can't believe I grabbed the wrong bag." Maddie re-wrapped the White Shrub and stuck it in the bag. "It's safe to assume that the S'morbs are laced with weed, too. I apologize. Ray is a cross between Emeril and Wavy Gravy."

"Honestly, I'm fine." He turned on the radio and Bruce Springsteen's *Dancing in the Dark* filled the car. Jackson turned up the volume.

When the song was over, Maddie said, "Can I ask you a question?"

"Sure." He turned off the radio.

"Does creating the sanctuary scare you? Do you find it overwhelming?"

"Not at all. I grew up in a family of entrepreneurs. Taking chances is in my blood. Are you scared?"

Maddie shifted uncomfortably in her seat. "I have to admit that as much as the project thrills me and what we'll be doing is what I've always dreamed of, the enormity of it does give me pause. You may have grown up with risk takers. I was raised in a household where caution and a traditionalist attitude were pervasive. Leaving the table before dinner was over made me nervous. What if my plate is taken away? Will someone eat my food? Crazy, huh?

"It's not crazy. It's called playing it safe and a good many people adhere to that principle and it serves them well. If they have regrets, then they weren't being true to themselves." Jackson looked at Maddie. She looked anxious. "Don't worry. Our sanctuary is going to be spectacular."

Maddie gently took the painting out of her tote bag. "I don't want to distract you, but I'd like to show you what I made before we get to Sycamore."

Jackson looked over at the eight-by-ten painting. A small black and white calf stood in a meadow, its eyes a deep blue-violet, the same color as Jackson's. "It's the calf at the sanctuary that was named after you."

Jackson had a strange look on his face. "Is it a hologram?"

Maddie looked at the calf, then put it back in her tote. "Sir, you are stoned."

"It hasn't been fifteen minutes."

"Everyone's different. When the freeway starts looking like a hologram, it's time to pull over and let me drive."

Jackson looked at Maddie. "First of all, thank you for the portrait of me as a calf. You totally got my eye color. Second, I…wait, what did you say to me?" Jackson glanced in his rear view mirror. His heart started pounding. "Is that a cop behind me?" He looked at the speedometer. He was going five miles over the speed limit.

Maddie turned around and, sure enough, a Highway Patrol car was a good ten car lengths behind them. "It is indeed. You okay?"

"Nope. Major paranoia is setting in. You need to drive." Without incident, he reduced his speed, pulled off at the next exit, and they changed places. By the time they got back on the road, Maddie was beginning to feel the pot's effects. She was grateful that she only took a small bite. She also opted not to tell Jackson, since he might force her to stop driving.

Jackson pushed the lever and moved the seat back to accommodate his long legs. "The last time I was stoned was five years ago. The chemo made Jackie nauseous, so she asked me get her some pot to help her get her appetite back. We had so much fun getting high. I bought her all the food she loved and together we had a feast."

He closed his eyes, then opened them and said, "If I got cancer, I wouldn't do chemo or radiation. I watched my wife slowly and painfully die while the doctors stuck a needle in her arm and pumped her full of chemicals. Chemo therapy. Chemical therapy. It's sick, really. Think about it. Cancer is the result of a weak immune system. Instead of getting the patient's body stronger, they infuse it with a toxic soup. It kills the good cells and it kills the bad cells. And when they're done ravaging the body, the good doctors don't recommend anything to build up the immune system which has been raped. Beaten into the ground. Jackie said food had a metallic taste for months after the chemo."

"I absolutely agree. A friend of mine was diagnosed with breast cancer and the doctors did everything they could to convince her to go the traditional route: slash and burn. She refused. Even her parents and friends were mad at her for making a decision they felt was foolish. She went on a journey of alternative therapies, switching to a raw vegan diet and meditation, visualization, and yoga. A year later, the cancer was gone. That was six years ago. She veers from the raw part every once in a while, but has stayed vegan and even wrote a cookbook." She quickly glanced over at Jackson. He met her gaze with very red eyes. "How are you doing?"

"Totally loaded. Off the charts loaded."

"Is it the kind of stoned where you feel like you may never come out of it?"

Jackson thought about it. A look of worry crossed his face. "Can that happen?"

"No. You feel like it, though."

"Shit. I do. How long do you think this will last?"

Maddie said, "It should be gone before we get to the sanctuary. Or not. Ray's pot is strong. It's a special strain that one of his friends grows. I think it's called Devil's Breath. I suggest you sit back and enjoy the experience."

Jackson stared out the window for what felt like an eternity. The scenery was a blur, yet the colors fascinated him. He watched a hawk flying over a field, scanning for its lunch. Suddenly, it dove into the tall grass and came out with something in its talons. "Whoa! Did you see that?"

Maddie laughed. "I'm driving, remember? What did you see that was so riveting?"

"Oh, you may not want to know. It had to do with a hawk."

"Did it catch something?"

Jackson nodded.

"The hawk has to survive. I'm glad I didn't see it, but it is part of nature."

"I think Trini likes me."

Hawk. Prey. Good segue. "You think? She *really* likes you. Can you blame her?"

"Am I what you ladies would call a catch?" He gave her a big, dopey smile, but Maddie thought he looked cute.

"As a matter of fact, I got together with the ladies last night and we were all exclaiming what a catch you were, but we also decided that Trinity is too young for you."

Jackson didn't answer. In her slightly altered state, she felt his eyes boring through her. It was uncomfortable and strangely satisfying at the same time.

Finally, he spoke. "You like me, don't you?"

"Of course I do! You're my sanctuary partner," Maddie replied, her voice higher than normal.

"You don't have to yell, Maddie. I'm right here."

Before she could answer, Jackson pointed to the roof. "I'm also here and over there and under the hood. I'm everywhere." Jackson leaned over Maddie and pushed the button to the sunroof. Once it opened, he looked up. "I'm even up there." He stared into the light blue sky.

Relieved that Jackson's attention span was being controlled by Devil's Breath, she turned on the radio and began hunting for a station. She stopped at the first one that had decent reception.

"You're listening to KRON, where we play the hits of today and oldie moldies of yesterday. Here's one I dusted off for all you grandmas and grandpas out there. Don't operate any heavy machinery listening to this romping tune."

A Summer Place by Percy Faith streamed through the radio. They looked at each other in disbelief. Maddie said, "I got chills!"

"Me, too, grandma. Look." He held out his arm and, sure enough, little goosebumps could be seen just under the light brown hair. "Gramps is going to lie back and take in the aural experience. See you when Percy puts the baton down."

As Maddie closed the sunroof to shut out the sound of the wind, Jackson adjusted the seat so it was almost horizontal. He turned up the sound and closed his eyes. Maddie wished she could do the same. Instead, she listened to the song for the third time that day and felt incredibly grateful that her life was unfolding in such a positive way. Even the thought of dealing with her eventual breakup with Charlie didn't seem so bad. She looked at Jackson, his eyes closed, smiling. She wondered where his mind was taking him. She had an urge to put her hand on his. Someday, she thought.

Maddie pulled the car into the parking lot at Sycamore Animal Sanctuary. She gave Jackson a nudge to wake him up. "We're here."

Jackson slowly sat up. Disoriented, he took off his sunglasses and looked out the window. "I am so thirsty."

"I bet. How do you feel?"

"Still off-gassing."

"That sounds gross."

"Sorry. In college, when we would be coming off an intense high, we would say we were still off-gassing, meaning we're not really stoned but we're not normal." He ran his hands through his hair and put his glasses back on. "Let's do this."

Trinity greeted them with a barely perceptible look of disappointment when she saw Jackson wasn't alone. Maddie caught it. She smiled extra big when shaking Trinity's hand.

"Could I trouble you for a glass of water?" Jackson asked.

"Me, too, please."

"Be right back." Trinity disappeared into another room and came back with two tall glasses of water. They eagerly accepted them, thanked her, and emptied the glasses in less than thirty seconds.

"Wow. Did you run here?"

"Feels like it," said Jackson. "Before we get into the nuts and bolts of sanctuary operations, I'd love to meet my namesake."

"Of course." Walking at a fast clip, Trinity led them to the cow barn where, in a small enclosure in front, stood a baby Holstein. Delighted that he had company, he trotted up to them, nuzzling Trinity with his pink nose covered with a smattering of black freckles. He looked up at her with his large brown eyes, his eyelashes long and white. "Hello Jackson Junior," she said as she petted him.

Jackson knelt down so he was at eye level with the calf. He put his hand out and Junior sucked on his fingers. "Is this normal?"

"For a baby it is," Trinity said. "Contrary to popular belief, cow's milk is for a baby cow. These little guys and gals are born and before they have a chance to nurse, the farmer takes them away from their mothers, leaving all that nutritious milk for humans. If the calf is male, he becomes a beef cow or is stuck in a small enclosure his entire life and becomes a veal calf. He's fed a low-iron diet so the meat retains its pinkish-white color. When the calf is eighteen to twenty weeks old, he's killed. Slaughterhouse workers report that as these babies are led to slaughter, they're still trying to find their mamas' teats, and suck on the workers' fingers.

"If the calf is female, she becomes like her mother, a milk

machine. She's constantly impregnated, her udder unnaturally large and heavy because of the growth hormones she's fed. An average dairy cow produces about 100 pounds of milk per day. That's ten times more than she would normally produce. After four to five years, she's done. She's dried up. She's sent to slaughter."

Maddie was aware of the dairy industry's inhumane practices. Jackson was not. As Junior continued to suck on his finger, he looked into the eyes of this two-week-old baby and felt a profound sadness. As his eyes welled up with tears, he was grateful to be wearing sunglasses. "Hey there, fella. Are you hungry?" Jackson looked at Trinity. "What do you feed him?"

"He's bottle-fed a calf formula. When Jackson Junior first arrived, we tried to introduce him to the other cows. Instead of socializing, he stood next to the fence and cried for his mother for days. It was heartbreaking. It took a while, but he started warming up to the other residents." Trinity pointed to a sheep in the meadow. "That's Wanda. She sort of adopted Jackson Junior. They hang out together. It's very sweet."

As if on cue, Wanda headed over to the barn and made a beeline for Jackson Junior. The calf nuzzled against her body while Wanda licked his head and face.

"I can't wait until we have our own stable of animals," said Jackson.

Maddie said, "I agree. Plus, we have the advantage of educating our shelter residents on eating a plant-based diet. Can you imagine the impact it could have when they leave the sanctuary and bring their knowledge and, hopefully, new diet to others?"

Back in the office, Trinity had lunch prepared for the three of them while she went over in finer detail the care of the animals, feeding routines, average monthly veterinary costs, and the various other requirements for running a sanctuary. Maddie wasn't sure if it was her imagination, but it seemed like Trinity was directing her instructions to Jackson, even though she was told that Maddie would have a hand in managing the sanctuary.

When they were ready to leave, Trinity said, "There's one more thing I want to show you."

Behind the office, in a cardboard box, lay a cat nursing four kittens. The mother was a calico. She was very thin and didn't look well. Trinity gently stroked her. "We found her in the box only last week. Up until then, no one recalls seeing her."

Jackson said, "Will the mother survive? She looks sick."

Trinity replied, "We're making sure she's well-fed by supplementing her food with vitamins. Believe it or not, she looked worse a week ago. I think she'll make it."

Maddie went to pet one of the kittens and the mother emitted a faint hiss. It was a weak attempt to protect her babies, but Maddie retracted her hand out of respect. "They're so cute, especially the calico. It reminds me of a cat I had growing up. Her name was Semi-sweet because she was. Sometimes, she'd let you snuggle with her and other times she'd scratch you for trying to pet her. What are you going to do with them?"

"Ironically, the only one that no one wanted was the calico. I shouldn't say that. The other three were chosen and little Semi-sweet here was left. Do you want her? I'd be happy to bring her down to you when I come to the sanctuary. I could time the visit with her weaning period, in a couple of weeks."

Maddie said, "Let me think about it. I have a boxer and I don't know how he'd react to a kitten. He's never been around cats before."

"Does he like to chase squirrels?"

"Not that I know of."

"That's a good start. Check out the ASPCA's website. They have a great article on how to introduce a cat or kitten to your dog. If it sounds like something you would like to do, let me know."

Maddie was touched. "Thanks, Trinity."

"You can call me Trini. All my friends do." Maddie was growing to like the woman until she saw her give Jackson a sly smile.

"We really should be getting back. Thanks again for all your help. You've gone above and beyond the call of duty." Maddie started to walk in the direction of the car.

"My pleasure. The more animal sanctuaries, the better. I dream of a day when we won't have to create homes for farm animals. Factory farms will be a thing of the past, a huge blight on human history."

Jackson said, "I hope that dream becomes a reality in my

lifetime."

"Fingers crossed."

While you're at it, keep your legs crossed, Maddie thought to herself. She almost laughed out loud at the absurdity of her attitude. Instead, she said to Jackson, "Do you want me to drive?"

"I'm fine, thanks."

On the road, Maddie pulled out a S'morb. "How about a little dessert?"

"You're kidding, right?"

"Yeah. Would you like to take it home and have it at a later date?"

Jackson thought about it. "I have to admit, it was fun once I relaxed."

"What do you mean? Once you relaxed, you fell asleep!"

"Before that. I remember our conversation and listening to Percy Faith. I forgot how everything is so much more intense when you're stoned. Tell you what. I'll take the loaded treat only if you and Charlie come over and eat it with me. I don't want to get high alone."

"Deal."

25

"Cut!"

Vicente wanted to wring Charlie's neck. It was the tenth take and the director could tell that his leading man wasn't into it. Rachel lay on the bed, her semi-naked body draped in satin sheets. She rolled her eyes as John walked over, deliberately holding his temper in check. He didn't need to look at his watch. It was late and he had hoped to wrap up the scene three hours ago.

"Too hot? Not cold enough in the room? What's the problem, Charlie?"

Charlie sat up and ran his fingers through his hair. His game was off. He couldn't concentrate and he knew why. Dating 'normal' women was easy. He didn't have to worry about their diet. They ate what he ate. They didn't share him with their children because they didn't have any. Conversations were simple. Easy to understand. With Maddie, Charlie was introduced to a different dimension, a totally alien lifestyle. If someone told him that he would be speaking at an animal rights protest, blasting a university researcher, he would have laughed at the absurdity of their claim. An older woman with teenage children, all of whom were vegan, seeped into his life. His heart. He was like a kid watching a sci fi movie for the first time with rapt fascination. He couldn't tear himself away from the screen and when it was over, he wanted more. He wanted Maddie and her loopy dog and her stoned son and activist daughter in his life.

"Hello? Charlie?" Vicente stood over him, eyes intense and tired.

"Give me a minute." Charlie went over to Grace, the make-up artist. "Can I borrow your cell?"

She dug into her pocket and handed it to him. From memory,

Charlie dialed. Three rings and she picked up.

"Hello?"

"Maddie, it's me. Charlie."

"Are you okay?"

"No."

Maddie sat up and turned on the light. Brightness filled the room and she squinted as it hit her eyes. She turned it off. "What happened?"

"I really miss you." He sounded like a lovesick teenager.

She looked at her alarm clock. "It's after two in the morning. Is the cast and crew tearing up Mendocino's bars, wreaking havoc, Hollywood style?"

"I'm on the set, wishing you were here. You want to come up?"

"Right now?"

"Sure. Why not? Live a little. Draw outside the lines. In less than three hours, we could be having hot, carnal sex. I miss that body."

Under Charlie's influence, Maddie didn't draw outside the lines, she created her own. Never in her life had she taken the chances she had or spoken her mind so radically. She also had never deceived so many people on such a grand scale. And now, one of the world's most famous movie stars was practically begging her to visit him on the set. At two in the morning. The thought of driving through the mountains in the middle of the night did sound romantic.

"Aren't you going to be on the set when I get there?"

"Hold on." Charlie yelled to Vicente, "If we get this shot, when will you want us on the set tomorrow, I mean later today?"

"Give me a scene I can use and we won't start shooting until the afternoon. One o'clock."

Charlie said to Maddie, "Get your little ass up here and we'll have until one."

Excitement started to build as Maddie anticipated their reunion. "I'll throw some things together and head out. I can't believe I'm doing this. It's crazy!"

"Good crazy, right? And don't worry about bringing a lot of clothes. You can go shopping and buy whatever you want. I'll see you soon." He was about to hang up when he heard Maddie say,

"Where are you staying?"

He laughed. "That would help. I'm at the White Pines Inn, room 45."

"Got it. Here's to extemporaneity."

"If you say so." Charlie thanked Grace for the use of her phone. Excitement and anticipation replaced his anxiety. He practically bounded into the bed, kneeing Rachel in the thigh. She let out a yell and rubbed her leg.

As Vicente shot the scene for the eleventh and last time, he was in awe of the radical turnaround in Charlie's focus. The actor nailed it. No one could hear his conversation with Maddie, but the director could guess whom he had called and the content of the conversation. Sex drive is a hell of a motivator.

Within ten minutes, Maddie had her overnight bag packed. She tried not to think about what she was doing. If she did, she was certain she would back out. Her feelings for Jackson were as strong as her desire to be with Charlie sexually. She hated how her libido shifted into hyper drive at the sound of his voice. She also loved how it felt to anticipate being with him. "So much for discipline," she said to Mick as he watched her put on makeup. "Do me a favor. Write a note to Ray and tell him what I'm doing." She stopped applying eye shadow and looked down at Mick. He cocked his head to the side and snorted. "Oh, yeah. I forgot you don't have opposable thumbs. Can't hold a pen. Never mind. I'll do it myself."

As soon as she got on the 101, Maddie called Priscilla.

For being awakened from a deep sleep, her friend sounded remarkably alert. "Massive accident. Parent died. Child injured. Just saying it better be bad."

"You got me into this sexy mess, so if I don't sleep, neither do you."

"Madeleine Mozart, I am not your therapist." Mr. Peepers was lying at Priscilla's feet. When she adjusted her legs, the cat swiped at her, then jumped off the bed in a huff. "Apparently, Mr. Peepers isn't, either."

"No, you're my dear friend who talked me into deceiving everyone so I could have the adventure of a lifetime."

"If that's what you called to tell me at…2:30 in the morning, you can start referring to me as your ex-dear friend." Priscilla heard a horn honk. "Are you in the car?"

"I am and that's not why I called. I wanted your advice because I think I'm getting in over my head. Charlie phoned me from the set in Mendocino and practically begged me to come up and visit him. That's why I'm in the car. Priscilla, I'm falling in love with Jackson, but can't get enough of Charlie in the sack. Am I totally blowing any chances I have with Jackson?"

"If I said yes, would you turn around and go home?"

"I don't know. In less than three hours, I can be having amazing sex and a new wardrobe. I'll tell you about that later. But if I don't go, I still have no idea if Jackson wants to be with me. Skinny Trini could be shagging him right now."

"Who?"

"Trinity, the owner of Sycamore Farms Sanctuary."

"Ah, yes. The one who had too much to drink that night at Jackson's and horked. I don't think you have to worry about her. For one, she lives too far away and two, I think Jackson feels she's too young for him. He wants a mature woman. Like you."

Maddie took a sip of her coffee. She wanted to make sure that she stayed wide awake in case the adrenaline rush wore off. "I'm so mature. Not only am I dating a man under false pretenses, I'm also having a full-blown affair with said man and he happens to be the stepson of my crush. When Charlie and I break up, will Jackson want to be with someone who's been doing the horizontal boogie with his stepson?"

Priscilla had a strong inkling that she wouldn't be softly snoring any time soon. She made herself a cup of tea and coaxed Mr. Peepers into coming back to bed. It didn't take too much persuasion to convince the cat to slip under the covers and settle in Priscilla's lap. Within minutes, he was purring. Priscilla was jealous. She rubbed her eyes and half-heartedly cursed herself for having such a needy friend. She had to remind herself about the time Craig broke up with her, abandoning her in Lake Tahoe. It was heart crushing. Without even asking, Maddie had dropped her kids off at Tommy's. Four hours later she'd arrived, listened as Priscilla ranted, then dragged her to the Hard Rock Casino where they gambled until six the next morning. They'd stayed another night at the hotel, ordered room service, watched movies, and even helped themselves to the premium spa treatment. All on Craig's credit card.

"Listen, M&M, you need to stop projecting and worrying about the future. If it's meant to be with Jackson, it will happen. You two are starting a business together. Don't you think working with him will endear you to him?"

"I guess. I know you're right. I just don't want him to think of me as the one who slept with Charlie."

"You should have thought about that before you slept with Charlie."

"I was being so good, too. If he hadn't given me the little cow, I'd probably still be chaste." She looked over at the speedometer. In front of it stood the black and white calf.

An hour and a half after she profusely thanked her friend and let her go back to sleep, Maddie pulled into the White Pines Inn parking lot. It was nearly five in the morning and the sun was still asleep. With little trouble, she found room 45 and knocked on the door, butterflies doing the rhumba in her stomach. She heard some shuffling, light fidgeting with the lock, then the door opened. To say that Charlie had bedroom eyes would be an understatement. Without saying a word, he took her hand and led her to the bed. Maddie was bracing for morning breath when Charlie began tenderly kissing her. Instead, he tasted like vanilla mint. She had to admit, the man thought of everything.

As Charlie undressed Maddie, his hands lingered on her skin. He unbuttoned her blouse and traced her breasts lovingly with his fingers. He even took off her necklace and replaced it with small bites and caresses. The effect was so erotic and her anticipation so acute, that when they finally made love, it felt like every cell in her body was electric. If she had known it was going to be the best sex she'd ever had, she would have driven even faster, regardless of the winding road with its hairpin curves.

As she lay in his arms, their breathing returning to normal, Charlie said, "You enchant me." She turned and kissed him.

"Thank you."

"Last night, I couldn't concentrate on filming. Vicente made us shoot the scene over and over. Rachel was on target every time. I was flat. I knew I wasn't on my game. I kept thinking that I wasn't going to see you for a week and it bummed me out."

Charlie got out of bed, went over to the picture window and slid it open. The sun was starting to rise in the east, shedding a milligram of light on the sky, just enough to bounce off the ocean. It shimmered as the waves crashed on the shore, their strength and might adding emphasis to Charlie's words.

"I've never dated anyone like you before."

"You're not the first man to say that to me." Maddie joined him at the window and let the cold ocean air whip around her naked body. "We vegans are a pretty intense group."

"It's not that. Well, your passion is part of it. It's your…"

"Riveting personality? Keen sense of humor? Stellar smile?" She plastered a huge smile on her face.

Charlie didn't smile back. He looked into Maddie's eyes and she got scared. She prayed he didn't say the L word. "I can express myself best when I read someone else's words. That's why I quote my movies so much. It makes me feel smart. Maybe that's one of the reasons I became an actor. But you don't have to worry about using other people's lines. You can express yourself really well. So give me a moment to say what I want without being interrupted, okay?"

Maddie nodded, suddenly feeling very small. After a while, he continued. "You *are* funny and have a beautiful smile. You also care about people and animals so much that you want to help them. It's that dedication and the love you have for your children. Ray and Kenzie are so much like you and I believe they're going to make a difference in the world. I wish I could be more like you."

Maddie didn't say anything. She didn't want to interrupt him again. Charlie said, "I'm done."

"You're wrong, Charlie Evans." She put her arms around his waist. "You do have a way with words."

Charlie hugged her. "Why don't we get dressed and grab a bite to eat?"

"Fantastic idea. I'm starving. There's a great vegan restaurant right up the street. It's called Ravens and it's at the Stanford Inn. Want to go?"

"I wouldn't dare say no."

It was chilly with a dampness in the air, but it felt good on their skin. Charlie and Maddie walked hand in hand to the restaurant. The manager had just flipped the sign to 'open' and enthusiastically welcomed his first guests. He seated them at a table next to the window. Their view was of the wooded area behind the restaurant. As they decided what to get, the smell of fresh brewed coffee and baked goods permeated the air. Maddie's stomach grumbled. Charlie laughed.

"Sometimes, it's nice going to a restaurant where I don't have many vegan choices." She looked over the breakfast menu. "I'm either going to have the chocolate chip pancakes with bourbon maple syrup and soysages or the Portobello Benedict."

"How about if I get the pancakes and we can share?"

"Yes!" Maddie leaned over and kissed Charlie. "So tell me about the filming. Is it going well? Where are you shooting today?"

"After we spoke last night, it went really well. So far, we've wrapped up five of the eleven scenes we're shooting up here. Are you familiar with Heritage House, the mansion off Heeser Drive?"

Maddie shook her head.

"It was one of the first homes built in Mendocino. I think they said the owner of a timber company had it built in 1851 for his family. It's really cool. It was renovated twenty years ago, but they kept a lot of the original furniture. We'll probably be shooting there for a few days, then we go to the High Tail Inn for a day or two."

"Is Rachel behaving herself?"

"She is. Everyone on the set is so glad I said something. She pissed off quite a few people. Now, she's a pussycat. Very tame."

"Have you ever been reprimanded by a director?"

"Oh, look. Here come our lattes."

After they ordered, Maddie took a sip of her almond mocha latte with two shots of espresso. She could feel the caffeine sliding into her sleep-deprived veins. Maddie wasn't a proponent of artificial stimulants, but she considered caffeine natural and an essential part of her morning routine. Plus, a cup of coffee was as comforting and familiar as an old pair of Levi's. "Uh-oh. Sounds like Good Time Charlie got a slapdown. What'd you do and what movie was it on?"

Charlie said, "It's a boring story."

"Try me."

Charlie sighed. He knew how tenacious she was. He wouldn't get peace until he told her. "Let me just say that I'm not proud of this at all. And I was in my early twenties. Very much full of myself and the testosterone was surging through my body at warp speed."

"This is going to be good."

"I was playing opposite Kathy Peters. At the time, she was only nineteen and a virgin. The director, Lou Gentry, told me she was off limits. Kathy's father was her manager and he said she could be in the movie if she was left alone sexually, especially by me. They were a strict Catholic family. I still tried everything to get her to sleep with me. If you can believe it, I even lied and told her I was a virgin, too, hoping that would make me more desirable."

"You? Lied? What a shock."

Charlie felt like he'd been slapped across the face. The tone in Maddie's voice went a hair beyond sarcasm. He wanted to ignore it, but it stopped him cold.

"I was kidding. It was a joke."

"Not funny."

"Charlie. I'm sorry. I'm sleep-deprived. Ignore half of what I say. Please tell me what happened."

Reluctantly, he continued. "Where was I? Oh, yeah, I told Kathy I was also a virgin. That did it. She agreed to go out with me. We set up a dinner date. At the restaurant, Kathy didn't show. The director did, and he was mad as hell. He'd found out about our dinner from the producer. I'd asked Kathy to keep our date a secret, but she'd been excited and told the producer who'd gone immediately to Lou. He threatened to have me replaced if I tried anything like that again. It was very humbling."

"Major smackdown, eh? Isn't that the Kathy Peters who's married to the porn star, Jeremy Wooden?"

"That's her. Just goes to show you that you can't protect your children, no matter how hard you try."

"Very true. I'm so thankful that Ray and Kenzie are amazing kids. I give them advice and steer them in the best direction I believe they should be going, but ultimately, it's their choice."

"Aren't you worried about Ray getting high all the time?"

"I am only because his father is a recovering alcoholic. Ray has the propensity to become addicted to pot. My gut tells me that he won't. I really believe it's a phase he's going through. Call it a mother's intuition. I've seen that kid go through a number of phases. When he was seven, he painted his fingernails hot pink and listened to Kiss. That lasted a few weeks. Then he was into growing his hair long and playing guitar and insisted I call him Slash. I could go on and on. Ray's going to reach a point where smoking is going to hinder his ability to think clearly."

"My mom told me the same thing. She knew I'd be okay despite my rocky high school years. Even the school principal met with her and expressed his disappointment in my failing grades. He told her that my concentration was lousy and I was disruptive in class. Nowadays, they would have said I had ADD. Mom knew I would do well in a subject I was interested in. I barely graduated. A few months later, we moved to Hollywood and I started going on auditions." He picked up the knife, pretending it was a cigar, and said in a Groucho Marx voice, "And the rest, as they say, is history."

Maddie said, "Henny Youngman?"

Offended, Charlie said, "Really?"

In her best impersonation of Groucho, Maddie took the knife from Charlie, put it up to her mouth and said, "If I held you any closer I would be on the other side of you."

"Not bad. Not bad at all."

After they finished eating, Charlie said, "What do you say we pay the bill and go back to the hotel for a little more R and R?"

"Rest and relaxation?"

"Rumble and roll."

Maddie raised her hand. "Yes, please."

A studio car came by for Charlie at 12:45. He made Maddie promise to come to the set and watch them film. He even gave her the driver's number so she would have a ride there. Despite the double shot latte, Maddie fell asleep within minutes of Charlie's departure. Her slumber didn't last long. The cell woke her and without looking at the number, she picked it up. In a sleepy voice she said, "This is Maddie."

"Are you okay? You sound sick."

"Jackson?"

"That's me."

"I was sleeping."

"It's 2:00 in the afternoon."

As she became more lucid, she found herself dreading where the conversation would lead. "I know. I'm in Mendocino with Charlie."

"Oh. Well then, I guess you won't be able to come to the sanctuary site. I'm signing the papers today and afterwards wanted to celebrate with my partner."

"Damn. I would have loved to be there."

Jackson tried to hide the disappointment in his voice. It nonetheless filtered through and made its way right into Maddie's heart. "When are you coming home?"

"I'm not sure. It was a spur of the moment thing. I can't be gone too long because I have a shift at the women's center Thursday afternoon. Why don't I call you when I'm home and we can plan to get together and have a belated celebration?"

"Sure. I ran our sketches of the sanctuary by the architect. He's going to use them to design the buildings and layout. He said he'd have something to show us next month."

"I can't believe this is all coming together so quickly. You're doing an incredible job, Jackson. Thank you."

"Aw, shucks. It's nuthin'. You have fun up in Mendocino. If you have the time, take Charlie to Glass Beach up in Fort Bragg. It's amazing."

"Glass Beach? Why have I never heard of it?"

Jackson relaxed a little. The tension in his neck eased slightly. "I don't know. There are three spots and they've been around for a long time. All were used as dump sites. Can you believe it? People threw their trash over the cliffs and into the ocean. Bottles, appliances, even cars. Right over the edge. I think it was in the sixties when they closed the sites. Most of the trash degraded and the metal was removed and sold as scrap. Over the years, the waves broke down the glass and pottery and tumbled those pieces into small, smooth, colored rocks. Thousands of colorful, odd-shaped stones are mixed with the sand. It's quite a sight."

"Sounds beautiful. Thanks for the tip."

"Tell Charlie I say hi. Have a safe drive back."

"I will and I will. Talk to you soon."

Maddie couldn't go back to sleep. She tried, but every time she closed her eyes, she heard that schmaltzy song from the seventies, *Torn Between Two Lovers*. As soon as it would come on the radio, which was often, she would change the channel. Now it was tuned into her head and as much as she tried to change the brain wave, she couldn't. Instead, she reluctantly left the super comfortable bed, showered, dressed, and went shopping. Charlie had left money on the counter dresser and insisted she buy whatever she wanted as long as she came to the film site. While she promised she'd be there, the insecure side of her dreaded meeting Rachel, the woman responsible for Maddie's failure to stay out of Charlie's bed.

Wherever she went in town, she was recognized. Some were admirers, like an elderly woman who high-fived her and said, "Way to go, M&M!" Maddie suspected that Charlie used the nickname in interviews. It sounded odd coming from a stranger. It was also nice to know that older women were vicariously living through her. Then there were others whose jealousy colored their view of a woman they didn't know at all. When Maddie was trying on clothes in The Mendocino Woman, she overheard two young girls whispering about her. She caught smatterings of the conversation, with the words 'old,' 'don't understand,' and 'grandma' standing out. As much as she tried to ignore it, she found it difficult to do. When Maddie came out of the dressing room wearing skinny jeans and a pullover V-neck sweater, the whispering stopped. While looking in the 3-way mirror, she surreptitiously eyed the 20-somethings who were over by the jeans rack. Before she returned to the dressing room, she turned to the girls and said, "I may be older than you, but I have experience and to a man like Charlie Evans, that means a lot, so stop badmouthing me, okay?"

Stunned, the girls nodded and left the store. Twenty minutes later, Maddie made it to the cashier. She was holding two pairs of pants, the pullover sweater and two shirts. As the salesgirl rang her up, she said, "I saw the lab protest on the news. I think it's great that you picketed the college. Charlie Evans' speech was great. I hope that asshole's grant is revoked."

"Me, too."

"So...what's he like?"

"He's very generous and funny. He likes doing impersonations and spouting quotes from his movies. He can be very sweet, too."

"Good to know." She rang up the sales. "Your total is $453.78."

Like it was second nature, Maddie nonchalantly pulled five, one-hundred-dollar bills out of her purse and handed them to the salesgirl. "Can you recommend a spa in town?"

As if on cue, the girl pulled out a business card from under the cash register. It was on thick white stock with gold embossed letters.

Maddie turned the card over, admiring its design. "You must get asked a lot, huh?"

"This is a resort town, so yeah, I do get asked quite a bit. Lily Flower is the favorite among the locals and tourists. Since it is off-season, I don't think you'll have any trouble making a reservation. Ask for JoAnne. I think she's the best."

Outside, Maddie placed a call to the spa and made an appointment. As she walked to Lily Flower, she was struck by how easy it would be to get used to this lifestyle. She didn't have to worry about how much she spent, there were no time constraints, and if she felt like treating herself to a massage or facial, she could. On the other hand, she felt guilty. While she was buying clothes and pampering herself, there were people surviving on a day-to-day basis. They don't know where their next meal is coming from. Many sleep on the sidewalk, turning store entrances into mini-rooms. She wasn't sure if she could justify spending so much money on a regular basis when others had nothing. She resolved to make a donation to the local homeless shelter when she returned home.

Twenty minutes later, Maddie pulled open the stained-glass and oak door to Lily Flower. She stepped into a tropical paradise with ferns, orchids, and assorted African violets sitting atop tables, in large floor vases, and on the receptionist's counter. The air smelled of lavender and lilacs with a hint of vanilla. The walls were painted a pale pink. The receptionist was an older woman with long blonde, curly hair. She reminded Maddie of Dyan Cannon. She even had a large, toothy smile.

"Welcome to Lily Flower. I'm Eva. How can I help you?"

"I called a little while ago and made an appointment for a massage and facial. My name is Madeleine Mozart."

Eva inspected her appointment calendar. "Here you are. You requested JoAnne?"

Maddie nodded.

"Why don't you have a seat and I'll get you a cup of our enzyme tea."

"Sounds lovely. Thank you."

Maddie sat down on the plush sofa. She was admiring a yellow and pink orchid sitting on the coffee table when Eva brought over a mug filled with a hot liquid. It smelled sweet and tasted like a cross between Genmaicha tea and roses. She'd barely finished it when a woman came up and introduced herself as JoAnne. Maddie followed her to the massage room. The diffused lighting, meditative music, aroma therapeutic scents, and lavender-infused sesame oil added to a massage that drew all the tension out of Maddie's body. JoAnne's hands were energetic. She intuitively knew exactly where to knead harder and where to push more gently. When Maddie thought it couldn't get any better, JoAnne delivered a facial that brought vibrancy and a radiance back to Maddie's face. As an added treat, she had her make-up professionally done by the esthetician.

Maddie left the spa feeling delicious. Her skin faintly smelled of lavender and her body felt light, like she could fly. If her feet were touching the ground, she didn't notice. The studio driver picked her up and delivered her to the other side of the town, where cast and crew were holed up in Heritage House. The three-story white Victorian with deep blue shutters and gold gingerbread trim sat on a small hill overlooking the ocean. It was surrounded by enormous cypress trees that looked as old as the house. Their limbs were twisted and gnarled as if a giant ogre had molded them to his macabre satisfaction. A fountain graced the front of the house, a rearing horse in the center, water streaming off its back and splashing onto gold orbs. Maddie stood outside the asymmetrical mansion, taking in its spires and spiral brick chimneys. One of the turrets at the east end of the house had a scalloped copper finish. On top sat a weather vane in the shape of a seahorse. As she stared up at its gleaming dome, she noticed movement in one of the windows. At first, it was difficult to make out the shape because the glass was dusty. As her eyes adjusted, she realized it was a young boy around five or six years old. He smiled and waved. Maddie returned the smile and waved back.

Finding her name on the guest list, the security guard let her in, then told her they were filming, so her silence was requested.

Maddie quietly stepped into the cavernous ballroom where the scene was being shot. She was at the far end of the action and could barely make out Charlie, dressed in a suit standing next to Rachel. She was wearing an evening gown. Whether it was because she was so relaxed or the energy in the room was overpowering, Maddie detected a sharp tension in the air. As much as she wanted to keep her inner serenity, it was unceremoniously broken by the foul mood of the room. Every crew member wore a look of disdain or disgust. Maddie wanted to get closer to the scene. She started to tiptoe ahead, when the first assistant yelled, "Picture is up. Everyone settle, please. This is picture. Camera ready?"

Maddie froze. She watched Charlie and Rachel perform through an opening between a camera and lighting equipment. Within minutes, the director yelled, "Cut!" Maddie took the opportunity to get closer to the scene. Two empty chairs sat side by side. She asked one of the grips if she could sit down and he nodded. Vicente stood next to Rachel, speaking low. His words were inaudible but the tone was clear. The director wasn't happy and, as a result, his discontent pervaded the room. Charlie stood by, hands on his hips, looking impatient. When he saw Maddie, his eyes lit up and he smiled. It was momentary. His scowl returned as the director turned to him and spoke.

Three hours later, Maddie was falling asleep in the chair. The thrill of being on a movie set devolved into tedium and extreme boredom. She almost cheered when the director called for a break. Charlie made a beeline for Maddie. He looked tired. Nothing that make-up couldn't fix. "Are you totally bored out of your mind?"

"Oh no, it's fascinating. Really."

"Really?"

"Some of it is."

"Very little is," Charlie said as he took her over to the director. "John. I'd like you to meet Maddie. Maddie, this is John Vicente."

They shook hands. John said, "Nice to meet you. Thanks for coming up and straightening this guy out. You've saved us a lot of money."

Charlie protested. "I wasn't that bad."

Rachel came up behind him and put her hands around his waist. "Yeah, you were." Uncomfortable, Charlie moved out of her grasp and stood closer to Maddie. If it fazed Rachel, she didn't show it. "And you must be Madeleine Mozart, our savior." Her sarcasm wasn't lost on anybody. The statuesque blonde with Grace Kelly-like features would have normally given Maddie an inferiority complex. Bolstered by Charlie's attentiveness, she felt like Rachel's equal. Maddie thrust out her hand and shook Rachel's hand.

"That's me. Just call me Saint Madeleine."

"I'll do that. How long are you in town?"

"I'm leaving tomorrow."

"You are?" Charlie looked disappointed.

"I have to get back for my shift at the women's center." Maddie put her hand on Charlie's arm. "You're leaving here soon, anyway, right?"

John said, "Saturday, if we can stick to the schedule. Excuse me, I'm going to grab a bite. Very nice meeting you, Maddie."

"Same here."

Charlie asked Maddie, "Are you hungry? We have a full-on buffet in the kitchen."

"I could eat something. By the way, who brought their son to work? I saw him in the turret."

Charlie and Rachel looked at each other. "Nobody."

"I saw a young boy in the window of the third floor. He was wearing suspenders. Who puts their kid in suspenders anymore? Maybe he's a local kid who got past the security guard. Or…"

Rachel cut in. "Don't you dare say it. I won't work under those conditions."

Charlie said, "You're afraid of a child ghost?"

Rachel stormed off in the direction of the kitchen. "John!"

Charlie laughed. "How did you know that Rachel is deathly afraid of ghosts? That was good."

Maddie got goosebumps. She rubbed her arms. "I didn't. There really was a kid in the window."

"Honey, this place is locked up so tight, no one can get in. The only entrance is the front door."

"How did the crew bring in all this equipment?"

"Through the service entrance in the kitchen. That was days ago. They've since locked that door. This house is sealed up tight. There's a lot of expensive equipment in here."

Maddie followed Charlie to the kitchen where the cast and crew were helping themselves to a variety of food on two thirty-foot-long buffet tables. There was a sandwich-making section, hot foods, packaged snacks, and even a soft-serve yogurt machine. After she and Charlie filled their plates, Maddie took out her cell and Googled Heritage House. She scrolled down the search results until she found one that sounded intriguing. She looked up briefly and caught Rachel glaring at her. She had to stop herself from putting up her hands and mouthing, 'Booooooo!'

"Listen to this. 'Heritage House was built in the mid-1850s for timber executive Franklin Cove. Ten years after Franklin, his wife Mirabelle, and their four children moved in, their youngest son was killed. Six-year-old Franklin, Jr. had been playing in the nursery. The nanny had gone to make lunch for the family, leaving the boy alone. In an attempt to get a toy train sitting on the top shelf, Franklin, Jr. had stacked up toy blocks next to the bookcase. When he stood on the poorly assembled blocks, he slipped and fell onto a toy schooner, the ship's masts impaling the boy right through the heart. He died en route to the hospital. Shortly after his death, the family moved out and had another mansion built on the other side of town. Legend has it that Franklin, Jr. can be seen in the house's nursery window, smiling and waving to passersby.' Shit, I saw a ghost!" Maddie looked up from her phone. "Can I tell Rachel or shall you?"

"Don't you dare. We can't afford to stop shooting. All those nice things that John said to you, he'll take back in spades. I'm serious."

"Fine. Just for the record, I don't like her. She has a real attitude. That, 'I'm better than you, live with it' attitude."

Maddie looked over at her and flashed her best fake smile. Rachel returned a better one. "She's good."

"Listen, lady. Don't make work more difficult for me. I told you she's behaving herself. Let's leave it like that."

"You're right. I'm sorry." She gave Charlie a kiss on his cheek. "How much longer do you think you'll be on the set?"

"Hard to say. You know you can stay as long as you like, but I totally understand if you want to leave. Filming a movie, especially the scenes that we're shooting, can be like watching water turn to ice." Charlie took a bite of his sandwich.

"I'll stay a little longer, then probably go back to the hotel and watch a movie. I talked to Jackson today. He told me about this cool beach in Fort Bragg with multi-colored glass mixed in with the sand. Do you think we'd have a chance to go before I leave?"

Charlie felt defensive. "Why did Jackson call you?"

"He wanted to celebrate the signing of the papers for the sanctuary property. I told him I was up here with you and he mentioned the beach. He says hi, by the way."

Charlie persisted. "How did he want to celebrate?"

"He didn't say. And chill out. He was excited at the closing. I am his partner and you're his stepson. He wouldn't do anything untoward."

She forgot about using big words when talking to Charlie. He had the same expression Mick had when she told him about her day. The only thing missing was a cocked head and a wet nose.

"Inappropriate. Unpleasant. Awkward."

"Got it." Charlie took a sip of water. "We're on a really tight schedule, so I don't think I'm going to be able to take that much time off to play." In a flawless impersonation of Cary Grant, he said, "But there will be plenty of playing around in the hotel room."

"Kevin Spacey?"

"You just love messing with me, don't you?"

"Uh-huh. You make it very easy."

Maddie got up to refill her water glass. On her way back to the table, she noticed a man sitting at the far end of the kitchen, head down, shoveling food into his mouth at warp speed. When he looked up, she was shocked. It was Lonnie Harber, one of Hollywood's sexy new screen stars. As he spoke to his peers, little particles of food flew out of his mouth. Some even got stuck in his jet black, shoulder-length hair.

Maddie returned to her table. "I didn't know Lonnie Harber was in the movie."

Charlie said, "Yeah. He's kind of a dick."

"Not to mention a human wood chipper. The man is consuming mass quantities of food and then is proceeding to talk, spraying everyone in the vicinity with food. He was great in that indie film, *Wildwood Junction*. So suave and dignified. I'll never be able to watch him in another movie without that image." She pointed in Lonnie's direction.

"Ten minutes!" the director announced. Some people took the opportunity to grab one more bag of chips or a handful of cookies before going back to work. After they finished their meal, Charlie grabbed Maddie's hand and took her through the kitchen, around the corner, and up a flight of stairs. In a small coat room off in the corner, they kissed. Charlie had his shirt halfway off when the five-minute warning bell sounded. Maddie put her hands around his naked waist, then helped him button up his shirt.

Maddie said, "Don't you hate it when that happens?"

In a voice thick with passion, he said, "Very much." Reluctantly, they went downstairs. Charlie estimated he'd be back at the hotel before midnight. He gave her a kiss, then resumed his spot on the set. He was immediately descended upon by the make-up artist. Rachel must have detected a mini-glow from Charlie because she shot Maddie a nasty look. Maddie smiled back and gave her a thumbs-up. Rachel turned back to the set, a key light illuminating her blonde locks. They looked like spun gold.

After almost four hours of sitting, then standing, then sitting again, Maddie called it quits. She summoned the driver and he took her back to the hotel. Once she splashed water on her face and put her new clothes away, she decided to take a walk downtown. The night air was cool and the ocean mist invigorating. She walked quickly, giving her legs a much-needed workout after being cooped up in a haunted mansion for almost seven hours, watching her boyfriend arguing with an American senator, dancing with his leading lady, and discussing politics with a wealthy dowager. Maddie hoped Charlie would never ask her to come to another shoot. The interesting aspects of filmmaking didn't make up for the overwhelming tedium of the waiting and re-shooting and then waiting some more.

Established in 1856, The Motherlode was a small bar in the middle of town. Busy year, Maddie thought, as took a seat at the empty bar. She scanned the bottles of liquor sitting on wooden shelves in front of a mirrored wall.

"What can I get ya?" A man who personified a salty sea dog stood in front of her. His voice sounded like he gargled with whiskey and thistles. And his ruddy skin and red nose indicated his love for the liquor he poured his customers. Maddie pointed to a tall, square bottle with pale yellow liquid inside. The bartender took the bottle from the shelf, his crooked fingers wrapped around the elegant-looking vessel. He poured it into a brandy snifter and said, "This was Mirabelle Cove's favorite drink."

Every hair on Maddie's arms stood on end. "Why did you tell me that?"

He shrugged. "I felt like it."

"I just read about her family. And about her youngest son." She almost asked him if he knew the Coves. The man looked that old. "I'm Maddie."

"Garmin." He poured himself a shot of Jack Daniels. "My great granddad played with Franklin Jr. My daddy told me that his granddad was supposed to be at the house the day Junior died, but he had the flu and couldn't go."

"You wonder what could have happened if he'd been there. I just came from Heritage House. You know they're shooting a movie?"

"Yeah, I know all about it. A group of them came in the other night. They must work hard because they play even harder. They were generous tippers. I'll give them that."

Maddie sipped the pear cognac. It was smooth and light with the faint taste of Bosc pears. "I saw Franklin, Jr. in the nursery window today."

"You're not the first. He seems to come and go all the time."

"Have you seen him?"

Garmin nodded. "Couple of times. He smiled and waved."

Maddie spent a good hour talking to Garmin, learning the history of Mendocino. When she left, she was slightly high from the drink and very knowledgeable about Garmin's family tree.

A strong wind whipped through the town, pushing through Maddie's clothes and chilling her to the bone. In the hotel room, she got ready for bed. She slipped on a pink and white striped teddy, then stood in front of the mirror striking seductive poses. Satisfied that the new lingerie was sexy enough, she got into bed. Her intention was to watch a movie, but exhaustion overtook her and she ended up falling asleep before the opening credits appeared on the screen. She was awakened by Charlie unlocking the door. Disoriented, she said, "Ray?"

"Senility hasn't set in yet, has it?"

Maddie sat up, then remembered where she was. "Oh, hi Charlie."

"Don't go back to sleep," he said as he closed the bathroom door. A few minutes later, he walked over to the bed and leaned over, kissing his girlfriend on her forehead, then her lips. "Nice teddy."

"I'm glad you like it because you bought it." She pulled him closer. "What time is it?"

"Time to have my way with you."

The alarm went off at 9:00 a.m. Maddie and Charlie groaned at the same time. He hit the snooze button.

"Please, sir, can I have more time?" Charlie said in a cockney accent.

Her back to Charlie, Maddie said, "Don't tell me I'm sleeping with Oliver." She turned over and spooned with her beau. Even now, it was hard to believe that she was in a relationship with Charlie Evans. She'd seen him unkempt. She'd heard every one of his bodily noises. She still wasn't used to being with him in public when he was approached by strangers or, worse, the paparazzi. Maddie also knew their union was ephemeral. And for that reason, she vowed to enjoy every bit of her time with Charlie. She didn't even care if his compliments were heartfelt or bet-driven.

Charlie took her hand and kissed it. "Ready to grab some breakfast?"

"That sounds divine."

"We can go back to Ravens, if you want."

"I want. I want."

Seated at the same table as the day before, Maddie took a sip of her coffee as she watched Charlie stab a slice of her buckwheat waffle, dip it in the maple syrup and fruit compote and stuff it in his mouth. She loved how he seemed to truly enjoy every vegan meal. He caught her bemused look.

"Sorry. Should I have asked before stealing your food?"

"I'm not mad. Really. I'm actually quite taken by how much you love vegan food. Please, have some more." Maddie pushed her plate closer to Charlie. He enthusiastically cut into the waffle.

"After you go to Glass Beach, you should visit the set."

"I told you I'm leaving after breakfast."

Charlie stopped mid-chew. He looked heartbroken. "One more day. Please."

"They're expecting me at the center. I don't want to flake on them."

"How about if I call your boss and tell her...It's a her, right?"

Maddie nodded.

He continued, "Thought so. I'll tell her that I'll make a donation to the center if they can manage without you for a day."

Maddie was dumbfounded. "You would do that just so I can stay another day?"

"You bet your firm ass I would. Will you?"

Maddie shook her head in disbelief. "How much is my firm ass worth?"

Charlie smirked. "We can discuss that later. Will you stay?"

Maddie nodded.

Of the three Glass Beaches, Maddie chose the one in MacKerricher State Park, close to Fort Bragg. It was enchanting. The rock formations jutting out of the surf and the tide pools rich with urchins, starfish, and hermit crabs were as fascinating as the smooth, polished, multi-colored glass. Maddie spent hours walking up and down the beach, sifting through the glass, even making piles of the colors. She took more than a few photos, texting them to friends, Ray, Kenzie, and Jackson. She left mini mountains of amber, green, white, and brown glass. There wasn't enough red glass to create even a small mound, so Maddie topped each mountain with a smattering of red glass. She found the experience meditative, plus it stopped her from spending more money. Even though Charlie insisted she buy whatever she wanted, she felt better pacing herself.

Another three-hour snooze fest at Heritage House, then Maddie set off to The Motherlode to have one more drink with Garmin. Before she reached the door, a barrage of sound tumbled out of the little bar's open door. Every Wednesday, a group of octogenarians from Mendocino and the surrounding area descended on Garmin's place, drinking to excess and playing darts, liar's dice, and poker. Garmin's hand was on the beer tap practically non-stop while his waitress served the hard liquor. When he saw Maddie walk through the door, his mood brightened. He motioned for her to come over. Wading through the old codgers, she had to endure leers and a few suggestive comments.

She scanned the room, guessing there were about seventy-five seniors in all. A few patrons who weren't part of the group kept to themselves.

Yelling above the din, she said to Garmin, "Please tell me these guys don't drink and drive."

"Hell, no! Most of the locals walk here. The ones from out of town are driven here by Walter's daughter. She picks them up in an old school bus. She calls it the Coot Express. They get dropped off at

7:00 p.m. and picked up around midnight."

"Stop monopolizing the beautiful lady, Garmin." Before Maddie could respond, a man with glasses as thick as the Hubble telescope and large, veiny ears held out his hand. Maddie shook it. "The name's Felix. What can I get you to drink, doll?"

Maddie said, "I'm Madeleine and I'll have the usual, barkeep."

Garmin winked and poured her a generous shot of Moulin's Poire Cognac. When he told Maddie's admirer how much her drink was, he clutched his heart. "You pretty, young dolls have expensive taste. Put it on my tab."

Garmin gave him a half-hearted salute, then went back to pouring beer. Maddie thanked Felix and took a sip. She savored it as the light amber liquid warmed her throat.

Maddie put the drink down and said, "So tell me, Felix, do you still work or are you retired?"

"Sweetie, I work every day at staying alive."

She laughed. "Is that what I have to look forward to?"

Felix gave her the once-over, his glasses magnifying his eyes, making them the size of avocados. Maddie felt like he could see every pore on her face.

"Doll, you have a long way to go before you hit my age. What are you, thirty-three, thirty-four?"

"Hey, Garmin, meet my new boyfriend!"

Garmin nodded even though he couldn't hear Maddie over the noise. *Boogie Woogie Bugle,* performed by the Andrews Sisters, blasted from the jukebox. Before she knew it, Felix grabbed her hand and led her to the dance floor. The only ones out there, they garnered attention from the rest of the patrons. Poker games were momentarily suspended, darts held back from being thrown, and even the Liar's Dice players watched as Felix and Maddie showed off their best boogie woogie moves. One hand on their hips and the other in air, their index fingers pointing up, they danced around each other. Felix began to thrust his pelvis back and forth. Someone shouted, "Be careful you don't dislocate your hip!" When the song was over, they received thunderous applause. Felix bowed, then took out a handkerchief and wiped the sweat from his forehead. And upper lip. And behind his ears. He took off his glasses and wiped off the fogged- up lenses. Back at the bar, he finished the rest of his pint of beer and ordered another one.

By the time Maddie left the bar, she had danced with five more octogenarians. She'd had a blast. Aside from harmless flirting, the men had great stories to tell about growing up on the Mendocino coast. Maddie shared her ghost story with them and that got more of a response than why she was staying in town. The men could care less about lights, cameras, and movie stars. They were more interested in talking about Heritage House and its spooky history.

As Maddie approached the hotel, she noticed their room was illuminated. She didn't remember leaving the light on and Charlie wasn't expected back for another hour. Cautiously, she opened the door.

"Where the hell have you been? I must have called you a dozen times." Miniature liquor bottles from the hotel room bar were strewn on the bed, their contents consumed. His clothes were rumpled and he had anger in his eyes despite his lack of focus.

Maddie's heart was pounding. The last time she'd seen Charlie that mad was in Portofino when she refused his advances. She couched the sarcasm, afraid he'd pounce on her, and settled for genuine concern. "I was at The Motherlode, the bar down the street. You said you wouldn't be done shooting until midnight or so."

"I was wrong. Yes, it happens. Charlie Evans is not always right. We got off a few hours ago. Why didn't you answer my calls?"

Maddie tried to approach him, but he backed away, stumbling over his shoes. He righted himself before he tumbled into the television stand. "Charlie, I didn't hear the phone. It was really loud in the bar. Honestly, if I had known you had called, I would have answered."

When she tried to comfort him for the second time, he let her come closer, then he put up his hand. "Were you talking to other men?"

Drunk or not, Maddie didn't like being questioned about her loyalty. Her attitude changed and she decided to have fun. "I was talking to a lot of men. I danced with them. We played darts and I even learned how to play Liar's dice."

Charlie had to sit down to stop himself from swaying. He looked up at Maddie. She wasn't sure if his eyes were watery from inebriation or grief. "Did you cheat on me?"

Maddie sat down next to Charlie. She put her hand on his. "Sweetie, if I were into octogenarians, you would never see me again."

"Goddamn it, Maddie. Speak English."

"Sorry. The average age in the bar was eighty-five. I was cavorting with men so old, their skin was see-through. I danced with a man who lifted his feet a total of eight times the entire song." She put her arms around Charlie. He laid his head on her shoulder, his breath hot against her skin. "You can trust me. I would never flirt or play around behind your back, especially since I feel like at least two wide angle lenses are focused on me nearly all the time."

Charlie snuggled in closer. "I'm not as confident as you think I am."

"Mostly swagger, huh?"

"Yup."

"What do you say we go to bed? It's late and I'm leaving in the morning."

"Do you have to leave tomorrow?" Charlie sat up and looked at her with sad, bloodshot eyes. He ran his hands through his hair.

Maddie nodded. "I do."

"Then let's make this a night to remember." Charlie made an attempt to grab her, but lost his balance and fell back on the bed."

Maddie laughed. "No offense, but I'm not having sex with a drunk man."

Charlie righted himself and said, "I'm an actor." He waited for Maddie to respond. Instead she gave him a blank look. "Don't you see, if I'm straight, I can act drunk and if I'm drunk, I *can*..." Again, nothing from Maddie. "Act straight! What do you say?"

"When you give it that nice, romantic touch, how can I resist?" Charlie was about to kiss her when she said, "One condition: I'm the director and if this isn't going well, I get to say 'cut.' No re-takes."

"In that case, give me some time to get into character." He closed his eyes and began involuntarily swaying.

Maddie chuckled to herself. She had a feeling she would be pulling the plug on his career as a lucid character. "While you're prepping for your role, I'm going to wash my face and slip into something much more comfortable. Don't fall off the bed."

Charlie didn't respond. He was determined to make this work. While Maddie brushed her teeth, she could hear him performing tongue twisters. He did a halfway decent job. She washed her face to his recitation of the alphabet backwards. He failed around K. Despite his difficulty, she put on her teddy, hoping that Charlie would succeed in playing his role to perfection, since she wouldn't be seeing him again for three days.

Clothes thrown on the floor, Charlie was in bed when Maddie entered the room. Leaning on his elbow, he said, "I'm ready for my close-up, Mr. DeMille."

"No close-ups without brushed teeth, Norma Desmond. Now git."

Charlie resisted. "I may lose my mojo if I get out of bed. Can you bring me the mouthwash?"

Maddie rolled her eyes. She returned with a mini-Scope bottle and a cup. Charlie took a small swig, swished it around in his mouth and spit it into the cup. He placed both on the nightstand, then held out his arms and flashed her an irresistible smile. "I am *so* sober."

If Maddie had any doubts about his acting abilities, they dissipated as quickly as she slid into his waiting arms. Charlie thrilled. Charlie was skilled. When they were done, she was ready to carve an Oscar out of the hotel's bar of soap. Her last thought before she fell asleep was that she was really going to miss him.

26

D riving home, Maddie reflected on her time in Mendocino. Her thoughts jumped from ghost boy to having a killer breakfast with Charlie at Ravens to boogieing with Felix at the bar. About halfway through her journey, she felt hunger pangs. She remembered stuffing the remainder of a breakfast scone into a napkin and fished around for it in her purse. Instead, she grabbed the partially-eaten S'morb from her drive with Jackson and, without thinking, finished the last three-quarters. It wasn't until twenty-five minutes later, when the road began to undulate, that she realized she had eaten the marijuana-laced snack. Maddie panicked. Highway 128 had some hairpin turns. She envisioned missing a turn and flying off the road to her death. At the next turnout, Maddie pulled over. The first thing she needed to do was replace the thoughts of trajectory and a fiery death with more peaceful images. She managed to get her heart rate back to normal by conjuring up last night's dalliance with Charlie. From terror to erotica in the blink of a very red eye, Maddie's libido took over her mind. Before she knew it, her heart rate was starting to climb again, but she didn't mind at all. Her confidence level boosted, she decided to get back on the road. Despite an empty highway, she made absolutely sure there were no cars coming when she pulled into the lane. In the mood for country, she put on a Kenny Chesney CD. When *You and Tequila* came on, Maddie's imagination kicked into overdrive. She saw herself in a bar on the beach in Mexico, sitting across from Jackson. He was wearing the obligatory country-western garb: white tee, faded jeans, cowboy boots, and a black Stetson. She was wearing close to nothing: a tank top and shorts. No bra. Long, beaded earrings in a Native American pattern hung from her ears. A bottle of tequila sat in the middle of the table. Two shot glasses, salt, and lime slices sat patiently in front of them, waiting to be tasted.

She knew she was getting into dangerous territory. She knew she should hit the delete button and let her mind flow with the music, but the scenario refused to leave. It began to unfold and details emerged. Jackson leaned over and played with her earring. He filled her glass, then his, with a sly smile. She picked up the cactus-shaped salt shaker, licked the side of her hand and slowly sprinkled the white granules on her skin. Jackson pulled her arm toward him, leaned over and slowly licked the salt from her hand, then knocked back the golden liquid and sucked on the lime.

Maddie grabbed her water bottle and took a healthy drink. She rolled the window down and let the cool morning air dry the perspiration from her neck and forehead. She yelled, "Sorry, Charlie!" inhaled deeply and willed herself to abandon the erotic scene. Her mind refused to listen. Instead, it amped up the visual. She was now licking salt from Jackson's hand, shooting the tequila, and sucking on the lime. As the song came to an end, Jackson kissed Maddie passionately. She felt his hands touching her body. Then she felt him on top of her. For the second time in ten minutes, Maddie pulled off the road into another turnout. It was an ideal location, partially hidden by bushes. No one driving past would suspect that the woman in the driver's seat was completely immersed in a sexual fantasy. And five minutes later, she was positive no one heard her yell out Jackson's name as she climaxed. Totally spent, Maddie closed her eyes and leaned her head back, relishing the state of bliss. She reached behind her seat and grabbed a tissue. Once cleaned up, she got back on Highway 128. Her cheeks were flushed and her hands slightly shaking, but she concentrated fully on her driving while singing along with Kenny.

Maddie was surprised when she opened the front door and Mick didn't greet her. Then she realized that Ray's door was closed, highly unusual when he wasn't home.

"Ray?"

No answer.

Maddie knocked on his door. "Ray?" She heard Mick get off the bed and come to the door.

"What?" Ray's voice sounded off. Muffled.

"Why aren't you in school?"

"Don't feel good."

The effects from the marijuana lingered, heightening her sense of dread. "Can I come in?"

"No. I just want to sleep."

Maddie respected her son's privacy and normally wouldn't push it. Not this time. She detected that something was not right. She opened the door. Mick jumped up on her, barking. She thought Ray would object, but he was silent as she came closer to his bed. She panicked when she saw blood on his light grey sheets. His partially exposed head revealed matted hair mixed with dried blood. His ear looked black and blue.

A scream rose in her throat, but she suppressed it. She had to stay calm for both their sakes. "What happened?"

Ray turned to face her and she nearly passed out. His right eye was swollen shut and a red gash appeared on his forehead. His lower lip was split and blood trickled out of his nostrils.

"I was at Jarod's place, hanging out. Some guys broke in, stole his plants, beat us up." Ray lifted his arm to his mother. She hugged him tentatively even though she wanted to wrap her arms around her son and make the hurt disappear.

"We need to get you to a hospital."

"No! I don't want Jarod getting in trouble. I'm okay. I just need to rest."

"Wrong. You could have internal injuries or a concussion. I'm taking you to the hospital." Maddie took out her phone and dialed.

"Tommy. Meet me at Marin General's emergency room. Our son was in a fight. I'll tell you more when I see you."

Voice shaking, Tommy said, "Can I talk to him?"

"At the hospital. We're leaving now." Maddie hung up and helped her son to the car. He was a good six inches taller and at least forty pounds heavier, and it was all Maddie could do to keep Ray propped up. His balance was compromised and he was leaning on her for support. Once she got him in the back seat lying down, she could breathe easier. The scene from the movie, *Airplane*, popped into her head: In the airport tower, Lloyd Bridges, tasked with trying to keep a plane from crashing, says, 'Looks like I picked the wrong week to quit sniffing glue.' In her stoned state, Maddie felt like saying, 'Looks like I picked the wrong day to eat weed.'

Ray tried to turn his head, but only partially succeeded. "Please don't tell the doctor about Jarod."

"Jarod. Shit. I forgot about him. How is he?"

"He's fine. The guy's built like a tank. I think he has a black eye and a busted nose."

Maddie could feel her anger rising. These two teenage boys had no idea how close they could have come to being killed, murdered over a couple of marijuana plants. "Someone needs to check on Jarod. He may be worse off than you think. When we get to the hospital, call him on your cell for me. I'll talk to him."

Thankful they lived only ten minutes from the hospital, Maddie pulled up to the emergency room entrance. She went inside and had an orderly bring out a wheelchair. Once Ray was wheeled inside, she parked the car. It was a slow day in Marin, accident-wise. The waiting room was nearly empty, save a woman holding her left arm close to her chest with her right and a crying toddler cradled in his mother's lap. A nurse met her at the door and brought her to the exam room where Ray was being treated. Another nurse had begun attending to her son. When she saw Maddie, a glint of recognition crossed her face. It looked like she was going to say something, then decided against it. She gently wiped off the dried, coagulated blood from Ray's head and face. She helped him take his shirt off. Previously undetected, Ray's exposed chest sported a bruise the size of a grapefruit. He winced when the nurse touched it. The nurse said, "That's quite a bruise. What happened?"

Without thinking, Ray began to speak. Maddie interceded. "We'd rather not say right now, if you don't mind." At the same time, her cell vibrated. She absently said, "It's Charlie," and was going to answer it, but decided not to, concluding that the timing wasn't right.

"Ray, give me your phone."

He slowly reached into his back pocket and handed it to his mother. "He's under Devil."

"Of course he is." Maddie shook her head and left the room. He picked up on the first ring.

"Dude, are you okay?"

"I'm not okay," Maddie replied. "This is Ray's mom and we're at the hospital. Jarod, first tell me if you're hurt, then I'd like to know what happened."

"I'm sore but okay. They broke my nose. I reset it. How's Ray?"

"Like I said, we're at the hospital. Ray's being examined now. I hope to God he didn't suffer any serious injuries. Ray told me you have a medical marijuana card. Why are you afraid to go to the police?"

"If the cops talk to my friends, they'll find out that I sell weed and I'll get arrested."

"How old are you?"

"I'll be eighteen in two months."

"Listen to me. The worst that can happen is you'll be charged with a misdemeanor and when you turn eighteen, the charge will be expunged from your record."

Jarod was skeptical. "And you know this how?"

"It happened to a friend of mine's daughter. She's in law school now. No police record. Please tell me what happened and if there's any chance these thieves can be caught."

Jarod went on to tell Maddie that he and Ray had been alone in the house. They'd been in his room, smoking weed, when they'd seen two guys jump over the backyard fence. The guys had gone straight for the plants, cutting them down with three-inch loppers. He and Ray had run outside to stop them. Ray had tried to talk to them. Instead, the thieves attacked them both. "Before they left, they threatened to call the cops and tell them that I was growing and selling weed if I said anything."

"Did you recognize these guys?" said Maddie

"I sure did. They buy weed from me. Jerry and Bill McKoster. Assholes."

"Jarod, you need to call the police. Tell them what happened. I'm going to let the doctor know, too. I'm sure he'll be filing a police report. Are you sure you're okay? I'd feel better if you went to the hospital just to get checked out."

"I'm fine." He hesitated. "Shit, I'll call the cops."

Tommy showed up just as Maddie finished her conversation with Jarod. His face fell when he saw Ray and his eyes welled up with tears. He grabbed Ray's hand and lightly squeezed it.

"Dad."

"Hey, kiddo."

The nurse continued to clean her patient's wounds. Every once in a while, Ray would wince.

Maddie said to Ray, "We'll be right back, honey," then they walked out to the hallway and she told Tommy what had happened.

When the doctor arrived, they followed him back to the room. Dr. Vashon introduced himself, then began his cursory examination. Ray flinched more than once despite being given medication to relieve his pain. As he poked and prodded the boy's delicate body, he asked him how he got the injuries. Again, Ray related the story. He kept looking at his father, hoping he wouldn't see disappointment in his face. Tommy remained calm and nonjudgmental throughout. At the moment, he was more concerned for Ray's well-being than his bad habits.

Two hours later, Maddie, Tommy, and Ray sat in the living room, Mick curled up at Ray's feet. Their son had two broken ribs; the gash above his black, blue, and red eye sported ten stitches; and his fat lip was already showing signs of shrinking. Maddie and Tommy sipped on herbal tea. Ray drank a smoothie through a straw. The police had left a few minutes earlier. They had gone easy on Ray, knowing he was more of an innocent bystander, even though he was one of Jarod's customers.

"I'm grounded, right?" Ray looked at his parents with dread in his good eye.

Tommy said, "When I was your age, I was arrested for underage drinking. I spent the night in jail and when my parents came to pick me up, I was told that I was grounded for two months. No friends, no television, no going out. It was harsh. As soon as the two months were up, I went to a rave with friends, got hammered, and passed out at the party."

"But Dad, you couldn't control yourself because you're an alcoholic."

"True, but I never thought about the repercussions if I was

caught drinking again. It didn't matter to me. How do you feel right now about getting high?"

Ray sat very still. He touched his closed eye and flinched. "I don't know if that's a fair question to ask at the moment. I'm flying high on painkillers. I guess I'll have to play it by ear. I don't consider myself addicted to pot. I've also gotten high almost every day since I was, I don't know, sixteen, so will I be jonesing for a hit? Honestly, I couldn't tell you."

Maddie said, "Time will tell if you've inherited your father's addictive tendencies. His point was that we could restrict your activities and impose tough rules, but you'll do what you want to when we're not around. You're a really bright kid, Ray, and we sincerely hope that you couch the weed smoking for a while. See how you feel. Experiment with being drug-free."

Ray started to cry. His shoulders shook and he put his head in his hands. Tommy and Maddie exchanged confused looks. Tommy went over and put his arm around his son. "Are you okay? Are you in pain?"

Ray shook his head. "Thank you both for trusting me. It really…means so…much to…" He began sobbing again. Maddie went over to Ray's other side.

"We both love you very much, sweetie." She looked over at Tommy and mouthed, 'drugs.' He nodded.

Maddie got up and went to the kitchen to make more tea. The phone rang. "Tommy, can you get that?"

He patted Ray on the back, then went over and picked up the phone. "Hello…no, it's Tommy…what? Son of a bitch…yeah, I'll get Maddie. Hold on."

He went into the kitchen and whispered, "Priscilla's on the phone. She said the story about Ray's hospital visit is all over the news. The entertainment news." He handed her the phone.

Priscilla wasn't happy, either. She told Maddie that on Entertainment Tonight, her godson's beat-up face was shown alongside Charlie Evans' handsome one with the caption, 'Jealous over son's attention?'

"Did Charlie do this to Ray?" Priscilla demanded.

"No! Charlie's been filming on location in Mendocino since

Saturday. Ray and a friend were assaulted by some kids who stole his friend's marijuana plants. He'll be okay, by the way, just banged up a bit. Why would they even think Charlie could do such a thing?" Then it hit her. She remembered how the nurse looked at her. Maddie could tell she recognized her from the tabloids. When the nurse asked her what happened to Ray, she didn't think much of it. Now it made sense. "I know who took the picture of Ray and is spreading the rumor. It's the nurse from the hospital. I wonder if she was paid for the story. Damn it! I hate living in a fishbowl. I want my privacy back."

"Calm down. It will be easy to dismiss Charlie as the perpetrator. His alibi is ironclad. As for having your privacy, that's a big no. Not until you and Charlie split up. I know Tommy's there but would you like me to come over?"

"I would love it."

"I'm leaving now."

Maddie hung up the phone and sat down next to Ray. She told him about the news story.

Ray said, "I thought it kind of odd that the nurse took a picture of me. You and Dad were talking outside. She said the doctor needed a photo for my file. Why would she think Charlie did this? I told the doctor what happened."

"It's a much better story for the tabloids, isn't it? I'm surprised he hasn't called yet." Then it struck her. "Shit. Charlie did call when I was in your hospital room, but I had the phone on vibrate. When it went off, I'm pretty sure I said out loud that it was Charlie. The nurse must have heard me and assumed I was referring to your injuries. Amazing how rumors get started."

Tommy was furious. "I told you dating that guy was a mistake. Now you've dragged our son into the spotlight."

Maddie was about to respond when Ray said, "Dad, it's fine. Charlie's been super cool. If it weren't for him, I wouldn't have met Floyd, so don't rag on him, okay? I can handle this."

"I just don't like your face plastered all over the news."

"It could be a lot worse. I could just be plastered, right?"

Tommy laughed. "Yeah. Right." He went over to Ray and gave him a kiss on his forehead. "I'll give you a call tomorrow to see how you're doing. I love you."

"Love you, too."

Maddie walked Tommy to his car. They both looked like they had hiked through an emotional tornado. Maddie had been craving a full night's sleep. It looked like the only way she'd be able to achieve her wish was if Ray slept through the night.

"I know it sucks that our lives are fodder for the news. I'm sorry. Obviously, it wasn't my intent when I decided to date a movie star."

Tommy replied, "I know. Get some sleep. You look like shit."

"You could use a makeover yourself, Quasimodo. I'll call you if Ray's condition worsens. Otherwise, know that he's in good hands. Talk to you soon."

Tommy nodded and then drove off, much to Maddie's relief. She was afraid he'd want to spend the night to be closer to his son. Maddie had just made it to the door when she heard a car honking.

"Can I park in the driveway?" Priscilla shouted from her car.

"Of course."

Maddie hugged her friend as she got out of the car. Feeling her warmth and strength unraveled the coil that was keeping her grief in check. Maddie nearly collapsed as she broke down in Priscilla's arms.

"Hey, there. It will be okay. I promise." The two women sat down on the front porch steps. She let Maddie have a good cry while she scanned the neighborhood and trees for photographers. Thankfully, she didn't see any.

Maddie pulled a tissue out of her pocket and wiped her nose. "I'm sorry. Everything seems so complicated lately, then I come home to Ray looking like he went ten rounds in the ring with Rocky."

"I thought you said he was doing okay."

"He is. And he's in good spirits, thanks to Percocet. I pray he's not hounded by reporters."

"Have you talked to Charlie?"

Maddie shook her head. "I bet he's still shooting. Speaking of which, I can't believe how boring it is, watching him and Rachel, the bitch, acting and doing take after take. I'd rather go to a baseball game. It's riveting in comparison."

They sat outside a few minutes longer, then went in only to find Ray asleep on the couch, Mick curled up beside him. The boxer opened one eye. Satisfied it was Maddie and Priscilla, he took a deep breath, his jowls vibrating on the exhale, and went back to sleep.

During the course of the evening, Maddie fielded calls from relatives and friends, assuring them all that Ray was fine and Charlie wasn't responsible for his injuries. Kenzie came over and stayed for an hour, sitting next to her brother while he slept, leaving when it was clear he was out for the night. When Jackson called, Priscilla insisted she talk to him and ushered Maddie into the bedroom for privacy.

Determined not to start crying again, Maddie sat on the edge of her bed and told Jackson what happened.

Jackson said, "Do you need company? I know Charlie would be there with you, if he could. How about sloppy seconds?"

Maddie wanted to say, 'It's the other way around.' Instead, she told him that Priscilla was keeping her company and had volunteered to be Ray's nurse so she could get some sleep.

"Didn't get enough shut-eye in Mendocino with my incorrigible stepson, huh?"

Maddie blushed. "That's not what I meant."

"Whatever. I'll call you later in the week to check on Ray. Tell him I say hi."

"I will. Thanks for calling, Jackson. I really appreciate it."

"Maddie, I'm always here for you. Remember that. Now get some sleep, okay?"

"Okay. Good night."

"Night."

"Jackson, wait!"

He had almost hung up when he heard her voice. "Did you say something?"

"Yes. I totally forgot to tell you what happened on my way back from Mendocino. Believe me, you'll appreciate this. I was about halfway through the mountains on 128 when I got really hungry. I remembered putting half of a scone in my purse, but when I tried to find it, I pulled out the partially eaten snack that Ray made."

"Tell me it wasn't the one made with pot."

"I wish. I ate the whole thing before I realized what I'd done. Not only was I totally high driving home, but I had to take Ray to the hospital completely blitzed. I'm bringing my son into the emergency room for injuries sustained as the result of a marijuana heist. Can you feel the irony?"

"I can feel it and smell it. No wonder we Northern Californians have such a crazy reputation. I have a feeling that our escapades with the famed S'morbs are just beginning."

"I think you're right." I hope you're right, Maddie thought. "Okay, you're free to go. Talk to you later."

Maddie hung up and rejoined Priscilla in the living room. She recounted her conversation with Jackson, then told her friend the uncensored version of her drive home under the influence.

"You didn't!"

"Oh, I most certainly did and it was seismic. Navigating a mountain road while ridiculously high was not fun. Then coming home and seeing Ray bruised and bloodied was surreal." She looked over at Ray soundly sleeping. His injuries made her shudder.

It was past 11:00 p.m. when Maddie finally got to bed. She knew it was a matter of time before Charlie got wind of the news and called. She held out as long as she could, then pulled the covers up to her chin and fell fast asleep. Her cellphone rang at two in the morning, pulling her out of a deep sleep. She reached for the phone.

"Hello?"

"It's me."

"Hey. I was wondering when you'd find out and call."

"I know it's really late. Sorry. How is he?"

"Good. Banged up but okay." Maddie rattled off the laundry list of injuries. She had recited it so many times that night, it rolled off her tongue like a well-memorized script. She also told Charlie how she believed the incident made it to the press. She was relieved to hear that Charlie's publicist ran damage control as soon as the rumor hit the airwaves and a follow-up report was made.

Charlie said, "If the weather holds up, we should wrap up here by Sunday. How about I stop by and bring dinner? Invite Kenzie over, too."

"Sounds delicious. Let me know what time and I'll see if she can make it."

"Get some sleep, Ms. Mozart."

"You, too, Mr. Evans."

Within minutes, Maddie was fast asleep. The next time she opened her eyes, it was nine in the morning. She heard laughing and barking. Slowly, she put on her bathrobe and walked in the direction of the noise. In the kitchen, Priscilla, Ray, and Jarod were eating breakfast. Sure enough, with the exception of bandages on his nose and some bruising on his arms, Jarod looked fine. He sat next to Ray, his arm draped over his friend's shoulders. When he saw Maddie, he got up and hugged her hard.

"I'm so sorry for what happened. Please forgive me."

Maddie was taken aback by Jarod's emotional apology. "I never blamed you, Jarod, but thank you. How did your parents take it?"

"They're heavily pissed. When they found out I was growing and selling, I thought my dad was going to have a stroke. I think I'm grounded until I qualify for AARP. They said I could come over and see how Ray is doing and apologize to you. I've got to get back." He turned to Priscilla. "Thanks for breakfast."

"Anytime. Be good, Jarod."

Priscilla went to the stove. "There are some pancakes left if you want them, M&M. Coffee's made, too."

"Sounds delish. Thanks." Maddie went over to Ray. "How do you feel, sweetie?"

"Like I got hit by a Prius."

"Huh?"

Ray lightly touched his eye. "It hurts, but it's not excruciating, like getting hit by a semi. Nothing a couple of ibuprofen won't fix. So I heard you ate the magic S'morb yesterday. Way to go, mom. I'd say you were acting strange yesterday, but I was so out of it, I couldn't tell."

Maddie shot Priscilla a surprised look. "You told him?"

Priscilla said, "I thought it was kind of funny." She brought over a plate of pancakes, along with a tub of margarine.

"Ha, ha." Maddie poured syrup on her pancakes and took a bite. "Don't you have to work today?"

Priscilla said, "I said I'd be in later."

"You're a doll."

"My pleasure. Finish eating and I'll change Ray's bandages."

"Sounds perfect. Blood and gauze make me queasy."

"Don't you mean blood and guts?" Ray said as he got up to follow Priscilla into the living room.

"No. The sight of gauze sticking to a wound makes my knees weak. I forgot to tell you, Charlie called last night to see how you were. He'll also be coming over with dinner Sunday night."

"He didn't say anything about Floyd, did he?"

"We spoke at two this morning. I don't think he's talked to Floyd, why?"

Ray said, "What if Floyd doesn't like that I was on the news over a marijuana theft and doesn't want to work with me anymore?"

"You're going to have to ask Floyd, honey. I hope the guy is not that uptight that he would rescind the deal. You are a teenager, after all."

"Yeah. We're expected to make stupid decisions, right?"

Priscilla said, "Absolutely. Now, get over here so I can clean up your boo-boos."

"Yes, Nurse Diesel."

Maddie savored her breakfast. The pancakes were light and fluffy. The coffee was strong and aromatic. She dipped a forkful of pancakes into the syrup and relished the flavor, then washed it down with the hot coffee. Despite her son's condition, the mood in the house was calm and peaceful. She felt good. Sure, she would be dealing with a break-up within the next few weeks. The tabloids would be awash in speculation and innuendo. For now, she would enjoy the ride.

27

Sunday night with Charlie and the kids was 99.9% perfect. That's how Maddie described it on the phone to her friend Tanvi, who demanded to hear the details. As she drove down to Jackson's lawyer's office in San Francisco, Maddie recounted the evening. It began when Charlie had arrived with dinner and a gift from the cast for Ray. Better than a get-well card, they all signed the front of a bright yellow Visit Mendocino T-shirt. Rachel sealed her autograph with a kiss, her red lipstick hugging the R. They'd eaten dinner and watched an advance screening of Bruce Willis' new movie, *Jamison Jones, LTD*. Kenzie talked her brother into letting them all collaborate on a new snack. Each had been allowed to pick an ingredient that could be obtained without going to the store. The result was a cookie made from almond flour, coconut flakes, toffee-flavored stevia drops, and coffee extract. Ray had added almond milk and a few other essential ingredients so the cookies wouldn't fall apart. They called it a RaChaMaKen and it tasted like a Starbucks fancy flavored latte. Maddie promised to save some for Tanvi and her family.

"That's it?" Tanvi said. "Give me the juicy stuff. I'm married, remember? I have to live vicariously through you."

"How graphic do you want me to be?"

"Almost to the blushing point."

"You're at work, right?"

"Uh-huh."

"I'm not on speaker phone, am I?"

Tanvi laughed. "Of course not. Just the PA system." Before Maddie could protest, she said, "I'm kidding. Come on, girl, tell me.

What's it like sleeping with the world's most eligible bachelor who sounds like he's totally in love with you?"

"Wrong. Let's just say he likes me a lot. I blush easily, so here's the PG-13 version. The man is the best kisser ever. I think he took Advanced Kissing 101 because I'd be satisfied if that's all we did."

"No, you wouldn't."

"No. I wouldn't." Maddie pulled into the Stockton Sutter Garage. As she cruised for a parking spot, she continued. "He makes love the way he acts. He puts everything he has into it for the audience. I give him a standing ovation every time. Damn it, I'm blushing. I also found a parking spot. I have to go, Tanvi. I'm meeting Jackson at his lawyer's office to sign sanctuary papers."

"I can't believe this is really happening. I'm so happy for you, Maddie."

"Thanks, my dear. Except for what happened to Ray, I'm so grateful."

"Yes, of course. Promise me we can meet for lunch soon."

"Promise. I'll call you."

"Okay. Bye."

"Bye."

Maddie made it to the lawyer's office on time. Jackson was talking to the receptionist, leaning on the desk, his back to Maddie. Once again, she found herself staring at his backside.

"Hi," she said as he turned to see who had arrived. Jackson smiled and came over to greet her. Much to Maddie's dismay, his hug was tentative, aloof. If he felt her stiffen under his embrace, he didn't show it.

Jackson said, "Roland is running late. He said it may be ten minutes at the most."

"No problem. I have all day."

"You're not meeting Charlie later?" Jackson tried to sound nonchalant.

"He's filming."

In the reception room, Jackson and Maddie went over the papers, Jackson demystifying the legal jargon so she would understand what she was signing.

"Did you have a chance to go to Glass Beach?"

"I did. What a trip that place is. I've never seen so much ocean-polished glass before." Maddie dug into her purse and pulled something out. "Open your hand." Jackson obeyed and she placed a red rectangular piece of glass in his palm. "What does it look like?"

Jackson held it up to the light. "A square?"

"It's a blank canvas. You can put anything on it you want."

"Thank you, Maddie. That was very sweet of you to think of me."

"You're welcome. I can't wait to see what you paint on a one-inch square surface.

The receptionist hung up the phone. "Mr. Henry will see you now."

Jackson rolled the red glass in his hands, then put it in his pants pocket.

Roland Henry's office was ultra-modern. His plexiglas desk rivaled the ornate multi-colored glass artwork on the expansive white walls. Short and rotund, wearing a custom-made three-piece suit, the bespectacled lawyer welcomed them into his office.

"So this is the woman made famous by dating your stepson. Who said connections get you nowhere?"

Maddie replied, "Nobody. If not for Jackson, I wouldn't be here today, living my dream. Nice to meet you, Mr. Henry."

"Please call me Roland." He adjusted his wire-rimmed glasses. "Good to see you again, Jackson. Why don't we go over the papers once more before you sign?"

Jackson and Maddie nodded. They spent the next hour discussing the legal ramifications of running a nonprofit organization for farm animals and for at-risk women and children. Roland prepared their 501(c)(3) document from the IRS, as well as the formation of the board of directors. Throughout the meeting, Maddie was struck by Jackson's reserved attitude. His usual friendly, warm personality was shelved. In its place was a more somber man.

As they left the office, Maddie said, "You want to grab lunch?"

"I really should be getting back. I have a lot to do."

Undeterred, she persisted. "Come on, Jackson. You have to eat. We'll make it quick and I know of this dynamite restaurant on Maiden Lane."

He hesitated. The more time he spent with Maddie, the harder it was to reconcile the fact that she was with Charlie and he couldn't do anything about it. He knew Charlie's reputation and that it was a matter of time before he broke her heart, but he also loved his stepson and interfering in his love life was out of the question. "I really should be going."

"Please? My treat."

"I am hungry."

"Good." They started walking to Union Square, navigating the sidewalk full of pedestrians. Many of them were tourists, but most were businesspeople on their way to lunch. Maddie buttoned her coat as the infamous San Francisco wind infiltrated her clothing, chilling her. "Have you known Roland long?"

"Not really. He came recommended by my agent. She said he's an expert in nonprofit law."

"He certainly knows his stuff."

A few blocks later, they turned left onto Maiden Lane. They passed a real estate office, a couple of two-story office buildings, and a sandwich shop. Each one had the old-fashioned Victorian architecture with gingerbread trim: the quaint cut and pierced frieze boards. Halfway down on the left, they walked into a restaurant that resembled a French café. A blue and white awning shaded the café's outdoor patio. Mon Petit Chou was authentic down to the French menu with English translations.

Jackson said, "Aren't the French rabid meat-eaters?"

Maddie nodded. "That's what makes Mon Petit Chou so special. It's vegan. The owners met at the Academy of Plant-Based Nutrition. They're both from the States, yet they love the rich food that the French are famous for, so they decided to veganize the most iconic dishes. Do you know what the name means?"

"My little cabbage. My mom was French. In America, we say sweetie pie or honey bunch. In France, they call their children cabbages. Vegans at heart, eh?"

"I wish."

Maddie had to talk Jackson into getting a glass of wine. They both settled on Frey Vineyards Petite Sirah. She was successfully lengthening her time with him. Whether he realized it or not, she didn't care, as long as she was able to be in his presence for the afternoon. As they waited for their meal, they discussed the timeline for the sanctuary's opening.

"I estimated that if all goes well, from the approval of the plans and permits to the construction, we'll be ready to open our doors in a little less than a year. Won't Ray be graduating next June?"

"He will and may I say this Petite Sirah is lovely jubley?"

"Is that sommelier terminology?"

"Mais oui." Maddie took another sip, closed her eyes, and smiled. "I love getting mildly altered. I'm still in control, but I feel like I'm in a semi-dream state."

"One glass of wine can do that to you? Poids leger."

Maddie cocked her head to one side.

"Lightweight."

"That's me. Especially on an empty stomach." She mentally recalled the last time she was this hungry. It was only last week on her way home from Mendocino. She looked at Jackson as he tore off a piece of sourdough bread and dipped it in olive oil. She flashed on her pleasuring herself on the side of the road. Jackson caught her staring.

"What?" he said.

She blushed.

"This should be good." Jackson smiled and waited for a response.

"Sorry. This one's staying in the vault." Maddie drained her glass. "I promise I'll tell you some day."

"It's that good?"

"Oh, yeah. It's really good. How you say in French? C'est magnifique."

"I will call you on it, you know."

"I know."

Two hours later, Jackson and Maddie left the restaurant. Her buzz had worn off and in its place was a slight headache. It was worth it. By mid-meal, Jackson returned to his charming, funny, extroverted self. As soon as Maddie got into her car, she began her acupressure ritual to eliminate the headache. She applied pressure on her eyebrows, massaged her ears and finished off with squeezing the skin between the thumb and index finger. Slowly, the pain in her head dissolved. Before she started the car, she called Ray.

"What's happening, Mom?"

"I was going to ask you the same thing. How are you feeling?"

"Fantastic."

"You're on Percocet, aren't you?"

"That's a big yup."

"I'm leaving San Francisco. Do you need anything at the store?"

"Do they sell hot girls there?"

"Only at Rexall in the East Bay, but I'm not going there so you'll have to settle for Soy Dream frozen dessert. I hear it's comparable."

"Fine. You pick the flavor. I'm easy."

Maddie started the car. "See you soon, sweetie." She hung up the phone and muttered, "Men."

His attempt to avoid spending time with her was thwarted. Jackson had to admit, it didn't take too much to convince him to join Maddie for lunch and the glass of wine was a pleasant change from his normal routine of eating a sandwich while painting.

As usual, he had enjoyed himself immensely. Their conversation had veered from Ray's condition and the future of his snack company to Jackson's upcoming gallery showing at the St. Francis Hotel in San Francisco. She reminded him of Jackie, with her upbeat personality and sarcastic sense of humor. Few women had interested him since his wife died. He shook his head, chiding himself for falling in love with Charlie's girlfriend. Despite the situation, he was thankful that they would be working together on the creation of the sanctuary. And even though he felt pangs of guilt for entertaining the thought, he wondered if she and Charlie would still be together by the time it opened. He was hoping his stepson's short attention span would kick into high gear and he would be back to dating starlets or models before long.

After greeting the dogs and cats, Jackson checked his phone messages. The first one was from his agent, confirming the reception the night before his gallery opening. The second was from Trinity. She sounded frantic. He listened to the message and, before it was over, he called his real estate agent.

"Hi, Lisa. It's Jackson Danoff. Can you confirm that we'll be closing escrow on the property the day after tomorrow?"

"Let's see." Lisa glanced at her day planner. "Wednesday at 10:00 a.m. We're set."

"Is it possible to occupy one of the buildings before we close?"

"Anything is possible, but it's not legal. What's going on?"

Jackson explained the situation, to which Lisa replied that the likelihood of the deal falling through was so slim that if he wanted to take that chance and modify or add to the property, she'd look the other way. After a heartfelt thank you, Jackson placed a call to Trinity and alleviated the young woman's angst. His next call was to Maddie. She had been home only a few minutes and was in the backyard reading when her cell rang. She saw it was Jackson and picked up.

"Calling to thank me again for lunch? You're welcome."

"Actually, I'm calling to let you know that we're bringing our first residents to the sanctuary tonight. Are you available?"

"Are you kidding? Of course I'm available. Wait, you haven't signed the papers yet. Can you do that?"

"Legally, no. Morally, most definitely. Besides, escrow closes Wednesday. I don't think one day will make a difference and my real estate agent gave me the green light."

"Great. So give me the scoop. Who are we rescuing?"

28

Before Maddie had learned about the egg industry, she'd thought of Petaluma, Sonoma County's southernmost city, as a charming town, once known as the Egg Basket of the World. The image on the city's welcome billboard was as natural and rural as an apple pie cooling on a windowsill: a large woven basket filled with eggs laid by happy, contented hens. How very far from the truth it all was. As the human population had grown, so had the demand for eggs. Chicken coops had been replaced with climate-controlled industrial buildings, housing thousands of chickens in tiny wire cages. Given antibiotic-laced feed to eliminate disease caused by intense confinement, hens were now forced to produce eggs at an unnatural rate. As a consequence of the environment, their typical lifespan of five to eight years had been reduced to one to two. When they stopped producing, the hens were removed from their cages and shipped off to the slaughterhouse. It is the first time that their battered, bruised bodies would feel and breathe outside air. And the last.

In a rented van equipped with a large cage, Jackson picked Maddie up and drove north to Petaluma, exiting at Washington Boulevard and driving ten miles west until they came to Aunt Lucy's Egg Farm. Trinity had received a call from a distraught neighbor of Aunt Lucy's. She'd claimed that there had been a lot of activity late into the night, uncommon for the business. People had been going into the industrial hen house and coming out with cages of chickens for hours. She hadn't been able to tell what was happening to the hens, but she'd heard a few minutes of squawking, then nothing. Early the next morning, she'd noticed the building doors wide open.

The farmer's familiar red truck was gone. Where the land had been flat, there were large mounds of dirt. A few dozen hens, most partially covered in dirt, wandered the property looking shell-shocked. The hens' feathers were sparse. Many were broken. The birds' skin was raw, bruised, and bloody. It took her all afternoon to make the decision to call Trinity. She'd wanted to make sure that the farmers weren't returning. Trinity had wanted desperately to drive down and pick up the hens, but she'd been afraid that the long journey could further jeopardize their health. Trinity counseled the helpful neighbor on handling and temporarily housing the birds until help could arrive. Then she'd called Jackson.

It was dusk when Jackson drove past the farm and into the first driveway on the right. He parked next to an old Dodge Neon in front of a slightly dilapidated ranch-style home. The faded yellow house with brown trim was badly in need of a paint job. Instead of a lawn, weeds and scrub dotted the patch of dirt. A tricycle and assorted toys were mixed in with the weeds.

A woman in her mid-thirties opened the front door. She was short and stocky. Her bleached blonde hair was haphazardly tied back in a ponytail. Over a faded floral print house dress, she wore an apron that said, 'My favorite meal is take-out.' The television could be heard in the background. She wiped her hands on the apron, then held out her hand to Jackson.

"You must be Jackson. I'm Angie Glider."

Jackson shook her hand, then turned to Maddie. "Angie, this is my partner, Madeleine Mozart."

Angie gave Maddie the once-over as she grabbed her hand and firmly shook it. Her eyes got wide. "Aren't you Charlie Evans' girlfriend?"

"That's me."

"Son of a gun. I almost didn't recognize you in regular clothes. You're usually all dressed up when I've seen you in the tabs. As a matter of fact..." Angie ran into the living room and came back with a copy of *In Touch* magazine. Charlie and Maddie were on the cover, sitting at a sidewalk café in San Francisco. Holding hands, both wore sunglasses and smiles. Maddie had to admit, she looked like a celebrity.

Jackson said, "If we could see the chickens, I would appreciate it. I'm sure you'd like to get back to cooking dinner."

Angie replied, "Cooking?" She pointed to her apron. "I thought you were the pizza delivery guy." She walked outside and over to the garage door. When she lifted it, the rescue hens began to murmur. It was more like a whisper as their weakened condition prevented them from being more vocal. They were huddled together in a corner, cordoned off with a makeshift barrier of cardboard boxes and lawn chairs. Old towels provided bedding. There was a bowl of water and another bowl filled with uncooked oatmeal.

Angie said, "Did the woman from the animal sanctuary tell you what happened?"

"Only that the farmers emptied the building, buried the hens, then took off, but she didn't know why."

"After I collected the survivors, I called the cops. Turns out, they were in violation of a slew of city codes. Instead of paying the fines and cleaning up the place, they decided to kill the chickens and leave town. They worked for a larger company. It wasn't even their house! They rented it from their boss."

Maddie shook her head. "Why kill the chickens? Why not just leave?"

"I'd hear them complaining to each other about how they weren't paid enough to take care of so many chickens. I think they did it to spite the company." Angie glanced at the hens. "Poor things. I don't know how they had the strength to dig themselves out of the dirt, but they did. Do you need help putting them in the van?"

"That would be great. I'll go get our gloves." Jackson went to the van and grabbed gardening gloves for himself and Maddie. Then he opened the back and released the latch on the cage. It was filled with straw bedding.

Gently, they picked up the fragile birds and placed them in the cage. Not one protested. After thanking Angie, Jackson and Maddie took off just as the sun set. Per Trinity's request, Maddie called to tell her that their rescue was a success.

An hour and a half later, under dark skies, Jackson pulled up to the gate of their future sanctuary. The real estate agent had left it unlocked for his arrival. Maddie felt an immediate kinship with the property. It was as if the land knew its purpose was to comfort and provide solace. The air was cool and still. The smell of sage and rosemary was prevalent. It reminded Maddie of growing up in the high desert, where scrub grew next to cactus. As kids, she and her brothers would play cowboys and Indians, zigzagging through the rough terrain, occasionally stumbling upon a scorpion or centipede.

A sliver of a moon barely illuminated the barn where they were headed. Jackson parked the van as close to the barn door as possible and left the headlights on to help them find their way. He also turned on his flashlight.

One by one, the chickens were transferred to the barn where Jackson had set up a very rudimentary coop with wood shavings for bedding. The flashlight was placed on one of the inside posts so they could navigate the space. It cast long shadows on the barn walls, reminding Maddie of a Salvador Dali painting. As Jackson placed the last of the eighteen hens on the shavings, she began to shudder and slowly flap her torn and nearly featherless wings. Dirt clung to her chest and neck. He lifted the battered hen and held it close to his chest, hoping that his warmth would soothe her. She looked up at him, her mouth opened. Then she closed her eyes as her head dropped down to her chest.

Maddie shut the van doors and came over to where Jackson was kneeling. The hen was in his arms. He looked up at her. "She died."

"Oh, no." Maddie knelt next to Jackson and stroked the bird's body. "She knew freedom for such a short period of time. Poor, sweet thing." She looked over at her partner. His head was bowed, close to the hen's. When he lifted his head, tears were running down his face.

"Why are humans so callous?" Jackson lay the hen down on the shavings. "We need to give her a proper burial."

As he stood, Maddie also rose. She put her arms around him. She felt his tears on her neck. They felt cool against her skin. She wasn't sure how long they were hugging when Jackson put his hand on her chin and kissed her. It felt so natural and right. But it wasn't and they both knew it. Jackson disengaged first.

"I'm so sorry," said Jackson as he turned away.

"It's okay."

"No, it isn't."

Maddie went over to Jackson. "No. It isn't. Look, it was a slight indiscretion. Charlie has make-out sessions with his co-stars. Hell, they even have to be in bed together."

"He's an actor. It's his job. I'm his stepfather. I've betrayed his trust." Jackson walked outside and over to the van. He grabbed a shovel that was hung above the cage and started walking around to the front of the barn. He started digging. Maddie stopped him.

"Jackson, look at me." Reluctantly, his eyes met hers. "I know you feel guilty and I don't blame you, but..." It was Maddie's turn to be embarrassed. "But I've been wondering what it would be like to kiss you since I met you and yes, as I say it I'm feeling really guilty, too."

Jackson said, "Do you love him?"

Maddie shook her head. "But I like him." She took the shovel from Jackson and began digging a small hole. "I don't think he has to know about this."

"You know in the movies when people do something very bad? It could be a murder or robbery or infidelity. One of them wants to keep it a secret and the other's conscience compels them to talk. The consequences are usually dire. I still think Charlie should know. I'll have to live with the consequences and I'm willing to do that so I don't hold this mark on my character."

"Come on. It was just a kiss."

Jackson put his hand on the shovel. Maddie stopped digging. "To me it wasn't just a kiss." He removed his hand from the handle. "I'll go get the hen."

Maddie mentally slapped her head. It was the perfect time to confess her love for him. Instead, she stood there like Tim Blake Nelson in *O Brother Where Art Thou?* holding a shovel and sporting a clueless expression. She wanted to say something when Jackson returned, cradling the hen in his arms, but it didn't come out. Instead, she silently helped him cover the bird, creating a small mound. Jackson found a large rock and placed it on the grave, hoping to deter coyotes.

"Do you think we should make a cross for her grave?" Jackson said.

"I don't think she was religious."

Back in the barn, the hens were secured as were the barn doors, ensuring their safety from predators. Jackson was unusually quiet, which created an uncomfortable tension between the normally talkative two. When they got in the van, Jackson said, "Why don't I take you home?"

"I don't mind sticking with the plan to spend the night. Charlie was going to come over in the morning..."

"And pick you up. I know. I don't think I feel like seeing Charlie right now. Or you."

Jackson looked straight ahead as he spoke. Despite her fear, she put her hand on his arm. He turned to face her and she could see the pain in his eyes. "I would like to go back to your place. There's something I need to tell you, but you have to promise me that you will keep it to yourself."

Intrigued, Jackson said, "Fine."

"Say you promise you won't tell another soul."

"I promise."

"Good, because this is a doozy."

29

Tanvi, Priscilla, and Sylvie waited patiently as Maddie dished out the pasta. They sat outside, the patio umbrella shielding them from the noon sun.

"How are the rescue hens doing?" Tanvi asked.

"Great. Jackson's over there right now building a chicken coop with his carpenter friend. What's his name? Bill or Bob…it doesn't matter. He said they'll have it done by the end of the week. That's a good thing because the barn is too big and we're afraid coyotes or raccoons will find a way to get in. You know the boards are old in that place. I think it was built in the forties. Or fifties. I don't remember. Jackson said as soon as he's done with the coop, he wants to renovate the ranch house. I told you there was a house, right?"

"What's going on?" Tanvi said.

"What do you mean?" Maddie replied as she sat down to her plate full of pasta Pomodoro.

"You're rambling. And when you ramble, it's because you're nervous. What's making you nervous?"

Maddie tsked. "Get out of here. I'm not rambling. You asked me a question and I was answering you." She looked at Priscilla, then Sylvie. "Am I rambling?"

They both nodded.

"Afraid so, my dear. Is there something you want to tell us?" Sylvie took a drink of water.

"Not off the top of my head." She dug her fork into the linguini and twirled it, then took a bite. "By the way, Jackson signed the papers a few days ago. We officially have a refuge for the abused and misused."

"Congratulations! That's very exciting." Priscilla was almost positive Maddie was hiding something. She didn't want to cajole her into talking about it because she suspected it had something to do with the bet. "Sylvie, how's it going with the new guy you met on the online dating site?"

Sylvie laughed. "I thought I told you what happened. First date was great. Rod was so charming, I chose to ignore his big gut and slightly acrid breath. I figured I could set his diet straight and he would lose the belly and the rank mouth odor. Second date was nothing short of a disaster. He took me to Hanover's for dinner. Are you sure I didn't tell you about this?"

All three said no.

"Okay. As we're being seated, we pass by a tank full of lobsters. Their claws were rubber-banded and their little beady eyes were looking around, probably searching for a way out. I swear one looked right at me. You know I'm not a vegetarian, but the thought of those guys sitting in a small tank waiting to be boiled alive sickened me. So we sat down and the waiter was about to give us the menus. Rod refused them and told the waiter he knows what we want. Then he tells me to go to the tank and pick out the two largest lobsters for us. I said no. I told him that I'm not condemning those beautiful crustaceans to a horrible death."

"Way to go, Sylvie! I'll make a vegan out of you, yet." Maddie patted her on the back.

Sylvie said, "Are you done, you zealous vegan?"

Maddie nodded.

"Good. Anyway, Rod the Bod asked me if I was one of those animal rights freaks because if I was, he would have never asked me out. The waiter was standing there looking like he wanted to make a mad dash for the kitchen. Poor guy. I stood up and said, 'If I had known you were an insensitive lout, I wouldn't have accepted a date with you and, by the way, maybe if you stopped eating animals your breath wouldn't smell like a carcass.' Then I got the hell out of there and called a cab."

The women all clapped. Priscilla said, "Good for you. You've never had a problem saying exactly how you feel. Also, I don't know anyone under ninety who uses the word 'lout.'

Tanvi said, "What does that mean?"

Sylvie responded. "A stupid person. A fool."

"Good to know. Are your online dating days over?"

"Hell, no. Rod's just a blip on the screen. I'll find my Charlie out there."

Tanvi said, "Sure you will. I forgot to tell you all that Ava called me the other day. She invited me over for lunch. I declined and told her that we're not friends anymore, then I called her a koothichi and hung up. It means bitch in my language."

"Hindi?" said Sylvie.

"Malayalam."

"Did you just make that up?"

"Sylvie, Malayalam is only one of over four hundred native languages spoken in India."

Sylvie whistled. "That's crazy."

"Not as crazy as me calling Ava a bitch. Where's my high five for doing that?" Tanvi put up her hand and the women followed suit.

Maddie said, "That koothichi has a lot of nerve calling you." She grabbed the pasta tongs. "More pasta anyone?"

"Yes, please," Priscilla said as she held up her plate.

Tanvi and Sylvie declined. They had to get back to work. Once they left, Priscilla said, "Spill the beans, woman."

Maddie pointed to the house. At first, Priscilla wasn't sure why they had to leave the backyard. It was in the mid-seventies and sunny. Then she remembered that paparazzi could be hiding in the trees or behind the fence.

Once they settled on the couch, Maddie said, "I'll only tell you if you don't get mad at me or judge me."

"You take all the fun out of our conversations. I promise I won't huff and puff and blow your decisions down. Shoot."

"I told Jackson about the bet."

"What the hell did you…Sorry. Continue."

Maddie recounted the night they'd rescued the chickens. "After he wanted to take me home, I knew I had to tell him. He was miserable and I couldn't stand to see him like that. We went back to his house and I told him everything, including how I felt about him. He was quiet the whole time. He barely moved. I made a point to look him in the eyes when I spoke. I honestly couldn't tell what his reaction would be, but when I finished talking, he said he could understand why Charlie would be part of a scheme that would benefit him to the detriment of others. What he couldn't understand is why I would go along with it and perpetuate the lie to everyone. What could I say? I'd wanted to date a movie star and live a first class life for a while? Yes. That's exactly what I said. I didn't want to lie to Jackson. If he was disgusted with me, then I had to accept that."

"What did he say?"

"He forgave me and we had amazing sex all night long."

"Really?"

"No. He said he wanted to sleep on it. I was relegated to the guest room and had a fitful night's sleep. The next morning, I went into the kitchen and Jackson was sitting at the table with his mug of coffee and toast. He looked introspective. He said he was grateful that I told him, but he still wasn't sure how he felt about the whole thing."

Priscilla said, "I don't blame him. I *would* think that he'd be relieved knowing that his stepson wasn't in love with you and the end of the relationship was not only inevitable but near."

"Except for the problem he may have with my deception. I'm not the sweet, innocent woman he thought I was."

"Sweet, definitely. Innocent? Ha!" Priscilla picked up her plate. "I'd better get back to work before they miss me." Priscilla went into the kitchen. "Is Ray back at school?"

"Yeah. He insisted that he was fine despite his sore ribs."

"Is he still getting high every day?"

"No. He told me and Tommy that he's going to lay off the weed for a while, especially after he discovered that his snack ideas are just as amazing when he's straight."

Maddie rinsed off the plates and put them in the dishwasher. "Did I tell you that Ray is meeting with Floyd and his partners this Friday? Tommy's driving him down to Los Gatos after school."

"That's fantastic. You realize that in a couple of years, Ray is going to be wealthier than both of us?"

"That's if his snacks are successful."

Priscilla said, "I know there are other stoner-related snacks, but

Ray's are healthier and made by a teenager. He's one of them. I think it's going to be a money-maker. Does he have a name for the company?"

"Not yet. He has until Friday."

"Tell him good luck for me."

"I will."

"We need the plans by Friday. Otherwise, the deal is off. Got it?" Charlie slammed down the phone. He turned to Rachel, who was standing next to him, her eyes filled with tears. "Don't worry, my dear. He'll do it."

"God, I hope so. Without them, I can't…I don't think…son of a bitch. Sorry, John."

"Cut! Take five, everyone."

Charlie removed his black gloves and walked off the set in the direction of the bathroom. He spotted his agent waving him over. He pointed to the bathroom and continued on his way. When he got out, Donna was waiting outside the door. She looked ecstatic.

"Visiting me on the set? You must have good news."

"Great news. Scorsese wants you in his next movie. Is that fantastic or what?"

As flattering as the offer was, Charlie had made it clear to Donna that he only took the meeting with the director to appease her.

"Sure. Have you heard from Gretchen? John invited her to the wrap party at my request. I wanted her to see me and Maddie together. In person."

"I haven't spoken to her. Promise me you'll do the movie for Marty if *Julia's Love Affair* falls through."

"After my speech at the lab protest, I practically convinced myself that I was in love with Maddie. What did you think?"

"Stellar performance, as always. If it were up to me, you'd have the part. Remember, though, we're dealing with Gretchen Brockner and she's not fond of you. Will you promise?"

"Give me time, Donna. I'm not committing to any other projects right now. Do me a favor and call Gretchen's office and ask if she'll be at the party."

Donna shook her head. "Fine. You're as stubborn as she is. How's the shooting going?"

"Good."

"When this bet is over and you dump the old lady, I'd like to set you up with someone."

"Who?"

"Whitney Hyland. Have you heard of her?"

"No. Actress?"

Donna nodded. "She's a fairly new client. Right now, she has a recurring role on *Timothy Tundra*. She's a real knockout. Twenty-four. Killer bod. What do you think? I can arrange a meeting when you're back in L.A."

Charlie hesitated a little too long.

"Okay. Where's the real Charlie Evans? Was he tossed into the ocean in Mendocino?"

"I'll think about it. Right now, I want to concentrate on being with Maddie and finishing up this film, though working with John is such a pleasure."

Vicente came up behind Charlie. "You knew I was back here, didn't you?"

Charlie turned and put his arm around the tall, lanky director. "Not a clue." He winked at Donna. "You know my agent, Donna Madden."

"Certainly," John said as he held out his hand. "Don't you represent Sydney Balachek?"

"Yes, I do. I met you when he was in your film, *Desert Life*. When was that, two years ago?"

"Almost three. When you see him, give him my regards. Nice to see you again." He walked toward the set. "Five minutes!"

Donna said, "I'll let you go."

"Don't forget to call Gretchen's office."

"I won't." With a wave, she turned to leave.

Back on the set, Charlie got in position. As the makeup artist attended to his hair and face, he watched as John spoke quietly to

Rachel. She nodded from time to time, then gave him a quick hug and joined Charlie. He also thought about his conversation with Donna. She was pushing hard on the Scorsese thriller regardless of his reluctance. He wondered if she didn't have an ulterior motive.

"Donna Madden is on the line," Gretchen's secretary announced over the speaker.

Gretchen groaned and stared at the phone with contempt. She picked up the receiver and pressed the button. "This is Gretchen."

"Hi Gretchen. It's Donna Madden, Charlie Evans' agent."

"And to what do I owe the pleasure of this call, Ms. Madden?"

She wanted to say, 'As if you didn't know, bitch.' Instead, in her sweetest voice said, "I was checking to see if you received your invitation to the wrap party for John Vicente's film."

"The one Charlie's in?"

"That's the one." After being in the industry for a few years, Donna had mastered the art of schmoozing. She preferred candor to false praise, but she was more partial to an affluent lifestyle over a dismal financial portfolio, so she lied.

"When is it again, dear?" Gretchen savored having the upper hand. She'd earned it from years of subjugation. She wasn't too surprised that she had become what she loathed. She chalked it up to human nature. The species is so incredibly flawed. This was one more chink in the DNA armor.

"Two weeks from this Saturday at Top of the Mark."

"Time?"

"Eight."

"Morning or evening?"

"Seriously?"

Gretchen replied, "Very."

"Evening."

"I suppose Charlie will be parading Ms. Mozart around like a prize."

"Whether she's a prize or not is up to you, Gretchen, isn't it?"

"It is. Lucky me. I'll see you then." She hung up without waiting for a response and walked over to her coffee table. The tabloids certainly were convinced that Charlie had met the love of his life. She picked up the latest *Us* magazine. Charlie and Maddie were caught in a romantic embrace outside his hotel. He looked smitten. And he was right, the media loved her name. 'Evans and Mozart Make Beautiful Music Together.' 'Maddie Mozart is Evans' Favorite Sonata.'

Gretchen should have known better than to challenge an actor. She realized now that she should have refused Charlie's request outright. Now she had to decide if she was going to make good on her promise. Gretchen went over to her bookcase and picked up the golden statue. She was certain *Julia's Love Affair* would be nominated for an Oscar. At the moment, she was having trouble seeing Danny's face. Would Charlie make him believable or would Depp be the ideal actor for the part?

30

She glanced at the clock for the umpteenth time. Thirty-five minutes to go before her shift was up. Normally, Maddie wouldn't be so impatient. Today was different. Ray had his meeting with the venture capitalists and Tommy would be picking him up in an hour. She wanted to be there to see him off.

The hotline rang. Maddie picked it up. "Marin Women's Center. How can I help you?"

The woman on the other line spoke softly as if she didn't want someone in another room to hear her. There was sadness and desperation in her voice. "I gotta get outta here. If I don't, he'll kill me. He said so. Please. What do I do?"

"What's your name?"

"Helen."

"Hi Helen. I'm Madeleine. Do you have any children?"

"No."

"Do you have transportation?"

"No."

"I can call you a cab and we'll pay the fare. Is it safe to leave now?"

"I think so. I think he's still asleep on the couch."

"Give me your address and wait outside."

"1430 Bayview Road, apartment 12, in Terra Linda. What if he wakes up and sees me standing outside? I know he'll come down and get me."

"Is there a store within walking distance?"

"Safeway's down the street."

"Good. Are you on a cellphone?"

"Yes."

"Tell me when you're out of the apartment building and I'll call the cab and have them pick you up right outside the Safeway entrance. Does that sound doable?"

"Yes. Will you stay on the phone while I leave?"

"Of course. You can do this." Maddie handled calls of this nature on a regular basis, yet she still got nervous. It was like watching a woman walking down a dark street in a horror movie. Would she make it to her destination or would someone attack her? Maddie didn't even have the convenience of sight, only sound.

Maddie could hear Helen open a door, then the sound of snoring. A few more seconds and she opened the front door. A man's booming voice startled both Maddie and Helen.

"Where do you think you're going?" Seconds later. "And who the hell are you talking to?"

In a timid voice, she said, "The store. We need…"

"We don't need anything and you didn't answer my question. Who are you talking to?"

The phone went dead. Maddie hung up and calmly dialed 9-1-1. She told the emergency dispatch operator what had happened and gave her the woman's name and address. When she hung up, she silently prayed that the police would get there in time. Then she went over to the large dry erase board in the front of the room and wrote down the woman's cellphone number in case her abuser called in. If he did, the volunteers were to answer the phone without an introduction so he wouldn't know whom she called.

With a few minutes left on her shift, Maddie decided to leave. Despite her professionalism at handling the call, it rattled her. She could only imagine the torment and suffering the caller had endured if she'd come to this point, contacting a shelter. She hoped it wasn't too late to help her.

Back at the house, Ray was filling a large rectangular pink bakery box with his snacks. His black eye was circled in a swirl of pale yellow, dark blue, and faded red and the swelling had gone down on his lip. He was slowly morphing back into his old self. Maddie threw her purse on the couch and went over to the dining room table where Ray was arranging his creations.

"I love the pink box. People see it and instantly think cookies, cakes, pastries. They automatically salivate. Did you come up with this idea?"

Ray laughed. "I hate to admit it, but I told a buddy of mine who works at Bea's Bakery to grab a box for me since I didn't have one big enough to hold all the snacks. Maybe I did it subconsciously."

"Sure you did. That's how great minds work." Maddie looked inside the box where there were three of each delicacy. "Tell me again what they're called."

Ray pointed to the snacks in the upper left hand corner. "These are the S'morbs. Those are the Lava Cookies."

"I thought you didn't like that name."

"It grew on me. Plus, I couldn't think of a better description." Ray pointed to a flattened snack. "These are the Frisbeets and those are Almond Mantras. I hope they like them."

"Sweetie, they're going to love them. Did you pick a name for the company?"

"I've come up with a few names: Totally Cool Snacks, Feed Me Now, Dude Foods, and my personal favorite, Heat Seeking Munchies."

"I think that's my favorite, too." Maddie went to the fridge and pulled out a can of coconut water. "Do you want to go over your speech again?"

"No. I'll have time to recite it in the car." Ray picked up his cell. "Dad should be here any minute." He went over to the mirror and combed his hair. "How do I look?"

"You're asking your mother? I always think you look handsome, because you are."

Three short horn blasts announced Tommy's arrival. Ray closed the box, taped it shut and gave his mom a kiss before leaving. She said, "Call me on your way home. I want to hear what happened."

"Will do."

Maddie stood by the living room window with Mick and watched Ray place the box in the back seat. Before he got in the car, he looked over at his mother and waved. She waved back and blew him a kiss. Whatever the outcome of the meeting, she knew that Ray would be fine. He would continue to cook and create and do what he loved. Maddie was hoping he would want to work at the sanctuary as the head chef. She picked up her cell and called the MWC.

"Hi Jeannette. It's Maddie. I fielded a call from a woman who was attempting to leave her abuser. I ended up calling 911. Her name was Helen. Do you know what happened to her?"

"I certainly do. The police brought her here a few minutes ago. Constance is checking her in right now. Her husband was arrested on charges of battery. By the time the police arrived, she had taken some punches to the face."

Maddie breathed a big sigh of relief. "Poor thing. I'm so glad she made it to the shelter. Thanks for the good news."

"Certainly. Enjoy the rest of your day."

"You, too."

Maddie finished the coconut water and threw it in the recycle bin. She turned to Mick. "How would you like to go for a walk?"

Upon hearing the magic word, Mick began jumping into the air. His small, erratic hops always delighted Maddie. As she went to get the leash, she felt a wave of gratitude wash over her. Children, dog, boyfriend, Jackson, even Tommy for being a loving father, made her feel blessed.

After the walk, Maddie fed Mick, then prepared her dinner. The house was quiet and she loved it that way. Living with a teenager was synonymous with noise. Between Ray's cooking music, homework music, friends, and video games, quiet moments were few.

Maddie was lying on the couch reading a book when Ray came home. She expected an exuberant, animated boy, mouth going a mile a minute, barely stopping to take a breath. Instead, Ray sat down next to her and said, "I don't know if I'm cut out for corporate America."

She sat up. "Talk to me, son. What happened?"

"The presentation went great. Exactly as I planned it. Floyd and his two partners asked me questions and I was able to answer every one. They also sampled the snacks. Terence didn't like the S'morb, but he admitted that he wasn't a marshmallow fan. The other guys loved them all. I was totally into the whole scene. Then I started asking them questions, like how much they would participate in the cooking process, how the distribution would work, and what they felt my involvement would be in the company's direction."

"Which name did they like?"

"None of them. They told me to do some more brainstorming and come up with a fresh crop of names."

"Where was your dad during the meeting?"

"He sat in the reception room. So anyway, the guys told me that as the financiers and connections for distribution they would have fifty-one percent control. They also wanted the option of bringing in other chefs to create new snacks. The company would remain vegan and the snacks would always be healthy." Ray sat back and put his hands behind his head. "I don't want to lose control of my creations. Sure, they have the money and the means to make the company successful, but at what price? What if they bring in another chef and we don't get along or he tries to take over the business? I don't think it's a good idea right now."

"Whatever decision you make is the right one for you."

"Thanks, Mom. Dad said I was passing up the opportunity of a lifetime."

Maddie said, "It's only an opportunity of a lifetime if you feel good about it. Otherwise, it's simply another one of life's choices. You trusted your gut instinct, right?"

"Absolutely. You know how excited I was to meet these guys. The reality of the situation hit me when I thought about sharing my passion with people who were only in it for profit. I'm not naïve. I realize that's what venture capitalists do. It's not how I want Heat Seeking Munchies to start. Besides, if I get wrapped up with these guys, how am I going to help you with the sanctuary?"

"Good point, son. I like the way you think." Maddie stood. "Did you have dinner?"

"Dad and I stopped at Veggie Grill." Ray got up. "I'm going to get some homework done and then go to bed. I'm beat."

"I'm sure most of your fatigue is mental exhaustion."

Ray nodded and walked off to his room with Mick in tow. A few minutes later, rap music could be heard emanating from behind the closed door.

It was almost 10:00 p.m. when Charlie knocked on the door.

"It's open!" Maddie yelled.

"You really should lock your door," he said as he latched it after him. "What are you watching?"

Maddie paused the DVD. "A documentary about Kurt Cobain's death. And I do lock the door. It was open because I knew you were coming over. How was work?"

"Boring." Charlie sat down next to Maddie and gave her a kiss. "Floyd texted me and told me Ray's not interested. What happened?"

Maddie explained her son's trepidation. Charlie was confused. "Does Ray understand that Floyd's firm could make him rich?"

"He does. That's not what he wants right now. He's seventeen years old. Give him some time to grow and mature."

Charlie shook his head. "Bad decision."

"Maybe for you. Ray's trusting his gut and his gut said no."

"What if his gut is wrong? What if he's passing up an amazing opportunity?"

Maddie started to feel her anger rise. "Intuition is never wrong. I suggest we change the subject."

"Aren't we testy?"

Maddie looked Charlie in the eye. "No, we are not testy. We are respecting someone's decision regardless of whether we believe it's right or wrong. That's what respectful people do."

"You're right. It's Ray's life, even though he is only seventeen and maybe an adult should point him in the right direction."

"When we first met, you told me a story about how you went on an audition for a blockbuster movie. The casting director really liked you and offered you the part. You said there was something off about the guy, so you turned it down, even though it would have been a breakthrough role for you. Remember?"

"Of course. I told you the story."

"It was your gut feeling that said, 'run away, run away!' You were nineteen. Tell me again what happened to the cast and crew."

Charlie rolled his eyes. "They were stuck on an island in the Caribbean for days when the film lost funding. You made your point."

"Are you sure?"

"Yes, M&M." He got up. "I'm going to grab a beer. Want one?"

"Yes, please."

"Do you mind if we watch the documentary from the beginning? What's it called again?"

"*Soaked in Bleach* and I don't mind at all. I've only seen about ten minutes of it. I heard that they show compelling evidence that Kurt was killed and didn't commit suicide."

"Compelling, huh?"

"Yup."

Charlie sat back down and handed a beer to Maddie. "I like that word. Compelling. I'm going to start using it. Ask me how my day was."

Playing along, Maddie smiled and said, "So, Tiger, how was your day?"

"I wish it was compelling, but it was boring. No wait...I was hoping it would be compelling, but instead it was really boring. Which sounds better?"

"The second one but I would say, 'I was hoping it would be compelling, but instead it was insufferable.' It has more of a zing to it."

Charlie repeated it. "It does. Thanks. I'll even give you credit."

"What a guy." She kissed him on the cheek. "Let's see what really happened to Kurt, shall we?"

Charlie nodded. "I'm ready to be compelled."

Jackson lay on his bed surrounded by critters. Bubbles and Georgie were spooning, an unusual canine position, but one they engaged in often. Ever since Hamlet had died, the two had been inseparable. It was as if they were convinced that Hamlet had left when they weren't looking and they'd vowed it wouldn't happen again. The cats were indiscriminately spread out over the bed; Velcro, the Persian, was lying alongside Jackson, his fluffy body keeping his left side heated.

Topic of Substance was a great read, yet Jackson was having trouble concentrating. The conversation he had with Maddie the other night took up most of his thinking space. It wasn't too hard for him to fathom his stepson participating in a scheme to deceive someone in order to get a movie role.

Maddie was a conundrum. Even though he could understand why she would go along with the bet, he was disappointed in her decision. To Jackson, it showed a slightly bent moral compass. If she had refused to participate, it would have displayed strength. Then again, they never would have met if she'd declined. Despite her decision, Jackson easily acknowledged that Maddie was passionate and had a big heart. Her volunteer work with abused women was selfless, as was her dedication to animals. As much as he wanted to convince himself that these qualities overshadowed her moral lapse in judgment, his mind was having an ethical tug of war.

Jackson laid the book on his nightstand and took off his reading glasses. He rubbed the bridge of his nose. Charlie and Maddie were probably together. It bothered him, a lot. He hated feeling resentment toward Charlie. Jealousy toward Charlie. He'd known the man since he was a teenager; Jackson was only eight years older.

Maddie admitted that there were a few times she wanted to come clean, to tell Charlie that she knew about the bet, but she never did. With the wrap party a week away, she was certain that the relationship she had grown to enjoy would end amid the celebration. She convinced Jackson that she was fine with the dissolution of her fabricated relationship and, if he was willing, she would be interested in exploring a new one with him. Jackson wasn't sure what to do.

He picked up *Topic of Substance*, determined to finish the chapter. He re-adjusted his body, slightly shaking the bed. Georgie lifted her head and looked at Jackson as if to say, 'Do you mind? We're sleeping here.'

"Sorry, Bud. I forgot I was on an equal opportunity bed."

As soon as he began reading, he remembered that he hadn't secured the chicken coop. He chastised himself for the oversight as he got out of bed and put on his bathrobe and slippers. With flashlight in hand, he turned on the outdoor lights and walked to the coop.

He shone the light in the chicken's house and counted the hens. They were all there, including Sherlock. He sat on the perch, a hen on either side. Satisfied, Jackson closed the door and locked it, protecting his flock for the night. As he walked back to the house, he passed by the bird bath. It was less than half full. He picked up the watering can and as the water filled it up he noticed the light bouncing off something shiny. Among the polished stones, there was a crystal heart. Jackson pulled it out of the water and smiled. Maddie must have put it there when she spent the night. He was tempted to hold onto it, but decided that it belonged right where it was.

31

Priscilla looked at her watch. "Dear, you've been in there a long time. I'm falling asleep out here."

Maddie re-adjusted the straps on the evening dress, then looked in the dressing room mirror. "Sorry. I didn't like the last dress at all. I think you're going to love this one."

"Hallelujah. Get on out here."

She stepped out of the dressing room and Priscilla put her hand to her mouth. "It's beautiful. You look stunning."

"Thanks. Working out at the gym has really paid off," she said as she twirled, letting the emerald-green soft satin dress swirl above her knees. "Now I have to find shoes and jewelry."

"Don't tell me. You got a bucket of money from your sugar daddy."

"Yes, I did. A veritable fistful of one-hundred-dollar bills. I'm going to miss this."

"No shit." Priscilla stood up and stretched. "Whatever happened to the brothers who stole the pot plants and beat up Ray and Jarod?"

"They were arrested and charged with theft and assault. Jarod was put on probation for selling to people without marijuana prescriptions and my formerly pothead son was given a citation for buying without a prescription. All said, Jarod and Ray got off easy."

Maddie went into the dressing room to change. After paying for the dress, the women headed over to the shoe department. Macy's selection of vegan shoes was better than most, but still lacked diversity and elegance. They decided to drive over to Berkeley, home of Moo Shoes, a vegan shoe store. She easily found a pair of Mia Mona dark green snakeskin print stiletto heeled pumps. Their last stop was

Sacrebleu, an established jewelry store a few blocks away. Maddie found a vintage pair of ruby earrings with a necklace to match.

"You are going to look smashing, my dear," Priscilla said as they drove over the bridge back to San Rafael.

"Thanks. I'm starting to get nervous, thinking about all the people who will be there, including Gretchen, the one who started this whole thing."

"Do you think Charlie will get the role?"

"If Gretchen has been looking at the tabloids, she'd have to concede that Charlie looks absolutely in love with me. All the articles point in that direction, too. If she doesn't give him the part, she's slimier than I thought."

"I know you've had a great time with Charlie over the past few months, but do you really think he deserves to win the role?"

Maddie gripped the wheel a little tighter. "I've gotten a lot out of this doomed relationship. Maybe Charlie deserves the prize. By the way, I'm going to the sanctuary site to check on the hens tomorrow. Want to go?"

"Will Jackson be there?"

"Yeah. He wanted me to check out what he built for the girls. He's really into getting them healthy. It's wonderful to see."

"I'm sure it is. I'll definitely come with you. I've been wanting to meet Jackson for a long time." She quickly added, "And I'd love to meet the girls, too."

At exactly 8:00 p.m., the doorbell rang. Maddie yelled, "Ray, please get that."

"Since when do you wear a suit to dinner?" Ray said as he checked out Charlie's attire.

Charlie walked into the living room and gave Mick a head rub. "Well, hello to you, too. I'm taking your mother to a swanky restaurant in Tiburon." He went over to Ray and looked closely at the cut above his eye. "It looks like you're healing fast. How do you feel?"

"Good. A little pain left in my ribs. Otherwise, okay." He hesitated, then asked nervously, "Have you talked to Floyd?"

Charlie checked his watch, then yelled in the direction of Maddie's bedroom. "We have reservations at 8:30."

From behind the closed door Maddie yelled back, "Be there in a minute."

Charlie turned back to Ray. "I did and he told me that, even though he was disappointed in your decision, he respected it. So did his partners. He also predicted that you're going to do just fine."

"Thanks."

"I told you he wouldn't be mad." Maddie came up to Charlie and gave him a kiss. "Don't you look snazzy?"

Charlie put his hand up to his heart. "Hello, beautiful." She was wearing the peach and teal patterned dress from Portofino.

Demurely, Maddie replied, "Hello."

"Are you ready for a great meal?"

"Very much so."

Twenty minutes later, Charlie pulled up to the front of Heaven's Gate restaurant. He handed his keys to the valet, then walked hand-in-hand with Maddie into the posh restaurant. The maître d' seated them at the booth with a view of the San Francisco Bay. The glow of Tiburon's lights bounced off the water, adding a magical touch to an already romantic evening.

The waiter came up and was about to hand them menus when Charlie said, "I ordered two vegan meals."

"Of course, Mr. Evans. Excuse me for the oversight."

"No problem. Thanks."

A couple seated to the right of their booth overheard the conversation. The man, in his late forties and sporting a goatee, snorted and said to his wife, "I told you he was a wuss." She looked in Charlie's direction and shook her head. Her short hair was streaked with silver. Her heart-shaped face was pleasant, with fine lines around her eyes and mouth.

"What an asshole," Maddie said. She was hoping Charlie would say something to the couple. Defend his honor, so to speak.

"Let it go, M&M. If I responded to every negative comment people made about me, I would be exhausted." He raised his voice.

"Besides, why would I waste my breath trying to defend myself against ignorant idiots?"

Diners at nearby tables were excited about Charlie's presence. Some had their cellphones out and surreptitiously took pictures of the movie star.

Apparently the husband and wife had been talking and didn't hear Charlie's remark. They were in the middle of a discussion when the waiter brought them their drinks, then asked if they were ready to order. The wife spoke first.

"I'll have the almond crusted baby back ribs."

"And I'm going to get the filet mignon, extra rare. Bleeding, if possible." He looked over at Charlie and smiled.

Charlie ignored him and turned his attention to his date. "Jackson tells me that you're going to the sanctuary tomorrow."

"I'm going to take Priscilla with me. I want her to meet Jackson and the hens. Did he tell you that another one died? I'm surprised so many survived."

Charlie smiled. "I see what you're doing. Very clever."

Maddie was clearly confused. "What are you talking about?"

"You're setting your friend up with my dad. I think it's great. I don't know if she's Jackson's type, but it's worth a try."

"That's not my intent at all. I want her to see the property and meet Jackson since he'll be my partner at the sanctuary. It never crossed my mind to set them up."

"I think you should. The old guy is lonely."

The waiter came back with their wine and, after Charlie tasted and approved it, poured two generous glasses. The timing was perfect. Maddie was uncomfortable discussing Jackson with Charlie. She had to be careful what she said and how she spoke of his stepfather.

"Cheers," Maddie said as she raised her glass.

"Cheers and here's to you, looking lovely tonight."

A few flashes went off, breaking the mood for Maddie. I won't have to deal with this invasion of privacy much longer, she thought. Unfortunately for Charlie, this was his life. She wondered who would climb into the girlfriend seat when she was gone. A tinge of jealousy popped up, like an inconvenient itch. She looked at Charlie as he sipped his wine. The man was a beautiful human specimen. Externally. She wondered how the real Charlie Evans would have treated her. What a silly question. The real Charlie Evans wouldn't have given her a second look. She laughed out loud at the absurdity of her situation.

"What's so funny?" Charlie asked.

Thinking quickly, she said, "I remembered a joke Priscilla told me earlier. Want to hear it?"

"Sure."

"A yuppie parked his Mercedes on the street and, without looking, opened the car door. Another car came along and hit the door, ripping it off the hinges, along with the yuppie's arm. A policeman comes by and the yuppie yells, 'Look what happened to my beautiful Mercedes!' The cop says, 'Are you kidding me? You lost an arm, for cryin' out loud.' The yuppie looks down at where his arm used to be and says, 'Look what happened to my Rolex!'"

Charlie laughed. "Good one."

A few minutes later, the waiter brought their salads. What looked like Feta cheese was sprinkled on top. Before they could object, the waiter said, "The chef specially made this cheese from tofu. He hopes you like it."

Maddie stabbed a crumble with her fork and tasted it. She said, "Tell the chef it's superb."

Barely loud enough for Maddie to hear, the goateed man said, "Just eat the real thing, for Christ's sake."

Maddie looked over at Charlie. She could see in his eyes that he didn't want a scene. It might have been because he wasn't confrontational or he didn't want bad publicity. She took a deep breath and then glared at the man. He smiled and then watched expectantly as the waiter brought his filet mignon to the table. Once the plates were set before them, the couple grabbed their utensils and eagerly cut into their meat. The husband carved a large piece of bright red beef and shoved it into his mouth, staring at Charlie the whole time. He chewed slowly and swallowed, then said, "That's what a real man eats, not rabbit food."

His wife laughed as she chewed the meat off the rib bone. A couple of patrons shook their heads. Others softly chuckled to themselves. Charlie was sure that Maddie was going to lose it and verbally accost the couple. Instead, she dug into her purse and pulled out pieces of paper. She looked through them, picked two and went over to the meat eaters. She placed a photograph of a cow hung upside down, its throat being slit while it was still conscious, next to the filet mignon.

"A real man eats cruelty-free food. Only a coward allows other people to torture and murder an animal so they can stuff their faces full of its flesh. And here's a photo for you, honey." She placed a picture of a pig being kicked in the face by a worker. "What kind of person willingly eats the ribs of a diseased, beaten, and abused being? Don't tell me. It's got to be someone married to an idiot like yours."

Cellphone cameras were working overtime.

The woman looked at the photo and gagged. She quickly got up and walked out of the dining area, not before saying to Maddie, "You horrid, horrid woman!"

Apoplectic, the woman's husband was ready to grab Maddie when the waiter intercepted him. "Sir, with all due respect, you started this feud. I suggest you sit down and finish your meal." He turned to Maddie, "I'm going to ask you to do the same."

"Of course. As long as this troglodyte keeps his comments to himself."

Seconds later, the maître d' came over. He went over to Charlie. "Is there a problem, Mr. Evans?"

"Not anymore." He looked at Maddie with pleading eyes. "It's over, right?"

"I'll be good if he will." She glared at the man as he crumpled the cow photo and handed it to the waiter.

"I'd like another table, please. Preferably at the other end of the restaurant."

The maître d' said, "That can definitely be arranged."

"Please let my wife know when she comes out of the bathroom." He gave Maddie and Charlie a final steely gaze, then followed the waiter.

Heart pounding, Maddie took her seat. She had to take a couple of deep breaths to calm herself. Charlie was about to say something as she put up her hand to stop him. When she felt settled, she said,

"That vegan feta sure is good, isn't it?"

In a hushed voice, he said, "You know this is going to be all over the internet. My agent is going to have a fit."

"I'm sorry, but that jerk was way out of line and I can only take so much."

"Did you have to be so…so vocal about it? And do you always carry morbid photos of animals around in your purse?" As soon as he said morbid, he thought of Gretchen and then he realized that he had to do damage control and quickly. Before Maddie responded, Charlie took her hands in his and in a normal tone of voice said, "What you did was courageous, standing up for your beliefs and the animals." He leaned over and gave her a kiss. Out of the corner of his eye, he could see the cellphone flashes. Disaster averted.

The change in his reaction wasn't lost on Maddie. It definitely made for a more pleasant dinner. "I keep pictures of the animals in my purse for just such an occasion. I've used them once before. Do you want to see the one of the chicken or turkey? How about the lamb?"

"I'll pass." Charlie took a bite of his salad and swallowed. "This feta is outstanding! I can't wait for the main dish."

Maddie had to laugh. Dating a famous movie star and having him beholden made the relationship easy. "I'm pleased you're so enthusiastic. I thought you were mad at me."

Charlie responded in a flawless southern accent, "How could I be mad at you for standing up for what you believe, young miss? What we all should believe?"

She rolled her eyes. "*Once a Gentleman*, right?"

Charlie gave her the thumbs up. "How did you know?"

"Believe it or not, it's one of my favorite movies. I thought you were from the south until I saw you on Letterman."

"Are you a fan, Ms. Mozart?"

"I guess I am, Mr. Evans."

With the exception of a young woman who came up to Charlie while they were eating dessert, requesting his autograph and declaring herself a vegan, too, the rest of the dining experience was uneventful. After dinner, they strolled along the shore. The lights from San Francisco lit up the night sky. It seemed to Maddie like a massive pile of pirate's booty: a tower of glittering gold.

With Charlie's arm around her shoulders, she relished the last few days, the last she would be spending with him.

"You want to go to Sam's Bayside for a nightcap?" Charlie pointed to the seaside restaurant down the street. The heat lamps on the outdoor patio emitted an orange glow, warming the smattering of people below them.

"Sounds perfect."

A young, attractive waitress seated them next to the railing. She slowly pushed her long, auburn hair away from her face as she took their order, spending a little more time with Charlie than with Maddie. While waiting for their drinks, Maddie went onto YouTube and typed in 'Charlie Evans.' The top video with almost 300,000 views was titled, 'Charlie's girl goes rabid vegan on carnivore.' They watched a replay of Maddie's tirade. Charlie hadn't seen the wife's reaction to the pig photo and, when he saw the grotesque, gagging face she made, he started laughing and made Maddie replay it a few more times. He turned to Maddie and said, "You horrid, horrid woman," impersonating the woman's voice to a T. A few people turned in their direction, startled at first by the 'insult.' When they saw Maddie laughing with Charlie, they realized it was in jest.

Charlie said, "Don't read the comments. There are some real nasty folks out there and they don't care what they say or who they hurt. I gave up reading reviews and people's opinions a long time ago. You don't need that negative crap."

"I am kind of curious, though."

"You have been warned."

Maddie turned off the phone. "I trust you. Why ruin a great night, right?"

"Exactly."

Drink in hand, Charlie said, "A toast to you, Madeleine Mozart, speaking out for what you believe in, despite being called a horrid, horrid woman. You are anything but."

They touched glasses as Maddie said, "Thank you, Charlie. That was sweet." She was about to drink when she noticed that Charlie's glass was still in the air. He gave her a look as if to say, 'your turn to toast me.'

Maddie raised her hot toddy once more and said, "To you, Charlie Evans, for your generosity, understanding, and flexibility. May the vegan Charlie thrive."

Satisfied, he took a long sip of his scotch, then licked his lips. "When you said flexibility, you were referring to how effortlessly I started eating like you, right?"

"Not at all." She smiled.

"That woman had it all wrong. You're not horrid. You're nasty."

"Cheers to that."

When Charlie lifted his glass again, the napkin stuck. Maddie noticed writing on the other side. She pointed it out. "What does it say?"

Charlie turned it over. There was smiley face, the condensation from the glass blurring half of it. "Kirsten. Call me. Her number is written in thick ink." He crumpled the napkin and threw it on the table.

Maddie was unfazed. "The little tramp wouldn't have propositioned you if she knew how great I was in bed."

"How much brandy did they put in your drink?"

"Enough."

Charlie leaned in toward Maddie. Slightly above a whisper, he said, "Please don't yell at her."

"I won't, but I do have a nice picture for her in my purse."

Charlie's eyes got big. "Not again. Please."

"Just kidding. I'm done educating people. The harlot should know, though, how disrespectful that is to me. We women should stick together, not try to steal away one another's men. It's very offensive. I will, however, defer to you and be a good girl."

"Thank you?"

"Defer means to accept someone's decision."

"I knew that," Charlie said defensively.

"Then why the question?"

"I was surprised you were going to be a good girl, that's all. I've used the word defer a lot."

Maddie was poised to say something sarcastic. She stopped herself. For over two months, the man formerly known as Charlie Evans the playboy was bending over backwards to please her. His selfishness wasn't irrelevant, but Maddie knew how difficult it must be for him to adjust to her lifestyle. She leaned over and kissed him passionately. "I'm sorry. I misunderstood."

A few minutes later, their waitress came over to the table. "Is there anything else I can get you two?"

Maddie picked up the crumpled napkin and handed it to her. "Another napkin would be nice, Kirstin. This one is very dirty."

Avoiding eye contact with Charlie, she replied, "Of course. I'll be right back."

When she was out of earshot, Maddie shook her head and said, "The bitch didn't even blush. How bold is that?"

"Pretty bold." He took another sip of his scotch. "Is Ray home tonight?"

"He's sleeping at Tommy's."

"Good. I want to show you just how flexible I am."

32

Maddie checked Ray's room and called for him before she was satisfied that she and Charlie were alone. While he was in the bathroom brushing his teeth, Maddie lay in bed, experiencing a lingering buzz from the hot toddy. Eyes closed, she put her hands up to her face and inhaled. The faint smell of Charlie's aftershave lingered on her fingertips from when she had kissed him at the bar. A celebrity in person was so much more powerful than the onscreen persona. At first, the thought of kissing Charlie had sent her into a tailspin, as the opportunity to date him seemed non-existent. After their trip to Italy, the novelty had begun to wear off and the bright and shiny movie star had been replaced with a real person. A person with a temper and an inflated ego and a less-than-stellar IQ. But she was happy. If it hadn't been for Charlie, she wouldn't have met Jackson and she wouldn't be about to become the manager of an animal sanctuary/women's shelter, a job she hadn't even dared to dream of. Maddie could only hope that her partner would forgive her for dating his stepson and think of it as a minor infraction and nothing more.

From the bathroom, in a Cary Grant accent, Charlie said, "I hope you're ready for me, my dear, because I am very ready for you."

"Bring it on, big guy."

"You're telling me that you can have mind-blowing, passionate sex with Charlie and still want to be with Jackson? What did I get you into?" Priscilla pulled down the visor and switched on the mirror, then applied her lipstick.

Maddie drove south on I-80, increasing her speed to 75 mph. "Is there something wrong with that? You're the one who told me to have fun and I am. Charlie's a distraction. I know we have no future together. Think about it. Once they're done filming, he's back in Los Angeles. He'll either be on the flight home elated that he was awarded the role of Danny in Gretchen's movie or he'll be pissed that she gave it to someone else, drinking down as many mini-bottles of scotch as possible in a one-hour flight."

Priscilla patted her friend on the shoulder. "I have to hand it to you, M&M. I wasn't sure if you could sustain a levelheaded romance with Mr. Wonderful. I don't know if I could. I would probably be plotting ways to keep the relationship alive. Do you think you'd still feel the way you do if you hadn't met Jackson?"

"I hope so. Remember, the man is using me. Even if he developed real feelings for me and wanted to stay together, how could I trust him? We're talking about Charlie Evans, the guy who made it his mission to date as many Victoria's Secret models as possible. I'd be constantly worrying that he would stray."

"I hear you. I also can't wait to meet Jackson."

Thirty minutes later, Maddie pulled up to the unlatched sanctuary gate. She got out of the car and swung it open. As she drove through and turned left at the split in the road, the main house came into view.

"Nice digs," Priscilla said as she took in the scope of the property. She pointed to the ranch-style house. "Is that where you'll be living?"

"According to the plans, that's where they're building the art studio. The house is in disrepair. It will be torn down. When you get the tour, I'll point out where my home will be."

Maddie parked next to Jackson's Prius. From the corner of her eye, she saw Jackson appear from the side of the house. He was in his work clothes, holding one of the hens. He waved.

Before they got out of the car, Priscilla grabbed Maddie's arm and said, "For the record, step-papa is hot! If you hadn't called dibs, I'd be hitting that big time. I'll try not to stare."

"Or drool. Apparently you have a problem with that. I spoke to Mr. Peepers."

They walked over to Jackson. He held the hen while extending his hand to Priscilla. "I finally meet Maddie's confidante. Jackson Danoff."

Priscilla shook his hand. "Nice to meet you, too, and yes, I've certainly heard about you." She looked at the bird. "And who is this?"

Jackson stroked the chicken's head. She looked up at him, eyes closed, reveling in the massage. "This is Estelle, so named because she reminds me of the woman to whom I sold my first painting, Estelle Quintara. And to answer the question that I believe one of you is going to ask, poor Estelle highly resembled a sick chicken. But instead of clucks, she had big bucks." The women groaned. "Sorry. That was bad." He said to Priscilla, "You want to hold her?"

"Sure."

Jackson carefully placed Estelle in Priscilla's arms. The hen tucked her head into her torn and nearly featherless wing as Priscilla petted her, tentatively at first. "You told me that the birds were in bad shape. I didn't expect them to be so battered. What happened?"

"Up to six egg-layers are kept in a very small cage. They can barely move. When they do, their feathers rub up against the cage walls and their cage mates. Estelle's beak looks strange because the tip was cut off when she was a chick so she wouldn't peck her cage mates to death from stress and boredom." Maddie turned to Jackson. "How are they doing?"

"Come see for yourself." The women followed Jackson up a small hill and over to the barn. He had renovated a small section for the hens outside and in. There was a gated area in the corner. A two-by-two foot door was carved out of the old wood side. Hay was scattered around the dirt and a shallow bowl of water sat off to the side. The perimeter was lined with shrubs. Sleeping, Estelle came to life when she heard her fellow hens. Priscilla placed her in the enclosure and watched her scamper over to the water bowl.

Maddie was thrilled. "It looks like they're all outside and loving it."

"Yeah. As soon as I made that door, even the weakest of them ventured outside. Most of them started to peck the ground and some gave themselves dirt baths. Amazing how instinctual those practices are. With the exception of being buried alive in Petaluma, these girls had never been outside until now."

Priscilla eyed the ragged group of survivors. She knew that Jackson and Maddie were used to their appearance. For Priscilla, it was painful to see. It was a far cry from the illustrations of hens on egg cartons and commercials. They all looked happy and healthy and robust, like they wanted you to take their eggs. Maddie had told her about the intense confinement of food animals, but witnessing them in person, Priscilla felt as shell-shocked as the hens. She didn't show it, but internally she was crying. She followed Jackson and Maddie into the barn. It was a large, cavernous building. The slightly musty odor was mixed with fresh hay and dirt. Jackson had built a makeshift chicken coop in one section of the barn. He had created a number of perches and ramps leading up to nesting boxes.

"I am so impressed!" Maddie walked around the coop admiring the handiwork. "How long did it take you to do this?"

"A couple of days with my buddy, Bob. Next to painting, I love building things. Take a closer look at the door."

Maddie and Priscilla went over to the front of the wood and wire structure and leaned in. Above the door, Jackson had affixed the piece of red glass Maddie had given him. A white egg with a yellow heart was painted in its center.

"It's beautiful, Jackson."

"Thank you."

Maddie told Priscilla the history of the red glass, then she segued into the story of the ghost boy at the filming site. "After I left, Charlie said a couple of other people saw the ghost, too, and even heard someone playing up in the tower. It completely freaked out the cast and crew. They couldn't wait to wrap it up and leave."

Jackson said, "Why don't we show Priscilla the rest of the property, then we can go back to my place for lunch?"

"Sounds great," said Priscilla.

The tour lasted a little over an hour. They took Priscilla to where the women and children's housing would be, Maddie's residence, the counseling offices, and then the recreation room. On the other side of the property, she was asked to imagine horse stalls, cow barn, sheep barn, and pig sty. The official chicken coop was adjacent to the sty and additional barns would be built as needed. After putting the hens back in the coop and latching their door shut, the three headed over the hill to Jackson's.

"He only lives ten minutes away, so tell me what you think of him fast."

Priscilla said, "The man is simply irresistible. He builds, he paints, he creates, and that ass. No wonder you were mesmerized by it when you first met him. It's a beaut. And his face ain't bad, either. I can totally see you two together. It's meant to be."

"I knew you'd like him. He has a knowingness about him and his calm demeanor makes me feel so comfortable. I wonder if he's forgiven me for dating Charlie."

"I didn't detect any rancor or ill feelings. When we get to the house, I'll find an excuse to go to the store so you can be alone with him."

"Perfect."

"Welcome." Jackson opened the front door and let Georgie and Bubbles introduce themselves to Priscilla. She knelt down and petted them as they licked and pawed her.

"Your home is beautiful. You didn't build this, too, did you?"

Jackson laughed. "No. I'm going to prepare lunch. Maddie, why don't you show Priscilla around?"

"You don't need help in the kitchen?"

"I'm fine."

Maddie directed her friend to the living room as Jackson headed off to the kitchen. She took her from room to room, dogs in tow. Every once in a while, one of the cats would appear in a doorway and swipe at Georgie or Bubbles.

"Your house is to die for and your paintings are stunning," Priscilla said as they entered the kitchen. "Maddie told me you were talented, but I didn't realize how accomplished you were."

Jackson was at the sink, washing lettuce. "That's kind of you to say. Have you taken Priscilla to the art studio yet?"

"On our way. Then I was going to show her the backyard. See you in a bit."

Maddie opened up the door to the studio and Priscilla gasped.

"This is an artist's dream studio. The man really knows how to do it right."

The light coming in from the picture windows shone brightly on a painting on one of the four easels. It was of the sanctuary hills. Small shrubs and weathered, gnarled oak trees dotted the landscape. At the top of one of the hills was a figure. Arms outstretched, head back, the long hair indicated that it was a woman. Priscilla looked at it closely, then said, "I bet that's you."

Maddie said, "I doubt it. She represents the women that will be living at the shelter. The freedom they'll feel. The exhilaration."

"No. That's you." Jackson came up behind her. He put his hands on Maddie's shoulders. "If it weren't for this woman right here, there wouldn't be a shelter or an animal sanctuary. I may be providing the financing, but without your compassion and dedication, there would be nothing. I'm going to hang it in the office reception area."

"I've never been in a painting before, let alone one so inspirational." Maddie reached back and touched Jackson's hand. She let it linger.

"You deserve it," said Jackson. "Are you two ready for lunch? I set up the table on the back porch."

"Let's eat." Priscilla led the procession up the stairs, Bubbles and Georgie trailing behind.

The conversation was light. Jackson asked about Priscilla's work. She asked about how he became an artist. Maddie enjoyed eating and listening.

Jackson said, "I think we covered all the superficial information. Let's address the elephant in the room, shall we? Or should I call it the Charlie in the room?"

The women automatically turned to the house, expecting to see the man himself standing in the kitchen.

"I was speaking metaphorically. Priscilla, why don't you tell me why you talked Maddie into playing the role of the starstruck woman, despite her obvious knowledge of the bet, which I find deplorable, by the way."

"Oh, boy." Maddie took a bite of her salad. "Love the salad."

Jackson smiled. "Glad you like it." He turned his attention once again to the woman in the hot seat.

Priscilla cleared her throat. Despite being rattled by the question, she respected Jackson for broaching the subject. She put up her hand, then took a long sip of water. She cleared her throat again.

"When Maddie called me at 11:00 that night and told me that Charlie asked her out, I was dumbstruck. In a good way. I love M&M and I think she's beautiful, so why wouldn't he want to date her? Then she told me about how he's using her to get a role. I mean, really. That stank. But the more I thought about it, the more I felt that my unemployed, uninspired friend, best friend, should play along. Why not? I figured it would be temporary. Charlie's in town for a movie. Maddie's in a rut." She turned to her friend. "No offense."

"No offense taken."

Priscilla continued. "What's the harm? Charlie's got money coming out of his ass. He's not going to miss a hundred dollars for a nice dinner or even splurging for the trip to Italy. It's chump change."

"You didn't think it through. Maddie has had to lie to everyone about the romance. Her friends and family. Charlie. Me. Is that right?"

"I think the end justifies the means."

"I got to hear this." Jackson leaned in closer.

"For a little over two months, your stepson has gone from being a fairly insensitive, ego-based jerk to one who's been introduced to a smart, funny, intelligent, and beautiful older woman whom he never would have looked at twice under normal circumstances. Again, no offense, M&M."

Maddie smiled and patted her friend's hand.

She continued. "Now Mr. Evans is somewhat more enlightened as to the plight of animals. He spoke at a protest! Come on, that's good for something. He's a better person for knowing Maddie, regardless of how it happened."

"Everything you said is true. I was distilling the event down to its purest form. The bottom line. And that is, Maddie, you agreed to be deceptive for gain, monetary and otherwise. That's what I have a problem with." He looked Maddie in the eyes. "I've never disputed that you are a deeply compassionate person or that you would do anything for someone you cared about. So, does the end justify the means? I'm leaning toward yes."

Maddie exhaled, feeling as if she had been holding her breath for days. Her shoulders seemed to soften. Her neck felt less tense. "I'd never say that I don't lie. And anyone who says that they don't, is lying. I tell little white lies now and again and I don't think that there's anything wrong with it, especially if it spares someone's feelings."

Priscilla said, "I hate to break up this little morality play, but I have to go to the store for a woman's hygiene product that I don't believe is hanging out in your bathroom cupboard. Is there a store close by?"

"There's a CVS Pharmacy about a mile away on Stanyan."

Maddie cut in. "My keys are in the side pocket of my purse."

"Great. I'll punch it up on your GPS. See you in a bit." Priscilla grabbed the keys and hurried out the front door.

Jackson stood. "Would you like a cup of tea?"

"Maybe later. Please sit." Jackson sat back down. "This may sound odd to you and my logic may seem convoluted, but if I hadn't lied to everyone about my knowledge of Charlie's bet, I never would have known the purity of your commitment to the truth. I sensed that you had integrity and now I'm sure of it. I don't know what's going to happen after the wrap party with me and Charlie and I don't know what will become of us other than our sanctuary partnership. I will tell you that if we become involved, I will be honest with you. Will I ever lie? If you wear something that I find ugly or unbecoming, would you prefer I tell you or keep my opinion to myself and instead tell you that I like it?"

Jackson thought about an evening over ten years ago when Jackie came home from clothes shopping. She couldn't wait to model a dress she had bought. She proudly walked back and forth in front of Jackson, awaiting his compliments.

He hated the dress. It was too short and the paisley pattern in lime green, pink, and orange didn't complement Jackie's complexion. It made her look sickly. She was so enamored of her purchase, Jackson couldn't bring himself to tell her the truth. Instead, he told her she was beautiful and looked sexy.

Jackson responded, "Since we're being honest, I'm going to have to go with smile and lie to me. I would rather shield my ego and pride from the truth. Your opinion means a great deal to me, but I've been on the receiving end of someone's less-than-tactful review of a meal I cooked or a favorite shirt I've worn. I wish I was more evolved and I could appreciate the truth and use it for my betterment. Alas, I have a ways to go."

"If you were too evolved, I doubt you'd give me a second look. Perhaps we could evolve together."

Jackson smiled. "I've never been in a quasi-love triangle before and never wanted to be. I have to say, even though I'm frustrated by the situation, I find it strangely exciting."

"Like jumping out of an airplane exciting?"

"More like training for a marathon and then anticipating crossing the finish line."

"I hope you win."

There was a knock at the door. Maddie said, "It's Priscilla. I'll get it." As she opened the door, she said, "That was fast. What did…oh, hi."

Both women's faces dropped at the same time. Trinity stood on the porch, overnight bag in hand. She was wearing skinny jeans tucked into red cowboy boots. Her black T-shirt was tight. A red bra strap was visible just outside the V-neck. Her blonde hair was in a high ponytail. She was holding the calico kitten. Maddie felt old.

"Jackson didn't tell me you were coming."

Trinity said, "He wanted me to check out the rescue hens and I thought this would be a good time to bring Semi-sweet. Is she adorable or what?" She handed the kitten to Maddie. "Can I come in?"

Maddie didn't realize she was blocking the entrance. "Sorry."

As Trinity walked past Maddie, she caught a whiff of her perfume. Opium by YSL.

"Hey there, Jacks."

Jackson put down the dishes he was carrying to the sink. "How was the drive down?"

"Easy peazy. I'm going to put my bag in the bedroom, the guest bedroom, and wash up."

When she heard the bedroom door close, Maddie said, "She's spending the night?"

"Maddie, she's a colleague. Nothing more." He took the kitten from Maddie and kissed it, then cradled it in his arms.

"Tell that to her. She likes you. A lot. Look at her outfit."

Jackson shook his head. "Believe me. Nothing's going to happen."

Maddie looked in the direction of the bedroom. "I don't trust her."

"Come here." Jackson went outside, Maddie followed. At the end of the garden, far enough away for privacy, Jackson said, "Trini is too young and immature for me. I'm telling you that nothing is going to happen."

Maddie was trying to be mature about the situation, but she was having difficulty keeping her jealousy in check. She imagined Trinity getting drunk like she did on her last sleepover and coming on to the unsuspecting Jackson. Or sneaking into his bedroom and slipping under the covers wearing a sexy teddy. Maddie was positive the slutty undergarment was in her overnight bag.

"What if she tries to put the moves on you and you've had a little too much to drink?"

Jackson looked up at the sky. When he looked back at Maddie, his eyes were stormy. "Your jealousy is unfounded, but now you know how I feel. Wait, you can't imagine how I feel knowing that you're intimate with my stepson every damn time he sees you. I assure you I'm not sleeping with Trini. You can't say the same for Charlie, can you?"

"It's not the same."

"No, it's not. You're having sex with a man who's using you."

Maddie felt like she was slapped across the face. She should have realized that her relationship with Charlie was uncomfortable for Jackson. Still, his comment made her feel dirty.

"You're right. I'm being selfish and petty. I'm sorry."

From the patio, Priscilla waved. "What's going on?"

"Be right there!" Maddie answered. She turned to Jackson. "I should be going. Thanks for lunch." She held out her hands and Jackson gave her the kitten.

Without waiting for a response, she quickly walked away.

"Who's the girl who answered the door and who's that?" Priscilla said as she petted the calico.

"Trinity, the woman who runs Sycamore Animal Sanctuary and this is Semi-sweet."

"She seems nice."

"Yeah. She's a real peach. Let's go."

Maddie gave Priscilla enough time to thank their host. In the car, Priscilla snuggled with the kitten and waited for an explanation. Instead, Maddie turned on the radio. Priscilla turned it off.

"Talk."

"I'm afraid if I do, I'll start crying and you know how I hate to cry in front of people."

"I'm not people. I'm your best friend. I'll give you a few minutes to compose yourself, then let me have it. You're human, my dear. It's okay to shed some tears."

Maddie told Priscilla what transpired. "Here I am moaning and groaning over this little vegan tart and I forget that Jackson has to live with knowing that I'm sleeping with Charlie. How insensitive is that?"

"This isn't a typical situation. Of course you're concerned that Trinity is going to try to seduce your guy, but he asked you to trust him and I do believe you're going to have to, since you two aren't dating."

"I know. Life was so much easier before Charlie Evans toppled my tidy, little world and stood it on end."

"Easy is so overrated."

33

Charlie insisted that he pick Maddie up in a limo. She didn't argue, especially since he'd paid extra for a fuel-efficient stretch. He told her that the mileage was on par with a Honda Civic. Priscilla insisted that she hang out during the day with Maddie for moral support, if nothing else. And Mick very much insisted on playing with and protecting Semi-sweet from anyone who dared to interrupt their love affair. He had been completely enamored of the kitten from the moment Maddie had tentatively presented him with the small ball of orange, brown, white, and black fur. When she saw how curious and gentle Mick was with her, Maddie felt comfortable letting them check each other out.

Waiting for Maddie to finish dressing, Priscilla watched Ray in awe as he moved about the kitchen with the grace of a dancer. He stirred a caramel-colored mixture in a bright green Le Creuset pot, then removed a head of iceberg lettuce from the fridge. Chopping, mixing, pouring. Ray made it look ultra-easy and fun. He didn't measure the ingredients. He simply shook the spice jar or poured liquids from the containers until it felt right to stop.

"Who taught you how to cook like this?" Priscilla said. She swished the olive around the martini glass, then ate it.

"No one. My parents were never enthusiastic about cooking. They weren't bad. They just kind of went through the motions. I thought some of the meals could be better, so I asked if I could help. Pretty soon, I was doing most of the cooking. It's like a game to me."

"You're a natural, like your relative Amadeus Mozart. He sat down at the harpsichord when he was three and started playing."

"I know all about him. He wrote his first symphony when he was eight. We're not direct descendants of his, you know."

"Get out."

"It's true." Ray grabbed an apple and began peeling. He deftly turned it clockwise so the peel would be one long piece. "My mom likes people to believe that our bloodline follows his lineage when in reality, our family tree begins with Mozart's great grandfather's second family. Amadeus had six children. Only two survived infancy and those two sons never had children."

"His genius came from somewhere. It's in the Mozart blood." Priscilla took a sip of her drink. "When you're done with the appetizer, I think you should try your hand at creating the perfect martini."

Ray stopped peeling the apple and gave her a disapproving look. "I'm only seventeen."

"Well, hurry up and become legal. The drinking community needs your talent. This martini is good, but I bet you could make it outstanding."

"You don't like my martini?" Maddie stood in the doorway. She twirled, careful not to spill her drink.

"Mom, you look sick!"

"Thank you, son."

"I second the motion. You're rocking that dress. I knew those shoes would look great with it. Are they comfortable?"

"For now. I'm sure in a couple of hours, I'll be hobbling. Getting back to the original question: what's wrong with my martini?"

"Nothing. It's good. I just think the Ray touch could make it stellar. Since he's still a lad, we'll have to wait for his gift to grace the world of spirits and libations."

Ray said, "When is Charlie picking you up?"

Maddie glanced at the kitchen clock. "In a little over a half an hour."

"Nervous?"

"Not as bad as before I had this little gem." Maddie held up her drink. "It's amazing how therapeutic alcohol can be if it's not abused."

Priscilla touched her glass to Maddie's. "I'll drink to that."

Maddie motioned for her friend to follow her to the living room.

After they sat down, Maddie said in a low voice, "Almost three months ago, I walked into this surreal, Felliniesque world. Tonight, it will be over."

"Are you sad it's ending?"

"Not at all. I really despise being followed by photographers and seeing my picture in tabloids with humiliating headlines. The only glamorous part of this experience will be tonight. I can't wait to see how it's going to end. Will Charlie get the role? I have a feeling Gretchen is going to snub him."

"Why?"

"According to Charlie, she can't stand him. I can see her giving the role to someone else and relishing Charlie's disappointment. Such is the wild and wooly world of the movie industry. And tonight, I get to rub shoulders and chat it up with these people."

Ray brought the appetizer in on a large platter. Lettuce 'cups' were surrounded by the apple skin ribbon.

Priscilla said, "I watched you make it, but I have no idea, aside from the apple, what's in it. Enlighten us."

"What we have here, ladies, is sautéed apple, Fakin' Bacon, marinated tofu, and shiitake mushrooms inside an iceberg lettuce leaf topped with rosemary, black salt, and cilantro. Help yourselves."

The three of them picked up a crisp lettuce leaf and took a bite.

"Sensational!" Priscilla said.

"Ditto. Son, you're amazing and you certainly didn't get your talent from me."

Priscilla said, "Apparently, he didn't get it from Amadeus either. I thought you were a direct descendant."

"I never told you that."

"You never didn't."

"That makes a lot of sense. Want another martini?"

Priscilla replied, "You know what I mean."

"With a name like Mozart, why wouldn't I want to keep the mystique alive? It's so much more glamorous than telling people that our bloodline comes from Amadeus' great grandfather's second family. Who the hell cares what their names are? Not one of them was famous."

"Methinks your mother is an elitist."

"Are you, Mom?"

Maddie pursed her lips and gave Priscilla a disapproving look. "Not at all. If someone takes the time to ask me if I'm related to the composer, I tell them the truth. If they don't ask, I don't volunteer the information. And in a convoluted way, I am related to Wolfie. We shared his great grandfather. Now if you'll excuse me, I need to reapply my lipstick before Charlie arrives." Finishing the last of her martini, Maddie went into her bathroom.

"You'd better hurry. The limo just pulled up," Ray yelled.

Mick left Semi-sweet and ran up to the window, barking. Priscilla stood next to him. She parted the curtains and watched as Charlie got out of the limo. She whistled.

"Just when I thought he couldn't look any hotter. Ouch!"

Ray opened the front door and let Charlie in. "Dude. Congrats on finishing the movie."

"Thanks." He saw Priscilla. "The last time I saw you was the night of your friend's party."

"Ex-friend. Sounds like you two are going to have fun tonight."

"I hope it's as memorable for Maddie as it is for me."

"I'm sure it will be."

Maddie walked in. The martini made her slightly unsteady. It also bolstered her confidence, which she was positive she would need plenty of tonight. When Charlie saw her, he was genuinely captivated.

"Madeleine Mozart, you look amazing."

She smiled. "Thank you. You look exceedingly handsome." She then turned to Priscilla and said, "Do you think he would love saying my last name if he knew?"

Charlie looked confused. "Knew what?"

"She'll tell you in the limo, right, Ms. Mozart?"

"Yes, Ms. Selfrante. Come on, Charlie. We don't want to be late." Maddie kissed Ray and gave her friend a tighter-than-usual hug.

As they settled into the limo, Charlie poured them each a flute of champagne. "What's the secret about your last name? You didn't change it from something embarrassing, did you?"

"I wouldn't think of doing that, Mr. Torregrossa." She clinked her glass against his. "To things not always being what they seem.

Long live illusion."

"O-kay. What's all this about your name?"

"Here's the scoop. Wolfgang Amadeus Mozart. Actually, his Christian name was Johannes Chrysostomus Wolfgangus Theophilus Mozart. Anyway, his only two surviving children were boys and they never had their own offspring, so his bloodline died with him. However, his great grandfather's side of the family did a ton of procreating and that's the side of the family I come from. Disappointed?"

"Why should I be?"

"I'm not a direct descendant of the only famous Mozart?"

"Sweetheart, you're..."

"Don't say anything cloying."

Charlie shook his head. "Why would I say something clawing?"

"Cloying. Sappy. Sugary sweet."

"Oh. Fine. Here it is: you're a special person no matter what your name is or who your relatives are or aren't." He leaned over and gave her a kiss. "Couldn't you have just said sappy?"

"I like the word cloying."

"Of course you do."

Maddie opened up the sunroof, then kicked off her shoes and laid her head on Charlie's lap. She looked up through the window and watched the flashes of orange steel pass overhead as they drove across the Golden Gate Bridge. She wanted to savor the moment, since she was almost certain she wouldn't be riding in a limousine again for a long time.

If Maddie had ever wanted to feel like a celebrity, this was the night. When word got out that the cast and crew of the movie were having a wrap party at the Mark Hopkins Hotel, the paparazzi had descended on the elegant building like vultures on roadkill. When their limo pulled up to the hotel's entrance, Charlie held Maddie's hand as he smiled ear to ear for the cameras. Flashbulbs were popping in every direction. One of the photographers shouted, "Hey Charlie, are you going to miss San Francisco?"

"More than you know."

"Are you going back to L.A. with Charlie, Madeleine?" another photographer shouted.

Not knowing what to say, Maddie smiled and tightened her grip on Charlie's hand. Once they were inside, she felt better. It was short-lived. As they waited for the elevator to take them up to Top of the Mark, someone tapped Charlie on the shoulder. They both turned. Dressed in a conservative deep purple pants suit, Gretchen Brockner had the look of a woman in complete control. She extended her hand to Maddie.

"I'm Gretchen Brockner. You must be Madeleine. So nice to meet you."

"The pleasure is all mine." Before the bet, Gretchen's films had been among Maddie's favorites. She still admired the woman's talent, but she'd never give Gretchen the satisfaction of telling her so.

Gretchen said to Charlie, "It's been a while since I've seen you. We'll have to catch up at the party."

Maddie could feel Charlie's energy level intensify. This was the moment he'd been waiting for since they met.

"Yes, we will." Charlie tried to sound nonchalant.

John Vicente stood at the entrance to the party, welcoming the guests. When he saw Maddie, he gave her a warm hug and whispered in her ear, "Don't let all these stars intimidate you. You're better than all of them."

"Thank you, John."

Maddie kept those words close as she surveyed the guests. She recognized actors from the film. She knew most of the other guests were comprised of the crew and their friends and families. She tried not to search for Rachel Swanson, yet found herself scanning the crowd for the blonde actress.

Charlie interrupted her. "Can I get you something to drink?"

"I'll come with you."

As they walked to one of the bars, Charlie was approached by his colleagues, congratulating him on a job well done. He returned the compliments. Every time, he introduced Maddie as if she were a prized possession.

"One chardonnay and do you have single malt scotch?"

"Glenfiddich," replied the bartender.

"Perfect. On the rocks, please."

Charlie stuffed a twenty-dollar bill into the tip jar and handed Maddie her drink. "There's someone I want you to meet. Actually, there are a lot of people I want to introduce you to, but this person is special."

Maddie followed Charlie through the crowd to the other end of the room. He approached a tall, slender woman with short, auburn hair. Maddie guessed she was around thirty-five. Were it not for her high cheekbones and dark green eyes, she would only be mildly attractive. When she saw Charlie, she held out her arms, almost spilling her drink.

"There's my favorite client," she said as she embraced him as if he were a long-lost friend.

"Maddie, I'd like you to meet Donna Madden, friend, agent, and all around great sport."

"Nice to meet you, Donna."

"The pleasure is all mine."

"You sound familiar," Maddie said. "Did you visit Charlie on the set in Mendocino?"

Donna shook her head. "No. Sorry." She looked over Maddie's head and smiled. "There she is."

Charlie and Maddie turned in the direction of Donna's gaze and watched as a striking young woman sauntered up to them. Her very short metallic frock was see-through, revealing a baby blue bra and matching underwear. The spike heels elevated her already tall frame to a little over six feet. Maddie could have sworn she heard Charlie's jaw drop. Without thinking, her eyes went to his crotch, expecting to find further evidence of his attraction. She chided herself for being so petty.

Donna took the woman's hand adoringly. "Whitney Hyland, I'd like you to meet Charlie Evans, who I'm hoping will be your co-star in Scorsese's next film." Almost as an afterthought, she added, "And this is Madeleine Mozart."

Whitney tried to act poised and self-assured as if meeting an international movie star was an everyday occurrence. Maddie could tell that underneath the young woman's stunning veneer, she was a bundle of nerves. Charlie's megawatt presence was no match for the neophyte.

"So this is the Whitney you've been telling me about. Nice to meet you."

"You, too." She nodded to Maddie, making Charlie's girlfriend feel like the court jester in a group of royalty. Donna explained how she'd met Whitney, recalling in droning detail their first introduction. Suddenly, Maddie placed Donna's voice: outside the nightclub where she'd first met Charlie. She wondered if it had been Whitney Donna had been talking to that night. If so, the agent was playing matchmaker with her clients.

Maddie interrupted Donna's story. "Please excuse me. I'll be right back." Desperate for a glass of water, Maddie went to the closest bar. She was standing behind a man nearly twice her size in width and a good foot taller. In front of him, Gretchen Brockner was talking to Lauren Titus, one of the co-stars in Vicente's film.

Lauren said, "I've heard great things about *Julia's Love Affair*. The buzz is that Charlie's playing the lead."

Gretchen turned around, checking to see who was within earshot. Maddie was completely hidden. Satisfied, she replied, "I don't know where that rumor started, but it's not true. I'm not sure who's going to play Danny. I may give the role to Depp."

Maddie left the line and went to a bar on the other side of the ballroom. For the second time that night, she was hit with a zinger. As much as she abhorred being the subject of a bet, she was more repulsed by Gretchen's inability to uphold her end of the deal. She took a long sip of her wine, contemplating whether she should tell Charlie what she overheard.

With water in one hand and her near empty glass of wine in the other, Maddie rejoined Charlie and Donna.

"Where's Whitney?" Maddie asked.

"Ladies room," said Donna. She looked at her empty martini glass. "Refill time. I'll catch up with you two later." She gave them both air kisses and was off.

Charlie took the glasses out of Maddie's hands and placed them on a table. He walked her out on the dance floor. The band was playing, *Fly Me to the Moon*. The vocalist did a dead-on impersonation of Sinatra. Normally, Maddie would have enjoyed the spontaneous dance, but her mind was elsewhere. After a few minutes, she said, "I've been dying to ask Gretchen about a scene in one of her movies. Would you go with me so I can talk to her?"

It was a strange request at an inopportune time, but Charlie was used to Maddie's quirks. "Whatever you want."

Thankfully, Gretchen had just stepped out of the ladies room, so she was alone. In her most innocent voice, Maddie said, "Ms. Brockner, I wanted to tell you what a big fan I am of your movies."

"Well, thank you, Madeleine."

"Please, call me Maddie."

"Okay. Maddie."

"I've always been fascinated by the scene in *A Little Time*, when the twins walk through the tunnel and enter a tobacco shop. At the risk of sounding ignorant, why did they end up there? I thought for sure they'd walk into a forest."

"If you remember, early in the film their father talks about wanting to own a tobacco store and he would have if the twins hadn't been born." As she continued with her explanation, Gretchen observed the couple before her. They both seemed so comfortable with each other. If she wasn't so skeptical, she would have sworn that Charlie was in love with this older woman.

Maddie nodded. "Of course. That makes perfect sense." She took Charlie's hand. "Charlie speaks highly of you, so I don't think he'd mind if I told you our news." She moved in a little closer. "He asked me to move in with him! Isn't that great?"

Maddie gave Charlie a big hug. She whispered in his ear, "I know about the bet."

Gretchen looked flustered. "That's...um. Well...congratulations. I'm...um...so happy for you both."

"Thank you. Now, if you'll excuse me, I have to visit the ladies room."

Charlie watched her walk away. The enormity of her confession rendered him speechless.

Maddie calmly walked into the bathroom. As soon as she locked the stall door, she broke down. As she cried, she could feel the lie drain from her body, flowing out through the tears and dropping like tiny raindrops from a storm cloud. Tension she didn't realize she had been storing dissipated. The purge lasted a good five minutes. When it was over, she felt diaphanous, like she was made of tissue paper. Certain she was the only one in the bathroom, she opened the stall door. One look in the bathroom mirror sent her into a panic until she remembered that she'd brought her makeup bag. It was a mini-emergency kit that held face-saving products. She grabbed a paper towel, wet it and held it against her eyes, hoping the cool water would reduce the puffiness and redness. She tackled her red nose next by applying a powder foundation.

Another five minutes of reapplying mascara, eyeliner, and lipstick, and Maddie felt comfortable enough to rejoin the party. She found Charlie sitting alone, nursing his scotch. Her first inclination was to hold his hand as she sat down next to him, but she stopped herself.

"Are you okay?" she said.

"I…" Charlie looked at Maddie. "Were you crying?"

She nodded. "So, what happened with Gretchen?"

"I got the part." He smiled weakly, the victory somewhat eclipsed by Maddie's admission.

"That's great! Congratulations."

"How long have you known?"

"Since the beginning. That's why I declined your invitation to leave the nightclub together and tried not to give you my number. You were very insistent."

John Vicente came up to the couple. "Sorry to interrupt, but Graham Norbert just showed up and I'd like to introduce you. He's the screenwriter I told you about, the one who co-wrote *Nathaniel's Dream*."

At Maddie's insistence, Charlie reluctantly agreed to go with John. She watched the men walk away and a sadness overtook her. She knew this would be her last night with Charlie Evans and her heart felt like it was losing some of its luster. Despite the circumstances that had brought them together, Charlie brought joy into her life. She didn't know if his courtship was an act. If his real personality wasn't as tolerant or as loving. Or as generous. Somehow, it didn't matter. She'd had fun.

"A glass of chardonnay please." While Maddie waited for the bartender to pour, Rachel Swanson came up beside her. She looked exquisite. Her blonde hair fell to her bare shoulders. Her body-hugging strapless dress looked like it was made exclusively for her figure. She gave Maddie the once-over.

"Where's your boy toy?"

"The one you tried to seduce, or the one who didn't want to have anything to do with you? Oh wait, they're one and the same. He's with your director."

Rachel huffed, "No need to get nasty. I was just kidding."

Maddie accepted her drink from the bartender, then turned to Rachel and said, "No, you weren't. Rachel, there's one thing we both have in common: growing older. Whether you'll have the means and inclination to slow the process is up to you. You'll either age gracefully, which I doubt because of the business you're in, or you'll get nipped and tucked and pulled and tightened. Either way, I hope you regret making fun of me because of my age. You're going to be there before you know it."

Flustered, Rachel nervously pushed her hair out of her face. "Actually, I think you look great for your age."

Maddie gave her a nasty look. "Can't you give me a compliment without attaching an addendum to it?"

"Can't you just accept it and move on?"

"No." Maddie turned and walked away. A little smile crept across her face.

Charlie and Maddie ended up leaving the party early. Both were emotionally spent. And both wanted to talk without being in a party environment. As soon as they got settled in the limo, Charlie started in.

"I don't know where to begin. I'm angry with you for playing along and using me. And I also don't understand how you could be with me, knowing that I was using you."

"That's a good question." Maddie readjusted her position so she was facing Charlie. She was thankful that her 'pressure valve' had been released at the party. Otherwise, she would have been a mess.

CAROL TREACY

"When I overheard Donna talking on her cell, telling Whitney about the bet, I was crushed. Your interest in me was a farce. I was your ticket to a role in a movie, for Christ's sake. You bet I was pissed. And hurt. And I felt like an old lady." Maddie put her head back on the plush seat and closed her eyes. When she opened them, she looked right into Charlie's slightly bloodshot blue eyes. "My first inclination was to refuse your dinner invitation, but I changed my mind. Why not play along? What did I have to lose? My dignity? Maybe. What I had to gain seemed so much more desirable. I would be dating one of the most eligible bachelors on the planet. I could speak my mind and know that you wouldn't dump me. Couldn't dump me. I admit I hated the lack of privacy.

"After a while, I began to enjoy being with you. You're funny and very generous. The more we hung out, the less I thought about why you were dating me."

Charlie smiled. "I had fun, too. I have to admit, I learned a lot about women being with you. Most of the women I dated would do anything I asked or wanted. Not you."

"You've got that right."

"You say that now. What if you hadn't known about the bet? Would you have slept with me on our first date?" Charlie grabbed an ice-cold bottle of champagne from the refrigerator. "Want some?"

"No, thanks." Maddie sat up and crossed her legs. "If I thought you were seeing me because you were actually attracted to me, I would have stuck to my three-date rule." Charlie frowned. "Don't look so disappointed. I like to think that I still have a semblance of decorum."

Seeing the all-too-familiar blank stare, Maddie quickly added, "Dignity."

"I knew that."

"No, you didn't."

Charlie took a mouthful of champagne. "I have to say that you weren't the easiest girlfriend I've had, but hands down you were the most fun."

"Really?"

"Hell, yeah."

"What about your diet? Will you become a vegan?"

Charlie said, "Good question. I'm leaning toward it, but I won't make any promises."

"Fair enough. Did you know that your choice to eat vegan for the last few months convinced thousands of people to try a plant-based diet? I heard it on Entertainment Tonight."

"Wow. That means I helped save a ton of animals from being eaten." Charlie held up his glass of champagne. "A toast to me and to you for bringing kindness and compassion into my life."

Twenty minutes later, the limo pulled up in front of Maddie's house. She put her shoes back on and grabbed her coat and purse. "So, I guess this is it."

"Is it?" Charlie went in for a kiss, but Maddie stopped him.

"Charlie, as Max said to Professor Fate, 'the jig is up.' You don't have to pretend to be attracted to me anymore. It's okay. As a matter of fact, I think you should ask Whitney Hyland out. She's a real..."

Charlie put his finger up to Maddie's mouth. "Yes, I'm leaving tomorrow for L.A., but I am very much attracted to you and would love to spend my last night in the Bay Area in your bed. Is that alright?"

The last night. When he said it, it hit her harder than she thought it would. She had been anticipating this moment since they'd begun dating and thought she was prepared, emotionally. She wasn't. She also wasn't about to turn away the man she'd been seeing for almost three months and was certain she wouldn't be dating again. "Sure. One more roll in the hay for old time's sake. Come on in, liar."

"Thanks, deceiver."

Charlie grabbed his overnight bag from under the seat, then told the limousine driver to pick him up at ten the next morning.

In bed, Charlie's touch, his kisses, his attentiveness felt more intense. It was as if a thin film of complicity that had covered his conscience had dissolved, leaving him vulnerable and honest. Maddie relished it. It was one of the few times that she felt like she was with the real Charlie Evans.

Maddie returned from the kitchen with two glasses of water. She handed one to Charlie as he sat up in bed. She said, "I want to thank you for not telling me that you loved me."

"No one's ever thanked me for not saying that before."

"And most likely no one ever will again. You could have played that card and you didn't. I appreciate it."

"Do you love me?"

"I like you a lot, but no, I don't love you." Maddie snuggled under the covers. "How's that ego holding up?"

"It definitely needs a boost. What do you say?" Charlie caressed her body.

Maddie glanced at the alarm clock. It was close to two in the morning and she was exhausted. Then she looked over at her soon-to-be ex. She had to admit, he was the sexiest man she'd ever been with, but hopefully not the last. "Push my button, Max."

34

The morning was almost too beautiful to bear. In addition to the rolling hills and proximity to the San Francisco Bay, Marin County had near-perfect weather. At least Maddie thought so. She relished cloudy days, rainy days, and most especially days like this one. A slight breeze moved around the seventy-three degree air, mixing with the faint scent of magnolia blossoms.

Maddie set up her easel on the patio. She was determined not to call Jackson. Painting would take her mind off the urge to pick up the phone. It had been two days since Charlie had flown back to L.A. She wondered if he'd spoken to his stepfather before he left. And if so, if he'd told him what Jackson already knew.

She left her cellphone in the house and turned off the landline ringer. Eventually, they would talk. They had to. They were partners. Maybe it was a good thing, having distance from Jackson. Charlie's scent, his aroma, still lingered.

Hours later, when she was satisfied with her painting, she brought it inside and leaned it against the microwave, then grabbed leftovers out of the refrigerator. Ray ambled into the kitchen. His bed hair and half-lidded eyes were proof that he had just awakened.

"Good afternoon," Maddie said. "Would you like some of this?" She held up the bowl of vegetable fried rice.

"Is there enough for both of us?" Ray yawned and stretched his arms in the air.

"Yes, but just in case I'll sauté some marinated tempeh and mushrooms."

"Sounds groovy. Someone was at the door a little while ago. The doorbell woke me up."

Maddie said, "Who was it?"

"I didn't answer."

Maddie rolled her eyes and went over to the front door. She opened it and sitting on the welcome mat was a large basket. It was covered in light blue cellophane, obscuring the contents. Maddie picked it up and placed it on the kitchen table. She removed the envelope taped to the cellophane.

"I bet it's from Charlie, the jerk who didn't even say good-bye to me."

"I told you he felt bad about that."

"Still, he could have called. Read it out loud."

"*Maddie, spending time with you was incredible. I will cherish it always. Please share these treats with your amazing son. He is one talented 'dude' and I know he'll be successful at whatever he does.*" She looked up at Ray.

"Sweet. Keep reading."

"*Also, please call Jackson. Yes, he knows. Love, Charlie.*"

"What does that mean?"

"Inside joke. Not important. Let's see what we got here."

Together, Ray and Maddie removed the cellophane. The basket was from Vegan Goodies, an online store. There were protein bars, cookies, faux meats, and snacks. It was a mountain of all things vegan. There were even peanut butter-flavored bones for Mick. And a catnip mouse for Semi-sweet. Ray unwrapped one of the bones and gave it to Mick. The boxer made a beeline for the living room rug where he proceeded to chew the bone with zeal and slobber. The mouse was placed in front of Semi-sweet who was tucked into the corner of the couch, sleeping.

"Why don't we skip the leftovers and gorge on all of this?" Ray said.

"I can do that. You start. I have a phone call to make."

Three hours later, Maddie arrived at Jackson's, her overnight bag stuffed behind the driver's seat. She didn't want to assume that she would be spending the night, even though their conversation earlier indicated that all systems were go. She reapplied her lipstick and brushed her hair, then fluffed it. Not because it needed it. Maddie was nervous.

She walked up to the front door and the dogs started barking before she could ring the bell.

"Door's open! I'm out back!" Jackson yelled.

As soon as she entered the house, Georgie and Bubbles barked and pawed her, their tails wagging furiously. After giving them attention, she made her way out back. The house smelled like apple pie and coffee. *A Summer Place* played in the background.

Jackson was at the patio table, working on a small canvas propped up on a table easel. His palette was full of vibrant puddles of watercolor and his left hand was holding a beveled paintbrush. He must have showered recently because his hair was wet and slicked back. Maddie wasn't sure why, but he looked even more attractive than when she first met him.

"Hey, slick," she said as she went around the table to get a look at his work. The pencil sketch of a hen was nearly hidden by shades of red and orange, brown and tan. The bird even had a shortened beak, a tribute to the rescued hens. "I like it…a lot."

"Thanks." Jackson ran his hands through his hair. "I'm thinking about recreating the Brylcreem look. A little dab will do ya."

"Wasn't that ad before our time?"

"Yeah, but my dad used to say it every time he greased up his hair with that stuff."

Maddie looked at his hair again. "I thought it was wet."

Jackson laughed. "It is. I was joking. I'd never put that goop on my head. So, how was the drive down?" He patted the seat next to him and Maddie sat down.

"Not bad at all. I ran into the obligatory traffic on 19th Avenue. Other than that, piece of cake."

"That's a funny expression, isn't it? What's so easy about a piece of cake?"

"Don't have a clue. Google it."

"I will. Later." Jackson got up and went over to the birdbath. He picked up the crystal heart and brought it back to the patio, laying it on the table. "My heart jumped when I saw this in the birdbath. It was a gesture of enormous compassion."

Maddie got tears in her eyes. "It's how I feel about you."

"One question: Are you going to miss the spotlight and the glamor of dating Charlie? Being part of the A-list circle is a rush."

"I have to admit, I had a blast. It's almost like being in another dimension. Like you're a breed above everyone else, even though they're more messed up than the rest of us. This may sound bizarre, but the air smelled sweeter."

"That does sound bizarre."

"I won't miss the total lack of privacy. I hated being judged 24/7. Most importantly, I won't miss the feeling that every woman is hitting on my boyfriend. Actually, it wasn't a feeling. It was always happening and I knew that I would grow to distrust Charlie. I don't want to live like that, under a constant cloud of doubt. And I also believe that eventually, after so many propositions, one or more of them would be pursued."

Jackson thought about it. "What if you knew for a fact that Charlie would never cheat on you?"

"I would never know. I don't think even Charlie would know. At the time, he could swear that he'd always be faithful. Two, four, ten years later, he won't be the same person who uttered that vow. Nope, I could never trust him."

Jackson looked at Maddie with a whimsical smile on his face. "Do you trust me?"

"No."

"Wow. That was blunt."

"I'm being honest, and that's how I want to be with you. Living with that lie stung, like a tiny splinter wedged in my palm. It felt great to get it out. I know I'm going to have to rebuild your trust in me, too. I'm simply saying that time will reveal your character. With the exception of a white lie now and then, I will tell you the truth. Even if sometimes it's candy-coated. I'm pretty sure I know where that expression came from."

Jackson picked up the crystal heart and turned it in his hand, feeling the beveled edges and smooth face. "Speaking of the truth, can you tell me now what made you blush when we were having lunch in the city?"

"Can you be more specific?" Maddie was drawing a blank.

"I asked you why you were smiling and you said you'd tell me later. That it was in the vault. Sound familiar?"

A small smile crept across her face. She did tell him that she would be honest. Maddie looked him straight in the eyes. "Yes. I do remember. It involves you, a fantasy, and a S'morb on my way back from Mendocino."

"This ought to be good."

"It wasn't good. It was amazing." When Maddie finished telling Jackson about her experience, he was the one blushing.

"I have a great idea," said Jackson. He went into the house and returned with a tray. On it was a bottle of tequila, two shot glasses, a shaker of salt and six slices of lime. "Are you in the mood for a reenactment?"

She nodded. "It's a good thing I'm wearing my Viva Zapata thong."

Jackson laughed. "You have one wacky sense of humor." He filled the glasses with tequila and handed one to Maddie.

"Get used to it, slick."

"I already have."

— THE END —